"Well, I hate you," she whispered.

He let loose a sideways grin. "You don't."

"Yes, I do," she said with a petulant pout, even as her arms moved to his neck and draped over his shoulders. *Bad idea.*

He took advantage, laying his lips on hers as he tugged her flush with his torso, pressing her breasts to his chest and slanting his mouth to deepen their connection. She enjoyed the smoky, whiskey flavor of his mouth and the way his tongue stroked hers, zapping electricity through her entire body like a hair dryer dropped into a tub of water. She touched his stubbled face, tugging him closer as she rocked her hips against one of his thighs.

Hopeless. She was completely hopeless when it came to him.

When he finally lifted his lips from hers, it was to breathe a command she wouldn't refuse. "My room."

Gloria didn't think. For once, she didn't think about their past, or other people, or the fact that she was jumping from the Frigidaire to the frying pan. She simply allowed him to link his fingers with hers and lead her up the mansion stairs to his guest ro

ACCLAIM FOR
JESSICA LEMMON'S NOVELS

A BAD BOY FOR CHRISTMAS

"A terrific read for any time of the year. With charismatic characters, stirring situations, and enough sexy to fill an entire town's worth of stockings, this latest in Lemmon's Second Chance series is 400-plus pages of Christmas magic."
—*USA Today*

"Connor and Faith are strong and complement each other, and their chemistry is explosive. Lemmon is an expert at the modern-day romance."
—*RT Book Reviews*

"Sexy and well-constructed...Likable and realistic characters with believable emotions, and the right balance of fantasy fulfillment, make for some good holiday heat."
—*Publishers Weekly* (starred review)

"Sometimes a book has all the elements that make it a perfect romance...Playful, fun, sensual, emotional, and sexy all describe this book and I truly can't wait to sit down and read it again."
—**GuiltyPleasuresBookReviews.com**

RESCUING THE BAD BOY

"An amazing read...Lemmon's knack for creating authentically flawed, vulnerable characters readers can identify and sympathize with shines again in her latest."
—*RT Book Reviews*

"Lemmon manages to make me swoon, laugh, and become connected to all of the characters in this small town...My biggest problem thus far is deciding which Bad Boy I love more."
—CaffeinatedBookReviewer.com

BRINGING HOME THE BAD BOY

"Clever, romantic, and utterly unforgettable."
—**Lauren Layne,** *USA Today* **bestselling author**

"Everything I love in a romance."
—**Lori Foster,** *New York Times* **bestselling author**

"4½ stars! A sexy gem of a read that will tug at the heartstrings...A heartfelt plot infused with both emotionally tender and raw moments makes this a story that readers will savor."
—*RT Book Reviews*

THE MILLIONAIRE AFFAIR

"Fast-paced, well-written, and impossible to put down."
—**HarlequinJunkie.com**

"Landon and Kimber's banter is infectious as their chemistry sizzles. Smartly written with a narrative infused with humor and snark, this modern-day romance is a keeper."
—RT Book Reviews

"I have always loved Jessica Lemmon's books and have enjoyed reading this series. She has again captured me with her magnificent writing and characters."
—NightOwlReviews.com

HARD TO HANDLE

"[Aiden is] a perfect balance of a sensitive, heart-on-his-sleeve guy who is as sexy and 'alpha' as they come...A real romance that's not about dominance but equality and mutual need—while not sacrificing hotness factor. A rare treat."
—PolishedBookworm.com

"[Aiden is] a fantastic character. He is a motorcycle-riding, tattooed, rebel kind of guy with a huge heart. What's not to love?"
—RomanceRewind.blogspot.com

CAN'T LET GO

"This novella was long enough to get me hooked on Aiden and Sadie and short enough to leave me wanting more... The chemistry between the characters is fan-worthy and the banter is a great addition. The writing style draws readers in."
—BSReviewers.blogspot.com

TEMPTING THE BILLIONAIRE

"A smashing debut! Charming, sexy, and brimming with wit—you'll be adding Jessica Lemmon to your bookshelves for years to come!"

—Heidi Betts, *USA Today* bestselling author

RETURN
OF THE

Bad Boy

JESSICA LEMMON

FOREVER

NEW YORK   BOSTON

Forever
Hachette Book Group
1290 Avenue of the Americas
New York, NY 10104
forever-romance.com
twitter.com/foreverromance

First Edition: April 2016

Forever is an imprint of Grand Central Publishing.
The Forever name and logo are trademarks of Hachette Book Group, Inc.

The publisher is not responsible for websites (or their content) that are not owned by the publisher.

The Hachette Speakers Bureau provides a wide range of authors for speaking events. To find out more, go to www.hachettespeakersbureau.com or call (866) 376-6591.

ISBNs: 978-1-4555-6650-1 (mass market), 978-1-4555-6653-2 (ebook)

Printed in the United States of America

OPM

10 9 8 7 6 5 4 3 2 1

To my amazing readers. Thank you for loving this series.
This one is for you. ♥

ACKNOWLEDGMENTS

Special thanks to the usual suspects: God for your abundant love and blessings; John Lemmon, the recipient of the Husband of the Year Award seventeen years and running; my agent and friend Nicole Resciniti; editor Lauren Plude for finishing this leg of the journey with me; and new editor Michele Bidelspach for adopting me. Everyone at Forever working behind the scenes to help this book come together, including the cover model who loaned his perfect features to Asher Knight.

Mountains of thanks to beta readers Lauren Layne, Shannon Richard, and Erin Nicholas—your input is always welcome. And to the readers who have accompanied me on this journey—thank you for sticking with me and for your letters and heartfelt messages. You are the reason I write! A few of you helped name Asher way back when, so thank you for that as well.

Lastly, thank you, Sam Hunt. You don't know me, but your music fueled this book. I can't read it without hearing your album *Montevallo* on loop in the back of my mind.

RETURN

OF THE

PROLOGUE

Last December
Pate Mansion

*W*ill you just— Gloria, dammit," Asher Knight, visiting rock god, client, and consistent pain in her ass, called from behind her. "Stop running!"

Gloria Shields had picked up speed on her way out of the ballroom of Pate Mansion. In tall heels and her strapless purple gown, she guessed she looked pretty good doing it. But she wasn't trying to catch the eye of the man following her; she wanted to get as far away from him as possible.

"Sarge!"

Dammit. A charity toy drive wasn't the time or the place for this conversation, but here they were.

"There. I'm stopped!" She spun, arms out and eyebrows aloft.

Asher, mouth agape like he was about to say something else, seemed to think better of it. But even as he shut his mouth, he moved toward her instead of away. Closer, closer. Until he had her back flat against the wall. She pressed her hands to the patterned wallpaper, wishing this were one of those mansions with a trick door she could disappear through.

No such luck.

Soft music trickled out of the ballroom as the doors swung open. Connor and Faith strolled out—Faith dressed in an amazing fuchsia gown and Connor dapper in his tux. Faith spared them a quick glance.

"We have company," Gloria mumbled, feeling her face redden as she looked away from her friends.

"I don't care." Asher shrugged.

She believed him. He cared about little.

Connor and Faith didn't stop to chat, instead continuing to the great room, where they disappeared.

"If I swore on a stack of Bibles, you still wouldn't believe me, would you?" Asher growled, continuing the argument that started at the bar moments ago. Gloria lifted her chin, displeased at how even his snarling lip was attractive.

She really hated that about him. Or wished she could anyway.

Her eyes grazed his all-black outfit, darted down to the cowboy boots, and snapped up to the dark, styled hair and eyes so deep brown she could get lost in them like an enchanted wood. They'd started out civilly tonight, but quickly deteriorated as their potent mix of oil and water— or, well, more like kerosene and a lit match—devolved into this discussion yet again. And, yet again, Gloria stuck to her proverbial guns.

"You don't need to swear anything," she said. "It wouldn't matter anyway."

He licked his lips, looking guilty about something. Probably fucking that brunette years ago. The skinny, groupie bi—

"Sarge, I don't want to fight with you about Jordan."

Jordan. Hearing her name sent jealousy paired with regret surging through her. The emotion was so palpable, Gloria could photograph it and sell it on eBay. She wished she could forget the other woman's name, or the fact that she'd found her outside of Asher's rental cabin in naught but a nightie. But, no, Gloria's mind was a steel trap that held on to every minute detail, especially things she preferred to forget. Every second of what happened—both good and bad— was tattooed onto her frontal lobe.

"There is nothing to fight about!" she hissed, trying to keep her voice low while being supremely pissed. "We are past tense. *We* aren't even a *we* in any other faction save for work." Her job was to be his agent and sell the children's books he penned. That was it. Hell, some days that was too much.

He placed a palm on the wall next to her shoulder, leaning in. Crowding her.

"We are always a we." She watched his tempting lips form the words, his voice a seductive murmur in the empty hallway. "No matter what." His fingertips touched her chin and she tried to jerk away. He didn't let her, grasping her jaw and gently but firmly turning her face to his. "How long are you going to try to resist me?"

Forever was the answer, but every time she saw him, the vow became harder and harder to keep.

"One more night, Sarge."

She let out a weak laugh. One that trickled to every part

of her warm-and-getting-warmer body that should be saying *No way* instead of *Yes!*

His fingers moved down her neck, leaving twin trails of heat on her flesh. His long lashes draped over hooded eyes filled with the promise of things Gloria hadn't let herself want in a long time. Namely, him. More specifically, sex with him.

"I beg of you. I'm a drowning man."

Those damn eyes. They muddled her mind. Cracked her foundation. She watched helplessly as her hands grasped the lapels of his tuxedo jacket and pulled him closer instead of pushing him away. He looked as good in this outfit as he did in anything else he wore...or didn't wear.

"Please." He clasped her waist, firm but gentle.

"Ash..." She was losing the ability to say no. Or maybe she'd lost it the moment she'd reached for him.

"I miss you, Sarge." Melted chocolate eyes, sincerity on his face...He was killing her. Absolutely killing her.

"Well, I hate you," she whispered, wishing she could mean it.

He let loose a sideways grin. "You don't."

"Yes, I do," she said with a petulant pout, even as her arms moved to his neck and draped over his shoulders. *Bad idea.*

He took advantage, laying his lips on hers as he tugged her flush with his torso, pressing her breasts to his chest and slanting his mouth to deepen their connection.

Oh God. So good.

She opened to him, savoring the flavor she hadn't tasted in years. Years was a long time to go without Asher's kiss. She'd kissed men before and since, yet none of them compared. But she wasn't going to waste her time thinking of them. The nice, hazy little brain vacation she was partaking in at the moment was the dominating sensation in her world.

So she enjoyed the smoky, whiskey flavor of his mouth and the way his tongue stroked hers, zapping electricity through her entire body like a hair dryer dropped into a tub of water. She touched his stubbled face, tugging him closer as she rocked her hips against one of his thighs.

Hopeless. She was completely hopeless when it came to him.

When he finally lifted his lips from hers, it was to breathe a command she wouldn't refuse. "My room."

Gloria didn't think. For once, she didn't think about their past, or other people, or the fact that she was jumping from the Frigidaire to the frying pan. She simply allowed him to link his fingers with hers and lead her up the mansion stairs to his guest room.

* * *

"Fucking perfect," Asher praised from over Gloria's head.

Of course it was. If there was one thing she had perfected, it was the blow job. He was propped, his head on a pillow, one hand nested in her hair, his fingers stroking her scalp. She continued tasting him, and he tasted really, *really* good.

Just like I remember.

She grasped his shaft, taking the length of him, which was substantial, onto her tongue. He groaned, his rings scraping her head as he continued to thread his fingers into her hair, and a thought came that she couldn't push away.

This is going to end badly. Not the blow job, but the evening in general.

He'd talked her into it because he was Asher Knight.

With a pair of assaulting dark eyes and charisma to spare, he could cause the mass swooning of every female within a mile radius without trying. After what had happened between them, she could almost *expect* trouble to follow wherever he went. But he couldn't resist her, and she couldn't resist him.

So here they were.

His hips bucked and she shut down the tumultuous thoughts and smiled around her work, pleased with herself for pleasing him so thoroughly. His breathing went shallow and he lifted the length of her black hair from her face so he could watch what she was doing. She sneaked a peek to see his mouth dropped open, eyebrows pinched together in a so-much-pleasure-it-hurt expression.

He was a beautiful, beautiful, sexy beast of a man, but that wasn't the only reason why she liked being with him. Asher pushed her. Encouraged her to let go, to give in, to stop, at least for a little while, trying to control every tiny detail of her life. When she was with him, she could be present in the moment. As present as he was with her now.

His fist wound in her hair and on her next upward sweep, he tugged her mouth off his cock. She licked her lips, arms still locked around his thighs, his leg hair tickling her breasts.

"Get your very fine ass up here and ride me." He gave her a lopsided smile, an irresistible tilt she couldn't deny.

Since she and Asher had imploded a little over two years ago, she'd been with other guys. And she knew he hadn't kept his hands (or any of his other body parts) to himself since she quit him cold turkey after the Jordan Disaster. But now that they were here and they were naked and she'd had him in her mouth and he'd had his mouth all over her…

God. She wanted him. *Still.* No matter what the truth or their past entailed.

She vowed to just be here in this beautiful moment, take her release, give him his, and move the hell on. Tomorrow she'd reinstate her "no personal stuff with Asher" rule and they could go back to the way things were. Only she'd be a little more relaxed having achieved an orgasm that was better than "okay."

No guy made her feel the way Asher did—out of control but in it, safe while taking a risk. He was a portrait of opposing forces, and for the moment, he was all hers.

Gloria crawled to meet him, sliding up his lean, muscular body. His chest and arms were inked, but she didn't take the time to trace the patterns of his tattoos. Instead she focused on the lazy smile resting on his lips as she straddled his thighs. His fingers found her center and stroked, but there was no need to get her ready. Turning him on had turned her on and right now—in this bed, at this hour—getting turned on was all that mattered. She couldn't *let* anything else matter. Not if she wanted to go back to business as usual tomorrow.

He gripped her hips instead. "Slow, Sarge."

Sarge. The nickname came about because Ash insisted she "barked orders" at him whenever she had her "agent" hat on. He'd never let it go and she secretly liked that he'd kept referring to her as such, even though they weren't together any longer. Or maybe not so secretly. She suspected he knew how much she liked it.

He made short work of rolling on a condom and lined the head of his cock with her entrance. She held her breath as he slid deep, and threw her head back, a gasp leaving her lips. She hadn't forgotten how great he felt, but she had tried.

Oh, how she'd tried. The last thing she'd needed after he'd wronged her was to remember what she'd be missing. Now there was no denying it.

Pushing onto her knees, she lifted off him and came back down, taking each of his nine inches—that rumor was one hundred percent true. She continued riding him, pressing her breasts together with the sides of her arms and resting her hands on his chest.

"That's it, honey." His eyes slid to half-mast, focused squarely on her swaying breasts. "Fuck me. *Fuck me.*" His command was more of a plea, and Gloria felt her lips curl into a smile. She liked having control over him. In the constant play for who would end up on top, this time it was her. Literally.

He took some of that control a moment later, sliding his hand from her hip to her lower back, his long fingers draped along the cleft of her ass as he drove her down onto him again. She closed her eyes, enjoying the sensations assaulting her body. The way she tingled from head to toe. The way her mind blanked and welcomed the oblivion; the rare moment when all she did was feel and not think.

Utter bliss.

"Give me your eyes," he said, his voice low and deep and broken.

"No," she breathed, keeping them closed.

She didn't want to connect in any way other than the obvious. Nothing beyond the slippery penetration that would give them each what they needed. An orgasm. Anything more was . . . dangerous.

His hand smoothed around her ass and at his next thrust, he anchored her to him, preventing her from moving. "*Yes.*"

Her eyes snapped open. She stared down at him, her fingers moving over his chest hair. She opened her mouth to argue, but the moment she locked onto his dark eyes, she froze. His expression was soft, open. Revealing everything he'd kept hidden from her since they parted on not-so-great terms.

"That's it, Sarge," he said like he'd hypnotized her. Maybe he had.

She wanted to close her eyes—wanted to break the connection tying them together like a strong, unbreakable band. She just…couldn't.

Both palms on her hips, he encouraged her off him slowly, using his hands to slide her onto him again. Oh, that was the best. The way he sank deep, then pulled away, making her anticipate the next entry. Her mouth dropped open and a sigh of satisfaction eked from her throat. She put pressure against his chest, using her hands to assist him in lifting off her again. When she impaled herself this time, she kept her eyes trained on his.

After a few minutes, their rhythm grew frantic. Asher's eyes and mouth lost their lazy forms as a fierce, almost animal expression took its place. With a growl, he plunged, slamming into her. Then he pulled out, abruptly dropping her to her back and entering her. Taking charge of her again.

"Oh!" she shouted, the sound sharp and satisfied.

"Eyes," he demanded when she focused on a spot over his shoulder.

"Ash…"

He grasped her chin, not forcing her but letting her know he wasn't accepting half measures. Not tonight.

She obeyed, watching him as he held her in place and stroked into her over and over.

"Could fall into those pools, Sarge," he muttered. "Blue

skies, ocean waves"—he paused to suck in a satisfied breath when she clenched around him—"irises in the spring. Windows to your soul."

Sweetness oozed from each word he spoke. She hadn't experienced many men being sweet to her in the past. But she had with Asher. His sweetness had a tang to it—a flavor she could taste on the back of her tongue.

"God, I missed you." His humor vanished as quickly as it came.

Her heart seized. She'd opened up for him when she'd given him her eyes. It was the tiniest crack, but he'd widened the gap. This was a bad idea.

A bad, bad, *bad-boy* idea.

"That's a song, baby." He grinned.

No way.

"Well, you're not stopping to write it down," she informed him between erratic breaths, trying her damnedest to regain footing even as she fell apart beneath him. This was sex for sex's sake. She needed to remember that.

"Fuck, no, I'm not," he said. "But you can help me remember."

Help him remember to write a song about her? No, she did not think so. It was one thing to be in his bed, to extract pleasure from him—to *give him* pleasure, to be on the receiving end of his teasing. It was another to have Asher pen a song about her.

No, thank you very much.

"My turn. On your back." She pushed against his shoulders, desperate to regain some control.

"Forget it." His eyes sparkled in that playful way she'd always admired. "I'm going to hold you down and make you come and you're going to look at me when I do it."

She lost the will to argue whenever he watched her this intently. This single-mindedly. And wasn't that what it had been like to be with Asher from the start? When she was with him, he was thinking only of her. She'd never been with a guy who was so undeniably present. Fleeting though it was...

Their gazes locked, and all of her softened. From her fingernails raking over his pectoral muscles to her heels resting on his ass. His playful spark shifted into something much more intense. He slowed his movements, lowering over her, and she realized there was no escaping the shared intimacy between them. It was there, carving a path into her very soul.

And she wasn't the only one feeling it.

Reverence was written on Asher's expression. He was in control, moving in and out of her, thumbing her nipple the way he knew she liked, kissing her while he plunged deeper and deeper still. Gloria, her legs wound around him, tilted her hips to accept every last inch of him.

She never looked away. She watched him. Up until the very moment her orgasm hit her with the intensity of a battering ram, rocketing through her as he came into the condom, his hips frantically pumping as he said her name. Not "Sarge" but...

"Gloria."

Over and over, he said her name until his voice was hoarse and scratchy. Until he dropped his forehead onto hers. He pulled out and fell to his side, his breaths shallow and labored.

"God. That was incredible." He wrapped a tattooed arm around her waist and tugged her close. She went, even as tears pricked the backs of her eyes—blue eyes he'd said he wanted to write a ballad about. Eyes she'd given him as requested while he'd literally rocked her world.

Eye contact during sex was a line they'd never crossed before, and now that they had, it was like a little piece of her had torn wide open. Her heart, if she had to guess. And Asher had taken advantage, reaching inside and extracting part of her.

Shit.

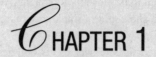

CHAPTER 1

Present day

$\mathcal{T}$he envelope in Gloria's hand was damp. Her palms were sweating, which was not attractive, but what was she supposed to do? July heat combined with walking toward Asher Knight's new Evergreen Cove vacation home had given her nothing but jittery nerves.

And not for any reason one might think. Yes, seeing him was hard and talking to him difficult after they'd "done the deed" last Christmas. Not helping matters, she'd since learned the reason *why* he'd settled on a second home here in the Cove.

He wanted to be closer to his son.

He'd purchased his house back in May, and then had deliveries made: equipment for the recording studio he was setting up. Furniture trucks from Cozy Home. His vacation home was beginning to look a little permanent, and Gloria wasn't sure how she felt about that. On the one hand, she got it...Asher wanted to be close to his son, and his son lived in the Cove. Which she couldn't think about without admiring the hell out of him.

He also wanted to be closer to his buddies, and one by one, Evan, Donovan, and Connor had settled here for the long haul. Hell, even Gloria had relocated from Chicago at the beginning of the year. The Cove had a way of doing that. Vacuuming you in and not letting go. It had the wealthy air of a vacation hot spot, and the laid-back small-town vibe without feeling like Mayberry. In a word, it was perfect.

Was being the key word. Before her client-slash-ex-slash-best-lay-of-her-lifetime moved in down the road, into the very house she'd dreamed of owning herself.

Before she'd moved here, she had her eye on this place. Her eye, her good credit, and every penny she could scrape together for an offer barely over listing price. She'd dreamed of moving into the luxury lakeside house, setting up her office in the back, facing said lake and the sea of pines, and living and working in the comfort of this gorgeous retreat.

Then the owner accepted a higher offer. A higher offer from Asher Knight.

Of course, Asher hadn't known that Glo had been waiting for an acceptance on the very same house, and *of course* he called, ecstatic about finding the "perfect" lake house. She casually asked him how much he offered and determined that coming up with enough to trump his offer would require her selling an organ. Or two. She didn't tell him he'd outbid her. Why? Easy. He'd have rescinded his offer. She did not need Asher Knight's pity house.

Since he'd moved in three weeks ago, she'd been avoiding coming over. Him she could deal with, even if she was uncomfortable. But here? Where she'd crafted a number of future dream scenarios in her head? That was going to be harder to get over...

"Come on, Shields," she grumbled to herself. It wasn't like her to become this attached...to anything. This pile of lumber was not hers, and that was something she'd have to get used to.

Asher's home away from LA sat on the edge of the lake, not a new build, but an older cabin that had been recently remodeled. The entire back wall was windows, so no matter what room you were in—dining room, living room, and kitchen—you could see out to the patio, to the dock, and the lake beyond.

At the front door, she took a steeling breath and knocked three times. She straightened her shoulders and tossed her hair, down in spite of the heat. Hey, a good hair day was a good hair day. When her long, black locks deigned to lie straight and smooth, she wasn't about to waste a ponytail holder.

She'd sent Ash a quick text that she was coming over to drop off a royalty check the publisher had accidentally sent to her agency instead of him. She could have mailed it, but then that was silly. No sense in delaying the inevitable. If they were kind of, sort of going to be neighbors, she was going to have to get used to—

The door swung open and Asher stood on the other side of it, all tall, dark, and sexy wearing a dark gray tank. His tattoos were on display, his torn-at-the-knee jeans slung low and fitting in all the right places. As usual, his wrists were adorned with hemp and leather bracelets, but he only wore a few rings today. Both on his left hand—the hand holding the phone.

He tipped his head, motioning for her to come in, glancing away before she had time to really get pegged by those bourbon-colored eyes. *Phew.*

"Yeah. I can handle it," he said into the phone. He strode away from her, barefoot, pant legs frayed, and Gloria's heart clutched. She hated her heart sometimes. Sure, she appreciated the whole "stay beating so I can live" thing, but where Asher Knight was concerned, her heart veered from its routine and decided to take up tap dancing instead. It was his gelled, sort of shaggy hair and the lazy way his eyes never opened all the way. It was the cross inked on his left arm and his who-gives-a-fuck style.

It was *him.* All of him.

She'd just have to learn to deal with her hectic-patterned heart because she was here to drop off a check and that was *it.* There wasn't any other reason for her to hang out in his house. Especially while he looked so—

He leaned on his kitchen island and she enjoyed the way his jeans showed off his ass. The way he crossed one bare foot over the other. The way he propped his chin on his palm and carried on his conversation...What had she been saying?

Oh, right. *Yummy.* She'd just have to learn to deal with him looking yummy. It was a fact of life. Like the weather. It was eighty-eight degrees and only nine a.m. and there wasn't a thing she could do but endure it. She'd have to do the same with him.

"Because. I'm Hawk's father and completely capable of handling him longer than a few hours."

Hawk. Father. At the mention of the name, and Asher's newfound role as parent, her stomach twisted. The envelope crunched in her hand. Asher turned in her direction, straightened, and pointed to the blender. In it sat some sort of green sludge she guessed was a nutritious drink. She wrinkled her nose. He mouthed the words "it's good for you" but she only shook her head vehemently. Good for her or not, she needed coffee.

"Listen, Jordan, I have to go. Check with your mom on that weekend and get back with me. I want him here. I want to get to know him."

Jordan. That name didn't make Gloria's stomach twist; it made her stomach toss. Like a tiny boat in a big, angry ocean.

"Yep," Asher was still speaking to Jordan as he moved across the kitchen to a single-serving coffeepot. He put the pod into the machine, pulled a mug from the cabinet, and pressed a button. "Okay. Later."

He ended the call and leaned a hip on the counter as the coffee sputtered into the mug.

"You really should drink my Green Goodness shake instead of a cup of acid." He gestured to the beautiful black brew rapidly filling the mug.

"I live on cups of acid." Gloria smiled brightly.

"Sarge. I want you healthy. Good agents are hard to find." A sideways smile tugged at his lips and it took everything in her not to remember kissing his mouth.

She accepted the mug from his outstretched hand, trading him for the envelope. "Your monies."

He tore it open and was silent for a handful of seconds as he studied the check. "Holy fuck."

"I know. It's bigger than we thought. Hitting lists makes big money, honey." She'd tacked on the "honey" with most of her clients, but with Asher, it sounded a tad…inappropriate? Probably because she didn't sleep with any of her other clients. It was a rule she'd enforced years ago, but then Asher came along and broke it. The way he broke everything else.

Like my heart.

She sipped her coffee, then blurted, "So, how are things with the coparenting?"

His eyebrows shot up like he was surprised she'd asked. She'd surprised herself, too. She'd made it her job *not* to bring up Jordan or Hawk. But she was trying to get back to normal—whatever the hell *that* was—and if he were any other client, she would ask how his personal life was going. It just so happened that this bit of his personal life intertwined with hers.

Which was unfortunate in every way.

Jordan was the groupie he'd slept with in his rented cabin in the Cove during Gloria's visit a few years ago. The same year Evan and his son, Lyon, moved here permanently. See, Gloria had made the *epically* bad decision—fueled by whiskey and undeniable attraction—to get physical with Asher. She'd shared his bed more than once...and then, one fateful night, the unthinkable happened. She couldn't sleep, so she went over to see him in the wee hours, and Jordan answered the door of his cabin wearing next to nothing.

Gloria had run straight to Evan's now-wife, then-friend, Charlie, and had a lovely and completely humiliating breakdown. Asher tried to convince her he hadn't taken advantage of Jordan's offer, but really, what was Glo supposed to believe? That a rock star with a penchant for easy women had turned down a cute groupie in a nightie?

No matter how many times he'd *actually* taken Jordan to bed, there was one undeniable, indisputable fact: It only took one time for them to conceive Hawk.

"She lets me see him for an hour or two," he said, "and

half the time won't leave him with me. I was trying to put off bringing in a lawyer, hoping we could work it out for Hawk's sake, you know?"

This was the part she couldn't be selfish about. He wanted to do right by his child, and that meant something to her—like way down deep. Glo knew too well how easy it was for some parents to discard a child, and here was Ash, fighting for time with his son. Every part of her admired that about him, and at a time she was trying not to admire him physically, knowledge that he was so much more wasn't easy to swallow.

"I'm an adult," he continued. "Hawk is my kid. I don't need supervision. I need *time*. Living in LA, I haven't spent a lot of time here. When I am here, she should let me see him." His brows arched in anger.

She nodded her understanding. For years, the biggest issue they'd had was arguing about whether or not he'd cheated on her. He'd been as adamant about his innocence as she had been about his guilt. Though, now her adamancy resembled petulance, because his story had never changed. Which meant he was telling the truth about sleeping with Jordan only once. Which also meant Gloria had blamed him unfairly for years.

She'd found out a few months ago, right around the same time Asher found out, that he'd fathered a child with that girl—Hawk was conceived prior to the nightie nightmare—and their biggest issue was suddenly dwarfed. Asher had a son. No matter how proud of him she was that he'd stepped up, that still hurt.

Gloria didn't *do* hurt. She was strong and tough and completely sure of herself.

Most of the time.

"You'll work it out," she said, but the sentiment sounded forced. She focused on her coffee mug, aware of him coming closer. So close she could smell his freshly showered, soapy scent. So close, she could almost recall what it was like when there had been no barriers between them. When, even before they'd slept together, he'd loop an arm around her neck and tug her close, and she'd lay her head on his shoulder. The way, *after* they'd slept together, his fingers would coast over her leg while they were sitting side by side and she'd smile at him and see all that dark, delicious intent blooming in his brown eyes.

Her thighs tingled. *Don't go there, Shields.*

"Wait'll you meet him," he said.

She snapped her eyes up to meet his. Asher having just settled in meant she hadn't had a chance to be around him. Not being around him meant she'd yet to meet Hawk.

"Hawk's great." Asher's face split into a grin. "I've hung out with him enough to know little dude rocks. Like his dad. You just wait."

There was evident pride in his voice and on his face, but her reaction was the opposite. Her shoulders curled in, her hands tightened around her mug. Meet Asher's son? Ho boy. Last thing in the world she was qualified to do. It wasn't that Gloria didn't like children; it was more that there wasn't a lot of proof she was good *for them.* Her history was comprised of two of the worst parental examples in the world and a handful of foster parents who hadn't won any awards either.

She may be willing to mentally pick up and move on while battling leftover-from-years-ago attraction to Asher, and she may admire down to her very bone marrow that he cared so much about his son…but Gloria getting to know a child that was half him and half Jordan? She wasn't sure that was a hurdle she was willing—or capable—to leap right now. Maybe after some time passed.

Like when Hawk was in college.

"Depends when he's here, I guess," she hedged. She put her mug on the counter and backed away from Asher, raising a shaky hand to push her hair behind her ear. "I've been busy getting book deals."

The excuse was a throwaway and they both knew it. Ash tipped his chin in acknowledgment, his smile more patient than anything.

She couldn't avoid Hawk forever. Hell, she'd probably have a run-in with Jordan herself at some point. Gloria had been really, really lucky she hadn't yet. But procrastination was her friend. She could put off that reunion forever.

Asher had proven as good at avoidance as Gloria. She'd been in his bed not seven months ago, and they'd managed to talk on the phone several times, neither of them breathing a word about it.

"I have to run—conference call in a few and I left my notes at home." All lies. She waved. "See you later."

His nostrils flared, but he didn't challenge her. Instead, he followed her backward steps to the front door and saw her out.

"Later, Sarge," he said, holding the door open for her.

Without looking back, Gloria paced to her car in her new cork-heeled wedge sandals as fast as her feet would carry her.

* * *

And she's off.

Asher watched Gloria's gorgeous hips sway all the way to the car.

Not like he could help it. The woman absolutely rocked him. She rocked him whenever she looked in his direction, whenever he heard her voice, and she'd rocked the hell out of him at the mansion in his borrowed bedroom last year.

Whenever he'd seen her since, it'd been almost the only thing he could think about. And, not gonna lie, when he'd signed the contract for the house he stood in right now, he'd thought about getting her naked and on her back again. Or on top of him.

Hell, both.

Neither of them mentioned last year, and at this point, he'd come to terms that the night at the mansion had been some sort of weird "time-out" before they'd both retreated to neutral corners. The narrow window when they could have moved closer to each other closed mere minutes after they'd orgasmed.

He wasn't expecting the bell to ding for another round any time soon.

Things between them had gone from hot and heavy to hotter and heavier until Jordan happened—which should have been a "one and done" situation. Ash met Jordan at a bar. She was a groupie and a fan. It wasn't the first time he'd taken a girl home to get laid, and it hadn't been the last. But Jordan came back to haunt him last year with news he didn't expect. Right about then, his world exploded before his eyes.

That explosion reminded him of when he'd played at this venue in San Francisco and the pyrotechnics for the encore performance of "Unchained" went terribly, horribly wrong. Just like that fateful night, he'd barely had a chance to process what was going on before everything around him was burning. In his and Gloria's case, the burn was a wild-fire, steadily destroying everything in its path.

He'd told Sarge about Hawk in January, having sworn his buddies to secrecy but knowing there was a fast-approaching expiration date. With his friends dating, then marrying Gloria's friends, someone was gonna spill and soon Glo would know and own Asher's balls. So he'd called from LA and broken the news over the phone. Not an ideal sitch, but he hadn't been able to tell her when he was here last year. He'd wanted to end on a good note, not further destroy things between them.

But then things had already been over by New Year's Eve. While Connor and Legs (Faith) were skipping through their snowy happily-ever-after in the courtyard behind the mansion, Glo and Ash did shots of liquor, avoiding watching their friends kiss during the ball drop and pretending not to notice they'd received pity kisses. Asher got each cheek kissed by Charlie and Sofie, and Glo had accepted a half-hug from Donny and a kiss on the forehead from Evan.

To think a few weeks prior, he and Gloria had been in that very house, sweating out the last bout of great sex he'd had. Before the intense moment at the mansion last year, he'd truly believed he had a chance to salvage things with her. Now, well, he had more shit to worry about than fighting or making up with Gloria. He had a son who came with an uncooperative mother, an album to write, and a dog to care for, and he was now the proud owner of two houses in drastically different parts of the country.

And if what he thought just happened had happened—Glo being hesitant about meeting Hawk—then there was no hope of getting on level ground with his agent again. Asher was committed to being a part of his son's life—a big part. To being a good father like his own father was to this day.

Gloria was right when she told Asher he'd make it work.

Despite his and Jordan's rocky past, Asher was going to *make* things work for his son and him. He and Jordan were a non-issue and had been since that one drunken night three years ago. Hawk was the gift Asher never could have seen coming. As long as he was breathing, he and his kid were coming outta this whole—regardless of drama with Hawk's mother.

Asher poured Gloria's coffee down the drain before he was tempted to finish it himself. Today was the last day of his cleanse, something he'd started so he could prep for the massive writing streak he'd have to do for his upcoming album. He wasn't about to throw in the towel on the final day. No matter how good day-drinking and writing songs on the dock sounded.

This was a new beginning for him. Learning "how to dad" wasn't exactly simple, and he needed to clear the decks. It was a bit of a California mind-set to start off this new chapter in life with a cleanse, but Cali had soaked into his skin since he'd become a resident more than a decade ago.

One more day and he'd be back to coffee and whiskey. He had this.

He dumped the rest of his blended shake into a glass and stepped out on the patio to look over his mini slice of paradise.

Evan was on point when he picked up with Lyon and moved here from Columbus. Evergreen Cove was in northern Ohio, right on Lake Erie. The town had a vacation feel and a family feel, and cycled through all four seasons. It was the perfect place to raise a family.

The town could at once feel traditional while not being small-time, and the Cove had the really cool vibe New York had where not every resident gaped because there was a

model who lived on this block or a rock star who lived on
that one. LA was a fine place to play and be and live, but
with his son here, Ash couldn't remain in California full-
time. He needed to be here for his boy. Since the Cove had
started collecting his friends, he figured he could crash with
them whenever he came to town. Evan, Donovan, Connor—
any of them would have taken him in for a few days. And,
hell, Donny had a ginormous mansion Ash had crashed in
several times.

But Ash didn't want that for Hawk. He may not be here
permanently, but whenever he saw his son, he wanted Hawk
to feel that permanence—have his own room, his own
things. Asher drank down part of the shake, chewing the
larger bits and scowling. *God.* Coffee would taste great right
about now.

His cell rang and he hoped it wasn't Jordan again. Small
doses was the only way to deal with that woman. Instead,
it was Veronica, the Cove's dog groomer. Wow. She wasn't
kidding when she said she wouldn't be long. He'd dropped
off Tank, what, two hours ago?

"Roni," he answered.

"Oh! Hi…um…Hi, Asher," she said with a laugh. He'd
picked the nickname. She liked it. She was also a little
starstruck, which he liked to encourage. "Tank is ready if
you'd like to come get him."

"Cool. I'll be down in a few. Pick you up something from
Cup of Jo's?"

She giggled again. Veronica was fortysomething,
friendly, and pretty. And married. But as flirting went, he
was open to making every woman he came in contact with
blush. That was his shtick and he was too good at it to stop
now.

"I'm good, thank you," she answered.

"It's for the best. I'd be tempted to buy a double espresso for myself." He made a face at the lumps sitting unappetizingly in the bottom of his glass. "I'll be there in ten."

"Okay." Another giggle. "See you soon."

He ended the call and rested one hand on the railing, the other closed around his glass.

The water sparkled, glitter on deep blue-green. This part of the lake wasn't mud-bottomed, which was awesome. They trucked in sand instead. And since the boats mostly scooted along the other part of the lake where the vacation cabins were, this part was also clear. Yep. Best house in town. Without a doubt.

He needed to have a party. Kick off his arrival. Part-time or not, he was here and the band would soon be here, and no matter where he was, Asher left an indelible mark. When the band arrived, they'd be pulling twelve- to fifteen-hour days, so may as well celebrate while the gettin' was good. Not that he was complaining. He loved song writing. He loved music. He loved his boys. And it wasn't like his bandmates would disapprove of a party.

Beach party, he decided while he leaned over the railing. To his right, the massive wooden deck had a set of stairs leading down to the shallows. There was a beach there—or used to be anyway, before it had become overgrown with brush. One call to his friends and they'd have it cleared. Connor could take the trees out, and Donny could build a fire pit right there by the water.

Straight ahead, the deck led out to a long dock that stopped in the deep. Deep enough to park a boat and deep enough to dive. Which meant his party could also include swimming. Bikinis optional, of course.

But the only bikini he wanted to see was Gloria's—preferably tossed over the edge of this railing and her out of it. Just thinking of her in a black string bikini, gorgeous, thick thighs and breasts barely contained, black hair blowing in the breeze and a pair of mirrored sunglasses hiding those blues...

Damn.

He received a nudge from his southern hemisphere and blew out a breath of defeat. He was so weak for that woman.

"Okay, then. Beach party," he said aloud. Cleanse or not, he could still fantasize about things he couldn't have: coffee, booze, Gloria Shields.

He finished off his green drink and turned for the house, depositing the glass in the sink and sweeping his keys from the counter. Off to get his accidentally acquired dog.

He seemed to have a lot of things in his life he hadn't expected to have years ago.

A son.

A dog.

A gorgeous agent with killer curves...

So far he was handling two out of three with ease. Two out of three wasn't bad.

CHAPTER 2

Gloria pressed a button on her cell phone and rubbed her overly warm ear. She'd been on back-to-back calls for the last three hours. She looked at the clock—scratch that, *four* hours. She really needed to invest in a headset.

It rang again, and she gritted her teeth, unable to spend another minute on the phone. Without looking to see who was calling, she silenced it, opened the drawer on the left side of her desk, and shut it inside. *Done.* She was so done with this day. It felt like it'd lasted two days already.

What had started with visiting Asher, then hearing about his *lovely* family, had been topped off with phone calls and contract negotiations and consoling one client who was crying because of bad reviews. The thing was, she enjoyed every part of her job. It hurt her when her clients were hurting. She believed in them so very much that when they hurt, she sort of absorbed it. She wished she could take it and hold it for them. Gloria could handle it. She could handle anything.

Asher and his offspring included?

Hmm.

She pushed out of her chair, stretched her arms overhead, and considered taking a break to tidy her office. She'd leased Sofie Martin's former office for Make It an Event. After Sofie relocated her business to the mansion with her hot mansion-owning bad boy, Gloria snapped up this downtown location. It wasn't a lakeside house with a wall of windows, but it was in the center of Endless Avenue, which had its own charm.

Once the business site was settled upon, Glo rented an apartment within walking distance. It was just a few blocks away, nothing too spectacular. But then after mentally crossing off what was now Asher's house, she figured where she rented wouldn't matter.

She'd buy a house on the lake eventually. Evergreen Cove had tons of houses on the lake. Wasn't like that was the only one.

But you wanted it to be.

That was the tired talking.

She rubbed her weary eyes and strolled to the coffeepot by the door. She fired up the machine and looked out the front window. She was comfortable behind that pane of glass, watching women in colorful dresses carrying shopping bags and smiling. Sometimes there were friends chatting over coffee from Cup of Jo's and sometimes there were families going in and out of the multitude of restaurants lining Endless Avenue.

Gloria had made plenty of friends here, which was part of the draw, but she'd admit, as they settled down one by one—Evan and Charlie, Sofie and Donovan, and now Faith and Connor—she'd begun to feel almost...lonely.

Yeah. Definitely, she was tired. She never let her feelings get to her this much. She poured a mug of coffee, sipped, and smiled as a couple walked by—vacationers by the look of their jaunty beachwear and floppy hats. She should be happy for what others had instead of pining for what she didn't have. Maybe she just needed to get out. She'd been working a lot lately.

Or maybe she needed to go on a date.

It'd been four months since her last "real" date, and that evening had ended with a one-night stand she'd chosen to keep that way. Thankfully, it was while she was in New York. She'd met a decent guy at the hotel bar. They'd parted with a wave and never exchanged phone numbers. The sex had been as sad as the story sounded in her head right now. Gloria hadn't been able to enjoy herself, and she suspected it showed.

Asher's fault. The last sex she'd had before casual New York sex had been with him, and it was the pinnacle of great sex. Hotel Bar Guy had a lot to live up to and he fell drastically short.

In several areas.

She quirked her lips in thought as the bell over her door rang. A man walked in, dressed in a slim navy suit and light blue shirt underneath, the collar open. He had a twinkle in his hazel eyes and enough blond licking through his medium brown hair to make him look harmless. That façade was his best and greatest asset.

Brice McGuire, one-man show at his own Chicago firm, Encore Music Agency, breezed into Gloria's life right when Asher landed the cover of *Rolling Stone*. He'd been at the magazine when Asher was doing his photo shoot and Glo had attended. They'd made small talk, learned they lived in

the same city and that their careers had the potential to over-
lap. Since then, Brice had sent her a few of his clients who
were writing books and she'd helped them along with con-
tracts. Brice was a good business contact to have.

"Gloria Shields." Brice smiled but it didn't quite hit his
eyes. His stubble was prominent and intentional. As was
the tattoo of his family crest on his right shoulder. Dealing with clients who were rock 'n' rollers meant he wanted
to be viewed as one of them. Staying dressed to the nines
while having an edge was absolutely on purpose. Brice had
the ability to be one hundred percent salesman, yet ninety
percent likable. As averages went, they didn't get much
better than that.

"Mr. McGuire." He'd called her a few weeks ago and said
he was planning a trip through Evergreen Cove. One of his
new signs—an up-and-coming band she couldn't remember
the name of—was here playing a few local bars. "This is a
surprise."

"I called, but it went to voice mail, so I decided to crash
in on you."

Ah. That was the call she'd ignored.

"You promised to buy me dinner if I came to see you,"
Brice said. "Where are you and your gorgeous legs going to
take me?"

And then there was the endless flirting. Brice was interested in her. She knew because he made a move every time
they talked. She'd never taken the bait. As tempting as it was
to bed a very attractive, highly successful man, she had to
draw the line at a man she worked well with. She'd blurred
those lines between work and play with Asher and the result
was not pretty. She did not want to climb back into that sinking boat.

"I have a few Lean Cuisines in the freezer back there." She shot a thumb over her shoulder. "You, me, and the microwave make three."

He plunged his hands into his pockets and shot her a grin that lit his eyes. And there it was. The reason Brice was tolerable. He wasn't exactly a sweet guy, but he did let his guard down every once in a while. "No way am I letting you pay me back for my generosity with a microwave meal. You'll have to do better than that."

He walked to her desk and picked through the papers there. She rushed over and snatched the corner of a contract, but he pressed his hand flat, keeping the paper trapped beneath his palm.

"Excuse me," she said.

"Professional curiosity." He moved his fingers over hers. "I'm personally curious as well, you know."

"Like you may want to try dating a man for a change?" She slipped the contract out from under his hand.

"Not that kind of curious." He shot her a look of derision. She was purposefully changing the subject and he knew the tactic too well. "I'd like to take you on a date, Gloria. I'm here for the night." His eyebrow lifted subtly.

"Well, I'm sorry to break your heart, but I'm not into the hookup scene."

"Who said hookup? It's a date."

"Playing dumb doesn't work for you, Brice." She used to date. But ever since she'd heard Asher was coming to town, she hadn't been out with anyone. The thought made her frown. Surely she wasn't subconsciously holding out for him. She tucked the papers into a manila folder she then filed on the other side of the room.

"But you're not really asking for a date," she told Brice

as she slid the file cabinet drawer shut. "You're asking me to sleep with you."

"I am. But I would take you on a date first."

Gloria laughed. So much nerve in this one.

He grinned. "That sounds like a yes."

"To dinner, *maybe*, but not to the second part."

"What if I extend my stay?"

She shook her head, but she was still smiling.

"What if I told you"—he came to her but this time hid his hands in his pockets—"that I plan on making you an offer you can't refuse."

"I'm not sleeping with you," she stated more firmly, meaning it.

"That's not the offer. I have a professional offer."

He had her at "professional." Gloria loved business. Loved deals. Loved offers. Just hearing the old "offer you can't refuse" bit was like waggling raw meat in front of a hungry lioness. But she wasn't about to show him her eagerness. That was a surefire way to get the short straw in any deal.

"Let's talk about it over breakfast," he amended. "I saw a cafe a few doors down. Interested?"

"Sun Up?" The diner was good, simple, and had outdoor seating. Plus great coffee.

"We can discuss my offer. I'll even pay."

She twisted her lips. It seemed simply having the thought about going on a date had called the Dating Fairy out of hiding. The perfect opportunity had just descended in the form of Brice McGuire. Even a business date was better than sitting in her office staring out the window. But Gloria was no dummy. She knew strings were attached to every part of his offer.

"This better not be a sex proposition," she said, letting him know she knew his tricks all too well.

"Come on." He gestured to himself as if to say, *Would I do something like that?* And the answer was unequivocally yes.

She rolled her eyes but accepted with, "Brunch tomorrow. Two o'clock too late?"

"For brunch, two is way too late, but for you, I'll make an exception." He gave her a quick nod, turned and pulled open her door, and walked out of it.

Gloria shook her head. Brunch was harmless. And nothing sexy happened at two in the afternoon. *And* it was a business date. Perfectly safe.

But the mystery offer was one she wondered about the rest of the evening.

* * *

"Shitty craftsmanship. Gotta love it." Donovan Pate, resident of the Cove and resident mason, pulled his head out of the fireplace. He used to build custom fireplaces for the hoity-toity Hamptonites in New York, but now he lived in his inherited thirty-five-room mansion with his event planner fiancée, Sofie. His talents were greatly underutilized in Evergreen Cove, but Donny himself had said he was tired of living like a nomad. Once he fell for Sofie, his life took a drastic left.

Asher tried not to be jealous, but he was.

Donny dusted his hands on his jeans. "I can fix it for you."

They'd been friends since Asher and his family used to vacation here when he was a kid. Donny was one of the few people who knew the real him: the Asher the tabloids would never see. Donny and Asher raised a lot of hell together. He, Asher, and Evan palled around and caused trouble during their vacation week for several years running. Evan's and Asher's families visited the same week every summer, but Donny was a local. The three of them spent as many days as possible attempting to drown each other in the lake and flirting with girls—hell, Evan had met his late wife, Rae, here. The three boys had later become christened by the local librarian and the newspaper as "the Penis Bandits."

Good times. He felt himself smile.

"I'd rather rebuild it for you." Donovan was frowning at the fireplace again, craning his head to take in the chimney, clearly unimpressed. "I can make it work, but fixing something this shitty isn't going to make it any less shitty."

If there was one thing about Donny, it was that he appreciated quality. He liked to suffer for his art. To be fair, the guy had done a lot of suffering as a kid routinely abused by his late asshole father, so that the man had any values and reverence for life at all blew Asher's mind. Asher would be lucky to have his friend fix or replace anything in his house. The man was a master.

"Don't get your hopes up for me returning in the winter," Ash told him. "I bought this vacation home for summer." He was hoping to get partial custody of Hawk and take him back to LA for the colder months. God help him if Jordan wanted to fight to keep his son full-time.

"Good luck." Donovan chuckled. "Everyone who comes here thinks they're here for the short-term." His eyes widened in comical horror. "No one escapes the Cove."

So Asher had noticed. The Cove sucked them in and morphed them into family men. Evan, Donovan, and Asher's new pal Connor had each paired off with a gorgeous woman. And now the Cove had another drop-dead gorgeous woman in its clutches—Gloria. Unfortunately, Gloria wanted Asher to drop dead, so them becoming anything resembling a pair was as unlikely as Asher grabbing a can of spray paint and decorating the library with penises again.

There was a time and place, and as much as he still wanted Gloria, he'd have to accept that their time and place had come and gone.

"Fine," Asher answered Donny, his tone harsher than he meant it to be. "Do it. Charge me a lot. I'm drowning in money."

"I know, I know. Celebrity."

"Beer?" Asher strolled to the fridge.

"Of course. I can't get a proper tour without a beer."

Asher cracked the tops off two bottles and handed over one of them. A bark sounded at the back door and he opened it.

"What the hell is that?" Donovan stood, beer bottle in hand, frowning down at the tiny dog that scampered into the house.

"Donny. Meet Tank. Yorkshire terrier by breed, badass by personality."

Donny abandoned his beer bottle to lower to his haunches. Tank barked, his tail moving back and forth in a cautious wag.

"It's okay, bud," Asher told the dog. "He's a good guy. Got a dog of his own."

"A big dog that would eat you up," Donny said, scratching Tank's chin. But she wouldn't at all. Gertie may be a Saint Bernard mix with pale blue eyes that matched her owner's, but Gertie would likely chew off a paw before she harmed a soul. She was a gentle spirit and the second best thing to ever happen to Donny.

Tank, on the other hand, had been left behind, and Asher, who had no desire for a toy breed that was better suited for a handbag than a lake house, ended up falling for the pup in a matter of days.

Tank allowed Donny to pick him up, licking his face with fervor. "I thought Yorkies had tons of hair," he said, dodging the dog's tongue.

Ash patted Tank's recently trimmed back. "He's not into that. Long-haired rock stars are too nineties."

Donovan plunked Tank on the floor and the three of them resumed the tour of the inside, moving quickly through the three bedrooms, three baths, and then back to the open-floor-plan kitchen and living room where the eyesore of a fireplace stood.

"And my favorite part." Asher stepped through the adjoining room, which took up the entire west side of the house and faced the hill and the rest of the lake. His house was private and that was great, but his favorite part was getting to set up the recording studio facing the sunset and the lake. Nothing but windows over here, and he'd had the fourth bedroom wall knocked out before he moved in to make the studio even larger.

"Nice. Soundproof?" Donovan strolled by the instruments—a few of Ash's guitars and the computer for mixing standing next to a keyboard he often used to incorporate the bassline.

"Totally."

"Incredible. This place is awesome." Donovan took a slug of his beer. "Needs a new fireplace, though."

"Yeah." Asher sipped his own beer and looked out on the

lake. "I'll be spending winters in LA, thanks. I could rent it out. Do people vacation here in the winter?"

"Oh, sure. The same way people flock to Florida for the sticky months of July and August."

"Smart-ass."

His buddy collapsed on a black vinyl sofa. With its square lines and wooden legs, it was very *Mad Men*. Asher picked it out online and had it delivered before he got here.

"How long you staying?" Donny asked.

"Few weeks. Month. Until we finish the album." Ash shrugged. "Hard telling." He sat on a stool next to a microphone stand.

"Is the band staying with you?"

"Hell, no." He smiled and lifted his beer. "They'll probably get a hotel and entertain the locals, if you know what I mean."

"That I do." Donovan leaned back on the couch, not looking the least bit upset that he was off the market. The man loved Sofie with an intensity that was enviable. Anyone who looked at them together could see the devotion between them.

Asher's parents had that. At one point, his dad endeavored to have a career like Asher had but settled down with Elana and raised a child instead. This propelled Ash to follow his dreams all the way to the stage...and fueled his decision to not get into anything too permanent with women.

Then Gloria stole a chunk of his heart. And Jordan had his kid. Fuck if he knew what to do about either of them.

"Willing to play a gig while you're in town?"

Asher narrowed his eyes, curious about the direction of this conversation. "What'd you have in mind?"

Donny lifted his brows. "Need a fourth groomsman. Would like it if that groomsman could also sing at the reception. Just one song."

"'Unchained,'" Asher guessed.

"Your big hit."

"I'll do both." He'd do anything for his friends.

"I'll get you details." Donny nodded and tipped his beer. It was like him not to get sentimental. It was also like him to change subjects before he did. "You plan on finishing the album, you might be here until winter."

"Nah. I'm going to churn this one out. I can feel it." He could, too. He already had piles of notes. Notes he'd woken up in the middle of the night and written down. He kept in close touch with the band, even when they were apart. It was nothing to have an online video chat with Alfonzo "Fonz" Rafferty, his bassist, in the wee hours after his wife was asleep, while they both strummed a few chords and talked out lyrics. The other two were better by phone. The drummer, Shiff, was a damn good lyricist, and Broderick Haines—Knight Time's newest band member, who performed backup vocals and guitar, and occasionally keyboard—came up with new songs in his sleep. Only thing was, Ricky never woke before noon. He was usually wrapped around a girl or two until then.

"It's nice here in the winter." Donovan stood. "I mean, if you can wrangle up someone to keep you warm. Shouldn't be too hard for you."

Asher snorted. "You looked around lately? The only one keeping me warm is Tank."

Donny bottomed out his beer. Ash did the same.

"Getting married." Ash shook his head. "I can't believe it." He never would've imagined his buddy settling down in the Cove, in the very house Donny grew up in—and hated.

Or maybe Asher couldn't believe it because he couldn't imagine it for himself. He was a fly-by-the-seat-of-his-pants rock star who was up for whatever, whenever. Granted, he'd buttoned up a bit since his boy came into his life, but he figured once they had a routine, he could be a dad when Hawk was with him and still be Asher Knight the rest of the time.

In theory, that was why things should have worked out with Gloria. She was a bit of a control freak, but he called to her wild side, and she answered by going all in on whatever idea he had. Like taking her to bed in Donovan's mansion that fated night.

Fated.

The word sparked an idea that didn't fully form. Asher grabbed a pencil and jotted the word on a notepad he kept next to the stool for that very reason. Maybe the spark was something. Maybe nothing.

"Before you find out from everyone else," Donny said, a small smile creeping onto his face. "She's pregnant."

"Fuck off." He took back being shocked over matrimony—Donovan being a father was the second most unbelievable thing he'd heard in the last year.

The smile didn't leave Donny's face. "She's it. She and I are going to have a family in that big house and a dog and I'll build her a white picket fence if she asks."

Asher leaned forward and slapped Donny on the arm. "Congratulations, man." He looked happy. Ash couldn't get over it. Had his brooding friend ever been this happy?

Donny eyed Tank, who had plopped down on a dog bed in the corner of the room. "How'd you end up with that tiny little dog anyway?"

"Same way you ended up with Gertie," Ash said of Donovan's giant mutt. "He adopted me."

Donovan shook his head but chuckled when he said, "And you think you're not staying? You have a dog and a house in the Cove. All you need now is the girl."

CHAPTER 3

*T*he next afternoon was bright and sunny and perfect when Gloria met Brice for brunch. Sun Up was packed, but he'd made reservations and snagged an available table outside on the patio. Now she perused the menu while Brice stirred a heaping spoonful of sugar into his espresso cup.

"You don't fit in here," he piped up.

Eyebrows arched over her sunglasses, she replied, "Thanks a lot."

He smiled. "You're too savvy. Too sexy."

"You're just saying that because you're buttering me up for something." She lifted her menu. "Speaking of which, the buttermilk pancakes sound good."

"I'm saying that because it's true. You're Chicago through and through. Don't you miss it?"

Of course she did. She'd called Chicago home for so many years, she'd have to tick them off her fingers to figure it out. "I don't not fit in here," she said instead.

The waitress returned to get their orders and Gloria splurged, going for the spinach and mushroom eggs Benedict while Brice ordered the chicken sandwich with a fried egg on top.

"The whole life cycle between two slices of bread," he commented after the waitress left.

"Gross! Stop." Gloria sipped her coffee and enjoyed the breeze coming off the lake. Weather like today's was ideal. Cool breeze, hot sun. "Evergreen Cove is like a more approachable Hamptons. The elite feel without the caviar. I like it here."

That was true, but while the Cove snuggled everyone she knew into its arms, Gloria sometimes felt as if she'd been left out of the group hug. Like she was forcing it by being here, struggling to belong while the evidence around her suggested otherwise.

Brice, for example.

"Okay," he said. "I'll admit I'm being selfish because I want you."

She sputtered into her mug.

"To work with me." He grinned.

"Oh, aren't you cute." She dabbed her mouth with her napkin.

"You think so?" Yeah, and he knew it. Brice was dressed in a suit sans jacket. A pale gray shirt was unbuttoned at the collar, revealing his clean-shaven neck below an equally smooth face. His belt and shoes were shiny black and his watch cost more than her car. His style was so different from Asher's. When Asher put on clothes, it was because he felt like wearing them. They called to him. Brice looked as if he'd preplanned every outfit with the day's purpose in mind.

It was odd how she found both options so attractive.

Like Chicago and the Cove.

Today she'd worn her usual micro-mini and a V-neck purple shirt that plunged low enough that her lace bra kept peeking out. She'd tugged up the neckline a few times since she sat down.

Brice noticed. She was used to male appreciation, so she didn't flinch. Can't put the girls on a shelf and expect the boys not to drool. Simple creatures that they are.

"Whatever offer you have, it'd better be a sweet deal." She lifted her mug to her lips. "I like working for myself. I enjoy making my own hours. Not reporting in at an office that sprawls over five floors."

She'd done that in her past life when she worked for the Dawn Lisner Agency. The place was massive and Glo had been so green. She'd learned the ropes under Dawn's tutelage, which she'd appreciated, but once she had it down, she walked away. It was a hard decision. She wasn't allowed to take any of her clients with her, so she had to start from scratch. But starting from scratch was what Gloria did best in life, and as she'd proven to herself shortly after, was also completely capable of in business.

He leaned forward in his seat and wrapped one hand around his espresso. "What I want, Gloria, is a partnership. You and me, we work our asses off. Imagine if we joined forces. Became a team. Double the clientele. Double our income. Probably triple it in the first year."

"Partners?" Gloria's throat closed off at the word. She wasn't a great partner. She was at best an "okay" friend. She blamed her upbringing. Dead dad plus druggie mom plus foster homes plus dropping out of high school hadn't exactly made a foundation for forging solid relationships. "Why would you want a partner?"

He was a lone wolf if she'd ever seen one.

"I'm crazy busy. I don't even have time to sit here with you." He grinned again, and she smiled at him and shook her head. "This is about being able to take a vacation. Being able to breathe. Sharing the load. And Chicago, no matter what you say, would look much better on you than this." He gestured at a group of twentysomethings with plastic cups full of beer at the outdoor bar next door. "Whatever is going on around here."

"It's a vacation town."

"Don't you miss the hustle?"

"I thought you wanted to relax."

Brice sat back in his chair, one arm dangling, the other hand on his espresso mug. Then he waited.

Gloria tapped her mug with her fingernail a few times before she said, "I...I just got here. I can't leave."

He sat up and leaned his elbows on the table. "It's not like you've dug in yet. You just got here a few months ago. Your apartment, your workplace, all temporary."

"I'll miss my friends," she said, but the argument felt weak. Wasn't she just thinking about how her friends had paired off? About how she was the one who was on the outside of the Cove's big hug?

"You travel. You'll make it happen." He shrugged with his mouth. "Think about it, Glo. You and me could make beautiful music together."

"You and I," she corrected.

"See how badly I need you?" He smiled again.

She sipped her coffee, disturbed that she should be adamantly refusing his offer and instead was considering it. She'd been here only a few months. Gloria Shields did not run. She stuck. No matter what. When her mother gave up everything for the needle, when her grandmother's mind splintered, when Gloria herself had to go it alone not knowing how or if she'd make it...

When the man you secretly lust after purchased your dream house out from under you.

"I don't run," she stated.

"If anything, you ran from Chicago. You'd be going back."

That silenced her.

Their plates arrived and Brice chatted throughout the meal about clients and the industry in general. About his new office in Chicago, his new apartment. About how he missed going to movies and enjoyed dinner cooked by someone other than himself.

"It's a lonely business," he said in a rare display of honesty.

It was.

"But it could be less lonely." Brice dropped his napkin on his plate like a gauntlet.

The offer and his level gaze clogged the air for a few tense seconds until his phone rang. It was the third time since their food arrived, and he'd ignored the calls until now.

He looked at the screen. "Damn. I have to get this."

She nodded her understanding.

"Mickey, hang on." He pressed the phone to his chest and dropped a hundred-dollar bill on the table. "Think about it, Glo. Chicago calls." He leaned down and kissed the corner of her mouth. "See you around."

She watched his confident exit from the restaurant as he talked on the phone and made his way to a car parked across the street. As he ducked into the rented sedan and pulled from the curb, Gloria was shocked to find that his offer had taken up a bit of her headspace.

She was more shocked to notice someone across the street watching her.

A scowling rock star dressed in jeans and a T-shirt with faded gray angel's wings on the front. In his hand was a leash and at the end of it a tiny dog.

Asher Knight did not look happy.

Not one little bit.

* * *

Who the fuck was that?

Asher's hand tightened around the bag from the pet store and Tank's leash, and as if the dog understood exactly what was pissing Asher off, Tank barked at the departing maroon four-door. Gloria met Asher's gaze from across the street, then lifted a hand to wave like she hadn't been making out with some guy in broad daylight.

Oh, hell no.

Rather than drag the dog, Asher palmed him and walked straight for Sun Up's patio, Tank tucked under his arm like a football.

"Refill to go, please," Gloria told the departing waitress as he put his hand on the railing separating guests from the general public. "Did you make a new friend?" she asked, nodding at the dog.

"'Bout to ask you the same thing."

She rolled her eyes.

He frowned. Behind his sunglasses, his gaze dipped to her low-cut shirt—her usual style, but he couldn't help wonder if she'd dressed with her lunch date in mind. The whole thing pissed him off.

"Oh my goodness." She stood and bent slightly, giving

him a view down her shirt—and his teeth sawed together at the idea of the guy who was just here getting that same view. She scrubbed Tank's face with her fingers. In a soft voice, she said, "Aren't you cute?"

Tank licked her face and wagged his butt against Asher's chest.

"He's a boy," Asher grumbled. "He's not *cute*. Who was that?"

"Well, excuse me." She pursed her lips, flashing him a look he couldn't read because her electric blue eyes were hidden behind her own sunglasses. "You're *handsome*," she said. To Tank.

"Takes after me," Asher said when Gloria kissed his head. *Lucky dog.* "Who *was* that?"

"No one," Gloria grunted. "Are you dog-sitting or something?"

"Sarge."

"Asher." There was a tense moment when she stood, fingers in Tank's fur, eyes on Ash, and he stood, dog in his arms, glaring back at her. The air crackled between them, same as it always had.

"He's mine," he said, ending the standoff. He was getting used to people being surprised about him with a toy dog. Rock stars weren't known for having miniature anythings.

"So *this* is the dog you told me about." She snuggled Tank a little more. "You kept him."

He'd told Gloria about Tank (at the same time he'd called to tell her about the house in the Cove), but not the truth. The truth was Broderick had been staying with him at the time. Their newest and youngest bandmate had hooked up with a groupie who brought the dog in her purse and left him there. Ash woke up the next morning with a wicked hangover and the dog followed him outside to do his business while Ash did laps in the pool. The dog followed him around the pool's edge for every lap. Tank was his shadow. The groupie never returned—Broderick was smart enough never to contact her again—and Asher kept the dog.

When Ash had told Gloria he'd found a dog, she'd responded, "Uh-huh. Some girl left him with you, didn't she?"

She knew him well.

Gloria, to-go coffee cup in one hand, opened the black gate separating the outdoor cafe from the street. Asher stepped aside and walked with her. "What's his name?"

"Tank."

"*Tank?*" Gloria snorted.

"Hey, his former owner had him in a pink collar with a tag that read 'Tinkerbell.' He's not effeminate. *Tank* is a badass." The dog smiled up at him, tongue lolling.

She snuggled the dog again and Asher caught a whiff of her perfume when she did. Gloria smelled like the beach and made him want to lean down and bury his nose in her neck. Speaking of...

"Were you at the beach today?" *With that dick.*

"No. I've been working all day." She frowned. "What are you doing here?"

"Doggie life vest." Asher lifted the bag in his hand, showing her the pet shop logo. "Not sure how much of a water dog he is but figured better safe than sorry."

"That's sweet."

"It's practical." He made a face...that she ignored.

"I'd better get back to work."

"You didn't answer me."

She lifted her sunglasses into her hair and let out an exasperated sigh. "Brice McGuire, okay?"

"Not okay," he growled. "Why were you having lunch with Brice McGuire?" Asher had seen Brice at the *Rolling Stone* photo shoot a few years back. The guy had tried to sign Knight Time years ago, before they'd hit it big, but Asher didn't trust him. Not with his career, and sure as shit not with Gloria.

"It wasn't lunch. It was brunch." She waggled her to-go coffee cup.

"Dammit, Sarge. He's trying to get laid. You don't see that?"

"And how is that your business?" Her voice rose enough that a couple walking by turned to look. Then they did a double take when they spotted Asher. He saw recognition on their faces. Thankfully, neither of them stopped for a photo or autograph. Now wasn't the time.

"Office," he said, pointing down the street to where Gloria's storefront stood.

Her nostrils flared, but she obeyed, crossing the street with Asher on her heels. Inside, he put Tank on the floor and the dog immediately put his black nose to the carpet to check the place out.

"Do not tell me you're dating that asshole," Ash said, picking up where he left off.

"Why do you care?" She held his gaze for a brief second, then tore her sunglasses out of her hair and threw them on her desk alongside her purse. She looked a little hurt and a whole lot gorgeous. He came close, and she took a step away from him. So he came around to the other side of her desk and stood even closer.

"Because I don't trust him," he answered, lowering his face close enough that a few more inches, he could touch his lips to hers. And damn, was that tempting.

Asher knew she dated. Hell, it wouldn't surprise him if she'd jumped back on the horse shortly after she'd returned to Chicago and he went back to LA, before either of them had moved here. Something had happened in that mansion bedroom, and by New Year's Eve it became clear that they'd both chosen to ignore it.

And what was *it*? Intimacy. A fuckuva lot of it.

They'd shared a palpable moment of connection. A connection he'd never felt with any other human being, and it had occurred between him and Gloria Shields. That wasn't the norm for him—not with any woman. Not even with Sarge. They'd slept together before and the sex was always awesome, but rarely that...close. Scared the shit out of him, but he'd been willing to explore it. See where it took them. Glo didn't share his mind-set. She shut down, started that shit about him cheating on her again, which he didn't even think she believed any longer, then ran for the hills. No matter how determined he was to win her over after, she wouldn't have it. The harder he pushed, the farther she ran.

"Brice and I talked about business, Asher." She thrust her chin up in an effort to get control of the conversation.

"What business?"

"I can handle Brice McGuire."

"I don't doubt it." Glo could handle a guy like Brice. "But I don't want you *handling* him."

"Well, I don't care what you want." They locked eyes. His lips curved. The power struggle continued.

God. Why did he admire that about her so much? Her snapping at him was a potent aphrodisiac. Maybe because in the past when she'd yelled at him, it'd led to her sleeping with him. Now it just led to more yelling.

But that didn't mean he couldn't continue trying to get her to change.

She started rearranging papers on her desk he'd just bet didn't need rearranging. "Are you going to Evan and Charlie's cookout tonight?"

Cue the subject change. Fine. He'd let her have this round.

"Yeah." More like a setup. Charlie's idea, no doubt. Downey sent him a text that read, *Wife invited Glo. Don't bring a chick.* He wondered if Gloria got a similar text from Charlie. "You bringing *Brice*?"

"I'm bringing *veggie burgers*. Is that on your cleanse?" She smiled. Syrupy sweet.

"I'm done *cleansing*. I'm back to being dirty."

She must have found it impossible to look at him because she started rearranging those damn papers again.

"Are you bringing someone?" she finally asked, eyes down, voice small.

"Yeah."

Her head snapped up, a dash of hurt washing over her features.

"Tank." Ash bent and lifted his dog into his arms.

"Oh." Her small shoulders dropped in what he suspected was relief. It was exactly the reaction he was hoping for. She wasn't dating Brice, and she didn't want to see Asher with anyone else either.

He couldn't help but feel cocky about that. Hey, a win was a win.

* * *

Once upon a time, Gloria was not Charlie's favorite person, but anyone looking at the two of them now would never know it. Glo got it—Charlie wasn't the first girl (and likely not the last) to have a jealous streak where she was concerned. The truth was Gloria used to have a little crush on Evan when she'd first signed him, so when Charlie and Evan were starting to "feel all the feels" three years ago, Charlie was sure Gloria and Evan had a past—a past involving them hitting the sheets.

Charlie had nothing to worry about. It never happened.

Ev may be hot, but he felt more like a brother than boyfriend potential. She'd known it the moment his lips hit hers—one drunkish kiss in Chicago a hundred years ago, before he and Charlie were ever a thing. Gloria and Evan had sobered on contact. *Yikes*. Platonic was the only way when it came to Evan Downey.

Nothing at all like the electric shock that vibrated the air in her office earlier when Asher Knight stood close to her. If only she could slot him into the "platonic" category as well. But of course not. Instead, everything about him drew her in. His dark eyes, sexy tattoos, even his adorable dog.

And he wants you in a way that parallels how much you want him.

Anyway.

Once Charlie learned that Gloria had zero romantic interest in Evan, they became fast friends, and the bond had only strengthened. Glo didn't make girlfriends easily, so making a long-lasting one was a bonus she hadn't seen coming.

She glanced out to the deck where Asher was gesturing with both hands—telling who knew what kind of tall tale. Evan stood, face lit by the fire bowl in front of them, and threw his dark head back to laugh. Asher laughed, too, a genuine, easygoing laugh that made him look gorgeous and approachable and like the very man she wanted to run out and throw her arms around.

She hated that.

Glo dumped a bag of shredded carrots into a large salad bowl as Charlie added a container of baby tomatoes.

"What are those two yammering about?" Charlie asked, tossing the leaves and vegetables together with a pair of wooden tongs.

"Who knows." Gloria leaned a hip on the counter and reached for her wineglass, taking a hearty sip of the red before noticing Charlie's huge hazel eyes on her, drilling a hole through her head.

"What? Do I have purple teeth already?"

"No. It's not…" Charlie shook her head. "It's just…" Those huge eyes narrowed in suspicion. "Is there something still going on between you two?"

"Me and Evan?" she joked. "Of course not, honey."

Charlie raised an eyebrow, suggesting she wasn't in the mood to play.

"I didn't think that was going to work," Glo grumbled. "You mean Asher."

"Of course I mean Asher." She set the tongs aside. "Since he arrived here, you've been…I don't know. Circling each other."

Wasn't that the truth. Gloria shrugged and prepared to insert some distance. That was her way. She and Charlie were friends, but it didn't mean Glo had to let her in all the way. Getting close to someone risked heartbreak when they left.

And they always left.

Charlie had said she used to feel the same way before she and Evan fell in love. That shared belief was one of the things she and Glo had in common. But Glo still found herself holding back, out of habit or maybe self-preservation. Or both.

Asher was a prime example of how getting close was a bad idea. If she'd never gone to bed with him, then he could have slept with all the *Jordans* he wanted and she couldn't have cared less. He could've repopulated the planet with groupie babies. But, no. She'd crossed the line. She'd let him kiss her. Then kissed him back.

"I'm fine," she lied.

"Uh-huh." Charlie set the salad aside, not sounding the least bit convinced.

Gloria lifted a tray filled with buffalo burgers and veggie patties and a few hot dogs for the grill. Lyon came barreling out of his bedroom right then, Tank hot on his heels.

"Mom!" Lyon may be Charlie's stepson, but he was one hundred percent hers. The whole "Mom" thing? Totally his idea. "We need a dog!"

"You have a fish." She smiled, then said from the side of her mouth, "Terror the Third." Yeah, they'd gone through a few Starving Artist Fair fishes since the original Terror went to the big aquarium in the sky.

"Fish can't fetch." Lyon had bronze skin, wild curly hair ("like his mom's," Charlie always said of her late best friend), and striking turquoise eyes. The eyes were all Evan. Gloria had once told Lyon he'd grow up to be "hot with two Ts" like his daddy, and even in his gangly preteen years, she couldn't take it back. Mark her words, the kid was going to be a looker.

"He makes a good point," Gloria put in. "You should get a big dog, though. One that's sturdier than a Yorkshire terrier."

"Tank's sturdy." A raspy, low voice washed over her and

made the hair on the back of her neck stand on end. *Asher.* Showing no concern for personal space whatsoever, he stood directly behind her, pressing his chest against her back as he reached around to snag a tomato from the salad bowl. "He's all dog, aren't you, buddy?"

Tank yipped his confirmation.

Asher ate the tomato, sliding his gaze to Gloria and then peeling his body away from her. Before her brains could leak out of her ears and she did something horrifying, like swoon, she went on the offensive.

"What BS were you telling Evan out there?" she asked.

His smile held. "Don't worry about it, toots."

He rested a palm on her hip, leaned past her, and lifted her wineglass. Gloria most certainly did not watch as he took a drink, then licked his lips when a single red droplet clung to his mouth. No, she did not. And she did not feel every internal organ lean a little closer to him while she forced her feet to stay firmly planted on the exact spot of the kitchen's tiled floor. Nope. That didn't happen, either.

"I'm here for the main course," he told Charlie, relinquishing the wineglass to Gloria and holding out his hands. Charlie handed over the tray holding the burgers and dogs.

"Sarge, follow me out."

"What? Why?"

"Because Evan is opening the whiskey and we're all doing shots." He sent Charlie a sharp smile. "Ace, you're invited, too."

"I'll stick with wine, thanks."

"Me too," Gloria said.

Lyon ran through the kitchen, Tank following. "We'll go out!"

"No whiskey for him either," Charlie put in. "Give me

this." She swiped the tray and walked out to the patio, leaving Gloria and Asher in the kitchen.

Alone. Intentionally, no doubt.

"Not like you to turn down whiskey," he told her.

"I'm trying to be a good guest. We fight when we drink whiskey."

"That's not all we do when we drink whiskey." His smile was penetrating.

No. He was right about that. They also kissed. And hugged. Full-body, no-clothing-necessary kind of hugs. The best kind. *Gah.*

"In that case, maybe I'll never have whiskey again," she said, elevating her chin.

"Someday, Sarge, you'll have whiskey."

"I mean it," she said, picking up on the whole double-meaning thing and trying to sound resolute. "No more whiskey for me."

He opened the back door for her and she walked through it, but not before he put his lips over her ear and muttered, "We'll see."

CHAPTER 4

After dinner, Asher and Evan sat, feet kicked up on the deck's railing. Lyon had gone to a friend's house to spend the night, leaving the adults to lounge.

Evan's house faced the lake, but the dock was farther down the hill, giving him an awesome view of both the water and the hillside of pine trees behind it.

"Nicely done on dinner," Asher said, tipping his beer.

"Grill master," Evan said.

He and Ash had done a few whiskey shots, and true to her word, Gloria hadn't imbibed. Stubborn, gorgeous woman.

"Gloria was on a date earlier today," Asher grumbled, looking straight out at the water beyond.

"Ah." Tank was curled up on Evan's lap, proving he was an equal opportunity suck-up. Then again, Evan had fed Tank half a hot dog, so the dog was loyal to only him at the moment.

"What do you mean 'ah'?"

"Explains why you were pouring it on thick all evening with her. You're lime-green Jell-O."

"I'm not jealous of a guy named *Brice*."

Evan snorted.

Asher felt his lips tug down. "And I was not pouring it on thick."

"Were too."

Okay, he was. But it wasn't like he'd been trying. It was Gloria. She was touchable. She had skin like silk and he loved the way she squirmed and how the pulse point in her neck fluttered to life when he was near. He knew he was pushing her boundaries big-time—the ones she'd outlined the day after they slept together at the toy drive. *"We're not doing that again. And we're not going to talk about it again. And we're not going to get close to doing that again."*

He'd never agreed. He let her say her piece and then hang up on him. Things were less tense by necessity—they had to work together, but now that he was back in town, fuck if he knew how she planned on avoiding him.

"Who's Brice?" Evan scrubbed Tank's ears.

"McGuire. Music agent and asshole."

"Asshole," Ev agreed. "I take it you being jealous of Brice McGuire means you've given up on your mission to bang every chick in the continental U.S."

"Piss off," Ash said, and Evan chuckled. Being on the road, touring, and having chicks approach him hadn't been something Asher turned down often. Okay, *rarely* did he ever turn them down. Ev knew that. Just like he knew Glo was the game-changer for Asher. And there was apparently no hiding it from his best childhood buddy.

"It's the kid," Evan stated.

"What's the kid?" Asher tilted his bottle again, eyes on the lake.

"Hawk. Having a boy of your own makes you want to be better, doesn't it? Makes you want to have things that are good and right. Things you want to keep close. For the long haul."

Asher faced his friend. Wisdom lingered in Evan's sharp eyes. He'd lived a lot of life. Lost his wife at a really young age, her death leaving Lyon motherless at age three. Evan had juggled fatherhood on his own until he moved here and fell in love with his wife's best friend. The transition couldn't have been easy, and from what Asher saw, Charlie had struggled to fit the change into her heart as well. Now they were a family. Evan and Charlie and Lyon deserved every bit of beauty they'd won.

No way would he bullshit his friend after Evan had laid out that much honesty.

"Yes," Asher admitted. "All of those things."

"You bought a house here to be closer to those things. Hawk. Your friends. *Gloria*."

"Did what I had to do." Ash shrugged.

"Didn't have to *buy*." Evan dropped his feet to the ground and stood. He deposited Tank onto Asher's lap. "Didn't have to keep this furball, either. But you did." He didn't wait for a response. "Gonna check on dessert. Ice cream?"

"Nah. Drink refill, I'll take." Nothing numbed out life's pesky questions like liquor.

Behind him, the door opened, female voices drifting out onto the air; then it closed again, shutting everyone inside. Asher stroked Tank's head and then his chin, wishing every relationship was as easy as the one he had with his acquired *furball*. But it wasn't. Hookups and breakups had happened to him more times than he could count. Women wanted him, wanted what he could do for them, and because he had a certain set of skills onstage, often were the ones seeking him out. Women came easy.

Except for one woman in particular. The one woman he wanted.

Asher hadn't lied to Evan the day he stood in Library Park and admitted Gloria intimidated him. She was hot as hell, and she was smart. Really smart. After he got a closer look at Gloria Shields, he wondered if maybe, in spite of his vast experience, he'd only been exposed to one kind of girl.

The kind of girl who wanted him for a night or for an hour and then never thought of him again. The kind of girl...like Jordan. Or the kind of girl like the one who slept with Broderick and abandoned her dog, for God's sake. Who did that? Tank snored lightly, already zonked out. Of course Asher had kept him. Dude had been abandoned once already.

Asher put his empty beer bottle on the deck by his chair, then pulled that same hand down his face in frustration. Jordan was one of those situations he'd replayed and replayed and *replayed* in his head, as if he could replay it enough to change the outcome. But he couldn't. She happened and they happened and then Hawk happened. When he'd learned about Hawk, something strange occurred. For the first time in history, he didn't want to change what happened with Jordan. He didn't want to alter a single thing because a tear in space and time would mean he'd lose Hawk.

That realization had sent him for a fucking loop.

He'd sat in Pate Mansion and confided in the unofficial fourth musketeer, Connor McClain. Asher and Connor were far from best buds, but Connor was a respectable family guy and Ash trusted him. So, New Year's Eve, while Gloria was spitting bullets at him from across the room, he told Connor what he'd learned: Asher was going to be a dad.

Then he'd vowed to get Gloria back, no matter what.

Now that Evan had gone all Man on the Mountain on him, Asher was considering what he pointed out. If he wanted to surround himself with all the things he wanted, wasn't Gloria one of those things?

Of course she was.

Soft footsteps sounded behind him and a second later, a square glass of whiskey appeared in front of his face. The hand was a woman's, and if not for the sparkling wedding band on her left ring finger, he may have thought for a second Gloria had brought him the drink.

No such luck.

"Thanks, Charlie." He accepted the glass and she took Evan's Adirondack chair, propping her feet onto the railing like he had, only in her case, she held her skirt to her legs. "Feel free to flash me. You know I don't mind."

Blond and beautiful, Charlie grinned. There was a palpable happiness to her lately and Asher loved seeing it. She was a great mom, and from the smile on Evan's face, Asher knew she was a great wife as well.

"How is the house coming along?" she asked. She and Evan had stopped by to see it the day he moved in, which was close to a month ago now.

"Good. Tank's right at home."

She reached over to pet the dog. The pooch got more play than anyone. "Have you seen Hawk much?"

"Not a lot. A few drive-by visits." He looked down at the dock and lake beyond. He missed his boy. Wanted to be way more present than Jordan and her mother were allowing.

"Well, I can't wait to meet him," she said. She meant it. He could see it in her genuine smile.

"Wish Sarge would have said that," he blurted.

Shit. Whiskey made him honest. Too honest.

"Well, she's not the kind to wear her heart on her sleeve," Charlie said with a small laugh. "I can relate."

"Ace, you're cellophane." He sipped his drink. "Your heart is in full view."

"Yes, well, I didn't allow myself to want good things for a very long time." Her smile turned sad but recovered almost instantly. "Gloria is a tough cookie. But she's *your* cookie."

He sipped his whiskey again and didn't answer. Charlie poked his arm and he looked over at her.

"It's your job to get her to crumble."

"This is some metaphor."

Charlie bit her lip like she was deciding whether or not to say more. Then she did. "She told me something the night she found Jordan at your cabin."

He may have slept with Jordan in the past, but he didn't sleep with her *that* night. The one time he did had been pre-Gloria. What he remembered about the night Charlie had brought up was waking to a knock and climbing out of bed to find Jordan closing the front door and Gloria peeling out of the driveway. The rest was history. Regret coated him, but the regret had nothing to do with Jordan. What he regretted was not running after Gloria, bringing her back into his rental, and keeping her there until she believed him.

"Can't wait to hear this," he grumbled, throwing back the rest of his drink in one burning swallow.

"She told me that night she'd given Evan bad advice. She told him I needed space, then she said girls like us don't need space. We need caveman-dragged by the hair."

"Caveman-dragged." If he tried to pull that shit, he could go ahead and sacrifice his balls to Gloria, too.

"That's what she said."

"What do you mean girls like you?" Far as he could see, girls like Charlie were the kind you grabbed and held on to with both hands. Evan saw that. So did his son, Lyon. The boy didn't waste time adopting her as a second mom. Smart kid.

"Gloria and I have family...issues." Charlie held his gaze. "We were both abandoned by our families in different ways, but it leaves a mark. Those are the people who are supposed to stick with you, you know?"

He did know. His family was supportive and loved him.

"So because we don't have that security, we need to be pursued. Pursued hard."

"You saying I haven't been trying?"

"Have you?" She stood from the chair. "And this other agent guy? Sounds like he started the race without you." Asher didn't have to wonder how she knew about Brice. Gloria probably told her. Those two had become close. "Better catch up."

"Caveman." He cast her a wry glance.

"Yeah. Show her who's boss." Charlie squeezed his shoulder and then let go. "She can handle it."

The back door opened and Gloria and Evan came out, arguing over who had more ice cream in their bowl. Charlie commented about how she was getting herself a bowl bigger than both of them and then they'd really have something to bitch about.

Ash watched the interaction with a smile, but his mind was on what Charlie had said—and how right she was.

Gloria could handle him. Hell, she *had* handled him.

He'd pushed her instead of giving her space last year at the toy drive. And look what happened. He got her into bed that night and experienced the sex—the connection—of his life.

Getting Gloria back was as easy and as difficult as setting his sights on her and running at her with everything he had. That's how he'd launched Knight Time. Not because he gave it a rest or a break, but because he dogged that goal until it had nowhere else to hide.

Shit.

He'd let Glo run him off.

"Sounds like he started the race without you. Better catch up."

He frowned.

Gloria harbored an attraction to him rivaled only by his attraction to her, so he'd have no problem reeling her in. But getting her into his bed was one thing.

Getting her to stay was another.

* * *

Gloria had long prided herself on her strength.

Born of Marlene and Steven Shields thirty-five years ago, it wasn't as if she'd had much choice in the matter. Her parents were raging alcoholics who had graduated to drug abuse before Gloria could walk. By the time she turned sixteen, the state, after repeat visits to their humble home, finally took her away.

Used to a house littered with needles, spoons, and unsavory visitors, Gloria was almost more terrified of suburbia. The glossy-magazine-picture life—manicured flowerbeds, hedges, fenced yards, and minivans in every driveway—was as foreign and unwelcome as she'd expected.

In a lot of ways, foster care was worse than living with her parents.

At her house she could come and go as she pleased. She'd been a little adult since age eleven or twelve, so her new "parents" making rules for her seemed more like a play for power than any real concern for Gloria's well-being. One by one, her foster homes gave up on her. They cited to the counselors that Gloria was difficult. Controlling. Unappreciative.

In their defense, they weren't wrong. It hurt, but she didn't absorb it. Nothing could rival being abandoned by the people who made her and should have loved her unconditionally.

"Have the changes to me as soon as you can, Cindy. Okay, thanks so much." She ended the call with the editor and slunk down into her office chair. It'd taken everything she had, but she'd secured her author a bump in advance and negotiated a book-signing tour on the publisher's dime. She sent a text to her client Millie Long, cookbook author and altogether kick-ass mother of three, that read, *We did it, babe. Have a cocktail.*

Then she dropped her phone and smiled, her smile fading the moment her e-mail binged, begging for her attention. If she started answering them, she wouldn't be able to stop.

She pushed away from the desk and rubbed her eyes, careful not to smudge her mascara, then stood to stretch. The door to her office opened and in walked the potential answer to her problems.

"Brice," she said, and with no small measure of shock.

She'd thought about what he'd promised at brunch. Double the income, a shared office... They could hire additional assistants to go through the submissions. She would have help navigating her treacherous e-mail inbox...

"I thought you were only staying one night," she said, caution outlining her tone.

From behind his back, Brice pulled out a bouquet of red gerbera daisies matching the shirt he was wearing. "I didn't want to go back to Chicago and leave such a hot deal on the table." He offered the bouquet. "I'm talking about you."

"I assumed." She accepted the flowers.

"Plus, one of my bands is in town for the Lakeside Dreaming party and I thought I'd be supportive and get completely wasted with them tonight."

Brice was wearing a pair of fitted tan shorts and boat shoes with a red collared golf shirt, and Gloria had to give it to him, he did look more laid-back than when he was in his slacks and button-down. And the tattoo on his arm peeking out from below the sleeve did make him look like he could handle things if they got wild.

"Well, have a good time," she told him.

"I plan on it. Because you're coming with me."

"I'm sorry to say I have about nineteen hours of work to do and only three hours before my eyeballs give out."

"You can't work all the time, Heels."

"What?"

"Your new nickname. You're always in heels."

She wrinkled her nose.

"It sounded cute when I was on my way over here." He smiled in an endearing way. "I'll keep working on the nickname thing."

But she already had a nickname. *Sarge.* Asher gave it to her back when she first signed him, and that nickname, said in Asher's scratchy, sometimes tender voice, was the only nickname she wanted.

Even though she told Brice, "You do that."

Because as things stood, she and Asher had separate lives. Well, as separate as they could have as a client with a house in town who shared cookouts with their many mutual friends.

Sigh.

"Look at you," Brice said. "Dressed for a rock concert already."

"A bonus of working for myself." She propped a hand on her black leather mini. "I can wear whatever I want." She'd paired the skirt with a sequin-studded hot-pink T-shirt sliced up the sides to reveal her toned tummy. Hey, she'd worked hard on her flat stomach. No sense in hiding it all the time.

"Trust me, Glo. If you worked with me, I wouldn't have you change a thing." His eyes cut down her body, and to her surprise, his appraisal didn't feel the least bit gross. Instead, his attention was...genuine. And sort of flattering.

"I sincerely have so much to do..." So much she didn't want to do.

"I know." He took her hand and drew her out from behind the desk. "Shut it all down, sweetheart. Come party with me."

Because his offer was tempting, if not a little charming, and she really did have a lot to celebrate considering her recent win for Millie, Gloria decided to give herself the treat and unplug early.

"Let me get my purse."

* * *

The big bash was outside of Evergreen Cove, the massive designated lawn area packed thanks in part to ideal weather.

The night was clear, with a light, warm breeze fluttering through the trees, and the setting sun made the water glitter like someone had thrown diamonds onto the lake's surface.

Gloria changed her outfit in spite of Brice insisting she was already dressed for a concert. She'd asked him to wait outside her apartment while she'd run inside and traded her skirt and heels for a pair of short shorts and flip-flops.

"I take it back. Maybe you do belong here," he'd joked when she came outside to join him.

The band was good, but the drinks were better. By the time she'd had three whiskey sours, she was relaxed and her work problems felt miles away. They'd be there in the morning, but she would deal with tomorrow when it came. Right now was about being in the moment.

She was swaying to the music—the band was covering an old Aerosmith song—when Brice palmed her hip and pulled her close. She smiled up at him. He was cute. In a professional/businessy sort of way. Then she frowned at the tattoo peeking out from under his sleeve. That part wasn't cute. It was hot.

She edged away, but he tightened his hold on her. "Dance with me, Gloria."

Well. Why not? She finished her drink and tossed the cup onto the grass alongside about eleven million other cups, then looped her arms around his neck and moved to the soft beat. He had rhythm, and she tried not to be impressed by his hips and the way they moved in sync with hers.

It'd been a long time since she'd been out without an agenda. Whenever she'd dated before, she'd spent most of the evening trying to anticipate what her date might do next, and further anticipate if she would turn him down or accept. She tried to decide if Brice would attempt to kiss her at the end of the night, and guessed he would, and decided to oblige him. Harmless kisses between potential business partners.

Hmm. That might be the whiskey talking...

"You made it!" Brice called out, making her jump.

Her eyes snapped open and she was released from Brice's hold so quickly, she had to adjust her weight to keep from toppling over. She pushed her hair out of her face to say, *Thanks a lot for the warning,* but found herself faced with Asher and, next to him, Evan.

"I was hoping you'd come out." Brice clapped Asher's shoulder. "Wasn't sure if you'd get the invite in time." The band's set ended and the crowd cheered. Brice paused in his greeting to Asher to whistle through his teeth. Gloria joined him, clapping halfheartedly, still perturbed that Brice's priority and attention had refocused on Asher.

"Looks like I'm too late," Ash said, his eyes boring into hers.

"Nah. They'll take thirty minutes and come back out. You're just in time to hear the last set," Brice said, oblivious to the silent conversation happening in his midst.

"Might be right on time," Evan said, hiking one eyebrow high enough to scold her.

Gloria wrinkled her nose. *Whatever.* She didn't owe either of her *clients* an explanation for what she did off the clock.

"Drinks on me," Brice said. "What can I get you?"

"I'll come with," Evan offered. "Glo?"

"Whiskey sour."

"Just whiskey," Asher corrected. "I'll have the same."

She nodded at Evan, and he and Brice made their way through the crowd—which hadn't thinned even a little despite the band leaving the stage—and walked in the direction of the bar. Gloria figured they'd get back about the time the band took the stage again, which left her with Asher in the interim.

"I didn't realize you were invited," she said over the melee.

"I see that." The corners of his mouth turned down.

"Why did he invite you?" she asked, curious.

"He wants me," Asher said, a bored expression on his face.

"No. He wants *me*." She pressed her fingers into her chest.

Asher leaned closer to speak to her and it took everything in her not to back away a step. Him close had a way of messing with her equilibrium...even more than the whiskey.

"I meant he wants to sign the band, Sarge. He's probably buttering you up to get to me."

"What?" she asked, slightly offended. "How egotistical are you?"

"I'm not being egotistical," he said. "That's a fact. And you're welcome."

Oh, he was too much. "I'm *welcome*?"

"Yeah. Now that I'm here, you won't have to touch him. He won't get within three feet of you." Stubble lined his jaw, fire burned in his eyes, and he stood close enough that his body heat blanketed her. "Promise."

"Listen, Asher"—she cleared her throat and tore her eyes away from his biceps, which were absolutely delicious and testing the limits of his T-shirt in the most distracting way possible—"I don't know what you think you're doing—"

"No, you listen." He palmed her hip much like Brice had earlier, but unlike Brice, when Asher touched her, her nipples perked up and every inch of her grew warm. Asher's nearness, one hand gripping her firmly as he looked down at her with dark hunger in his eyes, was so hot she couldn't think.

The crowd milling around them were having loud, drunken conversations, so he lowered his face to her ear to speak.

"I'm coming for you, Sarge." His hand moved from her hip to her lower back, his fingers splaying wide and slipping beneath the material of her shirt. "Bet you've never had anyone come for you, have you?" His nose moved along her ear, warm breath tickling her skin. "Bet you were a rebellious teen with a nose ring and a bad attitude and all you wanted was to feel good."

No nose ring, but the rest was scarily accurate.

"Well, guess what, honey?" he continued, his fingertips sizzling on her bare skin. "I'm going to make you feel good. I'm the only one who can."

He pulled his face away and she had to will her mouth to close. Her teeth clacked together as her brain scrambled to figure out what part she should argue with first. Wrenching a fist around his T-shirt, she tugged him close. A small smile played on his mouth, and his hand went higher beneath her shirt. He was anticipating a kiss, but she wasn't going to kiss him.

"Listen up, you arrogant bastard." Anger vibrated through her arms and a charge shot from her toes to the crown of her head. "You don't get to *claim* me. I'm not your property. I can do whatever I want." Because she wanted to wipe that stupid smirk off his face, she added, "And I can do *whomever* I want."

His lips flinched, but he didn't back away, stepping even

closer and touching the tip of her nose with his. Her vision was now swimming in dark hair, dark eyes, and the sexiest smirk she'd ever seen.

It's not sexy. It's stupid, remember?

But it wasn't. And the rest of her knew it. Her nipples tightened, her body tingled, and the hand she'd wrapped around his shirt began to sweat...

"You do me, Sarge. No one else," he said.

"I'm not"—she had to swallow around a very dry throat to finish—"doing you."

"Brice McGuire doesn't know how to make your body sing. I do." He slid his nose along hers and moved his hand from her back to her hair. She shivered. "Want me to make your body sing, Sarge?"

"We"—she closed her eyes to unscramble her brain, then opened them again—"decided not to sleep together again."

"You decided that." Awareness lit the depths of his gaze and he ran his fingers up the back of her scalp, causing goose bumps to cover her arms. "After."

After.

"Remember what happened after, Sarge?"

Of course she did. And judging by his sudden seriousness, he remembered, too. There was no doubting what happened after that night in the mansion.

Gloria had freaked right out.

HAPTER 5

Where the hell are you going?" Ash asked as she stood.

"I'm...I can't do this anymore, Asher."

"What?" He sat up on the bed, naked, hair all over the place and eyes wild. "Don't you fucking put that on."

She was attempting to slip into her evening wear while willing her knees to hold her up. That last orgasm had made her wobbly. Probably she should lie down and recover. But lying down meant lying next to Asher and she couldn't do that.

Dress on, she resumed the hunt for her shoes. "People are going to notice we're missing," she said, lifting the comforter from the corner of the bed and finding one of her shoes.

"I don't care."

Ah. She spotted the other one by the nightstand, half under the bed. She tugged it out with her toe and slipped it on, then balanced a hand on the bed to slip on the other one.

Asher propped on an elbow on the bed and frowned some more.

"Help me zip this, okay?" She turned, holding the front of her purple dress and moving her hair over one shoulder.

He climbed out of bed and stood behind her, and she closed her eyes so she wouldn't have to look at the damn near-perfect body she was refusing to climb into bed and snuggle with.

Leaning close, he whispered, "Don't do this."

Too bad she couldn't shut her ears.

"Zip." She worked up a glare, turned around, and shot him with it, then waited. He clenched his jaw but did as she asked. When he was done, he stood, hands on his hips, and glared back at her while she struggled to keep her eyes on his face.

"Why are you doing this?" His tone was just low and sincere enough to make her face heat.

"I don't owe you any post-coital snuggling, you know. I didn't agree to that."

"Yeah, Sarge. I know." His tone was weary. "You don't owe me anything. You've made that clear. Not even an apology for assuming the worst and being dead wrong."

"I saw her—"

"Yeah, you saw her. What you didn't see was me fucking her." He came closer and grasped her shoulders with his palms. "I did not sleep with Jordan after I slept with you. We fucked one time." He held up a finger. "Once. That's it."

Gloria frowned.

He dropped his hands. "Know what I think?"

She crossed her arms over her chest. She didn't want to know, but she figured she couldn't stop him from speaking.

"I think," he continued, "that you believe me. And I think you're going to continue to pretend you don't to save face, or try to ignore what just happened in here. And I'm not talking about the sex, Sarge. I'm talking about what happened. You're freaked. Hell, I'm freaked. But it happened and I'm not going to pretend it didn't."

Something had happened. And he was right. She was freaked. Because in the tender moments when he held her eyes with his, when he started babbling about song lyrics, when he admitted he missed her, she realized something else.

She missed him, too.

The sex that was supposed to be a reprieve from their usual bickering had delivered, but an orgasm wasn't the only gift. There had been a deeper undercurrent between them. One where they saw each other without the cover of for-show arguments and their egos getting in the way.

She'd been naked with Asher before but this was the only time she'd felt truly naked. She had to get the hell out of this room—out of this mansion—because she couldn't let him any closer. He was way too close already. She could so easily go from having a good time to falling, and falling hard.

After being hurt so badly the last time, there was no way she could allow herself to be that vulnerable again. So, yeah. She recognized that something happened. But she didn't have to admit it. Deflection was her only ally.

"We both needed that, but let's not make this into a thing." She went to a mirror on the wall under the pretense of fixing her hair.

"A thing?" He stalked up behind her. Still naked. Still beautiful. She tried to keep her eyes on her own reflection.

And failed. He was a study of shadowed, lean muscle. Cut abs, rounded pecs, tattoos—flowers, a skull, the cross on his arm—sketched permanently onto his olive skin. Just so sexy he made her teeth hurt. "Are you shittin' me right now?"

She so was. But giving in meant they'd continue this discussion. And then what? Asher was about to go home to LA. She was about to go home to Chicago. How could either of them act on the level of intimacy they'd just experienced? They couldn't.

She tore her eyes off his reflection and spun on him. "This wasn't a new beginning for you and me, Asher. You knew what this was before we came up here. A blow job and sex and then we both return to our regularly scheduled lives."

Her own words cut into her. Deep. Deeper than before because part of her was already too vulnerable to him. Dammit! Why hadn't she said no?

"You think that's what you are to me?" His expression was downright murderous.

She didn't think that. Part of her thought he might be the man who held the key to figuring out who she was. To letting her be who she was. The real her. Another part of her believed that Ash was the real him when he was with her. But none of this was practical.

They had too much between them. Past. Geography. More stubbornness than a herd of mules…

"I have to go," she said.

"Sarge—"

But she didn't let him finish. She threw open the door of the borrowed bedroom, collected her coat and purse, and ran into the frigid December air.

* * *

Gloria blinked out of the memory, feeling every ounce of pain and hurt she felt that night.

"I was really mean to you last year," she murmured.

"You're mean to me all the time, Sarge." Asher was still close and he used the hand in her hair to tilt her face to his. "I like it."

"You're sick," she said, giving him a small smile of her own. It felt so damn good to be held by him. To have her head cradled in his hand and his focus zeroed in on her— even in this sea of people, he made her feel like she was the only one who existed.

Out of her peripheral, she spotted Brice and Evan as they elbowed their way through the crowd.

"That was fast." She looked up at Asher. "They're back."

He didn't turn around or back away. Simply stood, one hand in her hair and one clasping her hip.

"We should probably—" She pressed her palms onto his chest, but Asher didn't let her push him away. He stamped her mouth with his, pressing her body against his hard, warm muscles when he did.

Somewhere beyond her swirling mind and the heat radiating between them, she was aware of Evan muttering, "Ah, hell."

Asher didn't stop kissing her, and she couldn't bring herself to stop either. She closed her eyes and enjoyed the flavor of his mouth, the feel of his firm lips, and the way his tongue knew when to spar and when to stroke.

No one kissed like Asher Knight.

He moved his mouth along hers, tilting her head with the press of calloused fingers to her jaw, and finished her off by gently dragging his teeth along her bottom lip. By the time he pulled his lips away and lowered her to her heels, her entire being was flushed and horny. If that kiss had happened anywhere but in public, they'd both have been wearing a hell of a lot less clothing by now.

Her fingers went to her lips as she slid her eyes to Evan, who still had his eyebrow raised, then to Brice, who looked a combo of confused and angry.

"Whiskey," Evan offered a pair of drinks held in one hand, and kept hold of a beer for himself with the other. Asher took the cups and handed Gloria one.

"Thank you," she mumbled, aware of three pairs of eyes trained on her.

"Cheers, Sarge." Ash tapped his cup to hers and tossed back the whiskey. She followed suit and they threw their cups to the ground. There was a twinkle in his eye that said he'd known exactly what he'd just done.

I'm coming for you, Sarge.

"Asher, I was hoping to get a word." Brice was holding his own beer and scowling.

Shit. Brice would probably expect an explanation from her, too. She didn't have one. And she didn't think saying "Because Asher" would get her off the hook.

"Glo, babe. Let's talk business." Evan moved to her, and she was grateful for the reprieve.

Whatever was about to happen, neither Brice nor Asher needed her input.

* * *

Hell, that was fun.

Not just kissing Gloria—that was always fun—but

putting despair and jealousy on Brice's proper mug. The jackass. After Evan had (smartly) moved several feet away, Gloria in tow, Asher turned to Brice.

"Nice setup, McGuire. Any band would be lucky to get this kind of gig."

"Feeling the heat, Knight?" Brice stood, one hand in his pocket, Solo cup in the other.

"What heat?"

The other man tipped his head in Gloria's direction. "She was having a good time with me before you got here. We were getting...close."

Asher's nostrils flared. "Didn't notice. I was too busy kissing her."

Brice laughed and Asher's tendons went taut. This guy dug under his skin. He was pursuing Gloria, and from where Ash stood when he'd first spotted them dancing, it was working.

"Come on, Knight. We both know that kiss was to put me in my place."

Okay, he'd admit partly to wanting to show Brice what Gloria meant to him, but once he'd put his lips on hers, Brice was the furthest thing from his mind. It'd been all about tasting her, melding with her, wanting her. He'd felt her give—go pliant beneath his touch—which meant he had a shot.

"Make you a deal," Brice said. "You bring the band over to me for representation and I'll stop pursuing Gloria."

Asher couldn't have heard that right. He took a step closer to Brice, fist curling at his side. "You're gonna want to rethink that statement, McGuire. You think I'd let anyone use Gloria for anything, you're a bigger asshole than I originally thought."

Hitting him would be ill-advised—his PR person would kill him—yet so satisfying. Decisions, decisions...

"I'm not using her at all." Brice was too calm. Asher didn't like it. Didn't trust it. "I was offering as a courtesy. I think she likes me."

"I think you might see things differently when I drop you on your ass in front of all these people." Ash tilted his head. Ill-advised or not, maybe just one solid hit. He'd break his nose and walk away. He was Asher Knight, after all. He may have a dog, a house, a son he was trying to get closer to, but that didn't mean his edge was dulled. When it came to Gloria, this bastard needed to know she was out of fucking bounds.

"You need a new agent." Brice sipped his beer, undeterred.

"So, not just an asshole, but a stupid one. You think I'd let you touch my band?"

"You're a smart guy. You know the benefits of being linked with an agent with my connections. And soon, when Gloria agrees to partner with me, she and I will share lots of things. Clients. A federal ID number. Chicago." He smiled smugly.

Chicago. Asher felt like he'd taken a punch to the gut.

"She just moved here, dumbass." But Asher's confidence had slipped a little. She'd partner with Brice McGuire over his dead body. "You have nothing to offer her."

Not in business. Not personally. Asher would see to it.

Brice didn't have a chance to respond because right then a very high-pitched squeal came from their left, followed by, "*Oh my God!* Are you Asher Knight?"

A blond girl, old enough to drink but Asher would guess

not by much, wobbled over wearing knee-high, sparkly pink boots. *Pink.*

Worst timing ever, but if there was one thing he wasn't willing to do it was snub a fan. He owed them. The fans made him who he was. They may forgive him for brawling in public, but not for ignoring one of their own.

"Tend to your groupie," Brice said.

Definitely hitting him when he was done.

Asher turned to the girl and put a finger to his lips. He did his best to look coy. "Don't tell, okay? I'm in disguise."

"Oh my God," the fan whispered this time. "I love you." She cradled her red Solo cup and judging by the size of her pupils, whatever was in there wasn't the only substance she'd had tonight. "Can I get a photo?"

"Sure thing, honey." Quicker they got this over with the better. He always had time for fans, but he also had Brice's face to smash in. Gloria took priority, and setting things straight needed to happen.

Ash went to the fan as she pulled a cell phone out and switched to selfie mode. In what he guessed was her signature pose, she pouted and snapped the picture while he gave a practiced smirk.

"Oh my God! Will you sign my body?" She tucked the phone back into her pocket. "I don't have a pen."

"Sharpie?" Brice offered, producing a black marker from his pocket.

Ash snatched it from him.

The blonde yanked the very low-cut neck of her shirt even lower and pointed out where she wanted Asher to sign. Tit. *Of course.* He scrawled his signature over her boob as requested.

He capped the marker and backed away while the girl

snapped a selfie of his artwork. She was something else. And he'd bet she started every sentence with—

"Oh my God!"

That.

"Thank you!" she said, forcing her voice to a whisper when he held his finger to his lips again.

"Welcome." He lifted his hand to wave and took a few steps away from her.

"I'm going to get it tattooed," she called.

"Send me a picture."

Her eyes glazed over the slightest bit. "Oh my God, really?"

Shit.

"Yeah, listen, honey, I gotta run." He glanced around, noticing a few people in the crowd looking in his direction and whispering to each other in a way he knew meant they'd recognized him. Lucky for him, right then the band took the stage. Which gave him the perfect distraction as the crowd moved forward in anticipation. Evan and Gloria came back, narrowly avoiding the crush of the crowd pressing closer to the stage.

"Time to go," Evan stated. He hadn't missed a thing. Probably knew that Asher was about to get into a fight with Brice.

"Yeah." Ash turned to Gloria. "Come on, I'm taking you home."

Her eyebrows pulled down. "I'm not leaving. I want to hear the second set."

"Uh, man." Evan palmed his shoulder roughly and Asher saw that the blond girl had met a gaggle of other girls who were looking over at him.

Fuck. He'd been made.

"Come with me if you want to live," Asher offered his hand, wanting to get Glo out of here and the hell away from Brice.

"I drove her here. I can drive her home," Brice said.

Asher turned to him and his fist balled automatically. Then he spotted some of Evergreen Cove's finest spread out along the edges of the crowd. The familiar face of Officer Brady Hutchins among them, who gave a chin lift like he'd also gleaned what was going on.

"Unless you wanna spend the night with Brice in jail, I suggest we go," Evan said close to Asher's ear. Totally had figured out what Ash was thinking.

Gloria either overheard or picked up on the tension. "I can't believe you. Either of you. Whatever. I'm done." She waved them off, then turned toward the stage and started hopping to the music.

Asher frowned.

Brice shrugged. "Say the word, I'll back off."

Asher leaned in close enough so Brice could hear him. "*No* is the word."

He forced a cocky grin he knew would make Brice wonder what Asher was up to, then walked to Gloria, clasped her hip, and put his mouth to her ear.

"See you soon, Sarge. Don't forget to miss me."

When he backed away, she looked up at him—a little dazed and not just from the whiskey. He knew her. No matter what McGuire tried tonight, she wouldn't touch him. Not after Asher had kissed her first. Which made coming out tonight worth it in every way.

"I'll be fine," she said, jutting her chin out.

"You are that." He winked at her and turned to leave, sidestepping Brice, who didn't look the least bit threatened.

Had to be a mind game he was playing. Ash wasn't falling for it.

"We'll see, Knight," Brice stated calmly.

That's when Asher found his smile. Like Charlie said, the race may have started without him, but after that kiss? He knew who was in the lead.

CHAPTER 6

*G*loria stepped outside her apartment and started off to work on foot. That was one benefit to living close. She'd walked to work often when she lived in Chicago, but in the Cove, the pace was different. Slower, more relaxed.

More...her?

Not yet, but it could be.

Brice thought she didn't belong here, but she wasn't ready to give up yet. It'd taken a few years to fit in after she moved to Chicago, too. Evergreen Cove hadn't accepted her yet, but the people who lived here had. And that was a start.

Speaking of people who live here...

Asher Knight, in the tattooed flesh, stood on the walk in front of her, Tank at the end of a leash, wagging his tail. Gloria had been watching her shoes while she walked and, until she lifted her chin, didn't realize she had company.

"Brought you coffee," Asher said, familiar lopsided grin on his face, cups in his hands.

Hmm. Suspicious.

Determined not to let him break her stride, she walked to him, accepted the paper cup, and bent to give Tank a quick pat. "What else?"

"What else what?"

She straightened and lifted the cup. "What else did you want besides to deliver me coffee?"

"Walk you to work," he said, leisurely pacing beside her. Tank toddled along, keeping up. The dog was good on a leash. Either he'd had training or learned that getting under Asher's feet did not produce a desired outcome.

"And..." She smiled, wondering when she'd become so weak around him. She used to not take any of his shit. She used to be able to look at him and swoon internally but resist him externally. Now his charm overwhelmed her, and she wasn't sure he was trying.

It was just...him.

"And find out how your evening went with Dickhead." A little of his charm slipped. Last night, she thought he was being immature and jealous, but today she could see it'd really bothered him when she'd stayed behind with Brice.

"I'm sure you already know," she said, eyes straight ahead as she drank her coffee. God. Cup of Jo's. How did they make a coffee better than any she'd ever had?

"I have a guess," he said.

"I bet you do."

Asher had kissed her last night to derail her. Both of them knew it, and neither of them had stopped it. There was a time that kiss never would have flown. A time when she wouldn't have spent the rest of the evening thinking about how amazing Asher's lips felt and how tempting he was to every female part of her.

After Ash had gone, Brice had asked her point-blank if she always made out in public and she'd laughed it off, saying, "He's crazy." When Brice drove her back to her apartment's parking lot, he leaned over for a kiss, and Glo had given him her cheek instead.

She'd lain in bed, wide awake thanks to the whiskey buzz jittering her system, and wondered if she would have kissed Brice if Asher hadn't kissed her first. Maybe. Brice was attractive enough, and she admired his business savvy. But if she was considering partnering with him, she shouldn't entertain that line of thought.

Asher had mentioned he thought Brice was using her to get to him. She didn't know if there was something to that or if that was Asher being jealous. Then there was the issue of her thinking about how he'd set his lips to hers on purpose and how she knew as a strong, independent woman she should *not* like that kind of display of caveman claiming, but she had. Just a little.

Asher needed ground rules.

"It was fine, thanks for asking." She sent him a glance and he narrowed his eyes. He wasn't getting any more out of her today, so he would just have to deal. "I didn't know you were back to drinking coffee."

"I'm on a bender. I like things that are bad for me too much to give them up for good."

She wondered if he placed her into that category, then considered it was she who had given him up. Once bitten and all that.

"You look hot today, Sarge," he said, walking beside her at an easy gait.

She should. She'd dressed in a white dress, red belt looped at her middle and bright red shoes. Sunglasses, black.

Lipstick, red. She flipped her hair off her shoulder, and before she'd thought about it, pulled her shoulders back with pride. *Damn*. He could get to her like no one else. Asher had invaded her space by moving here, then with his nearness at Evan and Charlie's house, and then by kissing her last night. Now he was in her head, complimenting her and making her feel beautiful and like she was the center of his world.

But that was fleeting, wasn't it? He'd leave the Cove and then she'd get her head back. She just needed to hold out until then. But she felt as if she was already losing that battle. If he kept showing up, she'd never regain control.

She stopped halfway to her office, in front of a sandwich shop. Reggie's Subs wasn't open yet, being that it was only nine in the morning, which made it a fine hangout for this conversation.

"Asher, you can't keep behaving like there is some contest between you and Brice," she said.

"Oh, I know there's no contest." He lifted one eyebrow and Gloria felt her lips purse.

"What do you call that kiss, then?"

With a slight shake of his head, he replied, "I call it an appetizer to the bigger main course I didn't get to have." He took her coffee cup and put it and his on the bench in front of the restaurant, then reached out to brush her jaw with his fingertip. "Like to make up for that."

Gloria swallowed, her throat thick. *Resist, resist.*

But she didn't want to resist, because she'd like to make up for it, too. She could easily make out with him right here. Right now. She opened her mouth to say the opposite—if there was any hope of surviving him she had to listen to her brain, not her female anatomy—but didn't get a word out. Instead, a haughty, exasperated woman's voice cut through the air.

"There he is."

Asher took his hand from Gloria's face and scowled over her shoulder. She turned around to find an older woman coming toward them on the sidewalk, reddish-brown hair coiffed above a summery yellow suit.

"Emily," Asher said, his tone flat.

Emily?

Tank let out two quick yips.

"We said nine in front of the flower shop," Emily said.

"Jordan told me ten," Asher replied.

"I said nine," came a higher, sharper voice. If hearing Asher say Jordan's name didn't shoot a dart of pain through Gloria's heart, seeing her did. The brunette carried a very little boy on her hip. A boy with big dark eyes, hair a shade lighter than Asher's, and wearing the cutest ensemble of a blue shirt with a sailboat on it and cargo shorts.

The whole family was here. Gloria's knees went weak.

"There he is!" Asher's face split into a smile. He looked to Gloria. "Sarge, hang on to Tank." The sheer happiness on his face made her heart pick up speed. She accepted the leash and Asher rushed to lift his son out of Jordan's arms. The dart of pain in Gloria's chest dulled. Seeing him hold his son and seeing him so happy to see Hawk caused conflicting feelings: a dab of admiration and a dab of envy.

"No matter, we're here now," Emily said primly.

"We did say nine," Jordan said, rolling her eyes. Gloria felt her lip curl. Emily must be Jordan's mother. They had different hair colors and styles of dress, but the two women resembled each other.

Asher put his hand on the boy's chest and rubbed. "Hey, kiddo. This is Gloria. Can you say hi?"

"Mama," the boy whined, reaching for Jordan.

"Just put him down," Jordan spat.

"Jordan—"

"Mama!" At Hawk's exasperated cry, Asher lowered him to the ground. Hawk ran not to Jordan, but to Emily, hugging her leg.

"He's tired this morning." Something about the older woman was downright hard. As much as Gloria wanted to be Team Asher, she kind of couldn't blame Emily. Her daughter had been knocked up by a rock star who hadn't appeared in his son's life for a while. Granted, Jordan waited to tell Asher about his son, so that was her fault. Gloria wondered if Emily knew the whole truth. She glanced over to see Jordan standing off to the side, texting like a teenager instead of behaving like an adult with a child to rear. Glo guessed she was around twenty-eight, twenty-nine, tops, and she further guessed that Jordan's mother had done much of the heavy lifting in Hawk's life thus far.

Gloria took a step back, planning on making her getaway as quickly and cleanly as possible. Asher didn't let her.

"Emily." He put his hand on Gloria's back and brought her closer to him. "This is my book agent, Gloria Shields. Gloria, Emily Trudeau."

Trudeau. Her name sounded as wealthy as she looked. Gloria nodded her greeting. "Nice to meet you."

"You've met Jordan," Asher said, his voice dipping slightly.

Jordan tucked her phone into the pocket of her shorts and gave Gloria a curt nod. Yeah, this wasn't the most comfortable reunion. Emily's eyebrows lifted as she watched the exchange.

"Did you bring your swim trunks, Hawk?" Asher asked, folding in half to lower to his son's level. "We're going to go on a boat and maybe swim later. Sound good?"

Hawk's eyes widened in a combination of curiosity and fear at the suggestion, or maybe he sensed he was about to be left alone with his father. Clearly, the two of them hadn't spent a lot of time together yet, given the boy's shyness. It broke Gloria's heart to see Asher have to work so hard to earn his son's trust. She'd had parents who hadn't tried at all. Hawk was lucky.

"A boat?" Emily bleated.

Asher's smile slipped the slightest bit as he stood. "I have life jackets."

"Well, who's going to watch him when you drive the boat?" She tilted her head.

"I am," Asher answered, frowning. "It's not a speedboat, Em. It's a pontoon. Like a floating living room."

"You didn't say anything about a boat," Jordan said. "If you're planning on going on that thing alone with him, we'll just take him back home."

"Gloria's going, too." Asher shot her a glance. "Aren't you, Sarge?"

Gloria felt her eyes go wide. Going? Out with Hawk and Asher? For a change, she was tongue-tied. She wound the leash in her hand, utterly speechless. Jordan's eyes narrowed to slits.

"She and I have to talk about a few book things," Ash continued, clearly unaware—or not caring—that Gloria was about to have an anxiety attack.

Jordan continued glowering, her pretty features turning harsh. "Hawk doesn't know her."

"He doesn't know me either," Asher bit out, and as much as Glo didn't want to spend family time with a family that wasn't hers, she also kind of wanted to high-five him.

Emily pressed her lips together.

Wow. What a sour bunch.

"Would it be okay if Gloria came with us?" Asher turned his attention to Hawk. "She's fun."

Gloria, aware that Hawk was looking up at her like she was a giant scary monster, decided to stop looking like one. Apparently, she was going on a boat trip, and as much as she resented Asher dragging her into this situation, she'd much rather agree and piss off Emily and Jordan. Who did they think they were mandating how Asher could spend time with his son?

Gloria pulled her lips into a pretty smile and lowered to the boy's height, balancing on her heels. "I'm super fun," she told Hawk.

He smiled at her and a dimple appeared in his cheek. Oh goodness, he was so cute. Tank ran to her side and licked Hawk's hand.

"Doggie!" Hawk giggled.

"Yep, and the doggie is coming, too," Gloria said.

Asher lowered to his heels next to Gloria and her chest grew warm. She sneaked him a glance and he smiled, clearly grateful.

"Doggie swims?" Hawk patted Tank's back and Tank barked. Hawk giggled, exposing that dimple again.

Ahh-dorable.

"Doggie doesn't swim yet, but he has a life vest, too," Asher answered, scrubbing the top of Tank's tiny head. He shot a glare at Jordan and Emily as he stood. "I know Hawk's had lessons. Not like the kid isn't accustomed to water. I'll be with him the whole time."

Glo stood beside him. It felt right standing there shoulder to shoulder with him. If there was one thing she could be on his side about, it was his right to be with his child.

"And what qualifies *her* to watch my grandson?" Emily clipped.

Gloria blinked a few times. This woman had a lot of nerve, and she guessed Emily wasn't used to things not going exactly as she planned.

"I have nephews," Gloria said, rather than let Asher answer. She could speak for herself, thank you very much.

"Nephews," Emily repeated.

"Yeah." A half-truth. Her best friend Kimber's son Caleb was turning four this year and Glo had known the kid since birth. Plus Lyon referred to her as Aunt Glo. Totally counted.

"She doesn't have to qualify to you, Em," Ash said. "I trust her and that's what matters."

Much as she didn't want to go with him today, and as much as she wanted to give him a hard time for puffing his chest out last night, right about now, Gloria was glad for his interference. She wasn't easily intimidated, but Emily was almost...mean.

Emily slid her a cold gaze and Gloria stepped a little closer to Asher.

"It's settled, then." He put a hand on Gloria's back again. A drove of tingles lit her from head to toe. The man drew women like flies to honey. She jerked her gaze to Jordan, then Emily. *Or WASPs*, she thought with a little smirk.

"I have Hawk's bag in the car. Snacks, swim trunks, a change of clothes." Emily gestured to a Cadillac parked on the curb.

"I have all that stuff at home for him, Em," Ash said with a sigh. He'd had this discussion before.

"It's already packed," Jordan interjected.

"Lead the way." Ash lifted his arms, apparently unwilling to go to the mat over such a minor issue. He followed

Emily, flashing a glance at Gloria with an accompanying eye roll. She gave him an encouraging smile she didn't feel. Like, *at all*.

Because now she was alone with Tank and Jordan and Hawk. Every part of her wanted to pick up the little dog and high step it to her office.

"Didn't expect to see you here," Jordan grumbled the second her mother and Asher were out of earshot.

"I live here." That feeling of running away faded into the familiar art of digging in. That's what Gloria did when she was challenged. Normally. She'd run away from Jordan before—the night she'd encountered her at Asher's front door.

God. That memory killed.

"You think you're going to insert yourself into my son's life?" Jordan snapped.

Hawk watched warily and Glo, in spite of anger saturating her very being, fought to keep her composure. That she did for Hawk. "He's not only yours. He's Asher's, too."

Tank barked his agreement.

"Just know your place." Jordan curled her lip.

Gloria let the slack out of Tank's leash and Hawk immediately squatted to play with the dog. His attention diverted, Jordan blurted, "I didn't sleep with him that night."

Gloria gaped, torn between telling her this was an inappropriate discussion to have in front of a child and hearing her out.

"I wanted you to think I did, but I didn't." To her credit, Jordan glanced at her son, who was repeating the word "doggie" and laughing while Tank licked his face. She looked at Gloria to say, "He said you didn't believe him."

She hadn't believed him at first, but now was a different story—not that she'd let Jordan reel her into this discussion.

"Too bad," Jordan said with a lazy shrug. "You're missing out. Ash is a great lay."

"Yes, I'm aware," Gloria gritted out, anger burning her cheeks.

"You and every woman he's ever met, honey." Jordan flashed her a smile suggesting she'd baited Gloria into that admission. "But only one of us shares his child." An evil smirk set in as Asher rounded the corner with a bright blue beach bag over his shoulder. Emily was giving him an inventory of what was in the bag, neither of them aware that Jordan had just sank her fangs into Gloria.

"Grandmother and Mommy will be back in a few hours, okay?" Emily smiled down at Hawk. It was the first genuinely kind expression Gloria had seen on the other woman's face. At least she loved her grandchild.

"Mama!" Hawk stomped his feet, and the first sign of tears appeared. Gloria's heart broke a little more despite her feeling incredibly out of place. Every last ounce of her wanted to run away again. Just make an excuse and bolt.

"What is it, baby bird?" Jordan lowered to her knees and Hawk started crying and saying non-words. "You're going to hang out with Daddy today. It'll be fun." She swiped his tears with her shirt, getting her clothes wet and snotty and not caring. The scene made Gloria wonder if she'd hallucinated the moment when Jordan had become venomous.

But she hadn't. Both Jekyll and Hyde had been there.

"I love you." Jordan kissed her son and Emily repeated the sentiment, patting his head. Gloria guessed the other woman would sooner die than lift her tailored jacket to swipe the tears from Hawk's cheeks.

Hawk continued stomping and crying and a few passersby turned their heads to look.

Asher brushed by Gloria, his face contorted into a mask of pain. This had to be hurting him, seeing that his son didn't want to come with him.

"Come on, bud. Let's hang out today, okay?" He lifted his son off the ground and Hawk continued to wail, kicking his legs as Emily and Jordan blew kisses and walked for the car.

"Tank," Gloria suggested over Hawk's cries.

Asher nodded.

"Hawk. Look at the doggie. He's excited you're coming." Ash physically turned his son away from Emily's SUV. Hawk sniffled and turned his head over his shoulder to find Tank. "You like him?"

"Yeah," Hawk said tentatively, tears drying on his face. The meltdown had ended as quickly as it started. Glo could only hope that was the last one today.

"Doggie! Down, down, down!" Hawk kicked his legs, and Asher deposited him on the bench, lifting Tank to sit on the bench with him. He snatched up the coffee cups before boy and dog knocked them over. Gloria accepted hers with a tight smile.

"This is cutting me to the quick, Sarge." He shook his head, his eyes on his son. "And it's not even his fault."

"He'll come around," she said, smiling as Hawk and Tank played.

"You think?" Asher sought an answer on her face, watching her for so many seconds, she started to sweat. There seemed to be another silent question in the depths of his eyes. A question about her, and whether she'd come around as well.

She didn't answer that question.

She didn't dare.

CHAPTER 7

*L*ord have mercy, he was tired.

On more than one occasion, Asher had spent the day on a boat with Evan and Lyon. He'd taken for granted that Evan knew his own kid and Lyon knew his dad. Hawk and Asher weren't strangers, but they didn't have the closeness a father and son should have. Not yet.

Also, Lyon was several years older than Hawk. Hawk was *three*. Age three must be synonymous with "tornado on two legs." Today hadn't been quite the relaxing outing he'd pictured.

He'd imagined getting his son in the water, them splashing around a while, maybe floating in an inner tube. And then watching Tank doggie paddle—in his own dog life jacket—while Hawk laughed and clapped. Since Gloria had let him talk her into going, he further imagined her on the deck of the boat, phone to her ear, that gorgeous white dress blowing in the breeze. Lifting just enough to give him a view of her delicious thighs.

Things had been less like the music video he'd directed in his head and more like a nightmare on the open water. Hawk was mad about *everything*. He cried when Tank came near, he cried when Tank ran away. He wailed because he wanted in the water, only to wail that he wanted out once he was wet. Gloria didn't spend the day on the deck watching the water and sending him flirtatious winks—how could she? Hawk was in mid-fit most of the day, making it impossible for her to excuse herself to take the constant incoming calls on her cell phone.

Surprisingly, the only moment of peace came when the three of them sat down to eat. Asher had no idea if he'd prepared Hawk's sandwich right, or if the kid even liked cheese sandwiches, or if Hawk would sooner throw his animal crackers overboard than eat a single one.

But Hawk ate. He ate and smiled and fed Tank half his food, which was fine by Asher (and extra fine for Tank) because for once his son wasn't crying. Gloria joined them, but she'd gone so quiet, he couldn't get a read on her. Not that he had the space to ask her how she was. While he drove the boat, she sat with Hawk and pointed out gulls. When Ash was with Hawk, she kept her distance from them both.

"I'm going to go," Gloria announced. They'd docked at Asher's house and he'd carried a sleeping Hawk inside, happy about getting to hold him and happy he was asleep in equal measures. His boy was sunned and surfed and cried out. Thank God. Asher was exhausted.

"Don't go," he told Glo. "Hang out. I'll make you a cocktail."

"A cocktail." Her red lipstick had since worn off, and her plump lips pressed into a line.

"Yeah." He let loose a tired smile. "We can sit on the deck and talk." God. That sounded great. Apparently not to her. Her eyebrows crashed over her nose.

"You know, you pulled me into this day with you and your son. I didn't ask for this. I didn't want it."

Fuck. He wondered if her silence meant she was pissed today. He gestured to the front door and Glo crossed her arms defiantly. He dropped his hand and lowered his voice. "Can we bitch at each other outside?"

God help them all if Hawk woke up right now.

She took in Hawk's temporary sleeping spot on the couch and then marched out the back door. Ash looked at the ceiling, then at Hawk, who was definitely snoozing, and followed her out to the deck. The second he was outside, she lit into him.

"You know what I'd like? I'd like *not* to be pulled into the drama going on between you and Jordan."

And we're off.

"Drama?" Asher gestured to the house. "That's my kid in there, Gloria. He's not drama."

"I don't mean Hawk! I mean you pulling me into a family day with you like I'm the girlfriend or something. I'm not. I had work to do! I have a life. I can't just...just"—she threw an arm in the direction of the boat—"go out and play with you whenever you feel like it."

"You could've said no," he said, raising his voice some. "Last I checked, you aren't accustomed to agreeing to things you don't want to do."

And wasn't that the fuckin' truth?

"You don't *own* me, Asher Knight. You don't get to be possessive when I'm on a date—"

"Come on!" he interrupted. "You want me to believe you're pissed that I interrupted your *date* with Brice McGuire?" He knew her better than that—hell, Gloria knew herself better than that.

"Yes, Asher. A *date*." She leaned closer to him, fire in her eyes, her hair wild from the wind. "You don't get to pull me into your life whenever you need help. I have a life, too."

"I know that." But she kept going.

"A life that is not in this house, that is not on this dock." She pointed at the wooden slats they stood on now. "A life that shouldn't be happening *here*, of all places."

Okay, she'd officially thrown him. "What does my house have to do with anything?"

"How about the fact that I saved every dime I had to buy it?" She pointed at herself, poking red nails into her white dress. "I put down an offer and you outbid me. I was supposed to be living and working here, not playing family with a guy who only wants me sometimes!" She quit speaking when her voice became choked with emotion. He heard it. He *saw* it.

It took him a few seconds to piece together what she'd said.

"You put an offer on this house?" he asked, pointing at the deck.

She sniffed, crossing her arms and looking past him at the lake. "Yeah."

"Why the fuck didn't you tell me? I would have pulled my offer and let you buy it!"

"I know you would have!" she shouted, dropping her arms and going red in the face. "I didn't want you to!"

He couldn't win. And he also couldn't keep from grabbing her face, tugging those lips to his, and kissing her with every ounce of passion and anger and whatever else flowed between them whenever they reached this point with each other.

Gloria responded like he expected, tugging his T-shirt in both fists as she dragged him closer. They'd always been a volatile mix, their arguing a twisted form of foreplay. But when Asher's hands went to her hips and pulled her close, he found himself softening and her softening against him.

She pressed those pillowy breasts to his chest and looped her arms around his neck as he tilted his head to the side to make out with her as thoroughly as possible. She let out a muffled moan and he splayed his hand across her back, tucking her into him.

She tasted like everything he wanted but couldn't have. Being this close wasn't enough. Not for either of them. He could tell by the sweep of her tongue in his mouth she felt the same way.

The sound of barking cut through the haze fogging his brain. Glo started to pull back and he groaned in disagreement.

"Ash," she said, pulling her lips from his, but he went for her again.

More barking. Gloria shoved him back and this time when he turned to the house to tell Tank to shut up, he saw Hawk had climbed off the couch and was on the move.

Shit.

"Give me one second," Ash said. "I have to get him."

But Gloria had already sobered. She stepped back, her top teeth sinking into her bottom lip.

"Don't move," he told her, then ran for the house. He was out of time, and he knew it. He scooped up Hawk, who'd narrowly missed pulling a potted plant onto his head, then propped his son on his hip and went outside. Just as he'd anticipated, there was no one there.

The only sound was the clop-clop of retreating high-heeled shoes against the deck as Gloria made her way to her car.

* * *

After the longest day in recent history, Gloria decided she couldn't eat another frozen dinner. She headed out to Salty Dog instead and ate comfort food in the form of a fish and chips basket with a tall Dr Pepper.

Diet be damned. It'd been a hell of a long day. In the parking lot, she dug into the bottom of her purse for her keys, pulling out a toy dinosaur instead. Hawk must have hid it in her purse today when she wasn't looking.

The toy brought back memories of the day and stress pulled her shoulders tight. Being pushed into Asher's day, him *pushing* her into his day, had frightened her in a way she couldn't categorize. Never in her life had she pictured herself hanging out with Asher's son. Asher and Jordan's son.

Gloria may be good with Evan's son and Kimber's son, but when it came to Asher, she worried she'd fail Hawk and fail him big. She didn't want Hawk to feel Gloria's animosity toward his mother and Gloria was afraid she radiated it even if she didn't speak it.

Hawk deserved the best. Every child did.

She smiled down at the T. rex in spite of her tumultuous thoughts. Today she'd been uncomfortable, and she'd admit it, a little afraid. Okay, a lot afraid. She hadn't had the most stable home life and today was a reminder of just how ill equipped she was when it came to hanging around with a toddler.

It'd all bubbled over into an argument with Asher—admittedly the last thing he needed after working hard all day to be a good dad. God. She could be so selfish sometimes.

Bonus: During her rant, she'd told him about how she put an offer on what was now his house. She wasn't supposed to tell him about the house. Yes, she'd dreamed of owning it, but sometimes things didn't work out. She was accustomed to pulling on her big-girl panties and dealing with things, so why hadn't she?

The stress of standing on that deck with the man she'd shared too many close encounters with, his sleeping child in the house, had pushed her over the edge. She'd lashed out at Asher, who had already had a hell of a day.

Both of them had.

She wasn't really surprised. They tended to bring out the worst in each other. And the best. As illustrated by the kiss that followed. The kiss was nothing short of amazing. Had Hawk not been there, who knows what would have happened.

You know exactly what would have happened.

With a sigh, she climbed behind the wheel of her car and jammed the key in the ignition. She threw her purse on the passenger seat, dropped the toy inside, and pointed for Asher's house. She'd return the toy and apologize. Those big-girl panties also meant she could admit when she was wrong.

She fiddled with the radio as she took left and right turns on autopilot, shaking her head at the song. It was about breaking up in a small town. The man sang about how he couldn't avoid her after they split. How he ran into her at stoplights, at parties, at the same gas stations...It paralleled her life so closely, she had to smile.

Asher Knight. The man she'd never be rid of.

She pulled into his driveway a few minutes later. Toy in hand, she left her purse and phone in the car. Soft strums from a guitar floated on the air, a song she didn't recognize. Goose bumps covered her arms when Asher's rasping, sexy voice accompanied the melody.

Like a hapless sailor drawn by sirens, she slipped off her heels and followed the wooden deck around to the back of the house. What she should do was climb back in her car and leave, because no good could come from her being around Asher when his crisp voice hit that one note that made her shudder.

He sang another line. Predictably, she shuddered.

Damn. That was the one.

At the corner of the house, she spotted him on the bottom step. From there, the deck shot out into a long dock in the deep part of the lake.

Gorgeous night. Gorgeous guy. Gorgeous song. Definitely, she should leave.

Asher's voice, low and heartfelt, sent chills up her spine. She listened to the lyrics as he sang. Something about "blue eyes and summer skies and floating around with you."

She thought of the night in the mansion last year and chills covered her arms.

That's a song, baby.

Glutton for punishment that she was, she stepped lightly across the deck. A few candles in metal buckets were burning and the light from the flames danced off his bare arms. He hadn't noticed her yet. Unashamedly, she watched him without him knowing.

He sang another verse, stopped, replayed a few chords, and hummed to fill the spaces between words. Then he leaned over and jotted a few notes on a yellow pad with a pencil she'd just bet was full of tooth marks. She'd noticed the habit the first time she was around him. Nerves didn't get to Asher Knight on the outside, but showed on his Number 2s.

"Knock, knock," she said softly.

He turned, eyes glazed from deep concentration, clearly surprised to see her.

"Hey." He dropped the pencil and set the guitar aside, leaning it on the steps. The instrument was like a loaded gun. Each strum, each chord, every word he'd sung bullets drilling holes in her chest. Or maybe she was being melodramatic.

"Didn't expect to see you here," he said.

"Brought you this." She offered the toy dinosaur.

"Aw, you shouldn't have." He accepted, sticking his finger into the rex's jaws. "Hawk."

Risking dirt on her white dress, she sat next to him on the step and put her shoes down next to her. Dresses could be cleaned. This was important. She'd been unfair and wanted him to know she could admit when she was wrong.

"I also wanted to apologize." She folded her hands together, arms resting on her knees.

He leaned, elbows on his thighs, and faced her, sending her a smile that made her weak all over. The same way he looked at her when they were in bed together.

"Not like you to apologize, Sarge."

That was, unfortunately, true. She hadn't given in where it counted with Asher. Opening up to him had always scared her right down to her toenails. *Time to grow up.*

Past time.

"I'm sorry," she blew out. She opened her hands and then clasped them together again. "I was mad and I overreacted."

He put a hand over both of hers. A small gesture, yet so big. And it made her want to scoot closer to him, which of course put her on the defensive again.

"You can't blame me. Not like you put me in the most comfortable position," she snapped, undoing the apology she'd just doled out, so she added, "Anyway, I'm okay now, and I wanted to make sure we were okay."

He watched her for a moment, then his lips curved in bemusement. He gave her hand a squeeze and let go. "We're okay, Sarge. You let loose with me and that's not a bad thing."

She bit the inside of her cheek. She did let loose with him. Of all the stress-induced moments of her life when she'd been able to hold it together, she came completely unglued when it came to Asher. Whether they were arguing or kissing.

She tightened her folded fingers, her nerves rattling. So…she could leave now. She guessed. But she didn't move.

"How'd the rest of your day go?" he asked.

"Busy." She tilted an eyebrow at him. "I feel like crashing. Or drinking a bottle of wine. Or going out dancing."

"Interesting mix." He smiled.

"You know me. Restless and don't know how to fix it." It was supposed to be a throwaway statement, but he didn't let it go.

"I do know you, Sarge." He stood, balancing the toy on the railing and extending a hand. "I know exactly what you need."

"Ash." She ran her suddenly sweaty palms down her skirt.

"It's totally innocent."

She didn't fully trust him, or herself when she was with him.

"Okay, *mostly* innocent." His smile broadened to a grin.

She put her hand into his. He held her fingers loosely against his palm and together, they walked down the dock.

"Beautiful night," she said as they strolled.

The stars glimmered in a navy sky and the pale moon shone, reflecting off the lake's placid surface. The back of the house faced a huge private portion of the lake surrounded by trees. Another mansion-style house was on the other side, another off to the far left, but unless someone had a telescope, he had privacy.

"You have a slice of paradise here." She lifted her head to take in the night sky.

"What was supposed to be your slice," he muttered.

She looked back at him. "I shouldn't have mentioned that."

"You should have mentioned it sooner."

"I have a place." She shrugged. "I'm settled."

"Don't want you to settle, Sarge." He held her eyes for a beat too long before saying, "Haven't seen where you call home yet, you know."

"No, and you won't, either." The retort came out like a bark. She didn't make it a habit to let people into her private space. She closed her eyes briefly, realizing she was being mean yet again. "Sorry, that wasn't nice."

"Nice doesn't suit you." He chuckled.

He knew her. He got her. She'd never known anyone like him.

"Where's Tank?" She needed a topic change with Asher's hand warming hers, the stars making her start to fantasize about dreams and a future and the view that could have been hers...He was standing so close. All she could think about was the kiss earlier.

"In bed." Asher's voice came out seductive, but it wasn't

his fault. His voice was seductive. It's why he was so great at what he did.

"Probably has his own room." She cleared her throat, nervous and not understanding why. Or well, yeah, she did. She wanted to kiss him again and things were suddenly... awkward.

"He has a crate but usually prefers furniture. After Emily came to pick up Hawk, Tank crawled into that crate and crashed. He had a big day."

Asher dropped her hand and stepped behind her, resting his palms on her shoulders and blanketing her back with his signature heat. No wonder girls cried and went nuts when he was near. He was like an element, but a new one—like water and fire mixed.

"Water's warm," he said, mirroring her thoughts. He ran his hands down her bare arms. "Had my feet in it earlier."

"I haven't swam since I moved here." She shivered but it wasn't the least bit cold.

"How can you live in a lake town and not swim?" he asked, his mouth close to her ear.

"I don't know," she breathed. "Busy, I guess."

"Maybe you should stop being busy." That low, sensual tone struck her nerves and made her close her eyes. His hands moved from her arms to the red belt looped around her dress. His fingers touched the buckle and she covered his hand with hers.

"Ash." A whisper.

"Let's get wet." He lowered his lips to her ear—her absolute weakness. His tongue flicked out and drew a circle and she felt her knees give. He anticipated her reaction, looping his arm around her waist to support her weight. The belt hit the deck next to her bare feet a second later.

$\mathscr{C}$HAPTER 8

$\mathscr{A}$sher bit her earlobe lightly, and she tipped her head to the side to grant him access to whatever parts he wanted to kiss. Because his mouth felt amazing, or because she was too tired to fight him, or because she missed him...Hell, all three.

Part of her didn't like to think too hard about consequences. She and Ash were compatible in that way. A large part of him didn't think hard about consequences either. She understood some relationships were temporary and just for fun and that was fine. Her family had been like that, her foster family had been like that, and she even had a few clients who had said "adios" after their temporary shared partnership.

People left. People moved on. It was an indisputable fact of life.

But Asher Knight—the very man who should have been a one-time thing, or at most a *two-time* thing—had somehow found purchase in her memory and her bones, and probably other parts of her she didn't want to acknowledge at the moment. If ever.

Behind her, his hands slipped up her dress, over both breasts, and then away, and she decided to hell with it. There was no way to avoid this. She knew it the moment she drove to his house on autopilot, the moment she spotted him with his guitar, the moment he offered her his hand. She was destined to end up with his mouth on hers again. That's where it belonged.

She lifted a hand and threaded her fingers through his hair as he continued kissing her neck. She kept her eyes locked on the stars, trying not to think about how good it was to touch him again, and how she hadn't forgotten what he smelled like, or how good he felt against her. Liked how she had someone to lean on. Someone she could trust.

Not hurting matters was the fact that the man was sex on legs. Watching him do anything led to imagining him naked. Another indelible fact was he was amazing in bed—and once she knew, she couldn't *unknow*.

Gloria could get a thousand kisses from now until the day she died, and she'd bet not a single one of them could rival the last press of Asher's lips to hers.

A tug on the back of her dress snapped her back to present. He pulled her hand out of his hair, drew the zipper down, and had her shoulders bared before she could think. Which was so damn refreshing after a day of nonstop thinking that she went with it. Warm, firm lips hit her shoulder as he moved her hair to the side.

"I missed that," she breathed. He knew how to turn her on. Better than anyone.

"I know." Another tug and the dress dropped to her feet.

She faced him. His eyes locked on her lingerie, matching white lace. She loved the fire in his eyes as much as she loved the answering fire in her belly.

"Sarge," he said, his voice husky, hands skimming over her waist.

"I know." She grinned.

He grinned back. A spark lit his eyes, and alongside the inferno of attraction burning between them, it was absolutely irresistible. She'd say yes to whatever he said next. He pulled off his shirt, exposing scrumptious abs and tats, and she was pretty sure she knew what was coming.

Until he said, "Skinny-dipping."

"What?" She took a step back from him and wrapped her arms around herself. "Forget it! There could be eels in there."

"Sarge." He flicked the snap of his shorts and dropped them, exposing a pair of V-lines above the black boxer briefs hugging his slim hips.

"Asher."

"Get wet with me." His eyes went to her panties. "I mean wetter than you already are because I know kissing your neck worked for you."

She narrowed her eyelids in faux anger. He was right—it did work for her. They were back on the familiar ground of attraction and playfulness, which was so much more comfortable than the intensity of a few moments ago.

"I don't have to do what you say," she challenged.

"No?" he asked, a feral light in his eyes.

She was feeling vulnerable standing this close to the water. She took another precarious step away from him and he advanced, crowding her closer to the edge of the dock. His lips quirked.

"Don't you dare." She held out a hand as he advanced.

"You'll like it." Another step forward.

"Asher, I mean it!" She skirted to the side, but he caught her. One warm arm locked around her waist like steel.

"No!" she whined, unable to fight his strength.

"Hold your nose." She heard the smile in his voice.

"Ash! Don't you dare! I mean it." She made a final, futile attempt to escape, but it was no use. Before she knew what happened, she was flying through the air.

* * *

Gloria's limbs went in every direction as she hit the water with the most inelegant splash he'd ever seen. It was *fantastic*. Nothing was more beautiful than when she let go. She was a planner and a control freak. So when he pushed her—this time literally—and she let him, well, hell...life didn't get better.

She popped out of the water and gathered enough oxygen to sputter, "You asshole!"

That was his cue.

He dove off the edge of the dock, disappearing beneath the dark water and popping up next to her as she was pushing her hair off her face. Her mascara was smudged under her formerly heat-filled eyes that now brimmed with anger.

Arm around her waist, he towed her in, getting a face full of water and some in his nose, when she drew back a hand and splashed him.

"I can't believe you did that!"

"Sarge." His tone said what he didn't. She should *absolutely* be able to believe that he did that. He swiped the water from his eyes. "Swim in." He tipped his chin toward the beach and let her go. In a few strokes, his feet hit ground and he lashed an arm around her again. "That's far enough."

She pushed at him but it was no use. He wrapped his hands around her ass and held on tight. "Not letting you go, so you may as well stop fighting me."

She paused and he paused and for a moment there was a flicker of awareness as his words hung in the air between them. She was wondering if he meant more than just here and now in this lake. And she wasn't wrong. He meant that in every way.

He knew it as soon as he'd seen her tonight. He'd been playing around with the lyrics for her song. The song he'd started hearing the melody to when he and Gloria were in bed last Christmas. Pieces of the song had hit him like a freight train—relentless and without warning. The same way seeing Gloria for the first time had hit him. Some instinctual part of him knew it was destined. Knew they were destined.

Sure, he'd tried to deny it. Tried to treat her the way he would any other woman. In theory, he should have been able to spend time with her, then move on. That's the way he'd been with girls since he was a teen. They traded their minutes for his minutes and then they let him go. Sex was a pastime he enjoyed. Drinking. Cards. Shooting the shit with his buddies. And sex. Sometimes the sex was on par with other hobbies, and sometimes it was better. And with Sarge? *Fantastically* better.

Sex was never as good as when he was with Gloria Shields. It was like she'd unlocked a part of him he never showed anyone. And when he saw who he could be with her, he was amazed. Had to squint because the potential of what lay beneath was too fucking bright for him to keep his eyes open.

Like now.

In the moonlight, Gloria, with her black hair, black lashes, pale skin, and piercing blue eyes, was so bright she was practically blinding. He towed her in, water sluicing between their bodies.

She wasn't alone when she freaked out the last time they were together. It was scary to see your future reflected in someone else's eyes. But she'd majorly chickened out at the very moment he became incurably intrigued.

He anchored his feet to the bottom of the shallow part of the lake. He knew where to dive, where to wade, and where to put his feet if he wanted to stand. He knew because he'd swam as often as possible since he'd been here. He'd always been a fish, but the way Gloria clung to him suggested she wasn't as comfortable in the black water.

"What's wrong, city girl?"

"You swear there aren't any eels?" Her eyes were wide as she scanned the surface of the water.

He bumped his budding erection against her leg. "Just one."

She gave him a bland look and he only smiled.

"Kiss me, Sarge. I need it."

She loosened her stranglehold around his neck, draping her arms at his shoulders instead. She watched him. He watched her back, admiring the elegant slope of her neck and all that black, wet hair sticking to her shoulders. Her cleavage and large breasts were decked out in a bra he could now see through. God bless the moonlight.

When his eyes returned to hers, blue gone navy, he kept them there, even though he was tempted to follow the drop of water rolling from her cheek to her lips.

Then she kissed him like he asked. No warning, no preamble, just laid her mouth on his and tightened her hold on his neck. He moved one hand to her back, flicking the clasp on her bra and releasing it on the first try.

She pulled a breath in through her nose but didn't stop kissing him or open her eyes. Long, ink-colored lashes lay on her cheeks. He knew because he'd been unable to take his damn eyes off her. He didn't want to miss a thing. As he moved the bra straps from her shoulders, she took her arms, one by one, from his neck. Bra off, he tossed the lacy garment onto the edge of the dock, and when he looked back, those gorgeous breasts, wet and beaded with water, were bobbing on the surface.

"I missed those, too," he said.

Gloria snorted. "You've had access to breasts I'm sure."

"Not yours." He cupped one and thumbed her nipple, taking her lips with his and wiping that smart-ass smirk off her face. He pushed his tongue into her mouth and she opened for him, wrapping her legs around his waist as he pinched and pulled at her nipple, his tongue dancing with hers.

Hell to the yes.

This was what kissing someone—what getting someone half naked—was all about. Only he wasn't mentally high-fiving himself as much as he was trying to keep from tearing off her panties and his boxers and plunging into her right in the middle of the lake.

Holding her body against his, he moved his hand south and slipped his fingers into her lace underwear. She pulled her mouth away from his, he guessed to suggest they slow down, or go inside, or stop altogether...but she surprised him by reaching beneath the water, holding on to his shoulder while she kicked, and bringing her panties out in one hand seconds later.

Asher's jaw dropped.

She squeezed the water out of her panties and tossed them next to her bra. Then her arms went back around his neck and she said, "Touch me."

Hot damn. It's like he was dreaming. "Cooperative" wasn't exactly a word he'd have used to describe the Gloria of late. Though, to be fair, she had come with him on the boat today. But he never could've imagined she'd come back to his house hours later and be naked against him, begging for his touch.

She didn't have to beg.

He moved his fingers to her pussy, waxed bare, save for a thin strip of hair at the seam. He traced over that strip and she bit her bottom lip, her eyes growing darker as her eyelids fell to half-mast. When he slipped his fingers into her folds, those eyes closed completely, her head falling back.

"That's it, Sarge. I have you." With her back arched, he had ample access to her breasts, so he leaned his head down and licked and suckled a nipple as he quickened his pace below the water. Water wasn't known for its lubrication, but she provided plenty, and he worked her into a slick, hot, shuddering mess in only a few seconds. He swirled his tongue over one nipple, then moved to the next hardened peak, biting her lightly and then kissing his way up her neck. When he reached the spot behind her ear, he licked and sucked there, too. A warm surge came over his fingers below and he thumbed her clit with renewed focus.

"Asher, yes," she breathed, and the sound of his name in her sweet voice was his ultimate reward. He plunged two fingers inside her, working her clit with his thumb as he bit down on her earlobe. Before she could moan his name again, she came, clamping his fingers with her inner muscles, clawing at his back, and pulling his hair.

His mouth left her neck to smile down at the sight of Gloria in his arms, cheeks pink, eyes closed, mouth open, breasts bare. He loved her naked. Getting to see the way her small shoulders gave way to an ample rack, then swept in at her flat stomach. And beneath the water were two thick, incredible thighs and a pussy he'd love to thrust into over and over and over *and over* again.

He kissed her mouth gently, nibbled along the jaw, but when he got to her ear, she tilted her head to stop his assault.

"I resent how good you are at that," she said.

"Nah, you don't. You enjoy how good I am at that."

Her eyes opened lazily.

"Written all over your face, Sarge." He smiled. "Let's go in."

She reacted like he'd asked her to take up stripping in her spare time. She covered her breasts with one arm, hiding them, which was comical since he'd just had them in his mouth. What she said, though, wasn't comical at all.

"I can't. I mean, I'm not going in."

"Why not?"

"Because if I come in, we'll have sex." Her brow furrowed.

"Promise?" He lowered his lips for a quick kiss.

"Then what?" She palmed his face, stopping his lips before they covered hers again.

"I'll make you come two or three more times and then I'll come and then we'll sleep," he answered. And really, how hard was that to figure out? Where was the argument? He couldn't see one.

"And in the morning?" she prompted. "And the day after that? And the one following that one?"

He pretended to think about what she said. "I think we

can negotiate number of orgasms, but I'm good with a one-a-day minimum."

Both hands on his chest, she shoved at him again but he held her tight. When her eyebrows met over her nose, he spoke before she could.

"You want to leave here and go home and continue dating Brice? You want to kiss him and fuck him instead of me? Or do you just want to make me think you are so I get jealous of what he's getting instead of me?"

"Oh, you think this is a contest?" She went from merely argumentative to good and pissed in a heartbeat. A charge shot through him, energizing him. If she was pissed, she was passionate, and he'd take that over her faux politeness any damn day of the week.

"I think you're trying to make it one," he said, baiting her.

"You left me alone with Jordan on Endless Avenue."

"To walk to a car across the street." He shook his head, unable to see what that had to do with this. "So?"

"So? So, it was the first time I was alone with the woman who…" She trailed off as if she was about to say something she didn't mean to…probably something revealing she'd rather him not know. He was so tired of her holding back.

"The woman who what, Sarge? Come on. We have been over and over this. Finally, fucking say what you mean."

"Fine. The woman who took you from me." Her voice trembled but he could tell she'd fought to keep it strong.

Ah, hell. His chest morphed into a sinkhole and swallowed his heart. He wrapped Gloria so close his nose was on hers. "You see her around here anywhere?"

Gloria held on to his neck but didn't answer.

"Do you?" he repeated.

Slowly, she shook her head.

"Do you see any woman other than you in my arms?"

She shook her head again.

"Right. Because when there's you, there's only you. And right now, there's *you*. I've told you a hundred times I didn't fuck her when she crawled into my window. She'd tell you herself if you asked."

"She did tell me," Gloria whispered.

"Seriously?" He pulled back to study her expression. Sincerity was written all over her face.

"Earlier today," she confirmed.

"So what's the problem?"

"The problem…" She looked up at the sky before pegging him with those blue eyes and shooting him straight. "The problem is that if I go to bed with you tonight, there's no guarantee you won't go to bed with someone else tomorrow."

He pulled his head back some so he could focus on her. She actually looked worried. "I could say the same to you."

"I wouldn't do that to you."

"I wouldn't do that to you either, Sarge. I *never* did it to you. You need to check your feelings against your facts, babe. I never had the desire to sleep with Jordan again. I didn't try to start a family just because she had my kid. Besides, if I married her, she'd be Jordan Knight. Like one of those New Kids on the Block."

Gloria blew out a brief laugh, and he could tell she didn't want to laugh. Her smile faded a second later.

"Point is, I don't want Jordan." He lowered his nose to hers again and squeezed her in his arms. "I don't want anyone else. I want you, dammit. And here you are."

"Ash."

"Sarge," he said, letting his voice drop low and his arms hold her tighter. "Let me blow your mind tonight."

There it was. As offers went, he couldn't make what he wanted any clearer. And when she gave her answer, it was equally clear and the exact opposite of what he wanted to hear.

"I can't," she whispered, then let go of him and swam for the ladder on the dock.

CHAPTER 9

 ofie pushed her sunglasses up and leaned her head back to smile up at the bright sun. "This. Is. The. *Life*."

"Totally." Faith smiled up at the sky as well.

Then the two of them laughed and clinked their iced tea glasses together. Next to Gloria, Charlie let out an audible sigh. They'd come to her office for Girls' Night Out— Charlie had kept her house for her photography work after she moved in with Evan two doors over. It was a great setup with a huge porch that emptied right onto a grassy/ sandy beach and the shallows of the lake. Sofie and Faith, both pregnant, lounged on chairs at the edge of where grass met sand with nonalcoholic beverages, which left Gloria and Charlie on the porch and in charge of drinking the wine.

"The babies are an epidemic around here." Gloria refilled Charlie's wineglass, then her own.

"Yeah." Charlie accepted her wine, her voice was as watery as her eyes.

Gloria cast a glance to the pair of friends several feet away on the beach. Faith laughed at something Sofie said. They were wrapped in conversation, not listening in at all.

"You okay?" Glo asked Charlie.

She nodded, but she wasn't. And because once Charlie had been there when Glo had a complete meltdown over Jordan, she turned her chair to her blond, sad friend and invited her to open up.

"Talk to me, Charlie."

Charlie cast a gaze at their friends, then lowered her voice. Eyes rimmed with red, she said, "Evan and I have been trying to get pregnant for a year...I haven't wanted to say anything in front of Sofie and Faith because I don't want them to think I'm not happy for them. Because I am." She shook her head. "It's just..."

Oh, shit.

Once upon a time, Gloria had been faced with a best friend confiding in her about an unplanned pregnancy. She hadn't given Kimber the sagest of advice. At the mention of something so quintessentially female, Glo nearly burst into hives. She sucked at advice for other people and was so terrified to steer Charlie wrong, she didn't want to say anything. So she lifted her wineglass instead.

"I'm really happy for them," Charlie sort of repeated. She sniffed and pressed her lips into a line.

Well. Damn. Gloria had to say something. She couldn't sit here completely silent like a jerk.

"I almost had sex with Asher."

"Oh my gosh." Charlie snapped her head around, her eyes growing wide. "What? When?"

"Night before last. I'm sorry. I know I should be comforting you, but I'm really horrible at it. You shared. I'm sharing. That's all I have to share." She hadn't talked to him since, which was perfectly normal and something she was trying not to freak out over. She refused to be the clingy girl. That wasn't her. She wasn't in the same zip code as clingy.

"What do you mean by *almost*?" A smile burst onto Charlie's face and it was like seeing the sun come out from behind gray clouds. That was more like it. The honey-blonde in the patterned yellow dress looked much more herself when wearing a wide smile.

Gloria raised an eyebrow. "I'm assuming you know what I mean by *almost*."

Charlie grinned. Yeah, she knew.

"Why do you look happy?"

"You have to tell me something." Charlie leaned forward and put her hands into prayer pose. "I beg of you."

Gloria sighed. She supposed she did owe her some details.

"We went swimming. Sort of. I mean, we started out in our underwear and then it turned into skinny-dipping. Then we were making out, and then…other things." Unbelievably, Gloria felt her face go warm. "But I didn't go all the way. And I won't either. I'm not giving in to him."

Again. Even though she felt like she already had.

"That's awesome. I think. Oh my gosh!" Charlie was still grinning. Which was unnerving.

"What are you two carrying on about?" Faith walked barefoot from sand to grass to the porch, Sofie on her heels.

"Yeah," Sofie said, sandals looped in her fingers. "What happened? Charlie looks like she just heard a huge secret."

"I didn't." Charlie drank her wine, but the guilt in her eyes gave her away.

Faith pointed at her. "Lies!"

Sofie scuttled to the nearest chair at the table and sat, her chin in her hands. Faith sat, too, but she craned one eyebrow expectantly while Charlie kept her wineglass tilted to her lips. Every pair of eyes was on Gloria.

Damn. It.

"Fine," Gloria said. "Asher and I—"

"Yay!" Sofie exclaimed.

"Did *not* sleep together last night."

"Sorry. I'm 'shipping." Sofie pressed her fingers to her lips, but behind them she was still smiling.

"But they *almost* did it," Charlie pulled away her wineglass to interject.

"Oh, you're close, then." Sofie angled a glance at Faith, who was frowning, then back at Gloria. "Wait. This is a good thing, right? Or no? I'm so confused."

"Glo?" Charlie asked, abandoning her wine.

"I managed to get away from him before we went too far." Gloria didn't have to look over. She could feel Faith's penetrative gaze boring a hole into her head.

"I don't see any reason why you should stay away from him," Charlie said.

"Besides the fact that he sleeps with every female who approaches him, including the one he cheated on Gloria with?" Faith crossed her arms. "I get it. He's a beautiful, famous man. And you have a past, but—"

"But this is also your past talking," Sofie said. "Asher didn't cheat. He didn't sleep with Jordan...I mean, not after he was with Gloria."

"Yeah, he didn't cheat," Charlie agreed.

Both of them had known the truth for so long. Gloria had really stayed in denial, hadn't she?

"But he did have a child with Jordan," Faith argued, crossing her slender arms over her small breasts.

That was a fact. An undeniable one.

"I married a guy with a child from another woman," Charlie said.

"That's totally different," Faith said.

"It is, but it doesn't mean things can't work out between—" Sofie started.

"Asher and I are not fucking!" Gloria shouted.

Her friends blinked at her like stunned owls.

"Sorry." She lowered her voice. "We had some fun, that was it. And Sofie and Charlie are right about Jordan," Glo said as an aside to Faith. "He didn't cheat. She told me herself, and trust me there is a lot of love lost between us, so if she could have lied to her benefit, she would have." But Jordan had twisted it to her benefit. She'd brought up Hawk to remind Gloria she had something Gloria didn't: a lifelong tie to Asher.

Everyone fell quiet, a gull cried in the distance, and water lapped the shore.

"I'm just going to see him when I see him," she continued. "And our seeing each other will *not* involve nine inches of Asher's finest asset as long as I have anything to say about it."

"So close," Charlie whispered with a headshake.

"Jordan really told you she didn't sleep with him that night?" Sofie asked.

"Yeah." Gloria reached for her drink, surprised to see her hand shaking from her mini-outburst. She drank down the remainder of wine in her glass.

"Nine inches," Faith said, her eyes glazing the slightest bit, sending all of them—even a reluctant and sexually frustrated Gloria—into giggles.

"So where are your guys tonight?" Gloria asked, desperately in need of a subject change.

"With yours," Charlie answered.

Gloria blinked slowly at her smug friend.

"They're getting ready for the party tonight." Sofie reached for a pita chip and dragged it through the bowl of crab dip from Abundance Market. That was the most addicting stuff Gloria had ever tasted in her life.

"What party?" Gloria asked.

Sofie stopped mid-crunch and Faith and Charlie gave Gloria twin wide-eyed "don't-you-know?" looks.

"The...big bash. With the band. Asher texted everyone this morning." Charlie's brow crinkled.

"Oh! Right. Sorry. I was thinking it was a different night." Gloria left a lame excuse for a smile on her lips and hoped to God her friends would stop looking at her like they pitied her. Like they knew the truth: that the man she'd refused to sleep with was possibly punishing her by not inviting her.

"Who sets a time for a party as 'nightfall' anyway?" Charlie asked with a laugh.

"I know, right?" Faith reached for a chip. "I'm glad we didn't change our Girls' Night Out date, though. Because we should never let boys dictate what we do."

Sofie fist-bumped Faith and Gloria felt herself getting further perturbed that she hadn't known about the party. Two days had passed and Asher hadn't bothered to so much as send her a text message. Then again, she hadn't tried to contact him. She'd gone home that night, simultaneously kicking and congratulating herself for sticking to her guns.

And so sexually frustrated, her vision was blurred. When she thought back to the way he'd held her and offered, "Let me blow your mind tonight," she had no earthly clue how she'd been able to turn him down.

Charlie steered the conversation into less choppy waters, and Gloria ate her crackers and cheese and drank her wine and smiled. But she seriously did not know what to do about this party thing. She wasn't invited, but an invitation was sort of assumed, wasn't it?

Well. Whatever.

She'd just show up. Invited or not, she knew where he lived.

* * *

Connor dropped another pile of cut branches into the huge fire pit by the lake. "That oughta do it."

Ash and the former military man hadn't been buddies back in the day—given that Connor was younger and more Donovan's friend than anyone else's, but they'd become unlikely friends over Asher's last several visits here.

Truth of it was, the landscaper helped everyone with everything. The moment Asher bought his vacation house, he made a call to Connor to get help with trimming back trees, planting flowers, and placing decorative rocks around his place—shit Asher knew nothing about.

And, yeah, landscaping was Connor's business, but he'd also texted Ash about other ideas he had for the place and didn't charge him any extra. Stand-up guy, and smarter than smart.

"Thanks, man." Ash clapped Connor on the back as he walked by.

Donovan came outside, Tank shadowing his every footfall. Asher saw why when Donny ate another piece of summer sausage sandwiched between two crackers.

"You're eating my party food."

"Taste-testing," Donny corrected as he chewed.

The crack of a can being opened sounded from Asher's right and he turned to see Evan slug back half the beer in a few deep guzzles. He let out an exaggerated, "Ahhh."

"I'm in. It's been a long, hot day." Connor went to the cooler.

The sun was low in the sky and everything was ready. Asher figured the band would straggle in later than late. They showed up yesterday. He'd met them at Salty Dog for shots, but when each of them partnered off with a few girls who'd come sniffing around, he took his leave.

He had Gloria. He sure as fuck didn't need a groupie in his bed.

"I'm in." Asher held up a hand. Evan tossed him a beer can and he caught it in one palm. He turned to look at the pile of sticks in the fire pit. "Light it up."

"Hell, yes." Donny tipped his head. "You're the one with fire in your pocket."

"I don't smoke. Why would I have a lighter?" Then, with a smile, Ash reached into his pocket and came out with a Zippo. The classic flip-top kind. He liked the weight of it there.

"I knew it. Old habits." Donny only shook his head.

Asher knelt to light the wadded-up newspaper beneath the sticks. He may not smoke any longer, but he liked having the lighter. And hey, bonus, carrying it wouldn't give him lung cancer. God. He never used to worry about any of that shit.

Thoughts like that made him worry he was losing his edge, but then he remembered he'd tossed Glo in the lake, followed her in there, and stripped her naked. He smiled to himself. Yeah, he still had it.

"Charlie says they will be here in thirty," Evan said, pocketing his cell phone. "Faith is driving. She and Sofie are in charge of our girls since they're not drinking."

Our girls. Ash didn't miss that reference.

"I hear congratulations are in order," Asher said to Connor, who had just finished off his beer. "You're gonna be a dad, too."

"Welcome to the crowd," Donny said.

Connor smiled and it was the most genuine expression. "I'm stoked. We had a false alarm last year, but this time, it's for real. I saw the heartbeat and everything."

"That's the best part," Donny agreed with a grin.

Evan chimed in with an ultrasound story of his own and Asher found himself watching the flames catch and feeling... something. Left out? Pissed off?

Both.

Jordan had been able to see Hawk's tiny, fluttering heartbeat on the monitor, and where had he been? Getting a blow job from some nameless girl? Screaming his face off onstage? Or something much more mundane like paying his taxes or sleeping off a hangover? He'd never know. Jordan had denied him the opportunity to experience his son's first heartbeats.

As alarming as it was to find out he was a father a year and a half after the fact, it was even more alarming to learn just how much he'd missed during that time.

"Shots?" he interrupted the guys.

They fell silent for a moment before Evan said, "Got it. Starting early tonight, I guess."

"It's a party, isn't it?" Asher chucked his beer can into the fire and crossed his arms. He needed to improve his mood, stat. Brooding was more Donny's thing than his. And it was a *party*. He was going to have fun, not think about how things kept going the way he didn't want them to.

"Whiskey?" Evan called over his shoulder, heading for the house.

Connor and Donny looked to Asher, who smiled.

"Whiskey," Donny confirmed.

"Yippee ki-yay," Connor said.

CHAPTER 10

*G*loria walked into the party behind Charlie, Sofie, and Faith. She was dressed in a casual summer dress—classic black and white striped—and comfy sand-approved flats.

She fit in, she knew half the people here, so why did she feel as if she didn't belong? She and Ash were friends at best, professional acquaintances at worst, and even if she *technically* wasn't invited, she could be counted as a plus one to any of the girls she'd arrived here with. So there was no reason she should be feeling—

"Ladies." Asher ambled up to their little group as they stepped onto the deck. He was wearing a tight, faded gray tee and black shorts and a smile so charming it made Gloria's heart ache with longing.

You turned that down.

Yeah. Well. She'd do it again, too. Life wasn't about feeling good. Life was about being smart.

He doled out cheek kisses to Charlie, Sofie, and Faith.

"Guys are by the fire." He gestured to the tall flames at the edge of the lake where Glo could see the outline of several bodies. Donny, the tallest, was easiest to spot. "Steer clear of the band, though. They're trouble."

"You included," Charlie said as she walked away.

"Me *especially*." Ash winked.

Charlie looked back at Gloria, seemed to decide not to ask if she was following, then grasped the handrail for the stairs leading down to the beach with Sofie and Faith behind her.

Asher turned to Gloria and her stomach bottomed out. Here it was. Do or die time.

"I'm crashing," she blurted. "But I don't eat much. So there's that."

"Feisty vixen." He put his hands on her hips. "You're always invited, Sarge. You're with me."

"I'm not *with* you, Ash."

"We'll see." Before she could argue, he put his lips on hers and blanked her mind. He slid a hand along her lower back, pressing her chest to his. His other hand went to her hair, threading up through the strands. The way he moved against her was like sex with clothes on. And she reacted by arching toward him, wrapping her arms around his shoulders and accepting his talented tongue into her mouth.

He awakened her inner wild teenager. Kissing Asher made her remember a time when hormones bounced around her body untamed and unchecked. When she'd sneak out of her foster parents' homes—pick one, there were three—and make out with a boy in the back of a car or in a basement while the parents were away. Kissing Asher felt as if she were breaking curfew in clothes she'd had to keep hidden deep in her closet—her shortest skirts. Her tallest shoes.

She pulled her lips from his, but he didn't let her go far,

holding her to him with one hand on the small of her back and the other on her ass. How'd that get there? She reached around and moved his hand from her butt to her back.

"PDA," she said, but her voice was more breathless than reprimanding.

"I'm a big fan." That lazy smile again.

She rolled her eyes.

"Lets people know you're with me." He grinned and she frowned, and then his eyes jerked to the right. "Hey! There he is." He straightened but held on to her. She pushed her bangs to the side and met eyes with Brice McGuire.

Brice McGuire on Asher's deck, ten feet away. *Really?*

She hadn't seen Brice since the night of the concert. Since the night she didn't kiss him good-bye and had played off the kiss between her and Asher like it was no big deal. Being caught making out with him just now put a chink in the armor of her credibility.

Asher extended a hand to greet him.

"Nice of you to invite Arrow's Flag, Knight," Brice said, pumping his hand in a professional shake.

Ah. So the band Brice represented was here. Made sense.

"And me." Brice skimmed Gloria from head to toe, stopping where Asher's fingers were wrapped around her waist. "Hi, Glo."

"Hi," she returned. Asher's grip tightened on her hip.

"Bonfire. Beer. Food." Asher pointed out the various stations one by one. "Make yourself at home."

Brice nodded at each of them before making his way across the deck.

"What was that about?" she asked.

"Mine, babe. Just making sure he knows it."

"I'm not 'yours,' Asher."

"Sounds like I need to make sure you know it, too." He cocked his head in challenge.

She huffed, but no words followed. What was she supposed to say?

"I'll deal with you later. You need a drink. Wine?"

"Sure." That she'd give in to.

He gave her one last squeeze, kissed her forehead, and released her.

She watched him go before turning to walk down the deck. She spotted the other band members of Knight Time at the corner of where the deck met the dock.

She'd met the band before at concerts, and when she'd flown to LA to see Asher right after he'd signed the contract for his and Evan's book, *The Adventures of Mad Cow*. Save for Broderick, the newer member. She hadn't met him yet.

One could line up the men of Knight Time by graduating degree of beard growth. First there was Asher Knight, who typically sported stubble that was about two days old. Broderick "Ricky" Haines was the scruffier one, with a pronounced mustache/beard combo that looked like it never quite filled in no matter how many days he gave it. Alfonzo "Fonz" Rafferty had a jet-black goatee that was trimmed and well groomed, and finishing up the pack was Harlan Shiff ("Just Shiff, doll," he'd told her the first time she met him), whose goatee hung off his chin a few inches. His hair was red-blond and there was a ton of it, thick and hanging down to his shoulders.

She approached Fonz. In a pair of black-framed glasses, he was dressed the tamest in khaki shorts and a button-down chambray shirt cuffed at the sleeves. Fonz was the married one, with a seven-year-old and a new baby and a wife at home.

"Gloria," he greeted, pulling her in for a hug that she accepted. Fonz was so damn normal. The rest of them were … not.

"How have you been?" she asked when he let her go.

He nodded rather than answered, his smile tight. Then he introduced the younger guy next to him. "Broderick. Gloria."

"Ricky," he insisted, taking her hand. "Hi, gorgeous."

"Hi," she said, unsure what to make of him yet.

"You know Shiff." Fonz gestured to the drummer.

"Of course."

"How are ya, Sarge?" Shiff didn't offer a hand or a hug, only lifted his cup in cheers. Then he moved stunning blue eyes to hers and held her gaze a little longer than social politeness merited. The lips buried under that long goatee stayed firmly in a flat line.

"Great to see you all," she said. "If you see Ash, tell him I'm on the beach."

"You got it, babe," Ricky said.

Okay, he was cute.

She spotted Asher across the deck talking to Brice's clients—the band who played the outdoor concert the night he and Ash had a pissing contest.

No sooner did she think it than Brice swaggered up to her.

"Heels," Brice greeted.

"I thought we agreed that nickname was silly." She folded her arms over her chest.

"You, maybe. I haven't let it go yet." A quick lift of his eyebrows, then, "Like I haven't let some other things go."

She readied for a confrontation. Just because the guy took her to a concert didn't mean she owed him a kiss good night. And she sure didn't owe Brice any explanation for what he'd spied her and Asher doing when he arrived.

Instead of saying any of those things, she was surprised when he said, "Think any more about Chicago?"

She blinked.

"I'll fill the spot I'm holding for you, and fast, Gloria. But you're my first choice." He put his free hand in his pocket, lifting the beer in his other hand to his lips.

"Well, I...haven't really had a chance to think about it." Plus she hadn't known there was an expiration date on the offer.

"You never know when I might change my mind, Heels," he said. "Did I mention the signing bonus?"

"No," she stated flatly, tilting her head in suspicion. "You never mentioned the bonus."

He smiled, flicking his eyes around the deck. "I will. Enjoy the party."

He walked away, leaving her with no more than that veiled offer.

Well.

That was interesting.

In an annoying way.

She turned to follow her friends, deciding that the deck was too filled with characters she couldn't tolerate to wait up here for Asher to return with her wine. As she meandered to the stairs, she thought about Chicago and how at home she'd felt there. And then she thought of Kimber, who still lived there.

Whenever Gloria had a problem in the past, she'd run to Kimber. They were best friends, but since she and Landon became an item, their son Caleb following shortly after, Gloria found herself backing away some. Simply because her friend deserved the time and space to focus on her family. And Gloria, even though she was Kimber's friend, was definitely a third wheel in that situation.

With Brice hinting that she should go back home, she

wanted to call Kimber more than ever. Even though Kimber admitted she'd miss Gloria, she had been one hundred percent supportive of Gloria moving to Evergreen Cove. If Glo laid out Brice's offer, she knew her friend would give her an honest opinion.

That's what she needed. Not only someone to talk to, but also someone to ground her. Someone who knew her well enough to know if Chicago was the right call. No judgment. Just honesty. She palmed her phone and tapped in a text: *Why don't you live closer? I'm going crazy and need you to tell me I'm not.*

Even if she was.

Because only a crazy person would fantasize about sleeping with a man who could see straight through to her soul while further considering moving back to the city she'd just moved from less than six months ago.

Crazy.

She slipped her phone back into the pocket of her dress, not expecting to hear from Kimber soon—she did have a very busy life with two businesses, a toddler, and a husband—then moved to the stairs leading down to the...

What the hell?

There, beneath the shadow of the deck and stairs, was Broderick, sliding tongues with a cute, petite brunette. Whose shoes looked so familiar...

Oh, man! Are you kidding?

Freaking Jordan. As in Hawk's mother, Asher's baby-mama, the Cove's resident scourge, *Jordan.*

Ricky's mouth left Jordan's and he was all smiles, saying what, Gloria couldn't make out. His hands were wrapped around Jordan's ass, and he didn't seem to be parting from her company anytime soon.

He also didn't notice Gloria at the bottom of the stairs, mere feet away from where they stood against the support beams for the deck. Which was why Glo heard Jordan clearly when she said, "I'm so glad to be rid of Hawk for the night." She wound her fingers into Ricky's hair. "I'd rather spend it with you."

"You won't be sorry," he told her.

"Seriously?" Gloria barked, her blood pressure shooting into the danger zone.

Jordan spun to face her as Ricky's head jerked up. The look of surprise melted off Jordan's face and was replaced with derision. "Sorry, honey. This one's taken."

"I don't care who you kiss."

"Hey, Gloria," Ricky said with a smile. A completely clueless smile.

She ignored him. Right now, her sights were set in on Jordan, who, in this moment, reminded Gloria of her own mother so much, she could feel resentment bubbling up.

Gloria's mother had made a habit of prioritizing men— and drugs and booze—over her own child.

"Can I help you?" Jordan asked.

"Did I hear you say you're 'glad to be rid' of Hawk for the night?" Gloria repeated as calmly as she could muster. "You can't even pretend to have your shit together, can you?"

Ricky looked back and forth between them, clearly confused.

"If you would like to discuss my son—mine and Asher's son," she quickly amended, "call my mother."

"Sounds about right. She's the one who cares for him while you go out and bed hop," Gloria growled.

Ricky's eyebrows disappeared into his disheveled hair.

"I don't recall this being your business," Jordan snarled.

"I know what you're doing." Gloria pushed the length of her hair over her shoulders. "You're manipulating Asher with his son to get what you want. But only when it's convenient for you. You don't even care if you spend time with Hawk, do you? Time Asher would open a vein to get with his son."

"Asher's son." Ricky's face went pale.

"Yeah," Gloria told him with a nod. "This is Asher's baby-mama."

"Fuck." Ricky took a step away from Jordan, pushed his hands into his hair, and looked like he might puke.

"Basically," Gloria said in agreement.

Not willing to give up, Jordan put a hand on Ricky's chest. "It's fine. Nothing is between Asher and me except for my kid."

"Keep it up, Hawk won't be between you either," Gloria interjected indignantly. How dare Jordan pull this kind of crap at Asher's party? And what was she doing here, anyway? "Asher deserves a chance with his son and you're damn lucky he hasn't taken his millions and pulled Hawk out of your custody. Oh, I'm sorry. Out of your mother's custody."

Jordan stepped closer, fists balling at her sides in agitation. Her stance was threatening but the fact that she had to crane her neck to look up at Gloria wasn't.

"Threaten me again, bitch," Jordan said, "and see what happens."

Gloria leaned closer, not the least bit intimidated. She hadn't hit another girl since she was fifteen, but she'd bet it was just like riding a bike. "Get the hell out of here before I toss your skanky ass out myself."

"Sarge." She heard Asher coming down the steps behind

her, but Gloria didn't take her glare off Jordan. "Fuck me. Are you kidding?" Funny, that was almost exactly what Gloria had said. "What the hell are you doing here, Jordan?"

"Oh, man." Ricky took an exaggerated step away from Jordan and made the very wise decision to save as much face as possible. "She yours? I didn't know."

She yours? Gloria's stomach tossed. Jordan *was* Asher's once. Just once, but once was too much. In a rush, Glo realized she'd overstepped. This wasn't her fight. This wasn't any of her business. Asher wasn't hers and she wasn't his. Abruptly, she turned, moving away from the three of them as quickly as she could with her shoes sinking into the sand.

"No, she's not…" Asher started, then to her retreating form, he called out, "Glo! Babe."

She kept going.

* * *

Fuck, fuck, fuuuuuuuck.

Jordan was a plague. How one tiny woman could cause him so much grief was beyond him. Asher gave up the drinks in his hands, wedging the cups in the sand and reaching Gloria in a few rushed steps. Jordan and Broderick were an issue he wasn't handling right now. Gloria was the priority.

"Dammit, Sarge." He caught her arm and steered her to the side of the deck, still far enough from the gang at the bonfire that no one would hear, and a few extra feet away from Jordan and Broderick—and whatever the hell was happening there.

"Yes?" Gloria stopped in front of him, raised her eyebrows, and waited.

"Yes?" He hated when she pretended nothing was wrong. As he'd learned over the years, this was her standard avoidance maneuver. "What was that all about?"

"What was what all about?"

"You threatening Jordan. What did I walk in on?"

She wouldn't look at him. "Nothing."

Beautiful liar.

He claimed her other arm and backed them deeper into the shadows, just under the edge of the deck. "That wasn't nothing. Tell me."

"You do this to me a lot, you know that?" She frowned at his palms on her arms. "This feels very similar to the toy drive last year. You pushing me into a wall in the hallway in the middle of a party."

His mind went to everything immediately following that moment and his veins caught fire. An answering heat in her eyes told him her mind had chased his to that same memory. The moment they'd gone up to the room and their kisses turned to stripping each other bare. The moment he'd laid his mouth on her naked body, and she put hers on his. The moment he slipped inside her and they moved in sync, their eyes on one another's as they felt every soul-exposing moment together.

Yet it'd been reduced to this. Arguing, lying to save face. He was sicker of it than dealing with Jordan, and that was saying something.

"I'd like to get beneath this layer of bullshit, so why don't we just stand here until you tell me what's going on?" He released her.

"That was for you!" She let out a dry laugh.

"Sarge, I don't need you to field Jordan for me. I can handle her."

"So can I." A mix of strength and hurt flashed across Gloria's features. He hated that. Hated more that he'd caused it. But there was no way to undo his past, to unknot the tangle he and Jordan were in.

"I can't change the fact that Jordan is around. She's part of my past. She's..." He lifted a hand and dropped it. "She's going to be around."

"I know that." Her weary tone suggested this wasn't her issue. Her eyes jerked to the crowd around the fire and then to the people mingling upstairs.

"Then why—"

"She's not a good mother, Asher."

He blinked. Last thing in the world he'd expected her to say. "Okay."

"I don't like the way she talks about Hawk."

He frowned. "What did she say?"

Gloria shook her head, looking frustrated and sad and something else he couldn't put his finger on. "I don't want to talk about it."

Suddenly, it didn't matter what was said. Only one thing mattered.

"What I walked in on back there was you taking up for Hawk?"

She pressed her lips together. *Damn*. He was right.

"Taking up for me?" he pressed.

She looked at her shoes.

Wasn't he the one who was supposed to be coming for her? Wasn't he the knight—literally—in this situation?

"Sarge." He palmed her face and forced her eyes to his. "You don't have to defend me, or Hawk. I can handle it."

Her eyes went wide and she shot him a look that, if he were a lesser man, may have killed him. His strong, tough girl wasn't used to anyone slaying dragons for her. She'd been doing it for herself for way too long. That strength was the very thing about her that drove him nuts, as well as what he loved about her.

Loved about her.

Yeah, he wasn't going to examine that thought too closely.

"Well, then I guess I'll just mind my own business." She tried to turn from him, but he didn't let her go.

"That's not what I meant." He took a step closer. "I know what you're capable of, Gloria. I just want you to be able to lean on me, rely on me. Let me fight a few battles so you aren't fighting them all."

There came the wave of hurt again, rolling through her eyes like troubled seas in a storm. He sensed she wanted to let go. She just didn't know how.

"Partially my fault," he said. And it was. He hadn't exactly stepped up for her in the past. "I haven't proven much to you, Sarge. That changes tonight." He had exactly zero experience with being anyone's hero. High time he started living up to it. Hell, *past* time.

"You don't have to do anything!" Her shout drew a few glances from their friends. She closed her eyes and held her arms with her hands. Closing off. Closing *in*. Protecting herself.

The reasons behind her reaction became ridiculously clear in an instant. She'd never had anyone stick anything out with her or for her.

Until now.

"Tough shit, Sarge. It's done."

She'd opened her eyes but refused to look at him. Somehow he had to get her out from behind her barrier. He could see she was uncomfortable. Probably because the dynamic had shifted between them. She would have one hell of a time accepting him calling the shots instead of her. Asher grinned. She was like a wild mare who needed to be broken. But he wasn't a complete idiot. Even a broke mare could kick his teeth in.

He grasped her hand and she accepted, weaving her fingers with his gently. Slowly. He started for the stairs leading to the deck, but she didn't move. Their arms stretched straight between them.

He tugged her hand the slightest bit. Once. Twice. Finally, she came to him. One trudging step at a time, but she came. When she was within reach, he leaned close but didn't kiss her.

Her eyes darkened and her lips parted. He put his forehead on hers and took a deep breath. Inhaling her, feeling her warmth. Her softness.

Still, he didn't kiss her.

"What are you doing?" she asked, her voice breathy.

The answer was simple. "Making you want it, honey."

$\mathcal{C}$HAPTER 11

$\mathcal{N}$o one's looking, Sarge." His grin was as Big Bad Wolf as they came.

Like that mattered? Like she was just supposed to follow wherever he led? Her mind turned over the conversation they'd just had.

"You don't have to prove anything to me," she said. Belatedly, but at least she said it.

"Yeah. I do. But first, I have to thank you."

"Thank me?" She was getting more uncomfortable by the second.

"Repeatedly." His eyebrows jumped and he tugged her hand and she followed.

God help her, she followed him up the stairs, past a scowling Jordan and mildly concerned Broderick, into the house, and straight to the main bathroom.

A night-light plugged into the wall was lit, and Ash didn't bother hitting the switch. He shut the door. Then locked it.

"What are we doing in here?" She swallowed, nervous, and backed away from him a step.

"Thanking you."

"For what?"

"Taking up for me out there." He palmed her hips.

"I was taking up for Hawk." She backed up another step and he went with her, pushing her to the wall beside the door. How did she keep ending up in this situation with him?

"Same thing," he murmured, then his lips crashed down onto hers.

There wasn't a single part of her—now that he'd preoccupied her mouth so thoroughly—that wanted to argue. The pressure had been building between them. What was about to happen? There was no denying it.

In a flash, he unzipped her dress and yanked it down, exposing her bra. He buried his face into her cleavage, just above the pretty little bow in the center. She dropped her head back against the wall. Fingers in the center of the bra, he tugged it down, suckling each of her nipples while her back arched to get closer to his heated mouth.

"Take this off," he said, then put his lips on hers. Shakily, she removed her bra and he pushed her dress to the floor. She stepped out of it, kicking off each of her flats. Anticipation had turned to expectation and she was vibrating with it.

Asher pulled off his T-shirt and pressed into her, his skin warm. She looped her arms around his neck and he kept his eyes trained on hers in the dimly lit room.

"Let's have some fun," he said.

She smiled. Yes. Fun. That's what sex had been with Asher before things became deep and complicated. *Fun* was just what she needed.

He smiled back, wrapping his hands around the backs of her thighs. "Legs around me, Sarge."

He lifted her and she wrapped her ankles around his back. Her back was pressed flat to the wall, and propped there only by his hips. Which was lovely, because that left his hands free. He thumbed her nipple with one hand and curled the other around her jaw, his lips hovering just over hers.

For one beat, then two, they shared the same air.

"Ash." Her voice shook. Her body quaked. "I can't stop." Couldn't stop shaking. Couldn't stop wanting him.

"God, I missed you." His deep brown eyes assaulted her.

The last time he'd said that, she'd told him she hated him. Nothing could have been further from the truth, and for some reason right now seemed to be the moment to tell him. "I never hated you."

"I know."

Winding her fingers into the back of his hair, she pulled his face to hers and kissed him, giving herself to him anew. He pushed his hard-on against her center and his tongue into her mouth and she wished he'd taken the time to lose the shorts before he put her against the wall.

She reached for the button on his shorts and fumbled with the zipper. He continued kissing her, launching his tongue into her mouth and out again as his calloused fingertips abraded her nipples and made her wet and so hot, she felt as if she'd fused to the tiled wall.

"Take these off," she said the second he let her breathe.

He lowered her feet to the floor and both of them wrestled with his shorts and boxer briefs until they hit the floor. Over his hip ran the script lyrics from "Unchained." Oh, she loved that tattoo.

Unchained. Finally free. Finally you. Finally me.

She ran her fingertips along the words, inching closer to his bobbing cock. That part of his anatomy held a lot of promise, and many good memories. She grasped the shaft and squeezed him lightly.

He palmed her breasts and put his mouth on hers again. And she did her level best to keep her eyes closed and her mind focused on the sensations of her body. The feel of warmth low in her belly, wet heat accosting the most private, secret part of her.

He kissed his way down, pausing for each breast and then licking a circle around her belly button. Her hands rested in his hair as he dropped to his knees. For a second, he stopped and rested his stubbled chin on her hip bone. She opened her eyes to find him looking up at her, lashes casting shadows on his cheeks, hair sticking up all over the place.

"I've dreamed of your taste." Expertly, he thumbed her clit. Her hips swiveled. His eyes left hers to focus on where he was touching her. He slicked his tongue along her center and her eyelids fell closed. She bit back the sharp moan clogging her throat.

"My memory is for shit," he mumbled, his lips tickling her. "You taste better than I remember." He repeated the motion, then his mouth left her and he took her hands in his. He was almost chuckling when he said, "Come on. Not going to make you stand up for this."

She let him pull her to the floor, where he laid her on top of a white rug next to the shower.

"What if someone wants in?" she asked, eyeing the door behind him.

"There's more than one bathroom in this house, Sarge." He lowered himself between her legs, tossing her knees onto his shoulders.

"Lie back," he instructed. When she did, he teased the insides of her thighs with soft kisses until her hips thrust.

"Oh, man." He tongued her inner thigh, agonizingly close to where she wanted him. "You are fun to tease."

"Please," she begged.

To her absolute delight, he gave in and licked her—one long, hot lick that made her back bow and her hands fist the rug.

"But more fun to drive crazy," he amended.

With his tongue against her, she blocked the thoughts about the party on the deck and the people who'd watched them walk hand in hand inside. Her hips pumped in time with Asher's ministrations, and all she could think about was how great it felt to have him there and how, for the first time in too long, her bones were melting. The man was a master with his mouth, and when he reached those talented fingers for her nipples, her orgasm peaked.

At his insistent lapping, she came, pulsing and writhing against his face, her voice lost. Asher slowed his pace, letting her ease from the massive release. Then he flicked his tongue against her and she let out a sharp breath, pushing her hands against his head.

"Fuck me," she breathed.

He didn't hesitate.

He moved to the drawer by the sink and pulled out a strip of condoms, tearing one packet from the row with his teeth. He rolled it on while Gloria held out her arms and made a "come here" motion with her hands.

On the floor with her again, he lifted one of her legs and pivoted his hips, pushing deep inside her and shoving her and the rug across the floor.

"*Yes.*" This was what it was like to be with Asher. Intense and unbelievably perfect. He filled her, consumed her, and didn't let up for one second.

With a grunt, he thrust forward, his hair falling over his forehead as he smiled down at her. He grunted again, this time paired with scrunching his nose and growling low in his throat.

Gloria couldn't help it—she smiled. "Animal," she said with a soft laugh.

"You make me an animal, sweetheart." He bared his teeth.

She kissed the underside of his chin. "Why do you feel so good?"

"Nine-inch cock," he answered immediately.

She chuckled.

"No laughing." He slammed into her again. She hadn't been exaggerating earlier when she'd mentioned Asher's length to the girls. He was hung and thick and as physically perfect as one man could get.

"Why do *you* feel so good?" He lowered his chest to hers and stroked into her again, his lips brushing hers when he said, "You're downright creamy."

God. So sexy.

"Finish us off," she panted, unable to take the build, the emotions, the *everything*. "We need to get back out there." He thrust again and she blew out a tortured yet pleased breath. "Before people start talking."

"Let 'em talk, Sarge." He grinned and she was one hundred percent sure that Asher liked the idea of everyone assuming they were in here doing just this.

"I'm going to have to sneak out the front," she half joked.

"No. You're coming." He thrust forward and stopped, buried deep and not moving another inch. "Not going." He pulled out, one long, slow pull. "Never going."

Her eyes sank closed as she savored another agonizingly perfect slide to the hilt.

"Say you're staying, Sarge, and I'll finish you off right."

"That's bribery," she somehow managed after another mind-melting thrust.

"Damn straight."

Another, and she felt her release crest.

"*Sarge.*"

"I'm staying," she said, her voice lifting as her orgasm overtook her—unexpected and overwhelming. He spiked the pace, holding on to her hip as he rode her to his own orgasm.

She shuddered against him, a faint sheen of sweat beading her brow and her upper lip and her belly where it rubbed against the bumps of his abs.

"Hell, yes," he panted against her lips, resting on his elbows and bumping his nose against hers, "you are."

* * *

That was . . .

That was . . .

Wow.

Yep. That was the word she was looking for.

Sex with Asher was *wow.*

She thought she'd remembered but her memory had dulled. She zipped up her dress and pulled on her shoes. To her surprise, the entire time they'd been in here—and they hadn't rushed—no one had come banging on the door.

"Why weren't we interrupted?" she asked, flipping on the overhead lights to check her hair and makeup in the mirror.

"Shiff," Ash answered, tugging his T-shirt over his head and running a hand through his mussed hair.

"Shiff?" She regarded Asher's reflection.

He shrugged. "Shiff saw us come in here. Probably rerouted everyone. He's good at that."

She blinked. "Is that his job or something?"

"No, it's not his *job*." Asher closed in behind her, wrapped his hands around her waist, and rested his chin on her shoulder. "He knows about you, Sarge. He knows how I feel about you."

"Oh." That was . . . sweet. And scary. All at once.

"You don't always have to assume the worst." He kept his eyes on hers in the mirror.

"Safer that way," she mumbled.

"Maybe." He kissed her neck and let her go, closing the bathroom drawer where he'd fished out a condom earlier. "But I don't like safe. And neither do you."

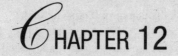CHAPTER 12

$\mathcal{G}$loria held her head high when she exited the house, Asher behind her. He palmed her back as they each ordered fresh drinks from the bar, then they walked down to the beach together.

She slipped away from him and made her way to Charlie and Sofie and Faith because that she could handle. Hanging on Asher in front of everyone...not so much. Bonus, she was pretty sure none of their friends had noticed they'd vanished for a while. She had no idea how long they were gone. Twenty minutes maybe? Thirty?

"Where have you been?" Charlie asked. Okay, *someone* had noticed.

"Eating," Gloria answered quickly.

Charlie was on the other side of Sofie and Donovan, and Asher was currently regaling a tale from his last show to Donovan, Evan, Connor, and Faith. That put six people between Gloria and Asher, and six people created *almost* enough distance for her to resume natural brain function.

If she stood next to him, everyone would figure out they'd just absconded to the hallway bathroom to do the nasty. Except it wasn't nasty. It was fantastic. And she'd agreed to stay tonight, which left a high probability they'd do it again.

Which made her feel out of control, wild. She liked and disliked that feeling at the same time. This whole Knight in Sexy Tattoos thing used to be fine, but now that she'd lost control, she felt...vulnerable.

"I need more wine," Gloria said to her empty cup.

"Me too. Why don't we stroll over to the cooler together?" Charlie smiled, looking very, *very* in the know. In a way, Gloria didn't want to talk about it. But in another way, she really, really did.

"Let's." She and Charlie turned from their friends, but they didn't notice. Asher was making explosion noises and big hand gestures and everyone was laughing. Ever the consummate entertainer, he was ironically providing enough distraction for Gloria to sneak out of his sight.

Not bothering with pretense, Charlie pulled a full bottle of white wine out of a nearby cooler and pointed to a blanket in the grassy sand near the lake. Torches burned all around, but most of the party had convened at the deck where music played—a sort of pop-up band had occurred between a few members of Knight Time and Arrow's Flag.

The setup on the beach, blankets and a few throw pillows, had not been taken advantage of yet. It was the perfect oasis away from the fire so she could talk about Asher.

Charlie opened the wine—screw-off top, but not a cheap bottle by any means—then sat. The Pinot Grigio was one of

Glo's favorites. Charlie filled their cups, wedged the bottle in the sand in front of their shared blanket, and waited.

That's it. Just waited.

"You know, don't you?" Gloria asked with a sigh.

"That you and Asher sneaked away after an interaction with Jordan and one of his band members and then didn't return for a very long time? What could I possibly know?" Charlie asked, her hazel eyes innocent.

Gloria stuck her tongue out.

Charlie laughed. "Do you want to talk about it?"

Did she? Gloria watched the ripples in the water on the lake. Probably caused by a fish or a turtle beneath the surface. Or maybe a turtle eating a fish. Sometimes the worst disturbances are hidden deep, the aftereffect muted despite the turbulence below.

She took a drink of wine. Now she was wallowing.

Gloria flicked a gaze over at Asher and said, "I gave in and I swore I wouldn't."

"It happens. I gave in to Evan, you know."

Heck yeah she had. Evan had caved Charlie's self-control repeatedly.

"I guess...I don't know what to say." Gloria pursed her lips.

"You thought sex would solve things but it only made things more confusing," Charlie offered.

"That about covers it."

"That happens, too." Charlie sipped her wine.

"Asher makes things confusing. He's...different."

"Different than when you were together three years ago?" Charlie asked. She wasn't wrong, but she wasn't completely informed. Gloria took a breath. And told her what she didn't know.

"Different from when I slept with him at the toy drive at the mansion *last year*."

Charlie's mouth dropped open. "No!"

"Yes." She smiled weakly and drank down her wine, reaching for a refill immediately. Charlie was wise to bring the bottle.

"Faith said she saw you two fighting in the hallway. She didn't say what she heard, just that she worried..." Charlie trailed off, but it wasn't hard to guess what Faith had ended that worry with. Faith had been on the tail end of a very ugly breakup at the time.

"She was worried about me being taken advantage of," Gloria guessed.

"Yeah, well. She had her reasons to think that way."

One of those reasons was that Faith's ex-fiancé was a dirty cheater who broke Faith's heart. Glo couldn't blame her for being wary of Asher, and even though Faith never properly voiced it, Gloria was incredibly grateful that she had taken her side so solidly. Charlie was another story altogether.

"I don't know what to make of you and Asher. I can see you want to be together so badly, but there is this huge wall you're standing on opposite sides of. With Evan and me, that wall was obvious. Rae."

Evan's late wife. Rae and Charlie had grown up together and were best friends—more like sisters. Rae had been gone four years when Evan moved to Evergreen Cove, but Charlie had battled guilt over falling for him.

"I didn't want to betray her," Charlie said. "I didn't want to feel any of what I was feeling. But I couldn't resist him." She grunted, a light, happy sound as she watched the pale moon over the water. "He wouldn't *let* me resist him."

"You put up a valiant fight, Charlie." Evan had been persistent. He'd tried to take the backseat when Gloria gave him the misguided suggestion to give Charlie some space, but it backfired and he'd gone right back to fighting for her again.

Smart man.

"Yeah, well. Don't we all?" Charlie turned her head and Glo followed her gaze to Sofie and Faith, who had put up valiant fights of their own. Sofie was sure she'd be able to move on after Donny went back to New York. Faith was sure she'd stand her ground and finally claim her independence. All of her friends had put up a fight only to crumble beneath the attention and love of their men.

But that was Evan. Donovan. Connor. Asher was a different breed of man. He'd built his life on a foundation of work hard, play harder.

"I don't think Asher is the forever type," Glo said, voicing her real concern aloud. "And to be honest, I get it. Because neither am I."

"Maybe you don't know yourself as well as you think you do."

"I think maybe *you* don't know me as well as you think you do."

"I think you don't want me to know you, but I do," Charlie said. "I also think that anyone who knows you well scares you." That truth came as such a surprise, Glo flinched. Charlie put a hand on Gloria's arm. "Girls like us, remember?"

Charlie was referring to the heart-to-heart they'd had the night Glo ran into Jordan in her nightie. Having nowhere else to go, Gloria had run straight to Charlie. She'd needed someone to talk to and she knew Charlie wouldn't turn her away.

"We need to be caveman-dragged," Charlie finished quoting.

"Asher isn't a caveman."

"No. But he's all man. And he is aching for you. He hates that he hurt you. Hates that he can't have a do-over. Except for Hawk. He wants his son. He wants to grow up. I think he has in a lot of ways."

"I take it he's had conversations about this in your presence." Gloria looked at the remaining wine in her cup.

Charlie didn't confirm, but she did say, "Evan is good for him."

Gloria didn't doubt it. Evan was an adult. He'd dealt with life head-on and as a result was a man who knew what he wanted. Being dealt so many low blows by the universe had made him who he was. But what about Asher? What did Gloria know about his past, his struggles, his life? She'd been trying to keep things with them on the surface.

Until the night the intimacy between them broke through. But the sex just now? Totally fun, and totally earth-shattering, but definitely not as vulnerable as last year.

Who were they when they were together?

"Sometimes I wonder if there are too many bumps between us to smooth out, you know?" Gloria wanted to eat her words the minute they fell out of her mouth. Damn wine. It made her sentimental. Made her look up at the stars and tell stories to herself. Make up future possibilities, and worse. It made her *hope*. She could feel the spark of it now flickering in her chest.

"There is a lot of water under Asher and Gloria Bridge," she continued, on a roll and not caring how she sounded. "I was seduced by the image of him the same as those girls up there." She tipped her chin to the dock where a gaggle of girls hung out. "Groupies aren't bad girls. They're just passionate. They fall in love on a superficial level with the idea of a sexy man singing his deepest thoughts and convictions. Then they follow blindly to the ultimate end."

Sex. Closeness. It was the only way to capture a man like Asher. He was like smoke. You could hold him in your hands for a limited time, then he'd slip from your fingers.

"That may be true," Charlie said, "but that isn't what you and Asher have. You have something else. Something that keeps you in each other's orbit."

"It's called a contract," Glo quipped.

Charlie grabbed the wine bottle and refilled her own cup. "It's called something else and I'm sure you don't want me to spell it out. But if I did, I'd say it started with L and ended with E and there are a whole lot of tumultuous, torturous, beautiful parts in between."

"Damn, girl." Gloria held up her cup and they bonked it against Charlie's in a toast. "You should write a book. Need an agent?"

Charlie smiled. "Do you want to get trashed? Just bottom out this wine and maybe one more bottle and pass out on the beach?"

Gloria, hand to her collarbone, pretended to choke up. "Charlie Downey, that's the most romantic proposition I've ever received."

"I need it," Charlie admitted, and her eyes filled with sadness.

"The pregnancy thing," Gloria said, venturing into territory marked with Do Not Enter signs.

"It's hard to want something and not get it while you watch everyone else around you attain it without effort." Her eyebrows pulled together. "That's unfair. And untrue. Things come as they come, and usually they're not easy for anyone."

"I feel like your observation could be about you having a baby or me having a relationship. Are you *sure* you don't want to write a self-help book?"

"I'm sure I don't want to tonight." Charlie lifted the bottle again and this time filled the cups to the top before tossing the bottle into the sand. "Bottoms up, beautiful."

"If I had a nickel."

Charlie laughed and Gloria laughed, too. She tipped her cup and made it her goal to finish every last drop of wine in it. And then, she'd do as Charlie suggested and open a fresh bottle.

* * *

Evan stood over the pair of girls passed out on the blanket on the beach and shook his head. "Well, well. What have we here?"

A soft snore came from one of them, hell, maybe both of them, and Asher smiled. Everyone but Shiff had gone home, or in the band's case, back to their hotels. Shiff was the unofficial bodyguard of the group and right now he was sitting on Asher's deck strumming a guitar really badly.

"Better get Charlie home." Evan raised his eyebrows at Asher. "Want me to take Glo, too?"

"I got her."

"She gonna be okay with that?" Evan asked, his expression bemused.

She'd agreed to stay. Ash assumed she meant for the party, not for the night. But he wasn't letting her out of his reach now that he had her here.

"I doubt it, but I won't take advantage of her passed-out state, so don't worry."

"Yeah. No need since you two sneaked away earlier."

Asher shrugged, refusing to answer.

"Not worried," Evan said, letting it go. "Make her Hangover Hash in the morning. Works like a charm." Evan's hangover remedy was a plate of browned potatoes, peppers, onions, cheese, and a fried egg—or in Asher's case, three—on top. Ash had sampled that fare a time or twelve. He and his buddy were no strangers to the hangover. Neither was Glo. Come morning, he refused to let her be filled with regret—over the wine or the bathroom sex. Both were way too good—way too fun—to regret.

"Good luck." Evan lifted Charlie into his arms, hoisting her easily, leaving behind the blanket she'd covered both herself and Gloria with. "'Night."

"'Night, man," Asher said. Even though it was more like morning. Four in the morning last he checked. He looked down at Gloria, on her side, black hair spread around her like ink leaked from a bottle. Her skin was pale, her lashes dark, her snoozing form lifting and falling beneath the plaid blanket.

She was beautiful and for the moment, she was his. It was everything he could want right now, all wrapped up in his bedding. He'd let her slip away from him after they'd come down to the fire to join their friends. She needed her space, and frankly, he could've used a little as well.

Sex with Gloria Shields had been fun, but this time no cracks in the universe had opened up and spilled out a vision of their future. No new lyrics to the song he'd been trying to recapture. He'd been so sure of what occurred between them last year, and now . . . where the fuck was it?

Mimicking Evan's move, Asher lifted Gloria into his arms, blanket and all. She stirred, barely, snuggling against him and blowing warm wine-infused breath on his neck.

"Not letting you away from me tonight, Sarge," he whispered, kissing the top of her head. He carried her up the steps and across the deck. Shiff quit playing the guitar when he spotted him, leaning the old Mitchell Ash had had since he was a teen against the stairs and standing.

"Everyone out?" Asher asked him.

"Yep."

"You didn't have to stay." He kept his voice down, though the way Gloria was snoring suggested she wouldn't wake even if he shouted. "But thanks for keeping an eye out." People at these kinds of parties tended to walk out with the silver if no one was looking, so the bandmates took turns whenever they were together keeping an eye on the place. "And for earlier."

Shiff's typical stone features split for a brief smile.

"Stay as long as you like. Spare room behind the studio."

"I'm rollin'." He nodded rather than do their typical low five/handshake since Asher's arms were full of Gloria Shields.

"Careful," Ash said, and he meant that in every way. No doubt Shiff was headed back to his hotel, where a girl or two was obediently waiting in his bed. Or maybe they'd started without him. With him, it was hard to say.

With Shiff on the road to wherever he was going, Asher let himself into the house. Tank lifted his head, having found a home on someone's shirt left behind. A woman's shirt by the looks of it. He could only hope it wasn't Jordan's or Gloria would go radioactive.

He carried Glo to his room at the back of the house and

laid her on the bed. Her hair smelled of fire and there was sand on her dress. He tossed the beach blanket in the hallway, figuring he'd deal with it later, and left her briefly—just long enough to check the house for stragglers and lock up.

No one else stayed. They were alone.

In his room, he stripped her out of her dress, then out of her bra, reliving the moment earlier when he'd gotten her out of her clothes. He left her in panties, telling himself that had been a mighty big ask of him, then he stripped down to nothing at all and climbed in next to her.

Out of the handful of times they'd slept together, she typically slept somewhere other than next to him afterward. So, in a way he lied to Evan when he said he wasn't going to take advantage of her in her passed-out state. He was going to cuddle with her, and he was going cuddle *hard*.

A thought that put a tired smile on his face as he curled against her and pulled a sheet over both of them. He wrapped an arm around her and she mumbled incoherently in her sleep. In a few seconds, Tank pawed the bed and whined, and Asher let go of Gloria long enough to lift the dog onto the bed as well. The furball curled up in the crook of Gloria's bent knees. Asher faced her, moving her bangs away from her forehead and trailing his knuckles down her cheek. Then he scooted closer, pressed his body to hers, and skin-to-skin, he fell asleep.

CHAPTER 13

*J*ackhammers. There were jackhammers in her head and cotton balls in her mouth. Gloria ran her tongue along the roof of her mouth and it stuck there. She held her skull and rolled over smelling musk and leather...

Asher.

Flashes of them naked in the meager night-light in the bathroom were interspersed with flashes of the bonfire and she and Charlie drinking and drinking and drinking some more.

She bolted upright, regretting it instantly, hands to her head like that might stop the pounding and sloshing. What was going on in there? She groaned when her phone rang a cheery little tune that made those jackhammers gave birth to baby jackhammers, all crying for attention.

She punched the screen and grunted into the phone. No hello, just a grunt.

"You're not at your office."

"Brice?" Her voice was hoarse. She pushed a hand through her tangled hair and bits of sand hit the sheet resting on her lap.

"Yeah. I brought you donuts from Sugar Hi and coffee from Cup of Jo's. You need sustenance. I saw you drinking your soul away last night on the beach, you know. I knew you had a rough night but was sure I'd see you by noon."

"It's *noon*?"

"Twelve forty-five."

Tank padded into the room and stood, front paws on the edge of the bed. He barked, one shrill, brain-piercing bark, and she shushed him.

"Go away," she whispered.

"I didn't know you had a dog."

"I don't." She covered her eyes with her hands. She needed coffee. And Advil. And about three more days of sleep.

"You stayed with Knight," Brice observed quietly.

"Not your business." She moved her hair behind her ear and her arm brushed against her bare breast. She blinked down at her mostly naked body, mildly alarmed. *Great*. She had almost no clothes on and was in Asher's house. Tank barked again. She made a shooing motion and he dropped his paws from the bed's edge to the floor.

"My offer to combine businesses was never contingent on you being with me in bed, Gloria," Brice said, sounding sincere. "Just in Chicago. Don't get me wrong, I'm jealous as hell a guy like Asher gets you and I don't, but I can live with it. I want you for your brains. Your beauty in my office is just a bonus."

In my office.

His honesty was so jarring, she simply sat in silence, fiddling with a corner of the sheet.

"Heels?"

"You're not giving that up, are you?" she asked with a small smile.

"I don't give up."

"I haven't decided yet, but I will." As soon as she gave herself two seconds to think of anything but her to-do list and Asher Knight.

"Okay, sweetheart. I'm going to drink both these coffees and be ridiculously productive today. But I have extra donuts. If you wander into work today, call me. My hotel is close and I deliver."

"Thanks."

"Sure thing."

They said their good-byes and Gloria put the phone back on the nightstand. Brice brought her coffee and donuts after seeing her drink herself into oblivion on the beach. And he did it after he saw Asher kiss her in plain view. It was possible Brice had also seen her steal away with Asher into the house for mid-party sex.

Brice claimed to want her professionally, but she'd bet it could be a personal something, too, if she could summon up a single feeling for him that wasn't platonic. Is that what her life held if she returned to Chicago and worked with him? Could she finally stop sleeping with the rock star who continually made her feel too many combating emotions?

Still, last night...She knew she couldn't get that kind of sex with anyone other than Asher.

You taste better than I remember.

No way would she have let Brice sweep her into a bathroom in the middle of a huge party and strip her bare. No way could she have had her mind erased so thoroughly as to let him go down on her while she had a brain-freezing orgasm.

Only Asher.

As scenes from last night looped in her head, she felt her pulse stir between her legs, throbbing insistently and begging her to give herself a moment's relief against the pressure. She trailed her fingers between her breasts, then over one nipple as she pictured Asher's tongue doing just that. Her eyes fell closed and she circled the hardening bud once more…

"I can help you with that if you like."

Her eyes flew open to find Asher leaning against the doorway, arms folded over his chest like he'd been standing there all day.

"I was…" She put her hand in her lap, unable to invent a single excuse for what she'd been caught doing. So instead, she said, "Come here."

He didn't hesitate, pushing off the door frame and skirting Tank. He put a knee on the bed, dipping the mattress under his weight, and took her nipple on his tongue. *Oh*, that felt so much better than when she'd touched herself. His attention was solitary and dedicated. Wet and warm.

"How ya feelin'?" he asked in the gap of time where he moved his lips to her other breast and kissed here there, too.

"Better." She palmed the back of his head and he pushed her onto her back. He lowered his body over hers, looking a lot like he had the first time she'd met him. Black jeans, black tee, necklace with a cross on the end dangling between them.

Each time she saw him, he stole her breath. She'd written the reaction off as being starstruck at first, but he was so much more than that to her. He always had been. He depressed the mattress more when he put another knee on the bed. He was wearing his cowboy boots, which meant he'd gone somewhere.

"Where were you?" she asked, her voice tight with lust.

He lowered his denim-clad legs to her bare ones and because he fit there so nicely, she wrapped one leg around his waist and pulled him close.

"Getting you breakfast." He kissed her nose. "It's on the counter."

Well she'd be damned. Two men had brought her breakfast this morning.

"Donuts?" she guessed.

"No, ma'am." His mouth edged in whiskers quirked.

Why was he so sexy? *Le swoon.*

"About half of Sun Up's brunch menu," he said. "Sure you don't want to eat it while it's hot?"

How sweet was he?

"Or...I could eat you while you're hot." He lowered his face again, swirling his tongue around her nipple. "You taste good, Sarge."

Okay, sweet *and* crazy sexy. That was a better way to describe Asher.

"I want you," she stated. She saw no reason to deny it.

He put a kiss on each of her nipples before trailing his tongue down her body and around her belly button.

"You have me." He fisted her panties with both hands.

"I want you *inside* me," she reiterated.

"Ah. You had a taste and you want more."

"So cocky."

"Nine inches, Sarge." He winked, thick lashes closing over one sparkling whiskey-colored eye. His sin-filled smile was enough to make her come on demand.

He stripped her of her panties as he stood from the bed, undoing his belt and unbuttoning his button-fly jeans next. A pair of black boxer briefs hid an erection she reached for and palmed.

Asher grunted, his arrogance swapping out for so much want, she felt downright powerful. She let him go and wandered her fingers along his flexing abs and then to the tattooed lyrics over his hip: *Finally you. Finally me.*

How appropriate.

Boxers gone, he climbed over her, wasting no time grabbing a condom from the nightstand.

"You have those everywhere," she observed.

"Always be prepared."

"For me?" She felt her cheeks heat. And she tried to think of something to say to make her sound less like she was asking for a compliment.

"Especially for you." He put his lips on hers and without warning, tilted his hips, sliding into her inch by precious inch.

She kept her mouth sealed with his, pulling air in through her nose. She loved the feel of him here with her, so *present* and perfect and exactly what she needed when she needed it. Propped on his elbows, he moved within her as she explored his chest with her hands, running her fingertips over the petals of the flowers on the tat on his chest, then along the leaves.

"Gimme your eyes," he said. "We didn't get to do that part last night."

Look who hadn't missed a thing that had occurred between them.

His request took her right out of the moment they were sharing. She wanted him desperately, but just as desperately, she feared connecting with him any way other than physically. Especially in broad daylight—she had no way of hiding from him now.

"Can't. I have a massive headache." An excuse, but also the truth.

"Working on fixing that for you," he breathed, slipping in and out of her again.

"Oh, there. *There*." She tilted her hips and he hit the spot again—the spot that promised to erase her headache, possibly make her forget she had a head.

He slowed his pace, not thrusting as deep this time. "Sarge."

"Don't hold my orgasm hostage," she growled. Then she grabbed his nipples. "Or else."

Asher's eyebrows went up. "You're going to give me a titty twister if I don't comply? Low, Gloria. Even for you."

She smiled, liking his teasing and the way he could have fun doing anything but especially during sex. She loosened her hold, unable to go through with her empty threat. "Just don't force my hand. I need a release and you're..."

"Great at it?" he finished.

"I was going to say convenient," she lied. She tilted an eyebrow up at him in challenge. A challenge he didn't accept. He wasn't into arguing with her right now and he proved it by sinking into her again, deeper. *Harder*. Her mouth dropped open as sweet, sweet bliss poured through her bloodstream.

"Givin' you what you need," he said, repeating the motion that caused a pleasure-filled moan to sound in her throat. "But you have to give me what I need."

She wrapped her arms around his neck and held on... then she turned her eyes up to his, holding his gaze.

"There she is," he murmured, something gentle lighting his eyes.

He thrust into her again and again, turning her inside out. When her orgasm crested, he picked up the pace, knowing exactly how to give it to her. Only then did she shut her eyes, throw her head back, and let her mind erase. She sank into the black oblivion, every part of her pulsing and pounding as Asher continued his seductive slides.

"Once more for me, Sarge," he said, breathless, his fingers brushing her jaw.

Her headache was gone, her entire body buzzing. And that must have been what ultimately made her obey. She opened her eyes and met his again. The smile on his face was tender. As tender as the kiss on her lips while he continued his sweet assault. His release followed a few pumps later, while she held on tight. And this time, she watched his eyes squeeze closed as a guttural male growl tore through his throat. The muscles in his shoulders tensed, his arms coiled, and his thick lashes flattened against his cheeks.

All she could do was think the same word over and over: *This.*

This was why she wanted to have sex with Asher. Not just the promise of feeling really good, but knowing she made him feel just as good. Existing together in a space and time where no one could touch them. Where nothing else mattered. This moment.

His eyes opened and a slow smile crawled across his lips. He pulled out and she gasped as he left her, curling onto her side and hugging the pillow.

He said nothing, just padded into the hallway while Gloria stared at the black Fender guitar on a stand in the corner of the room. Minutes passed and her buzz faded into a pleasant sinking feeling and, dammit, that headache. Still there after all, just blissfully numbed out thanks to a powerful orgasm.

The sound of rustling and Tank's tags rattling on his collar drew her attention to the doorway. Asher Knight stood buck naked save for bracelets, rings, and a necklace, bags of Sun Up takeout in both hands.

"Breakfast in bed?" He grinned.

* * *

"This is the life," Gloria said around a mouthful of breakfast. Asher smiled to himself and dug another bite of fried potatoes out of the foam container. Glo wasn't afraid to eat. She had three containers open in front of her. One contained potatoes and sausage, the other eggs and biscuits, and another was a bowl of gravy. She'd been rotating through all three, taking a bite of each one in turn.

Ash stuck with Sun Up's version of Hangover Hash, but there was a container he hadn't started on yet filled with pancakes. He polished off the potatoes. "We can do this as often as you want."

When she was quiet for several seconds, he looked over to find her examining her food with her plastic fork like it held the secret to life. He elbowed her gently and she looked up at him, slapping a smile onto her face.

"No, we can't," she said. "I'll gain fifty pounds."

Deflection. He should have expected it. He'd been lucky last night—luckier this morning, and not just because he'd *gotten lucky*. She wanted him, didn't resist him, and looked him dead in the eye while he made love to her. Last night was about breaking her down, keeping things light. Light seemed to be what she could handle. Today was about pushing and getting her to trust him. Open up to him. He'd won that battle, too, but damn. What he wouldn't give if she'd shut off her brain and lean on him all the way.

"I have work to do," she said, dipping a bite of biscuit

into the well of gravy. She was still naked. Hell, they both were. Gloria naked in his bed eating was a gift he'd gladly give himself every morning. Fifty extra pounds or no.

"Do you take days off, ever?"

She pretended to think about it, eyes turning to the ceiling. "No."

Tank yipped from his spot on the floor and Asher answered by breaking a piece of bacon in two and feeding it to him.

"Today's Sunday, Sarge. If God rested on Sunday, even you can take one off every so often."

"God didn't have my demanding clients." She smirked.

"No work today."

"But—"

"I mean it. I am a client, so you'll do as I command." He pushed his food aside and leaned over. Against her mouth, he said, "Let's eat pancakes in bed instead. I'll show you things that can be done with syrup you never dreamed possible."

She let out a loose laugh and he felt like he'd won the best gift on earth. Her palm hit his chest and she pushed him away. "I don't think so, buddy. I have to catch up on the work I've missed out on since…"

Since she'd stepped into his house to deliver a check that'd gone to her instead of him. He'd like to find whoever made that mistake at the publishing house and kiss him or her for that error. Glo had been avoiding coming to his house, and now he understood the deeper meaning behind why. But since then, she'd visited a handful of times, and he'd been able to get her naked almost every time.

He let his gaze drop to dark, raspberry-colored nipples perched on two large, gorgeous breasts. She cleared her throat to get his attention, but he only shook his head, refusing to look away.

"Not falling for that, Sarge. I feel like lookin', I'm going to look."

Her fingers found his chin and tipped it up. He was greeted by arched black eyebrows, pale skin, and a full, kissable mouth. She was a pinup dream girl. Especially with that thick shock of bangs dusting her forehead and her long ink-black hair flowing over her shoulders. She had a mad case of bedhead and he absolutely loved it. There was something inviting about her with her mascara slightly smudged under her eyes and her lipstick gone, her clothes missing. She was softer than ever. Even while trying to be hard.

Catlike blue eyes held his like she'd forgotten why she'd tipped his chin in the first place. He let himself sink into those depths and let his mind wander to the syrup that he'd much rather pour onto her than his stack of buttermilks. He slammed his mouth over hers, and Gloria squeaked, shifting on the bed and trying to hold herself so that they didn't end up rolling around in their breakfast.

He slid his tongue along hers and she let him, holding his face with her hands while they kissed. She probably wanted to stop him, so he made it his job to keep her turned on enough so she forgot she wanted anything but his mouth on hers. His mouth all over her.

His hand went to her breast and he kneaded until her nipple pebbled under his touch. He reached behind him and blindly felt around in the plastic to-go bag, keeping his mouth on hers so she couldn't argue. When he came in contact with a small foam bowl with a plastic lid, his fingers slipped on something sticky and he knew what he had. Real maple syrup. He'd paid extra for it instead of the corn syrup shit, thinking of nothing more than how fantastic his pancakes were gonna taste. Now? Now he couldn't care less about the flapjacks. But he had plans for the syrup.

He pulled his mouth from hers and tore the plastic lid from the bowl with his teeth.

"Oh no. No, no." She pushed against his shoulders.

He spit out the lid and flashed her a grin. "Trust me."

She shook her head, but a smile crested her mouth. "You can't—" She sucked in a breath as he poured syrup on her breast, watching the sticky drops spill over her nipple and drip down her stomach, onto the sheets half covering her where she sat cross-legged on the bed.

He set the syrup container aside, balancing it as best he could on the bed within arm's reach, and began to lick her clean.

"Asher." Just a breath. A lilting, hot breath that made his cock jerk to life.

He cleaned every bit of syrup off one nipple, then moved down her stomach and licked the path of sticky stuff to her belly button. Her hands were in his hair, pawing at him as she panted, her breaths tight. He may have given in to her request for a quickie this morning, but that meant skipping over a part of her he'd wanted to taste but had been denied.

"Hang on," he said. Any other time, he'd have swiped every bit of food onto his bedroom floor and yanked Gloria's ankles until she was flat on her back, leaving the mess for later. But a niggling in the back of his mind reminded him that Tank would eat every bit of food that hit the bedroom floor and Asher really didn't want to spend the rest of his Sunday at the emergency vet with a sick dog.

He worked fast, shoving containers into the plastic bags

and tying them off before dropping them to the floor. As an afterthought, he dug out a pancake and threw it into the hallway. Tank padded after it and Asher shut the bedroom door behind the pup. Then he turned back to his girl.

Glo sat, legs still crossed, fists pushed into the bed. Her hair was wild, her eyes filled to overflowing with want, and her breasts lifted and fell with each ragged breath she took.

"'Bout to make you dessert," he announced, stalking toward the bed.

She shook her head and made a feeble attempt to back away when he put a hand on her thighs. Before she worked up a protest he knew wouldn't be sincere, he buried his other hand in her hair and captured her mouth. Then. She *melted*.

He felt it—the way her bones loosened, the way her head lolled as he kissed his way down her throat. Even the hands that had been braced to hold her upright had moved to hold him instead. And he liked that a whole hell of a lot. He liked her a whole hell of a lot. And he was about to enjoy eating her pussy a whole hell of a lot.

He had all day. May as well make it count.

* * *

Asher's tongue moved against her clit, one insistent push after the other. The thoughts in her head ceased like she'd suffered brain damage. And maybe she had. She'd been determined to maintain control where he was concerned. With the sticky remnants of maple syrup on her breasts and his mouth moving in a tantalizing rhythm between her legs, she could say, without a doubt, she was no longer in control.

He was treading heavy, overtaking her the same way he had when they'd first been together. And because of the brain-damage-like effect, she couldn't for the life of her remember why she didn't want this.

So she didn't stop him.

She lay back and let him devastate her, bringing her to orgasm once, then twice. The last one causing her to twitch and stir and shake. Hand in his hair, she tugged. When he didn't stop, she sat halfway up in the bed and pulled his hair, but he only delivered blow after delicious blow and she came again, hard enough to see double.

"Ash," she begged. "Ash, please." A pathetic whisper. "Stop, please…"

Finally, he slowed, finishing her off with one long lick, and lifted his head. She still had a hold of his hair and he grinned up at her, lips glistening, devilish glint in his eye. "I'm gonna fuck you again but this time, slower."

"Please." She was supposed to follow that with something along the lines of *Don't. I can't handle any more,* but instead just left it at *Please.* Because Asher was Asher and the promise of getting fucked by him was too good to turn down.

He reached for a condom and she closed her eyes, anticipating and wanting and trying not to think. Then he pushed deep and thinking became impossible. Sensitive from his oral assault, he felt extra good as he moved within her. His grunts and moans of appreciation were plentiful, telling her she felt extra good to him.

"From behind," she said from her closed lids. Because she couldn't take it if he did the "Gimme your eyes" thing again. She was raw and open and feeling way too much. If he took what she gave him, she might never get it back.

He pulled out and palmed her hip. "Roll over, and stick your ass in the air."

She obeyed, hugging the pillow close and arching her back. He slid into her and right about then she nearly shot off the bed. He'd embedded himself in exactly the same way he had seconds ago, but in this position, she felt it deeper. Way deeper.

She let loose a moan of complete and utter enjoyment and abandon. Followed by more begging. And she threw in his name and an "oh God" while she was at it, because it was simply impossible to keep quiet while she was being brought to yet another powerful release under his control.

His hand smoothed over her bottom, thumb sliding between her cheeks, just a glance, a subtle touch. She clenched her inner walls, squeezing his cock. He groaned. She smiled into the pillow and squeezed again. Asher's answering groan told her he was close.

"Harder," she panted. "Harder, please."

He complied, slamming into her, pulling the backs of her thighs against the front of his, the slapping of their flesh causing sweat to bead on her upper lip. The harder and faster he went, the tighter and tighter she wound.

"Yes! Oh God, oh God!" She was shouting now, bringing down the walls of her mind as they crumbled into dust and the world faded from Sunday morning breakfast in bed to erotic black and white. Sensations buzzed through her body as she clawed the sheets. Asher growled behind her, taking her there while spending himself until he could no longer move.

She dropped to her belly and turned her head to the side, her labored breaths blowing her hair from her face. He fell over her, his sweat-slicked torso glued to her back, his hand on her hip, still pulsing and embedded deep inside her.

"That," he panted into her ear, having as much trouble catching his breath as she was, "was more fucking like it."

Gloria gathered enough oxygen to let out a weak laugh. One that Asher returned.

 CHAPTER 14

$\mathcal{S}$un sparkled off the lake, making Gloria squint, even from behind a pair of aviator-style sunglasses. The warmth soaked into her skin, covered only by a black string bikini and white sarong tucked in at her hip. Lifting a hand to shield her eyes, she looked out at the trees, the water, and the speedboat that zipped by, and she smiled.

Last weekend had been decadent. She'd packed a lot of great sex into two days, after all, but she found herself looking forward to today almost as much.

"Look who I found!" came a shout.

Gloria lowered her hand and spun around. Asher was walking down the dock with a tall man with a cleft in his chin next to a four-year-old with matching dark blond hair. Bouncing ahead of that man by about twenty feet was Gloria's very best friend in the entire world.

"Kimber!" Gloria climbed off the boat to meet Kimber Reynolds—now Downey—on the dock.

"Hey, gorgeous!" Kimber let loose a sharp squeal as she grasped on to her, her bright red hair tickling Glo's cheeks.

"You look beautiful." She did, too. Dressed in a vintage find from her shop, Kimber wore a white skirt covered in a banana-leaf pattern, a bright yellow top, and coordinating chunky plastic jewelry on her wrist and neck. Glo held her at arm's length. "I didn't realize how much I missed you until just now."

Kimber had texted her back the day after Asher's backyard party. Once Glo and Asher had stopped having *all the sex*, Gloria retreated to the deck with a strong cup of coffee. There, she'd had a brief text conversation about how she needed to bounce a few ideas off Kimber and how she and Asher were spending time together.

Kimber hadn't asked her to expound. Probably because she had already guessed what Asher and Gloria were spending time doing.

"It's so nice to have a break," Kimber said now.

Gloria turned to Landon, Kimber's tall, bespectacled, deliciously built ad-exec husband. He owned Downey Design, an advertising firm in Chicago. He and Kimber had been together almost as long as Caleb had been alive.

"Hey, Glo." Landon pulled her close for a half-hug and kissed her forehead.

And to think she'd once tried to convince Kimber to keep her distance from him. She still cringed thinking about how wrong she'd been. Luckily, neither of them held it against her.

"Who's that?" Landon asked the boy at his side, shaking his hand in his own.

"Glo!" Caleb shouted, letting go of his father's hand and wrapping his arms around her leg. She smiled and lowered to greet him, stroking her fingers through the fire-red hair he'd inherited from his mother.

Kimber took her son's hand.

"Asher rented us a boat," Gloria said, gesturing toward him.

"I see that. Thanks, Ash," Kimber said with a smile that, while it wasn't exactly unfriendly, still held a note of force. Gloria's fault. Over the years, she hadn't exactly shared flattering stories of the rock star. But like Faith, Kimber was being protective of her, and she loved that about her friend.

Landon's and Asher's paths had crossed several times over the years. From the Downey family vacations in the Cove, to weddings, funerals, and birthday parties. Landon extended a hand in formal greeting. "Nice to see you again."

Asher shook Landon's hand and muttered, "Glad you could come out."

Gloria could tell Asher was nervous. Unsurprisingly. Landon, though not in his typical sharp suit and tie, carried an air of intimidation with him. Until you got to know him. He had a dry sense of humor and a hell of a lot of warmth.

Glo just hoped those two found something to talk about while visiting this afternoon.

"So, what's the plan?" Kimber asked, her arm being yanked repeatedly by Caleb, who clearly was ready to go.

"Pick up Hawk, get a boat, and hit the lake. I figured we could grab lunch at the marina," Asher said. "On me."

Gloria felt her heart swell. Asher had been the one to insist that Kimber bring her son when she came up so that Caleb and Hawk could play.

Voices came from the side of the house and Evan, Char-

lie, and Lyon appeared on Asher's deck next. Gloria practically felt Asher's nerves dissipate. Having his best friend
here would help get him through today.

"Uncle Landon!" Lyon shouted. Landon bent and accepted a bear hug from his nephew.

Evan strolled in and clapped his brother on the back next
and Charlie offered her cheek for a kiss, then embraced
Kimber and Caleb. The gang was all here...almost.

"Let's go get my boy," Asher announced.

Gloria, for once not caring who was looking, took his
hand and walked with him to the car.

* * *

Please, God, let Hawk have a good day.

Asher pulled into the Trudeaus' driveway, Evan behind
him in his SUV with everyone else. Beside him, Gloria
squeezed his hand.

Man, he liked when she had his back. He hadn't seen
her much this week, save for Wednesday when he'd stopped
by her office unannounced with lunch. He locked her office
door, left the sandwiches on her desk, and led her to the back
room. There, he found a sturdy table and made good use
of her thirty-minute lunch break by having sex with her for
twenty minutes of it.

She hadn't exactly been avoiding him, and to be fair he'd
been busy most days and nights with the guys in the studio. He may have spoken too soon about the album "writing
itself" because he'd hit a few snags in the process. The
guys extended their stay for the month, renting a big, fancy
house on Peak Point where they'd parked their asses semi-
permanently. Asher had gone over there a few times to play

and plan to see if the change of scenery would help. It did and it didn't. They were resuming practice tomorrow at noon at his place and had committed to locking themselves in the studio until midnight if necessary.

Because of the busy week, he'd missed seeing Glo. Having her here, her hand in his, was nice. Something he could get used to.

"Be back," he said, sliding out of the car and leaving her behind. He strolled to the front door and knocked, waiting for Emily to appear, her slim eyebrows high on her forehead, looking at him with her usual mix of disdain and mistrust. What Jordan had told her, he had no idea, but he had a long road ahead with Hawk's grandmother.

He blinked in surprise when Jordan answered instead, wearing a bathing suit, a robe open over it. She smiled up at him brightly. "Hi."

"Hey." He frowned. What was she so chipper about? "Came to pick up Hawk."

"We're ready." She left the door open and he spotted a pair of beach bags leaning against the wall. One big and pink, one small and blue.

We? What the hell? The last thing he wanted was a fight, but he couldn't allow this to happen. "I came to pick up Hawk. Not you."

She raised an eyebrow.

"Broderick won't be there," he said.

"What's that supposed to mean?" Like she didn't know. She propped her hand on her hip and scowled. God. She looked like her mother when she did that.

"I have friends out there, Jordan. Let's not make this hard." He scrubbed his chin with one hand.

"I don't see why I can't go. Hawk's my son."

Hawk, picking up on the tension, went quiet and ran behind his mom. This was exactly what Asher did not want. He didn't want to fight with her in front of Hawk and he didn't want her pissed at him, driving a bigger wedge between him and the child he should be bonding with.

"Can you just let me take him for the day?" He unclenched his jaw to force out, "Please?"

"What is he begging to do?" Emily swept in from a huge window-lined living room full of floral furniture and wispy curtains.

"He wants to take Hawk on a boat trip, which I agreed to, but I did not agree for him to bring along Gloria."

He wasn't going to respond to that.

"My friends and their families are out there," he told Jordan's mother with as much patience as he could muster. Hard to believe, but of the two of them, Emily was the reasonable one.

"And *Gloria*," Jordan put in. She narrowed her eyes. "I don't approve of her being around my son."

"I swear to—" He looked at the ceiling and swallowed the rest of that sentence. It wasn't easy to figure out a kid-friendly way to say, *She is none of your fucking business.*

"You're going to have to trust him, sweetheart," Emily cut in, her tone curt.

Jordan snapped her head around to look at her mother while Ash stood, speechless and stunned.

Emily, unfazed, continued. "Asher is Hawk's father. Gloria seems like a nice woman. You'll have to trust his judgment."

"Trust a rock star who sleeps his way around the country?" Jordan bit out.

Hawk shrank away from his mother's tone while Asher's

blood pressure skyrocketed. Nice to know this was the way she talked about him to his son when he wasn't around.

"Jordan Bethany Trudeau." Emily stepped closer to her daughter, her voice low and lethal. "Do not be crass. Keep in mind while you're throwing stones from your glass house that you also climbed into bed with this man."

Asher gave Hawk a tight smile and hoped to hell his kid wasn't picking up on anything that would traumatize him in his later years.

"Really, Mom?" Jordan stomped away, flipping her hair over her shoulder. Hawk followed, calling, "Mama," and Asher felt his heart chip at the corners.

He blew out another breath and pulled his hand over his face. *Fuck*. This was going as well as he'd expected.

"I didn't mean for…" He shook his head as he tried to think how to end that sentence. "Any of it."

And wasn't that the truth.

"I love my kid," he reiterated.

"But not his mother."

"No." He didn't love Jordan. Love had nothing to do with anything that happened between them. Ironic considering he felt the genuine pull of love toward his son.

"Look, Mr. Knight, I feel like you're both trying to do the right thing, here." Emily looked in the direction Jordan had stomped off in a huff. "You more than my daughter. It's fair for you to spend time with Hawk. And she should let you and stop trying to mandate when and how. Your lives are separate but together and that's the biggest challenge. I love my daughter and my grandson, and I want what's best for them both. Unfortunately, the best thing for Hawk is not the best thing for Jordan. The boy needs his father."

"I agree." Which is what he was trying to do. Spend time with his son. He'd be damned. Emily got it.

"But you can't keep showing up like a part-timer."

Okay. Maybe she didn't get it. He pulled in a deep breath.

"Jordan and I are raising this boy," she said, "and you're getting to go out and show him the fun side of life. There is another side. Getting him to eat. Sleep. Dealing with tantrums and his recent fascination for the word 'no.' If you expect him to respect you as a father, you need to start being one to him."

"I have asked Jordan to let me have him overnight and the answer is the same every time. She doesn't trust me. She doesn't know me." Asher felt his ears turn red. God, he was pissed. "I don't know what kind of game she's playing, but she wasn't invited to my house last Saturday. And I sure as shit didn't expect to see her at my party, making out with my friend, then getting into a catfight with Gloria."

"I beg your pardon?" Emily's brow creased. "Saturday? Making out? She told me she went to her friend Leanne's house on Saturday and they went to a fair and then a concert that evening."

What was Jordan, fifteen years old? Why would she lie?

"I don't have time for this," he said honestly. "I have friends out there, and my girl is waiting for me. I want to take Hawk out today. My friends flew in from Chicago with their four-year-old and I'd like him to hang out with a kid around his age. Jordan is not going. I'm not dealing with her drama, and I refuse to put Gloria in a bad spot."

Emily stared him down for the count of five.

Asher stood, arms over his chest, and waited her out.

"Jordan!" she called, holding Asher's gaze. "Bring Hawk down here."

A few minutes later, Jordan appeared in the foyer, Hawk in her arms. She put him down when she saw her mother and Asher standing close.

Emily bent and smiled at her grandson. "Do you want to go play with another little boy your age today?"

Hawk's face split into a smile. "Yeah!"

Asher's heart swelled. He'd give anything to put that smile there more often. It was better than his son crying whenever he was around.

"Mom!" Jordan sputtered.

Emily ignored her. "Your daddy is here to take you to play. Do you have your bag?"

Hawk ran to the blue beach bag. He hoisted the bag onto his shoulder, or attempted to, anyway. Asher, his heart feeling even bigger and more tender from Emily referring to him as Hawk's "daddy," took the load from his son.

"Ready, kiddo?" he asked.

"Yeah!" Another smile. Dimple and everything.

He extended a hand and Hawk put his tiny palm in his. Together they walked for the door.

"Be careful, honey," Jordan said, bending to kiss Hawk good-bye. Hawk didn't let go of Asher's hand, and he saw that as another inch of ground gained.

With a nod to Emily, he said, "Thanks." Because without her, this would have ended differently. Probably badly. "I'll have him back by eight or nine tonight."

"Fair enough," Emily said.

Displeased, Jordan pursed her lips, but she knew better than to take on both of them. Asher may have gained an inch, but he still had miles to go.

* * *

"Mimosas!" Charlie came out of the cabin to where the girls had set up a trio of lawn chairs and beach towels on the fantastically huge boat.

Gloria turned her attention from the sight below in the water. Asher held on to Hawk, who splashed around in the lake. Landon had climbed in with Caleb, too, who wasn't as used to the water. He was clinging to Landon like a barnacle. Evan and Lyon swam like freaking fish—like there never was a day they weren't in the water.

"Thanks." She accepted her champagne drink.

"To friends," Charlie said, lifting her flute.

"And family," Kimber chimed in. They toasted and Gloria joined them, but her heart pinched. Family wasn't something she had, but these two did. They'd married brothers and became sisters.

Gloria sipped her drink, trying to concentrate on the sun and the gorgeous day and not her maudlin feelings. Her eyes went to Hawk, who grinned up at Asher. Her heart pinched harder. *Family.*

"He's good with him," Kimber commented, her eyes on Asher.

"You sound surprised," Glo said.

"I am…a little." The redhead smiled, looking a tad guilty. "Everything I know about him is from you and you didn't make him sound like much of a catch."

No, she guessed she hadn't. Gloria had called Kimber on several occasions and yowled about his horrible behavior.

"Don't get me wrong, Evan spoke in his defense, but I didn't side with him. Brother-in-law or not, I'm on your side."

"I know." Best friends. This was why God made them.

"Sisters." She held up a fist for a bump that Gloria returned. Maybe she had family after all. The center of her chest grew warm.

"I wasn't necessarily on Asher's side," Charlie said, looking slightly chagrined.

"Hon, you have to take his side, because you have to take Evan's side," Gloria said, giving Charlie an out. "And you should. Evan is a solid guy. If I were a better human being, I would have listened to him. But, in case you haven't noticed, I don't really listen to anyone."

Nope, she was on an island. But she was the one who'd marooned herself there, so really, she had no one to blame but herself. Gloria had been a rowdy teen who had learned early she couldn't lean on her mother. That was why she didn't cling to her foster families. They may have been decent people, but she didn't get to know them. She didn't *want* to know them. As a result, she'd bounced from house to house to house for the next year and a half.

She stroked Tank's fur. He'd smartly taken a spot under one of the benches in the shade. He had his doggie life vest on, just in case, but Glo couldn't imagine a scenario where he'd voluntarily get in the water. He wasn't a sporting breed, even though Asher seemed to be in firm denial that Tank wasn't a lake dog.

"You had something pressing to talk to me about," Kimber prompted.

Charlie gasped, her eyes wide. "Is it about sex?"

"With her and Asher, it's always about sex." Kimber laughed.

Gloria had confessed to Kimber when she called. She was her best friend. But there was something she'd been keeping from everyone.

"Ace!" Evan called up. "Get in here!"

"I will in a minute!" Charlie called back.

"Just leap off the top deck. I'll catch you." Evan grinned, treading water while Lyon swam around in a life vest. He'd argued about putting it on, but Evan argued harder that he should. Lyon was a great swimmer but a rambunctious kid. There was no way to keep eyes on him all the time and Evan knew that.

"You're crazy!" Charlie smiled.

"Crazy for you, baby," he said, and winked.

Gloria's heart turned to mush.

Next to them, Kimber chuckled. "Could he be more full of crap?"

"Doubt it," Charlie said. "Do you mind if I tend to my husband and son? Unless you need me?"

Gloria waved her off. "Get in the water. Kimber can field this. It's a Chicago question anyway."

Charlie made her way down to the lower deck of the boat. When she was gone, Kimber's green eyes met Gloria's blue ones.

"Chicago?" she asked.

"Brice McGuire, the music agent?" Gloria said. Kimber nodded, knowing who Glo was talking about. "He offered me a partnership if I move back to Chicago."

She wasn't sure what kind of reaction she expected from Kimber, but a frown wasn't it.

"What?" Glo asked.

"Don't get me wrong," she said. "I miss you like crazy, but you came here because you wanted a change. You were going to live in a house on the lake like you dreamed, remember?" Without waiting for her to answer, Kimber glanced at Asher and back at her. "And what about whatever you two have?"

"I'm not sure what we have." She watched Asher lift Hawk out of the water and splash him back into it. God. So cute. Both of them.

"It's something, though." Kimber tilted her head.

"He's going to be in California part-time. It's not like he'll live in the beautiful house I wanted for myself." It'd be empty all winter. Like her, she imagined. Wow. She was downright *morose* today. "You don't think I should take Brice's offer?"

Kimber put a hand on Gloria's arm. "I think you should give this a chance."

"This," Gloria repeated, watching Asher get splashed in the face courtesy of Hawk kicking furiously. "Evergreen Cove? Or Asher?"

"Yes," Kimber said with a smile.

This time when Glo looked back to Asher, his hands were on Hawk, but his eyes were glued to hers. Even with the distance between them and the people surrounding them, they shared an intimate, quiet moment.

He made a diving gesture and then mouthed the word "Jump." She gauged the distance from railing to water and bit her lip. When her eyes went back to him, he shouted up at her, "Do it!"

"No!" she shouted back.

He laughed, and she smiled, because wasn't that just like her? Part of her really, really wanted to. Wanted to just let go, fly off the edge of that boat and land in the water below. Problem was, she didn't know what was under that murky water. She couldn't be confident she would land unharmed.

And wasn't that the metaphor for her life? Gloria only leapt when she was sure she'd land safely. Anything else was too risky. She'd been wrong about Asher when she'd been sure he'd tire of her. He didn't. And she'd been wrong about herself when she thought she'd be able to let him go without missing him. She had.

Being that wrong messed with a girl's head.

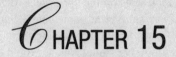

CHAPTER 15

Kimber, Evan, Charlie, Gloria, and all three kids were in the water, leaving Asher on deck with Ev's brother, Landon.

Asher knew Landon, of course, since he'd known Evan, but he'd only met the guy a handful of times. There hadn't been a lot of opportunity for one-on-one time with him, that was for damn sure. The advertising executive, even dressed down in shorts and a T-shirt, carried himself in a way that made Asher think he didn't care for him all that much.

Fuck if he cared. Being in the spotlight since forever meant some people didn't like him and some people did and there wasn't a lot anyone could do to change their minds.

Which was why it perplexed him so much when he tipped Jack Daniel's into a glass and held up the bottle in offering. "Whiskey?"

Landon met his eyes through a pair of sunglasses, mouth a flat line. "Sure."

Well. This should be fun. Asher handed Landon the glass and then poured himself a double.

They each took seats on the upper deck, overlooking the water. Gloria was smiling at something Kimber said, her hands around Hawk. Seeing her helping him splash around in the water made Asher smile. And here he'd been worried about her wanting to meet him.

"She's a natural with kids," Landon commented, sipping his drink. He was squinting, his cheeks drawn up under his sunglasses. He wasn't smiling, and Ash wasn't sure if it was the drink he disapproved of or the company. Until Landon added, "You ain't so bad yourself."

Asher's brows lifted. He hadn't expected a compliment—especially one that casual—to exit Landon's mouth. The guy was serious all the time.

"Yeah. Takes practice." Practice that wasn't easy to get with Jordan fighting him every step of the way. His lawyer wanted to draw up papers, but before Asher dropped those in her lap, he wanted to see if they could work out things amicably. Maybe with Emily involved, they'd be able to.

"Takes being there."

Oh, here we go.

"Yeah." Asher drank his whiskey and waited for a lecture. A lecture he wasn't going to sit here and take. He didn't owe Mr. Millionaire Ad Exec any explanation for—

"How's the album going?"

Stunned again, he blinked over at Landon, who had stopped watching the water to look in Asher's direction, brows up.

"It's…uh…it's fine. It's good. It's going."

Landon chuckled. "Fine, good, and going. Sounds like my last campaign. Fucking Cheese Bitz redesign. Almost killed me." He held up his hand and pointed out a shallow mark. "See that scar? Got that in the pitch meeting."

In spite of himself, Asher laughed. Maybe he'd had this guy wrong. Landon, though the oldest and the most buttoned-up Downey, was still a Downey. And if he was ten percent of who Evan was, Ash should expect to like him.

"Creative process is a wily beast," Landon said, lifting his drink again.

"I'll drink to that," Asher said, then did.

"Sometimes the ideas flow smoothly and other times you can't figure out how to put one thought after the next."

"Or one note after the next," Asher said. "I have one song that's working, but the band and I are butting heads on the rest. I don't know. Maybe we're sick of each other. We've been together a lot of years. Except for Broderick."

"The new guy," Landon said with a nod. He must not have missed Asher's shocked expression. "I know my Knight Time. 'Ballin' by Summer' is my favorite song."

"Unchained" he would have expected. It was his biggest, most popular song. But "Ballin' by Summer" was a song off their third album and hadn't gotten any radio play.

"You're blowing the idea of you being a stiff suit out of the water," Ash admitted with a shake of his head.

"Yeah, well, you blew the one of you being a shallow dick out of the water, too." It was a compliment and Asher took it as one.

"Thanks."

Landon sat up in his chair. "Gloria tell you she's a foster kid?"

That was a segue if he'd ever heard one.

"Sure." *In so many words.* "I don't think it's a secret."

"It's not," Landon stated simply. "Her mom was a drug

addict. Heroin, mostly. Gloria was taken out of the house when she was sixteen. She never graduated high school."

Asher shifted in his chair. He'd known about the high school thing because he'd asked. She'd attained a GED and then taken some business classes in college, only to become an agent and excel, first working for someone else, then for herself. But then, Gloria was a badass, so it didn't surprise Asher that she excelled even with a stacked deck.

"She told Kimber to break things off with me when Kimber was pregnant."

It was such a personal statement that Asher felt a sharp prick of shock at the confession. "Bet she's not your favorite person."

Landon shook his head. "Wrong. She's pretty close to the top of my list."

She was at the very top of Asher's. Though right now, Hawk was vying for space and winning. Frankly, he'd like them both at the top. He could handle them both.

"I'm trying to figure out how to ask you your intentions without sounding like her father," Landon admitted with a quirk of his lips.

"Too late."

"She's Kimber's best friend, so I look out for her."

Damn. Asher liked that. Liked that Gloria had people who were looking out for her. A thought sparked and before he could decide if he was being opportunistic or just smart, he said, "There's a music agent nosing around her lately. He's interested in a partnership with her back in Chicago."

Landon grunted, brows lifting. He hadn't known.

Asher debated asking, then figured what the hell and asked anyway. "Think she'll move back?"

"Have you given her a reason not to?" Landon let the question hang, sipping his whiskey.

"A few." They hadn't breached that topic specifically. He was planning on returning to LA, so it wasn't like he could ask Gloria to hang out here waiting for him when he came back every so often.

"Maybe give her a few more." Landon finished his drink and rested the glass on the deck.

Asher did the same, then stood up and looked over the railing. Gloria was holding on to the straps of Hawk's life jacket, letting him kick and splash but not letting him go too far. He liked the look of her with his son way too much.

She tilted her head back and blew him a kiss.

"That's what I like!" he called down to her.

"Yeah? Come and get it."

"You got it, Sarge."

Her mouth dropped in surprise, but he saw the spark of admiration there, too. She should have expected it. He'd never turned down that offer from her yet and wasn't starting now.

"Going over," he informed Landon, but Landon was already pulling his T-shirt off.

"Race you to the bottom." Landon put a foot on the railing.

Asher tugged his shirt off next and the two of them climbed over the railing and threw themselves over. He came up for air to find Landon already slicing through the water to Kimber.

"You lost," Evan pointed out.

"Depends," Asher said as he cut through the water to Gloria. He wrapped his arms around her and collected his reward.

"You're crazy!" she told him after a kiss that ended too soon.

"Crazy!" Hawk parroted.

"That's 'Daddy' to you, kid," he joked.

"Daddy!" Hawk repeated.

Yeah, Landon may have won the race to the water, but it was Asher who won the day.

* * *

"Thank you so much for inviting us." Kimber shouldered her bag. "I think the hotel is calling our name."

"I wish my place was bigger. I totally would have asked you to stay with me."

"No, you wouldn't have," Kimber said with a laugh. True. Glo didn't let many people into her personal space. Kimber was an exception to that rule.

"But I would like to be the kind of person who would have offered," Glo amended.

"You don't want any part of this when he wakes up at six a.m., honey, trust me." Kimber gestured to Caleb, currently in Landon's arms, his head on his father's shoulder, snoozing soundly.

"Yeah. Save yourself." Landon winked behind his glasses, and Gloria smiled up at him.

"Thanks for bringing the entire family." She hugged him, careful not to wake Caleb, and then embraced Kimber. When Landon started for the car, Glo pulled Kimber's arm to keep her from going. Evan and family had already gone home, and Asher was inside with Hawk.

"You promise to keep me sane?" she asked her friend, taking advantage of their alone time.

Kimber hugged her again. "I know you, Gloria Renee Shields. I know you better than you know yourself some days. You feel like you're losing ground by giving in, but the only way to trust him is going to require you giving in to him every once in a while. Take it from this old, married lady. The secret is—"

"Don't you dare say compromise."

"I was going to say fantastic sex." Her red brows arched, her expression so sincere, Gloria held her stomach and laughed.

"Seriously, though." Kimber blinked bright, green eyes. "No matter what hardships occur, you keep it hot in the sack and you'll end up A-okay."

"This is why I love you."

"Well, duh." With a wink and a wave as she walked away, Kimber headed around the deck to the driveway. Gloria stood outside until they pulled away, arms crossed, teeth on her bottom lip.

Through the windows at the back of Asher's house, she watched him move away from a sleeping Hawk, stroking the boy's hair gently and picking up Tank when he tried to jump on the couch. Dog in his arms, he came outside and Gloria let the moment freeze while she thought about how perfect this setting was.

The house she'd dreamed of living in. Asher. Hawk. Tank. What if this was her destiny? Being a part of something permanent and lasting and deeper than she'd ever experienced in her life...Could she accept that, as big and scary as it was?

"I hate to wake him up, but I promised to have him home by nine." Asher put Tank down, who trotted off the deck and to the grass to do his business.

Asher palmed her jaw, lowering his lips to hers. She lifted an arm and held him, kissing him gently, and then not so gently when his tongue pushed past her lips. They made out for a few minutes until a surge of heat infused her every last nerve ending. He pulled away and gave her a wicked smile.

"Don't leave," he said.

"Unfair," she breathed. How was she supposed to leave after the promise that kiss held?

His cell rang and the fire in his eyes flickered.

He answered his phone with, "Yeah." A pause. "That works. See you in a minute." He ended the call and thumbed Gloria's chin, his eyes going to her lips. "Change of plans," he said. "Emily was out this way, so she's picking up Hawk."

"She's very involved in his life."

"More involved than his mother." He turned to check on his son, still zonked out. "Had a run-in with her today." He shook his head. "She didn't want Hawk to hang with you."

Gloria bit her lip. Probably because she'd put Jordan in her place at the party. Which was not Gloria's job no matter how justified her reasoning.

"My fault," she admitted.

"No one's fault, Glo. This is the deal. But I need you to do me a favor."

Gloria cringed.

He only chuckled. "Just go out and say hi to Emily when she gets here. Show her what a class act you are."

"Asher..."

A horn honked and Tank barked sharply.

"You can do it," he assured her, then kissed her, palmed Tank, and carried him inside. "I'll wake Hawk and bring him out in a few."

Class act. Right.

Gloria had changed from her swimsuit/sarong pairing into a casual summer dress and heeled sandals. Her hair had air dried in thick waves, but she was presentable. Maybe not presentable enough for Emily Trudeau, but there was only so much she could do on short notice. She rounded the deck to the front of the house, where a maroon Cadillac was parked.

Emily had just turned off the car and was climbing out. The older woman wore a prim and proper black and tan dress, which made Gloria feel underdressed. By the look Emily ran down Gloria's body, it was obvious the other woman wasn't impressed.

"Asher is waking Hawk now. He's pretty beat after a long day."

"Oh." Emily looked to the house.

"He had fun, though. We ate lunch and swam."

Emily said nothing.

"He and Caleb played most of the day. I think they really hit it off." Gloria cleared her throat, wondering what the heck was taking Asher so long.

"Caleb is one of your nephews?" Emily asked.

"Oh, well, honorary," Gloria said, feeling badly about fudging the truth before. He's my best friend's son. I've known him since he was born."

Emily assessed her again, staying quiet and making her feel uncomfortable. Gloria began resenting playing nice with this woman who was clearly going out of her way not to be nice to her. If Gloria was able to lay things out for everyone else, there was no reason for her to walk on eggshells around Jordan's mother.

"Next time, maybe Hawk can stay overnight," Gloria said. "He's going to be a bear when he wakes up." She didn't know that, but it made sense. If she were fast asleep after the day they'd had and someone jostled her out of her nap, she'd be a monster.

"That would require me trusting that Mr. Knight is capable of handling him overnight," Emily said. Which pissed Gloria right off.

"And I'm sure Jordan was a natural," Gloria quipped.

Emily blinked, straightening her shoulders. "I'm not sure what you think your role is, Ms. Shields." She narrowed her eyes. "But Hawk is not your child. It's up to his parents to decide what's best for him."

"And you, apparently." She was so sick of this back-and-forth. Of playing nice.

Emily stepped closer. The woman was Gloria's height, so they stood eye to eye.

"I'm Hawk's relation," Emily stated. "His grandmother. Asher referred to you as…how did he put it this morning? Oh, right. His *girl*."

His girl. Gloria liked that. But Emily saying it made it sound so…tawdry.

"I'm not sure what rights are afforded to you as his *girl*, but I'm guessing it does not include making decisions for my grandson."

Stung, Gloria opened her mouth to retort, but no words came out.

"These so-called nephews of yours. Have you ever had them overnight?"

She felt her face go red. The answer was no, she'd never had Lyon or Caleb overnight. She wasn't about to admit it, but her silence said more than she could have.

"Maybe you should ask yourself why you are not trusted with your nephews' care before you insist on being trusted with Hawk's?" Emily raised her eyebrows haughtily. She had the answer she needed.

The front door popped open and Asher came out, bag in

hand. Hawk hung on to him much like Gloria noticed Caleb hanging on to Landon earlier. Asher and Hawk looked so natural together, her heart lurched.

Asher moved to Emily's SUV and strapped a half-asleep Hawk into his car seat.

Emily spared a look over her shoulder. "Not such a bear after all, is he, Ms. Shields? Guess this worked out just fine."

"Nah, he's too tired to be grouchy." Asher gave Emily a smile. And why wouldn't he? He had no idea what had gone down just moments ago. "Thanks, Em."

She hummed softly, probably trying to decide if she should tell him everything that had just transpired. She must have thought better of it, however, because even though she glared at Gloria before shutting the car door, she said nothing more.

Gloria and Asher watched the Cadillac reverse out of his driveway and vanish down the tree-lined road.

"What was that about?" he asked.

"It was her letting me know I have no business in Hawk's life," she answered. It sucked, and she wanted to bitch about it.

"That's bullshit."

Earlier she would've agreed. Now she wasn't so sure.

"Is it? No one has ever asked me to so much as babysit. Not even Kimber and she's my best friend." Tall pines shrouded Asher's cabin, looming and black in the nighttime sky. Gloria walked beneath the covered porch and sat on the bench by the front door. "What's that say about me?"

"That you're busy and your friends respect your time." He sat next to her, elbows on his knees.

"Or maybe it says the runaway daughter of a drug addict isn't a fit person to leave your children with." She faced him.

"Sarge." Anger seeped into his features.

"It's the truth," she whispered. This was the kind of crippling fear that crept in while she was sleeping. The thing that made her a dater rather than a settle-downer. The thing that was keeping her from getting too close to anyone. To Hawk...to Asher.

"You know I don't think that." He put his hand on her leg.

"I don't want you to feel sorry for me." She pushed his hand away and stood.

"I don't."

She shouldn't have shared that with him. She shouldn't have given her fear a voice. And now that she had, she was embarrassed. Uncomfortable. Before she could escape inside, he pulled her onto his lap and wrapped his arms around her waist.

"Stop struggling," he said into her ear when she attempted to wiggle away. "I want you to listen very carefully."

He released her waist and turned his hands over, silently asking for hers. Asher had great hands. Calluses decorated his fingers and palms from guitar playing, and on every other one, a silver ring. Tonight he wore a leather cuff on one wrist, a handful of hemp bracelets on the other one. She put her palms in his and watched as he threaded their fingers together.

"Deep breath, Sarge."

She took one, feeling more relaxed and grounded in his arms, her hands laced with his.

"I trust you with Hawk as much as I trust myself." His low voice rumbled down her spine. "You're capable and smart. You're honest and you care about everyone more than you'd dare admit." He kept their hands linked as he wrapped his arms around her. "I don't know what the fuck to say to you about this," he mumbled into her hair. "Every part of me wants to apologize for putting you in this situation, but then that makes me feel like I'm apologizing for Hawk and I would never wish him away. No matter how difficult this is for you, I wouldn't change it—because I want you here."

She blew out a short laugh. He was so right, and in typical Asher fashion, so damn honest about what he was thinking and feeling.

He let her loose and turned her on his lap. Dark, earnest eyes studied her.

"It's a lot to ask, I know. But maybe I should actually ask."

Her smile erased as her heart beat a samba against her breastbone. Subtly, she shook her head. Whatever he was going to say seemed dangerous . . . because she wasn't ready. She was beginning to believe she'd never be ready.

"Do this thing with me," he said. "With me and with Hawk."

"Thing," she repeated, because what else was there to say? A panic attack was brewing. Because this "thing" wasn't a small thing. Maybe she should point that out. "That's a big ask, Asher."

"It is what it is, Sarge."

"You want me to . . . what? I already hang out here."

He dipped his chin into a nod. "That's a start."

"I have a job, a life. I can't start something."

"Little late to regret starting, isn't it?" he asked, and she heard frustration leak into his tone. Which made her hackles go up.

"I like my space." She slipped off his lap. Something about fighting with him was familiar. And much more comfortable than talking about playing family. "I like to be alone," she continued. "Maybe I need to understand who I am in the Cove. Nothing is permanent here yet. Not my apartment, my leased office building..." She swept her arm at the house and encapsulated Asher with it. He wasn't permanent either. He could leave any time. "I need to know who I am when I'm not attached to you."

"Attached?" He stood and scowled down at her. "You're not attached, Sarge. And don't act like you don't already know exactly who you are with me. You let go with me. You push yourself with me. You let me push you." He loomed over her. "You want that."

"Your spontaneity has boundaries, Asher. It's not always cute." She folded her arms over her chest and mentally dug in. "Not everyone can be a big kid all the time."

His lip curled. "Big kid."

"Yeah." It was the wrong thing to say, but she straightened her shoulders anyway and stuck by it.

A muscle in his cheek ticked. "At least I'm not a coward."

She dropped her arms and her mouth fell open with it. "Do you know what I've been through in my life? Do you have any idea how brave I am? How tough I can be?"

"I know exactly how tough you can be, Gloria," he said, his voice rising. "You won't stop trying to prove it to me. Have you ever considered that it's braver to trust someone to catch you if you fall?"

"How can you catch me when you're the one pushing me?" she snapped. And there it was. The felling blow.

He backed away from her, his lips flattening and his eyes straying to the sky. She felt a pinch of regret, but something in her—that innate stubbornness saying she'd won this round—refused to take it back.

"I have work to do," she said.

"Do it, then." He turned for the front door, pausing with his hand on the knob to add, "If you decide to leave, lock up."

The door slammed, leaving her on the porch. Even the crickets fell silent at that parting jab. *If you decide to leave...*

Now what? Well. She wasn't going to run away after that challenge.

"I have a laptop," she grumbled to herself. "I can work from here."

She marched inside, shouldered her bag, and headed for the couch. Through the window in the studio, she watched Asher prop the guitar on his lap and pluck in earnest.

She settled into the cushion and stared unseeing at the screen, wishing she could hear him play through the sound-proof windows and door. Wishing a lot of things. She opened her computer, having no idea how they'd ended up here or where they'd end up with each other tonight.

Typical, she thought, then began answering her e-mails one by one.

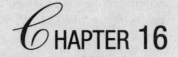 CHAPTER 16

Asher had gone into his studio to work off his frustration from yet another argument with Gloria, not sure why he was bothering to argue with her at this point. If she was so hell-bent on being problematic, why did he care?

You know.

That thought he ignored.

He spent the next hour writing and playing and living in bliss. Right in his sweet spot. Feeling every note in his bones, losing time and space as he hummed along with each strum. Lyrics came and he jotted them down, then closed his eyes again to return to the music.

After who knew how long, Gloria walked into the studio. He looked up from his notes. With leftover creative bliss saturating his bloodstream, it was hard to look at her and feel anything but want.

The almost pedestrian gray dress with faded white polka dots rode high on her thighs, and the front crisscrossed over her breasts, showing ample amounts of cleavage. Tall shoes sat at the end of her tanned legs, red toenails peeking out. Her ink-black hair was down, windblown from the boat, and an oversize pair of black-framed glasses were settled on her pert nose. She was a recipe for a hard-on if he'd ever seen one.

She took off her glasses and rested them on the table he was leaning over. He set his pencil next to them.

"So...I'm done," she said, looking around the studio instead of at him.

"Yeah."

"Are you mad?" she asked, craning an eyebrow as if to say, *Not that I'd care if you were.* But she did care. That was Glo. She cared; she just didn't want to admit she did.

"You're hard to stay mad at," he admitted.

A small smile, then, "I know the feeling."

"Wanna make up?" he asked, meaning it.

Her smile grew and she met his eyes with her penetrating blues. "Maybe. What do you have in your bag of tricks?"

"Hmm. Romantic walks on the beach are so cliché," he said. His eyes scanned her dress, down those legs and up again. He felt a smile inch across his mouth. "But now that I'm looking at you, maybe a few romantic slaps on the ass are due."

One eyebrow crawled up her forehead, then dropped again. "Whatever, Knight."

"You'd deserve it for that shit you just pulled."

"You don't get to punish me."

"No, you do that on your own." No one else could keep Glo down because she was too busy doing it herself. He reached over to the keyboard and pressed a button for a bass drum, adjusting the tempo and volume. "Let me find a good rhythm."

"If you think I came in here so you could spank me, you have another thing coming," she said, her voice going a little higher.

He stepped around the instrument and came to her. She liked to be pushed. He had no problem pushing her. Heat stole her cheeks and that fire he loved so much lit her eyes.

"I'm not into the rough stuff."

"Not rough, Sarge." He reached around and palmed her lower back, pulling her close enough that her breasts brushed his torso. She was warm and kind of grouchy and that was exactly the way he liked her.

She palmed his chest but didn't push him away, resting her hand there instead. "I'm not a kinky girl, Ash." His name came off her lips on a breath and his smile widened.

"You sure about that?"

Blue eyes went wide. She wasn't sure.

He slipped his hand lower, giving one rounded ass cheek a squeeze, and then slipped beneath the soft cotton of the dress to touch her bare skin, edged by a silky pair of panties. Pedestrian on the outside, but bad girl beneath. God. He loved this woman.

"It's not kinky. It's fun," he said, pushing the words through a clogged throat. Love. Where the fuck had that come from?

"For you, maybe."

"For me, definitely. But for you, too, sweetheart." At the drum's next beat, Ash drew the fabric up, exposing her skin to the air. In the windowed room, he could see her reflection on the pane. And God, she was beautiful, her hair arrowing to a point down her back, black panties doing little to cover the expanse of her ass. With his other hand, he gripped the material of her skirt and held it up. And on the next beat, drew back his hand and delivered one sharp slap onto her ass cheek.

"Oh!" Her hands clutched his T-shirt but didn't push him away, she dragged herself a little closer. Her mouth was dropped open, her eyes wide and curious. She liked it. It was written all over her face.

"Told you." He waited for sass, but instead, she emitted a brief sound that was half whimper and all permission. On the next drumbeat, he spanked her again.

She sucked in a breath this time and kept her gaze locked on his. "Why"—she had to clear her throat to finish—"do I like this?"

He was grinning now and damned if he could help it. "Because you trust me not to hurt you." He rubbed his palm over her backside, silky panties and equally silky skin. "Because you're a kick-ass, take-charge woman who secretly wants to be taken care of. Because you're safe and this is fun."

"Oh." She darted her eyes away.

"Now let's try it with you over my knee."

"What? No." But she was smiling. Curious.

He led her to the couch. She walked with him. Great sign.

"I didn't know this *thing* we were doing involved me over your knee."

"You want to talk terms, Sarge?"

She rolled those beautiful eyes.

"I'll talk terms," he said. "My terms are you by my side every spare moment you have. My terms are no matter what we spent the day doing—dealing with Jordan's shit, or Hawk being impossible, or you being grouchy—that we always, always make time to be us."

Her lips parted.

"There's nothing more 'us' than me pushing your boundaries." He sat and rubbed his palms over his denim-clad knees. "Bend over, beautiful."

* * *

Strong, tough, independent women did not bend over a man's knee for a spanking.

Right?

Asher leaned back on the slim leather sofa and propped his arms on the back, a crooked tilt to his mouth, fire in his expression and the promise of satisfaction—the really good kind—in his dark eyes.

Right???

Her bottom still stung the slightest bit from that last slap, and it had the by-product of sending a flood of warmth through her stomach and between her legs. Beyond her hectic heart, the keyboard ticked off the steady beat of a drum.

Asher stretched his arms toward the light switch over his head, his black T-shirt riding high and exposing an army of hard abs. He flipped the switch and the room fell into blackness. Outside, she could see the dock, the lake beyond, and a fat, pale moon—full—lighting the beach below. Inside the dark studio, she could make out the outline of a fantastically talented rock star who wanted to use his hands to turn her inside out.

She squirmed with anticipation. He offered a palm.

She took it.

"We're going to leave your dress and shoes on," he murmured in her ear as she bent over him. "But lose the panties."

Her breath caught when his hand slid under her skirt, wound around the scrap of silk, and tugged her underpants to her feet. She dragged them off and laid over him, elbows on the couch, anticipation and nervousness switching places to the beat echoing in the room.

He ran his hand through her hair, moving it over one of her shoulders.

"Asher."

"Shh-shh. No talking." He rubbed his palm over her bare backside, moving in slow, sensual swirls.

"Of course I can talk."

Snap! One sharp slap landed on her butt cheek before he started that rotating movement of his hand again. She gasped, unable to hide her shock... or how much he'd just turned her on.

"I say you can't." His voice was low and playfully sinister. "Right now, Sarge, you're not the one giving orders. Embrace it. You're going to lie here, and I'm going to do what I want to you. When I'm done—and only then—you can speak. Although," he added, and she heard the humor in his voice—the smile around his words, "if you'd like to answer with 'yes, sir,' I could completely get into that."

"Don't push it," she said, followed by shocked, "Oh!" when he slapped her ass again.

"What was that?" And now he was rubbing again.

"Yes, sir," she said with a smile of her own. She clasped her hands and bit down on her thumb.

"Fuck. I like that, Sarge," he said reverently.

So did she, but she didn't say so. Instead she did what she hoped would turn him on even more. She wiggled her bottom and purred, "Yes, sir."

His hips lifted, and she felt the hard ridge of his erection bump into her belly where she lay over him. Both of them were enjoying this, and quite a bit of her enjoyment was coming from the fact that for once in her day, she didn't have to be in charge of anything. Even her own needs. He was taking care of them for her.

He drew back and delivered the hardest crack yet.

"Ow!"

She felt his stomach move with laughter. Then that laughter stopped when he ran his fingers along the seam of her and found her wet and ready. He slipped over her folds, spreading her wetness and making her squirm. His touch—his attention—was only making her hotter. *Wetter*.

He pulled away and delivered another slap. Before she could recover from the shock of it, he drove two fingers into her and began fucking her. He continued moving in and out, slicking her wetness everywhere and making her want him inside her. Not his fingers—*him*.

"You have a beautiful ass, Sarge." His other palm was resting over her bottom and she pushed back against his hand.

"Asher," she breathed, but he didn't stop. She crawled back so she could reach his belt buckle, then flipped the silver piece open and went for his button-fly.

"Not done with you yet," he announced, turning her on still.

"I want you in my mouth."

"Not gonna argue with that."

She didn't think he would. She fumbled with the buttons, growled how there were too many but finally reached his cock. She dropped her head and tasted him, while he continued moving his fingers in and out and playing her clit with his thumb. The room filled with her hums of pleasure and the sharp sound of Asher pulling in air through his teeth.

He reached a hand inside the front of her dress, plunged

it past her cleavage and bra, and fondled her nipple. That, the heady, salty taste of him, and the loving attention being given to every part of her, tumbled her over the edge.

She bucked, squeezed her eyes closed, and moaned around his width. Only then did he stop. Only then did he lift her off him. And when he did, his made it clear what he wanted.

"Ride me, honey."

* * *

Maybe Asher was being sentimental, but there was something about the way Gloria rode him, her hips swiveling, her skirt pooling around his thighs, and her breasts bared—now that he'd pulled down the top of her dress—that made him not want to come just yet.

In fact, he was wondering how much longer he could get her to continue like this—her nipple on his tongue, his fingers wrapped in her hair, her pussy clenching around him and letting go as she bounced up and down on his lap.

The spanking had been fun. Fingering her had been more fun. Getting his cock sucked, infinitely more fun. But having her on top of him, moving slow, her eyes hooded and satisfied, her mouth slightly open—

Fuck him.

It wasn't only fun, but soul-crushing. In the best way.

In the years since he'd been a rock star—rock god, he oft argued flippantly to his friends—Ash had had a lot of tail. Pussy wasn't hard to find on the road and groupies were a dime a dozen. Because of this, he had a lot of experience and those experiences were sometimes good, sometimes better than good. What they never were was what he had with Gloria.

She was complex and a pain in the ass and beautiful and inviting. She didn't want to be coddled and she liked sex and she refused to show her vulnerable side. There were so many layers to her, he wondered if he would ever get them all uncovered if he started this second and investigated until the day he died.

And that was what he wanted.

He'd dared her earlier to do this "thing" with him, but now that she was on top of him, he knew what he wanted this "thing" between them to be. He wanted her by his side—in bed and out. He wanted what Evan had. What Donovan had. What Connor had. Those guys had women who loved them, who stood by their side and would raise their children with single-minded dedication. And by the looks of his buddies, they were getting plenty more than loyalty and friendship from their girls. They were getting it good in the bedroom.

With Gloria, Asher always got it good in the bedroom. But he'd also like Glo giving them a shot outside of it, too. He'd like to have both those oars in the water at the same time, thank you very much. In the bedroom and out. Hot sex and a long-term girl.

Arguably, this decision was being made mid-sex and really close to orgasm, but because he'd had a lot of orgasms, he could tell this wasn't his cock talking. This was about Gloria. She was the only woman who had ever made him have thoughts like the ones he entertained right now. Anything longer than a night or two on the road wasn't something he'd ever been up for.

One cushy breast against his face, he let loose her nipple and slid his tongue to the other. She tasted like heaven and smelled like sunshine. He had one hand on her ass and pulled her back down each time she rose up. Tight...she was so tight, his head was about to explode. She rested her palms on his shoulders and continued riding him, but there was one thing missing.

"Gimme your eyes."

"Not now, Ash." She pinched her eyelids closed in concentration. Or in avoidance. Probably that last one.

"What happened to 'yes, sir'?" He rolled her nipples in his fingers, watching her face contort with pleasure. She made a high-pitched sound and he grinned. "Eyes, Sarge."

She opened them. And he could die right then. Even not knowing her layers. Even not uncovering all that she was. This moment was perfect and he thought he could just pass on to the afterlife completely whole...

Okay, that was probably the sex talking.

"Why?" she panted, moving at a faster clip, her breasts bouncing in his hands.

He pinched her nipples and watched her eyes dilate. "Because I love to see you turned on."

"Oh, I'm turned on."

Another thrust.

"I love those blues."

Her lashes fluttered as her mouth dropped open.

He drove her down again, one hand on the small of her back, the other holding her hair away from her face.

"I love you, Gloria."

What.

The.

Fuck?

She stopped moving at the same moment he felt his face get hot and his head scramble and his balls tighten.

He'd seriously just said that out loud. Unrehearsed.

Thinking fast, he made an on-the-spot decision—like that time in St. Louis when Broderick played into the chorus of "Unchained" when it was the bridge and Ash had to cover. Sometimes you had to play through and hope that no one noticed, or at least if they did, would be quick to forgive and forget.

Dropping that three-word bomb was as unforgettable as things could get, but Asher wasn't about to let a slip of the tongue mess up what was happening right now. Not when they were both this close to finding heaven. He pressed his hand more firmly into her back, flipped her over so he could flatten her on the couch, and drove into her, deep and hard, making sure she felt it.

A sharp sound left her lips, approval written on her face. Over her head, he held on wherever he could—the couch cushion, the arm—anywhere to gain leverage and drive into her again.

"Like that?" He didn't need to ask, but he did need her focused on coming and not on anything else.

"Yes." The agreement was quick—a rushed breath of acceptance. He'd take it.

"Good."

She molded her palms around his bare ass, lifting her heeled sandals to his thighs just over his jeans. He was mostly dressed, save for the boxers and jeans pushed to his knees, but he was still able to work her into a lather.

A moaning, keening, blue-eyed lather.

She was still looking at him and he could see the conflict raging in her eyes like an on-field battle. He'd told her he loved her and she hadn't forgotten even now. While they came apart and together at a frantic pace, she was wondering if he slipped or if he meant it.

Asher hadn't said it on purpose, hadn't thought it out beforehand, but now that he'd said it, he knew...

He meant it.

Certainty reverberated in his bones, the same certainty he felt when a song came in a frantic rush of creativity and he just knew it was gonna be a hit.

Didn't mean it didn't freak him out. In a lot of ways he was in the middle of an identity crisis he couldn't stop from coming. He meant it, but could he follow through with it? It wasn't lost on him that he'd bounced several times before in his life. Until Hawk. Now he knew he wasn't going anywhere.

What about with Gloria? Could he guarantee he wasn't going anywhere where she was concerned? She did her best to push him away and at times he'd swear she was testing him. If he wanted easy, she wasn't the girl for him.

But he didn't want easy. He wanted fire and spark and a sharp edge that cut.

He wanted *her*.

There was no other woman for him, and he should know. There was no other man for her and she should know that as well. Problem was, he didn't think she knew. He didn't think she knew he wouldn't leave her. She was probably already thinking of leaving here tonight. Running to keep from talking about it.

As he stroked into her deeply, she threw her head back in a long, throbbing orgasm, and he tried to decide if he was going to let her run.

"Sarge," he muttered, pushing into her once more, then twice, finishing them both off. Her with her eyes closed and a sharp cry, him with a long, satisfied groan. He lowered his lips to hers and kissed her. She kept her hands on his ass, tilting her chin and tasting his lips as well. She didn't seem to be in a hurry to get away from him and he wanted that to be a good sign.

As things went between them, though, the good never lasted long. He'd like it to last a few minutes after he pulled out and let her off this couch.

CHAPTER 17

*S*he didn't stay.

Not long anyway. She'd excused herself to the restroom, which made her remember sex during the party, then she retrieved her beach bag from his bedroom, which made her remember sex after the party. When she came into the kitchen, she found Asher leaning against the counter, hand in a bag of chips.

"I'm going to go," she said. "Big day tomorrow."

He finished chewing, dropped the bag on the counter, and came to her, dressed in only jeans and jewelry. It was so appealing, she couldn't even understand it.

Probably the pecs had something to do with it. The flower tat. The cross. The fact that his abs looked like a hilly landscape. Ridiculously attractive man.

"Good night." She darted for the front door. He let her. That was the most surprising part.

She'd left last night and he didn't say anything to try to

stop her. She fully expected the patented Asher arm-grab as she walked for her car, but it never came.

She got away.

This morning, she'd woken in her own bed, hair wild after sleeping on it wet from her shower last night. She went to bed completely sated and relaxed and woke this morning agitated and restless, her mind spinning from all the things she still needed to do.

Yes, even on a weekend.

Dressed and ready, she moved to the dining room table to grab her laptop only to find it wasn't there. And the reason it wasn't there was because it was in her bag that she'd left next to Asher's couch.

In her rush to escape him and the *I love you* he'd dropped like a grenade into her lap, she didn't look around before she left. She'd been too preoccupied with getting out of there.

She bit her lip and considered she could go to the office and work on her desktop. Then she further considered she could also man up, show up, and get her belongings like a big girl.

She wasn't one to run and hide—well, not for long anyway. She could face him and handle the fact that—

Her phone rang from its home on her kitchen counter. She unplugged it from the charger, sighing when she saw Asher's name.

"Hey," she answered.

"Morning, Sarge." His voice was raspy and low and she could picture him sitting at his breakfast bar, bare feet on the rungs of the stool, black boxer briefs and jewelry—nothing else. Bedhead and sleepy dark eyes.

Kind of made her wish she had stayed.

"It's almost noon."

"Still morning," he said. "Your bag's here."

"Is it?" No sense in telling him she'd already figured that out and was debating coming to get it.

"Yeah." She heard the smile in his voice like he knew. "Band will be here in a few for lunch. You can eat with us."

"No, that's not—"

"Glo."

In a rare show of acquiescence, she pressed her lips together and listened.

"You don't have to avoid me in the morning because you gave in to me at night."

Did she do that? *You do and you know it.*

"See you in a few," he said.

"Okay. Bye."

"Bye, Sarge."

She collected her purse and keys and locked her door behind her.

* * *

Smoothies.

Never in her life did Gloria think that four adult rock stars would be sitting around the bar in the kitchen drinking fruit smoothies at twelve-thirty. Weren't rock stars supposed to open bottles of whiskey or tequila before they tuned their instruments?

"Bananas have no business in health drinks," Shiff stated with such authority that Gloria began to wonder at her own enjoyment of a banana-strawberry shake like the one in her hand right now.

"Don't be an idiot. Bananas are the foundation of any

good smoothie," Fonz stated. "Have you ever frozen them? Mixed them with cocoa and agave nectar? Tastes just like a Wendy's Frosty."

"Fuck off," Shiff said. He and Asher had split the latest batch—spinach, apple, celery, lemon juice, and honey. Ash had a glass in hand while Shiff drank directly from the blender.

"It's true," Fonz said. "Ask Broderick."

Broderick, cheeks full as he swallowed down his own banana-strawberry shake, shook his head. "Don't get me involved in this."

It continued a few more minutes. With a lot more swear words than necessary for such a tame topic. Gloria finished off her shake and went to the sink, feeling a presence beside her that could only be one man.

The same man who stripped her bare, body and soul, last night.

I love you, Gloria.

"We should get started," Shiff announced.

"Be right there," Asher said. One by one, Fonz and Broderick and Shiff took off for the studio—or as she'd forever remember it, *the confessional.* Who made a loaded pronouncement after doling out kinky spankings?

Asher Knight, apparently, she thought with a quirk of her lips.

Asher touched a fingertip to the corner of her mouth and she turned her attention to him. *God.* He looked amazing. Of course. His hair was its usual dark, styled mess, and he wore black jeans, a black tee, and his black cowboy boots. A necklace with an oblong crystal hung halfway down his chest and he wore rings on nearly every finger. Leather bracelets were cuffed at both wrists, no hemp ones today.

"How do you decide which jewelry to wear each day?" she asked, leaning on the sink with one hip.

"Whatever moves me, I choose that. Then if it doesn't call to me the next day, I take it off, trade it out."

She was having a hard time seeing that as anything other than a simile for them. Would he trade her out, too, once she didn't "call to him" any longer?

This was his fault. He'd developed a case of the I-love-yous and now she had to deal with the aftermath. Only it couldn't be fairly called a case of the I-love-yous, plural, since he'd only said it once. And unless he was going to bring it up right now, he didn't seem to have the urgent need to talk about it again.

Which was fine. Because neither did she.

He lifted his fingers to a button on her shirt. It was a plaid button-down, fitted, hot pink and black and white plaid with some really cool embroidery on the sleeves in the shape of fleur-de-lis. She'd paired it with short black shorts that barely covered her thighs and tall wedge black sandals.

"Hang for lunch," he said, dropping his arm to his side.

"I have to work."

"Laptop's here." He raised an eyebrow.

"Asher."

"Sarge." He drew in a breath through his nose and blew it out. Then his hands were on her waist, dragging her close, and he dropped his head to hers. She waited for a conversation to start or for him to tell her she was being difficult and cranky, which would start an argument, but he said nothing. Just stood there, eyes closed, forehead on hers, and held her.

So she lifted her arms and circled his neck.

"Why don't I get the pizza when it gets here," she said.

He opened his eyes.

"The room is soundproof. You'll never hear the bell."

"You have to work," he said.

"Laptop's here."

A smile nudged his mouth and dropped quickly. She lifted to her toes and kissed him, just a soft kiss of greeting that she hadn't been able to give him when she got here because they had an audience of three.

He tweaked her chin with his thumb and reached for his wallet, dropping a few large bills on the counter. "That'll cover tip, too," he said. Then he watched her for a second. "Thanks."

"Sure," she said.

He said no more, leaving her and Tank to shut himself in the studio with the guys.

"Just you and me, pooch," she told Tank. Then she sat on the couch next to the dog and pulled out her laptop.

* * *

The doorbell rang at four o'clock, and Glo finished typing and put her laptop aside, sliding the stack of cash from the countertop to pay the delivery guy. But when she opened Asher's front door, she saw it wasn't the pizza guy.

It wasn't even a guy.

The woman on the other side of the threshold had chin-length dark brown hair and stood a few inches taller than Gloria. The other woman's brown eyes were sharp, her lips a firm red line.

If she didn't look like she was in her fifties, Glo might wonder if she was a groupie who'd crashed band practice.

"And you are?" The woman's eyebrows craned as she eyed Gloria up and down, and then she blinked the slowest blink ever. Gloria did the same, inspecting the other woman's outfit. She was dressed in a slim, fitted pair of black pants and a white shirt tied in a knot at her trim waist. In one hand, a black clutch.

"Who I am isn't your concern until I know who you are," Gloria announced coolly. She should be the one asking the questions, considering she was the one standing inside Asher's house.

The other woman lifted her chin and eyed Gloria down the slope of her perfect nose. "If you're a groupie, I suggest you tell my son to put his pants on because his mother's at the door. I'm not going to pretend I approve of this sort of thing, but I know he's into pleasing the ladies and all I have to say is that it just figures because his father is incredibly good in bed as well." She delivered this speech calmly and Gloria once again tracked her eyes down and back up again.

Mother.

"Oh my God," Gloria said.

Right then, the pizza guy appeared on the walk. "Hey," he announced; then his face fell as he took in the stance of the two women on either side of the door. "Uh... I have a supreme deluxe, supreme veggie, a pepperoni and banana peppers, a Hawaiian—"

"Yes, here you go. Keep the change." Gloria thrust the cash into the guy's hands, took all five pies from him, and smiled at Asher's mother. "Come in, Mrs. Knight. You can share my pizza if you like spinach and artichokes and hot peppers."

Gloria turned to put the pizzas on the counter, hearing the door close and the slap of flip-flops as the older woman made her way into the kitchen. She turned to face the other woman, arm out, hand offered. "Gloria Shields, I'm—"

Before she could get any more out, Asher's mother raised her arms and laughed. One sharp *ha!*. Then she wrapped Gloria in the kind of hug that was reserved only for people Glo had known for a minimum of twelve months. A big, tight one. She patted the woman's shoulders with her fingertips awkwardly.

"Elana Knight," Asher's mom said, holding Gloria at arm's length. "I'm so glad you're not one of those bitches I usually find in his house and have to shoo out so I can come in."

Usually. Gloria winced, even though she didn't mean to.

"Oh. Shit." Elana's face fell. "I've spoken out of turn. I thought you two were—"

Gloria didn't get to hear the end of that sentence because the door to the studio popped open and Shiff bellowed, "Lanie!"

One by one, the band filed out and embraced "Lanie." They all seemed to know her, even Broderick.

"Ricky. I love your hair long." Elana lifted handfuls of his hair and cradled his jaw briefly. "There's my boy," she said when Ash sidled up and hugged her.

"You're early," he said, and his eyes went over his mom's head to Gloria. A smile played just behind the stubble. So, he'd known his mother was coming and hadn't bothered to tell her. Interesting.

"Yes, well. We came in for vacation now instead of waiting. Your father was sick of being at home. Yard work is getting to him." She made a shooing motion to the guys. "Go eat your pizza. Gloria and I are going out for a sophisticated lunch."

"That so?" Ash asked, his eyebrow hitching, eyes still on Glo's.

"Oh no. I'm good with pizza, really." Going to lunch with Asher's mom? Nightmare! Waking, living, breathing, walking, talking *nightmare*. Gloria wasn't good with moms, as proven by Jordan's mother last night.

"Don't be ridiculous. We'll have something gourmet. With cocktails. I have to fuel up if I expect to get my shopping done," Elana said. "Ash, that reminds me. The party is Thursday, six sharp. Emily, Jordan, and Hawk will be there. And you all are invited." She swept a hand around the room to include the band.

"Wouldn't miss it," Shiff said with a smile.

Tired of being left out, Tank began scratching at Elana's leg and she bent and picked up the little dog. "Hey, grand-pup."

Elana was having a party and Emily, Jordan, Hawk, and the band were invited. That was . . . weird.

"Are you buying those little cream puffs? Please say yes." That from Ricky, who paired his request with folded hands.

"If you're good." Elana pointed to let him know she meant it, then handed him Tank and turned to Gloria. "Grab your purse. Let's go."

"Mom," Asher said. He came to Gloria and draped an arm around her. "A minute, guys?"

"Yep," Shiff answered, taking the pizza boxes—Gloria's included. Fonz and Broderick, Tank in tow, followed him into the studio.

The second the door shut, Elana told Asher, "You can't expect her to hang around drinking whiskey and eating pizza while you all practice."

"I don't expect her to do anything, but I'm sure her idea of a fun Sunday afternoon isn't trolling through the market in search of proper party decorations."

"Sure it is. She's a girl." Elana threw a hand at Gloria.

"Mom."

"Asher." Her eyebrows lifted, then lowered as she watched her son. And the reason she watched him was because he'd moved his arm down to Gloria's waist, tucked her in close, and squeezed.

"Go with her." He lowered his lips to mutter, "You'll have fun."

Gloria parted her lips to argue, but he kissed her, keeping her from speaking. He kept his lips locked to hers so long, she had to pull air in through her nose. Even in front of his mother, she couldn't stop her hand from clenching his T-shirt or her eyes from sliding closed.

Damn him.

When he lifted his head, he was smiling, mischief twinkling in his eyes. "You girls have fun." He placed a kiss on his mother's cheek as he passed by. Elana was nearly as tall as her son, even in flats.

"This yours?" Elana picked up a slouchy black purse that was, in fact, Gloria's. Clearly the decision had been made. Gloria was going shopping with Asher's mom.

Whether she wanted to or not.

CHAPTER 18

The last place on the planet Gloria belonged in was a Toys "R" Us. Whenever she'd attended baby showers in the past, she'd strictly been an online shopper. And usually sent a gift card. A store full of children's toys made her feel as comfortable as she had in seventh-grade softball: not at all.

Elana had mentioned shopping for the party. Why they were picking out board games and stuffed toys was a mystery, until she finally interrupted Elana's decision over which Lego set to buy him with, "I thought we were buying decorations. Why are we shopping for Hawk?"

Elana paused, Lego boxes in hand, and blinked over at Gloria. Then she smiled. "You know what? I really like you." She put both boxes in the cart along with several other items she'd picked out for him and started off toward the register. "I haven't met my grandson yet. I intend to meet him.

And I'm not meeting him without making up for all of the birthdays I've missed."

At the counter, Elana unloaded the toys for the teenaged cashier who looked like she'd rather be getting dental work than spending her Sunday here. Gloria didn't hate being here as much as this girl, so there was that.

"Emily is easier to deal with than Jordan," Elana said. "Maybe it's because she relates to me grandma to grandma. Though she seems the type to prefer the term 'grandmother,' doesn't she?"

"I've heard her refer to herself as such," Glo said. "But the only preference of hers I'm sure of is that she does *not* prefer me at all."

"Why the hell not?" Elana asked, her brows pinching. The cashier mumbled the total. Elana kept her eyes on Gloria's face while she handed over a credit card.

"It's nothing." Gloria was quick to shake her head and play down her feelings of inadequacy. "I'm...I don't really know what I am in this situation. She wasn't wrong about me not having any experience with children."

Elana huffed, signed for her purchases, and dropped her credit card into her purse. "I'm not sure about that." She then paused at the door to address the cashier, throwing a clipped, "Thanks, hon. And listen, you smile through this day and you'll be much happier for it," over her shoulder.

Outside, Elana strode to a kick-ass white convertible and stowed the bags in the minuscule trunk. Once behind the wheel, she took her time weaving through the back roads of Evergreen Cove.

"Groupies are a dime a dozen, sweetheart," Elana said. "Asher's dad used to be in a rock band in his twenties. Did you know that?"

"Ash mentioned it."

"He never made it big-time, but that didn't stop the local girls from trying to get into his pants."

Gloria smiled at Asher's mom's frankness. "And did they?" She pushed her hair away from her face, whipping in the warm lake air as Elana took a curve smoothly.

"Fuck no! He had me."

Gloria chuckled.

"And Asher has you."

She didn't know what to say to that.

"I know all about you, Gloria Shields," Elana said to the windshield, her hair blowing, sunglasses on. "He's been chattering about you since the first time he met you. Smart, intimidating, beautiful, and a badass." She spared Gloria a glance. "That's an exact quote."

Words. There were no words for this conversation. Gloria focused on the road and kept her lips pressed together.

"You don't think you're good enough to care for Hawk?"

Since that was a direct question, Glo didn't have a choice but to answer. She did so with a shrug and a head shake.

On Endless Avenue, Elana parked in front of Sugar Hi and put her convertible in Park. She arranged her hair in the vanity mirror and said, "Let's discuss this over dessert. I sense this is going to be a long answer. And I intend for you to share everything with me."

* * *

Gloria cradled her coffee mug and eyed the crinkled wrapper that once held a Devil Dog. She ate every last bite of it while Elana had chosen a carrot cake cupcake that looked equally luscious.

"Okay, let's hear it." Elana sipped her coffee.

"Where to start?" Gloria asked her mug. She imagined being questioned by Elana Knight was a lot like being captured by the KGB. If she tried to lie, Elana would know.

"Where are your parents?" Elana asked.

Ah, so they were starting with the ugliest topic of all. Elana wore a no-BS look on her attractive face, eyebrows lifted in genuine curiosity. Gloria had no idea why she trusted this woman. But she did. And so she decided to tell her the unvarnished truth. A rare occurrence considering Gloria rarely opened up to anyone, but in Elana she sensed a kindred spirit.

"My father died of a drug overdose when I was twelve. My mother's recreational use became a daily habit and eventually, because I stopped showing up at school, Children's Services found out she was unfit and took me away at age sixteen."

"Foster care?" To her testament, Elana hadn't flinched.

"Yep. I had three homes over the next year and a half. By then I'd aged out or, well, close enough."

"Were they abusive, your foster parents?"

Gloria shook her head. "They weren't. I sensed that they were more interested in the paycheck from the state than in reforming a misbehaving teenager, but that's fair. I was not a good girl. I'd sneak out at night. I had a lot of boyfriends."

Elana's head moved up and down in a subtle nod. Her intense stare was unnerving.

Glo averted her gaze to her hands wrapped around her cooling coffee and tapped the porcelain with her fingernails. There it was. All the ugly. She braced for judgment.

"And you think this makes you unqualified to be with my grandson?"

"Well, it's not in the plus column," Glo said with a wry smile.

"Yeah. It is," she snapped. "Sounds to me like you know exactly what not to do with a child."

"I'm...sorry?"

Elana sounded almost angry, which threw her.

"What not to do is often more important than what you do," Elana said. "I bet you would never ignore a child, especially if he was misbehaving. I further wager you'd avoid getting too close unless you knew for sure you were going to be in that child's life long-term." She sipped her coffee. "If you've been avoiding spending time with Hawk, maybe you should reconsider."

"I haven't avoided him," Gloria said, feeling her face grow warm. She hadn't exactly been actively seeking a relationship with him, had she? "Not on purpose," she mumbled.

"You're nuts about him, aren't you?" A sly smile played on Elana's lips.

"Hawk?"

"Well, that's an eventuality." Elana waved a hand. "I'm talking about Asher."

Gloria felt more exposed than when she'd shared her home life. She swept a hand through her hair and licked her lips.

"Out of the boys in your past—the ones who did you wrong and a few who tried to do you right but you pushed away—Asher is the one who's stuck, isn't he?" his mother asked. "Stuck in your heart like gum in your hair. Even when you tried to push him away, he stayed, didn't he?"

"He went back to his life," Gloria hedged.

"Back to the girls who meant nothing to him," Elana amended. She rolled her eyes. "Bitches."

Because the backs of her eyes were burning with an emotion she didn't want to name, Gloria blew out a laugh to cover.

"How can I say this delicately?" Elana paused, thought, then confessed, "I can't. So I'll just say it." She leaned on her elbows on the small table. "Asher tires of girls very quickly. Always has."

Awesome.

"But you? He always had a spark in his eye when he mentioned you."

Maybe more than a spark. *I love you, Gloria.*

"Then, today…" Elana grinned and sat straight in her chair. "Today, I saw flames. He's gone for you, gorgeous, so you should prepare for that."

Wow. This woman didn't miss a thing.

Elana stood and extended her hand. Gloria looked at it, unsure how to feel about anything she'd said or done. Elana snapped her fingers and Gloria took her hand and stood from her chair. Elana then linked Gloria's arm with hers. "If you had been my teen, I'd have let you know you were loved. That's on them, sweetheart. Not you."

Then she winked and they walked to Elana's car arm in arm, Gloria biting back the sharp, so-good-it-hurt stab of emotion in the center of her chest. The feeling that someone cared about her.

Someone saw her.

Someone *got* her.

Finally.

* * *

Tank was hiding beneath the sofa in the studio, clearly uncomfortable with the level of voices, the tension slicing into the air like razor blades. Asher knew this, but he also knew he could tend to his dog later. Right now, he wanted to bash Fonz's face in.

Broderick and Asher stood on one side of the studio, Shiff and Fonz on the other. Broderick had hold of Asher's arm, one hand wrapped around his biceps. He was murmuring something like, "Chill, man. Just...let's take a walk."

Shiff was standing near Fonz, frowning down at him with such a look of displeasure, he may stop protecting him and let Asher beat his ass after all.

"Couldn't keep your mouth shut?" Fonz said, eyes on Broderick, fists at his sides.

"Fuck, I didn't know it was a secret!" Ricky said, his voice climbing. "I thought maybe you and your wife had some kind of open, on-the-road arrangement!"

Asher took his eyes off Fonz to glare over at Broderick. "You don't let go of me in two seconds, I'm going to beat your ass after I beat Fonz's."

Wisely, Ricky let him go.

"You are one to fuckin' talk," Fonz barked at Asher. "You get more tail than all of us combined."

"Not a cheater, Fonz," Ash said, taking a step forward. Tensions had run high in the studio today, everyone grumpy and worse for it. Finding out this bit of news about a friend he thought he knew, a friend who did the whole family thing and did it well, sent Asher boiling over.

Fonz clamped his teeth, a muscle ticking in his cheek. Ash had him there. Of all the girls he'd had, never did he have one when he was seeing someone. He rarely saw any of them exclusively. Except for Glo.

"You two need to mellow," Shiff advised.

"I'm not working with this asshole," Asher stated.

Fonz's wife, Pam, had been like a sister to the band for a lot of years. She'd trailed along on tours—several of them—until she'd gotten pregnant with Fonz's first child. And now, after she'd just given birth to kid number two, Fonz decided to get fresh pussy on the road? Unacceptable.

"Get out," Asher said, giving him a clear path to the door.

"My pleasure."

"Guys." This from Ricky, who backed to the studio door, hands raised. "Come on, this has nothing to do with the songwriting, right? This has to do with personal stuff, so let's shelf that and get to work."

"Business not pleasure." Fonz strolled by, cocky glint in his eye. Ash may have let him go, too, if he hadn't turned to face him and blurted, "Like you could ever keep it in your pants, you fuckin' hypocrite."

Asher lunged, then pulled back an elbow and delivered a punch directly into Fonz's face. On contact, Fonz's lip split. But he didn't waste any time whining. He turned on Ash and started swinging. They crashed into the keyboard, turning it over, and Fonz knocked his Fender to the floor, kicking it under the sofa when he scurried to knee Asher in the nuts.

Ash barely moved out of the way. Tank, head down, scurried out from under the sofa to avoid being kicked by either of them, since legs were scrabbling and Asher was currently holding Fonz by the scruff of his shirt.

"Get the dog!" Ash yelled.

Ricky was on it, scooping up Tank and carrying him out of the room.

Asher was aware of a huge shadow leaning over him.

"Swear to God, Shiff," he yelled. "You don't let this play out, I'll tangle with you next."

"Like to see you try," Shiff said. "But I respect you, boss. Fonz?"

"I can handle him," he said, not taking his eyes off Asher.

"On your own." Shiff left the studio.

Fonz's glasses had come off. He had Asher by the collar just like Asher had a hold of his. "What's your plan, Knight?" he asked, voice strained from holding his head off the floor.

"Beat your ass and feel better that justice was served," he answered between clenched teeth.

"Gonna beat Pam's ass, too?" A trickle of blood ran from the side of Fonz's mouth. "She started this shit. That's why we separated last week."

Asher felt his face go cold. He loosened his hold the slightest bit.

"Yeah. You didn't know that, did you? We didn't want to tell everyone, because it's completely humiliating to find out your wife is banging your brother and has been for two years."

Two years.

"Will?" Asher blinked. Fonz's older brother, Will, was a dick. Pam never liked him, often complained about him. And she'd started sleeping with Will behind Fonz's back? That raised a whole other set of uncomfortable questions.

"Yeah." Fonz let go of Ash's shirt, dropped his head on the ground, and held up his hands in surrender. "Now you know."

Ash let him go and eased off him. Once he was on his feet, he extended a hand. Fonz slapped it away and pushed himself up, using the bottom of his vintage Aerosmith T-shirt to mop the blood off his chin.

"Your boy?" Ash asked, and Fonz knew just what he meant.

"He's mine. For sure. She told me the day Thane was born. We've been trying to work things out, but she told me she's in love with Will." He swiped his lip again, put his hands on his hips, and looked at his shoes.

"Fuck," Asher breathed.

"That about covers it," Fonz said.

Asher pulled a hand over his face. He'd gone to blows with one of his best friends over a misunderstanding. There wasn't much he could say about it except for, "Sorry about the lip."

Fonz waved him off. "I shoulda said somethin'."

"Your business."

"Yeah."

The studio door popped open and Shiff put his head inside. "Girls are back. You good?"

Ash and Fonz exchanged glances and Fonz gave a chin-bob.

"Good," Ash agreed.

"You want to tell Shiff and Ricky?" Ash asked Fonz.

"Yeah. I'll tell 'em."

Ash left him behind to do just that as Gloria stepped into the living room. All he wanted to do was bury his nose in her hair and hold on tight. It was possible he was having some sort of creative meltdown, and just seeing her made him feel like there was hope.

"Hey," Gloria greeted.

"Hey," Ash returned.

"I'm heading home, sweetheart," his mom said, appearing behind Gloria a second later. She leaned close to whisper something to Gloria. Seeing the two women he loved most on this earth close, and seeing Gloria smile, made his heart squeeze.

"You staying, Sarge?" he asked.

"If you want me to."

"I want you to," he said. He did. He needed her here.

His mom came to his side to kiss his cheek. "See you Thursday, kiddo."

"Later, Mom." When she left the house, he pointed to the studio. "Gimme a minute?"

"Sure," Gloria answered.

He nodded and pulled the studio door shut behind him, but not before he gave Gloria a wink that held the promise of more to come later.

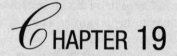

CHAPTER 19

Asher's minute turned into a half hour, and then a full hour.

Gloria had checked her e-mail, returned a few phone calls, and then gave up on working. Today had been a bust, but only in the business sense. She couldn't bring herself to regret spending time with Elana.

Gloria and Tank walked the length of the dock. She turned to look over her shoulder toward the house. Night had fallen and the boys were still in there, but none of them were playing instruments, which she found odd.

It looked more like an impromptu therapy session. Fonz sat on the couch, elbows on his knees, while Broderick sat at Shiff's drums, flipping a drumstick end over end. Shiff stood by the door, arms folded like a sentry, and Asher sat on a high stool, guitar in his lap but not playing.

She felt a little guilty spying, but how could it be consid-

ered spying if the room was nothing but windows and they'd
left the lights ablaze?

Immediately she thought of last night in that room. How
Asher had killed the lights, giving them privacy from…
well, no one, actually. Nothing but trees and lake and
moon—though tonight it wasn't full. She couldn't tell what
it was because clouds had swept in, making the orb a fuzzy
yellow circle set in black.

She lifted Tank in her arms and carried him down the
steps to the beach below. She scrubbed his tiny ears and he
licked the underside of her chin, his tail wagging enthusi-
astically. At least no one could debate she was good with
dogs. Once on the shoreline, she released him and he toddled along beside her, no interest in running off.

"Me and you both, pup," she told him. Where Asher was
concerned, weren't they both at home here in paradise?

And what was she doing here? Waiting around for…
what?

A repeat of last night?

Hmm. Of course a spanking/lovemaking session on the
couch would be lovely, but that wasn't why she was here.
She was here because shc was guilty of what Asher's mother
accused her of: Asher was stuck in her heart.

As much as it scared the shit out of her, she could also
acknowledge that Elana had said a lot of things that made
a lot of sense. Glo had been failed by her parents; this she
knew. But she'd also been failed by her foster parents, and
that wasn't something she'd ever fully acknowledged.

If Gloria Shields was one thing, it was accountable. She
had no problem owning her mistakes. She had no problem
squaring her shoulders and admitting she was wrong and
toughing out whatever retribution after things went south.

But maybe…

Maybe she'd been hasty to take the blame. To shoulder the weight. And because of that tendency, she'd been too hasty to deliver it as well. She'd made a snap judgment about Asher the night she'd found Jordan at his front door. Gloria had brushed him off, determined to lick her wounds and move on. But she'd never entirely moved on, had she? Mama Knight hit that nail on the head with a sledgehammer.

Out of the boys in your past—the ones who did you wrong and a few who tried to do you right but you pushed away— Asher is the one who's stuck.

Boys had come and gone in Gloria's life as Elana suggested. The ones who did her wrong—a lot of those—and the one or two who tried to do her right, but Gloria had quickly pushed them away. Then there was Asher, who she'd thought had done her wrong, but he'd actually done her right.

And she'd pushed him away, too.

Glo was sitting in the sand next to Tank, stroking his clipped fur, when Tank went alert, pointed ears standing straight out, and barked a happy *yip!*

"I see you're taking care of our girl," came Asher's voice, growing ever closer.

A tingle at her back spread across her shoulder blades. The promise of Asher too much for her body to ignore. She held her knees, arms around her legs.

"Good boy." Ash's hand appeared, scrubbing the dog's face and scratching his chest. Then Asher lowered himself behind Gloria, stretched his legs out on either side of hers, and took her hands apart so he could link her fingers in his.

His heat, his presence, his smell. Everything about him was stuck in her heart. *Like gum in your hair.*

"Glad you stayed." He nuzzled her ear and goose bumps spread down her arms.

"Seemed serious in there."

"Was."

"Did you have a breakthrough?"

"Kinda."

She opted to let it go, but he gave her more.

"Fonz and his wife, Pam, have been married for twelve years. Together for sixteen."

"Sixteen." Fonz didn't look much older than Asher. "High school sweethearts?"

"Yeah." He spread his fingers and then squeezed her hands tighter. "She and his brother..." He sighed and Gloria didn't make him say any more.

"Oh no."

"Yeah. They tried to work through it. Didn't happen. Their new baby is their baby and not his brother's, so that's good. But he's got a mess on his hands." He let out a self-deprecating chuff. "Almost as big a mess as I got on my hands."

Gloria drew in a breath. Maybe it was the nightfall or maybe because she'd already exposed her underbelly to his mother today, but Gloria decided to open up and admit something he deserved to hear. Much as she was willing to take her lumps and admit her wrongs, she'd never done that with him. Because the fallout potential was nuclear. But no risk, no reward. So here it went.

"I never should have pushed you away," she said.

Asher stayed silent. Probably too shocked to speak. Her heart picked up speed, but she forced herself to continue.

"I think I wanted it to be true," she said, her voice just above a whisper. "Because if I had a good reason to walk away, then I could move on. I wouldn't have to address the things I'd started feeling."

"What things?" he asked, his lips brushing her ear.

"*Things*." She shuddered. He let go of one of her hands to slide her hair aside. Then he placed a soft, openmouthed kiss on her neck. She drew in a breath, her skin cooling when his lips left her.

"I let you go." He reclaimed one of her hands, brushing her thumb with his and resting his chin on her shoulder. "Thought I could move on. I was trying to get over you, too."

"Groupies," Gloria whispered, but her smile felt sad.

"Less than you think. As meaningless as you'd guess. You?"

"A few guys. Boring dates. Short nights."

"Back on the horse."

They'd both tried to move on. They'd both failed and somehow found themselves in one another's orbits again.

"This is a very politically incorrect conversation." She blew a laugh out of her nose. "Aren't you supposed to say you regret everything? Aren't I supposed to say I waited for you because in my heart I knew you'd come back?"

"We're real, Glo." His low voice threaded around each of her ribs. "That shit isn't."

"I don't like regret," she stated.

"Then don't regret anything. I don't. You're you and I wouldn't change a fucking thing about you."

* * *

"Except for the feisty part," Gloria said. "The mean part. The—"

"Especially those parts." He released her hands to lay

her on her back on the sandy shore. Moonlight bounced off those killer blue eyes and highlighted her black hair. He propped himself on one elbow and smoothed her bangs away from her eyes.

He put a hand around her chin to hold her eyes to his. "Every ounce of you that's you and every ounce of me that's me. I wouldn't change 'em. Know why?"

She shook her head.

"Because then we wouldn't be the same us we are right now, and this? Sarge, this is worth everything. All the pain and misunderstanding and the mess we've been tangling ourselves up in for the last three-plus years."

Her eyes welled and he thought that might be the first time he'd ever seen her get emotional and get him at the same time. He'd broken through. He'd peeled back not one layer, but a dozen. And because of that, he smiled down at her.

She looked almost comically alarmed. "Don't."

"Don't what?" His smile grew.

"Asher. Please don't complicate—"

"I meant what I said last night."

She let out a gusty sigh. His girl. She made everything hard. Including him.

He released her chin and undid a button on her shirt. "Still mean it. I'll mean it until we're eighty years old and bitchin' at each other about who forgot to take out the trash."

He undid a second button and she swallowed, her throat working and her eyes blinking overtime, trying to keep those tears at bay.

"Tell me about Chicago," he said, placing a kiss on her collarbone and undoing another button.

"Wh-what?"

"You're thinking of partnering with Brice," he said, unbuttoning another.

"I'm keeping my options open."

Damn. Stubborn. Gorgeous. He opened her shirt, tickling the skin of her belly beneath a white tank top.

"Am I one of those options?" he asked.

She bit her lip. "You're going back to LA."

He scooted lower to kiss her belly and she sucked in a breath. "I'll be here a lot, Sarge." He rubbed his nose along her soft skin. "God, you make me crazy." She smelled like spice and sass and he wanted to bury himself in her and forget his own name. "Like it if you stick around and keep making me crazy."

She didn't say anything, and he didn't continue. He just wanted her to know that he knew. She held his head with one hand while he unsnapped her shorts and drew the zipper down. He climbed her body and kissed her mouth and she returned it, tipping her chin and closing her eyes. Tank ignored the both of them, curling up on a discarded beach towel, probably from when Broderick had come out here earlier to get some sun and had fallen asleep.

That meant Ash had Glo to himself. Just him and the moon.

He pushed his hand into her panties and slicked her with his fingers, pressing against her clit as he stroked her.

"Ash," she moaned, her back arching. There was a catch in her throat and sand in her hair.

Perfect.

"Yeah, baby."

"You make me crazy, too."

"That mean you're trying me out for a while?" Another stroke.

Her answer was a softly hissed, "*Yes*."

"Good girl," he praised, then slipped two fingers inside her and pumped once, twice. She arched closer, mouth open, shirt riding high above her gorgeous, flat stomach.

"Show me, honey."

"Show you what?" she asked, writhing as he stroked into her again.

"Tits, Sarge. My hands are busy. I have one hand holding me up and the other..." He allowed himself to trail off and slid into her again.

"Ohhhh, I know what your other hand is doing." Breathing tight, she sat up on her elbows and made short work of shedding both shirts and then unhooking a white lace bra that must match the panties scratching the edge of his hand. He had no idea how women stood to wear something other than cotton, but God bless 'em, because lace and silk were hot.

With her breasts exposed, Asher scooted higher and took a nipple on his tongue.

"I want you," she said, the sweetest three words ever. So far.

"I know, sweetheart. You're soaked." He gently pulled his fingers away and yanked her shorts off, unbuckling his belt and undoing his fly next. He dug a condom out of his pocket—the one he'd put in there after the guys packed their shit and left. He'd had an idea he'd find her out here. And he'd had a better idea of what he'd like to do to her when he found her out here. He'd do that now.

Condom on, he spread her legs and embedded himself within her. This...this was a helluva lot better than his fingers.

"I could live here," he said.

She laughed, a throaty, loose sound. The intensity swept off her face. She looked happy, and making her happy made him the same way.

He grinned. "Ready for the ride of your life?"

"Let's have it, cowboy." She looped her arms around his neck, grinning back.

And then they rode. They started out laughing and enjoying how much fun they had together, and then things went the way of serious. She grew quiet and intense, but this time in a good way as he worked her to her orgasm and him to his own. Once they were done, he gathered her clothes and lifted her into his arms. Then he carried Gloria into his house, Tank at his heels.

There was sand in his bed and probably in places sand had no business being, but it was worth it because Gloria was also in his bed.

In his bed and smiling sleepily and this time, staying.

He'd trade sand in his bed for that. He was beginning to think he'd trade just about anything for her in his bed. His apartment, his home—the one in LA, for example.

Before he slipped off to sleep, he thought back to Donny's words when Asher had first arrived in the Cove. For the first time, he didn't blow off his friend's assessment. Asher might be staying after all.

If everything he needed was here, then the rest would work itself out. He wouldn't lose this—lose her—again. No matter how hard she pushed.

* * *

Thursday brought rain, a warm rain that cleared quickly. It left behind heavy clouds and gray skies, but his mother re-

fused to let the weather dampen the party. The rental was
the same one they rented whenever they came here over the
summers when he was a kid, only now the rental was owned,
his mom and dad taking the plunge and signing the papers
on it this year. They told Asher they'd be here more often because of Hawk and that Hawk having his grandparents close
was important.

Asher agreed.

Being at this house reminded him of the days when he
met up with Evan and Donny, when they proceeded to wreak
havoc all over town. One summer night in particular, Donny,
thanks to his drunk old man, gained access to the liquor cabinet and stole a bottle of booze. They drank. Donny puked.
Then he sat and played lookout while Evan and Asher spray-
painted the brick walls of Mrs. Anderson's library with graf-
fiti penises. Seemed like the thing to do at the time.

They even made the newspaper. And whoever was working at the paper at the time allowed the headline to read
PENIS BANDITS STRIKE AGAIN! Elana was not impressed. And neither was Donny's old man, who didn't give
a rat's ass about the library but lit into Donovan with a belt
the next day when he found a missing bottle of whiskey.
Evan's parents had a good chuckle over breakfast, Asher had
heard. And that was very similar to the way Asher's father
had reacted. Elana had given Asher hell about civic duty
and responsibility, but Leland Knight had leaned back in the
lawn chair on this very deck and said, "He's okay, Lanie. Let
the boy be a boy."

That summed up his dad's feelings on just about everything. Laid-back. Easy. Leland had always supported Asher
as well as his dreams. It was his dad who had put his first
Fender guitar in his hands. It was his dad who had taken

Ash to his local shows. Leland had planted the seed of a dream that had later bloomed. Not the local music scene dream, but the *big* dream. To become a star. Go on tour in other countries. Have a band that stayed together for decades not just through one or two albums.

By the time Asher was eighteen, half that dream was a reality. Knight Time started local, but that wasn't where they stayed. Staying in Michigan was never an option. And so he moved, relocating to LA with a head full of dreams and his pockets full of change and crumpled dollar bills from a jar on his dresser. He had almost nothing, but he and his buddies were willing to take that leap together.

And his dad? Never the least bit jealous that Asher had realized his dream. Never upset that it was his son and not him up in the spotlight wearing leather pants. That was what made Leland a great dad. He was supportive and understanding.

"Fucked up shit right here, son," he said now.

Asher smothered a smile at the lip of his beer bottle and took a swig. He knew exactly what his dad was talking about, because he followed his father's eye line across the huge wooden porch to Emily Trudeau and Elana Knight, glasses of wine in hand, discussing what, Asher didn't want to know.

Jordan stood, Hawk on her hip, a look of disgust on her face. She sent Asher a scathing glare.

"How come whenever she does that, I feel like grinding my molars to dust, but when Gloria looks at me like that..." He didn't finish, just blew out a whistle.

His dad laughed. "Felt that same way about your mom. Once she flashed those dark eyes at me, no other girl could turn my head."

Asher's dad leaned an elbow on his lawn chair and propped his feet on the railing in front of them. The deck was on the second floor, a set of stairs leading down to a sandy beach where a volleyball net stood. Their house wasn't as private as Asher's, but then they hadn't come here looking for privacy. They'd come here to experience the season, and in the Cove, there was no better way to experience summer than a beach teeming with vacationers.

Leland Knight was still long and lean, his tattoos from back in the day faded but plentiful. He was the picture of an aging rock star, one who had gone on to become a welder by trade and an artist at heart. He crafted huge statues and sold them to people who had money to burn. Elana ran the business side of things, no slouch in the number-crunching department. His folks were perfect together. Complemented each other in a way that was both beneficial for their futures and obvious to anyone looking in.

Asher wanted that but never dreamed he'd find it. Now, despite jittering nerves at going all in, he wondered if he'd found that with Glo.

"Ready to stake your claim with the agent?" Leland slid Asher a look that said this news was a little late. "The groupie ain't gonna like it."

Asher shook his head. "Dad, you have to address her by her name. She's Hawk's mom. We owe her that much respect."

Leland grunted but acquiesced with a, "Yeah, guess so."

"Ash!" came a voice from the sand below. One look over and he confirmed the call came from Ricky. "Get your ass down here."

He tossed a volleyball into the air, but before he could catch it, Fonz knocked it away. Ricky started swearing, Shiff called to Fonz that he was open, and Fonz threw the ball to Shiff.

"Idiots," Leland said, but he did so with a smile on his scruffy face. His pop loved the band like his own kids, even though he called Ricky "the Minion" when he wasn't around.

Ash held up a peace sign to let them know he'd be down in two minutes. Shiff threw him a nod.

"How's the album?" Leland asked.

"Slow go."

"Sometimes that's how they go. Granted, I only cut two back in my day, but that second one was enough to drive me to drink." He tipped the beer bottle to his lips, took a pull, then lowered it and added, "Never stopped."

"Fonz is having some home life problems," Ash told him. "Took him to task about it because I thought he cheated on Pam. She cheated on him."

"Lotta that goes around," his dad commented. "Don't do that shit, Ash. Not worth it. Once you snag a good woman, there's no greater way to break her spirit than inviting another bitch to your bed. Gloria has a spirit like a wild stallion. You don't want to hear this, but she reminds me of your mom. She won't take your shit."

"Tell me something I don't know." Asher polished off his beer.

"Don't quit going after her even when she caves, son."

Ash dropped his beer bottle in a box for recyclables and faced his dad.

Leland sat up and shoved his sunglasses into his graying hair. "Still fightin' for your mom. She likes to think she doesn't need me to. She does."

He could relate. Gloria would sooner die than allow anyone to believe she had a weak spot. She did, though. Her weak spot was Asher.

Leland tugged his T-shirt off and chucked it onto the lawn chair. "Let's ball."

Ash followed his dad's lead and tugged his shirt off. Then they jogged down the stairs to the beach. On the way, Ash passed Glo and her lips curved into an appreciative smile. He gave her a wink and flexed his pecs, but kept jogging.

His dad noticed and punched him in the arm, a low chuckle echoing in his chest.

"Come on, old man. Let me show you how it's done," Asher told him. And then got prepared for the fight of his life. His dad may be nearing sixty, but he still had it.

CHAPTER 20

Gloria's mouth went bone dry at the sight on the beach. Ricky, Fonz, and Leland were on one side of the volleyball net, while Shiff, Asher, and Connor—who, along with Faith, had been invited since Faith had taken on the task of helping to pull together some last-minute details for this event—were on the other. The men were shirtless, sweaty, and had a combined body fat of around eight percent.

The clouds decided to part about ten minutes into their game, and thanks to the sun, they'd put on their sunglasses and kicked off their shoes. That meant the six men on the beach wore one piece of clothing each—whatever style shorts they'd chosen for the party.

"It's like a blur of tattoos and flexing muscles," Faith mumbled next to Gloria as they leaned on the railing upstairs. "Gosh, they're pretty."

Gloria smiled. She was glad Faith was here. She and Faith didn't do many things alone together, but she could see them doing more. Faith may not have the family history Gloria did, but her mom was no picnic. She was detached and kind of mean, from what Glo had gleaned. Apparently, some moms just sucked.

"That is a beautiful sight," Elana Knight commented, leaning next to Faith to look down at the game in progress.

But not always, Gloria mentally amended. Because Elana was the coolest mom she'd ever met.

"Your husband is a hottie," Faith said, waggling her brows.

"I'd talk. Your military man is a catch and a half," Elana commented on Connor. "I can't thank you enough for helping with the planning for this, and within three days. It was a lot to ask and you should've overcharged me."

"Come on. I wouldn't do that."

Faith wouldn't. That was another thing Glo liked about her.

"We had to impress." Elana stole a glance at Emily and Jordan, who were standing under a small tent by the wine bar. Gloria had wanted to refill her glass for the last half hour but hadn't braved that duo just yet. "No one expected a surprise grandbaby."

Gloria snorted, gripping the railing. Wasn't that the truth.

Elana leaned past Faith to say, "I hear you over there, Glo."

She leaned past Faith to retort, "How'd the talk go with the Trudeaus?" Hawk was at Jordan's feet and she was standing over him like a mama bear, daring anyone to come close and try to take him away. She looked tired and mean and at that moment sliced a glare over at Gloria.

"'Bout like you'd expect," Elana said. "Emily scowled a lot and Jordan looked like she just put something awful in her mouth."

"Like Ricky?" Gloria joked.

Faith laughed loud enough that Jordan snapped her attention to them again, looking like she had tasted that same awful thing.

"I need a refill," Gloria said to her empty wineglass. She'd only had one—and that was about three fewer than she needed to deal with Jordan. Unfortunately, Jordan and her mother were clogging the bar. "Do either of you need one?"

"I'm good," Faith said with a wave of her hand.

"You be good, too, Gloria," Elana said, her brows crawling up her forehead. She meant it.

Glo smiled. "I can handle it."

"That's what I'm afraid of." Elana gave her a wink. Then she looped her arm in Faith's and dragged her to the house, saying, "Let's talk about the anniversary party for Leland and me next spring…"

Gloria walked to the bar with her empty glass, noting that Emily was already narrowing her eyes. She went behind the bar and unscrewed the cap from an open bottle of white.

"What do you want?" Jordan snapped.

"Just wine," Gloria answered.

"I'm not sure what you're doing here. This gathering is for Hawk's family."

Gloria gritted her teeth. This was going to go on. And on and on *and on* unless they buried the proverbial hatchet. As long as Gloria was seeing Asher, she was going to see Hawk, and for now, that included seeing Jordan.

"Maybe we should talk." Gloria sliced a look over at Emily, then down to Hawk, who looked adorable today in his little khaki shorts and T-shirt. "Alone," she added.

"Whatever you have to say, you can say in front of my mother." Jordan cocked her head and put a hand to her hip. By her leg, Hawk said, "Mama!"

"Jordan. Try to be an adult." Emily stepped in and took Hawk's hand. "Come on, honey," she said to her grandson as she led him across the deck.

Gloria watched Emily and Hawk go, then turned back to Jordan. An expression of disgust contorted the brunette's naturally pretty features.

"We can stop grinding the ax any time," Gloria said. "I'm here for Hawk and Asher. I don't want to keep fighting with you."

"You have two minutes to say whatever you need to say. Then I'm taking my son and leaving this house."

At the threat, Gloria's anger spiked. Jordan's son was also Asher's son, as the woman constantly and conveniently forgot. Hawk deserved better.

"Are you sure you're able to make that decision without your mother?" Gloria asked, her anger barely veiled. "She seems to be in charge of your comings and goings." She could swear she saw a vein pop out in Jordan's forehead. Perhaps she should also take Emily's advice and try to behave like an adult. "I'm sorry." Gloria came out from behind the bar. "I don't like you and that comes through."

"Trust me." Jordan let out a humorless laugh. "The feeling is mutual."

"I know, and that's okay. I don't want to take Hawk from you. I just want what's best for him." Gloria licked her lips before admitting, "When I overheard you at Asher's beach party, something you said struck a nerve and that wasn't entirely your fault."

"Who I have sex with is my business," Jordan snapped, missing the point. Did she and Ricky have sex? Because that would be *bad*.

"You made it everyone's business when you were trying

to do it beneath Asher Knight's deck." Not the point, but Gloria couldn't help herself.

"I don't care what you think about me."

Also not the point.

"You have a son." This was Gloria's original reason for bringing up that evening. Being a mother was a privilege.

Maybe sharing something woman-to-woman was the best way to get Jordan to stop defending herself and actually *listen*.

"You are a mother. I had a mother—*have* a mother," Gloria quickly corrected. It wasn't always easy to remember that her mother wasn't dead. Her mom had been living with a random boyfriend in a shitty part of Chicago a few years ago, still on drugs, but then Gloria lost track of her. "Anyway. You're a better mother than mine."

Jordan's agape mouth closed. Probably surprised at the unexpected compliment.

"My mother had…has problems," Gloria continued. "Sometimes children take on those problems. Hawk has enough stacked against him without everyone bickering over him."

"And what do you call this?" Jordan gestured between them, one hand still on her hip.

Okay. So none of this was sinking in. That was fine. Gloria had another tactic. Nice wasn't working. Neither was reason. For Hawk's sake, for Asher's sake, someone needed to get through to Jordan—the woman who thought the most important part of this discussion was her being able to have sex with whomever she wanted. Keeping her voice low and doing her best not to loom over the petite brunette, Gloria came closer. Jordan was either being purposefully obtuse or just didn't get it.

Glo's money was on the latter.

"You'd better start acting like you care about him, Jordan. Or he'll know. He'll grow up knowing the only one you were looking out for was yourself. He'll know your priority was to get laid and wield some power play over his dad. He'll know you pushed him off on your mom and let her do the heavy lifting. And he'll know," Gloria finished, her voice stronger than ever, "that Asher tried to get involved, but you didn't let him."

As Gloria talked, Jordan's face grew redder and redder. Now her fists were balled at the sides of her prim white dress.

"Asher doesn't get to take over!" Jordan screeched. "*I* did the hard part. *I* carried Hawk for nine months, and *I* was the one who gave birth to him!"

"Yes, you were! And good for you!" Gloria said, unable to keep her temper in check any longer, or her own voice from rising. "You're a mom and that is amazing. But your job doesn't end after you push out a baby!" A charge like a shot rang through her limbs, but she kept on. If there was one thing she believed in her gut, it was that Hawk deserved a mother who cared about him. "You are responsible for Hawk and his happiness for the rest of your life. You can't just shrug him off whenever he's inconvenient!"

A small crowd had gathered. Elana came to stand at her side, but she didn't tell her to be quiet. She slipped an arm around Gloria's waist. Comforting her. Elana knew that Gloria's outburst had a lot to do with her own past, her own mother.

"I think it's time we all took a breath," Elana stated calmly, rubbing Gloria's back. At that soothing touch, Gloria blinked herself out of the rage-filled trance she'd been in.

Oh God.

What had she done? She jerked her eyes around to the crowd, Emily and Hawk, Jordan, Elana, and Faith off to the side. Gloria had made a scene. She'd let Jordan—and Elana, and Emily, and Hawk—see her ugly side. Her *weak* side.

"I'm sorry," Gloria pressed her fingers to her mouth.

"You damn well will be," Jordan snapped. At her outburst, Hawk started to cry. Jordan went to Emily and took her son into her arms. "Let's get away from these people, sweetie. You don't need any of them."

"Yes, I believe that is for the best." Emily glared at Elana. Elana elevated her chin. Whatever truce had been reached between them had just suffered an instant setback.

My fault. Gloria's hands began to shake.

Emily, Jordan, and Hawk entered the house from the patio to let themselves out.

"What the hell?" Asher said as he climbed the patio stairs, finding his friends and family gathered and Gloria encircled in his mother's arms. "Sarge, what happened? You okay?"

She nodded. She was okay, but the rest of this wasn't going to be.

"I'm so sorry," she whispered to both Asher and Elana. To everyone. Fear and regret washed through her. She let Jordan get to her. Let herself lose control.

"Everything is fine," Elana stated, her hand rubbing Gloria's back. "Sweetie, why don't you go lie down? There's a spare bedroom across from the bathroom in the hall."

"No. I'll just go home." She stepped away from Elana.

"You don't have to do that." Elana's brows bent.

"I want to." She needed to get out of here. "I'm sorry for ruining your party."

For potentially ruining everything.

"You ruined nothing, doll. This is life. Shit happens." Elana gave her arm an encouraging squeeze. "Ash, leave Tank with us. Our granddog can spend the night and you can get Gloria home."

"I drove," Gloria said. "I can take care of myself."

"I'll follow," Asher said, brow furrowed. "We need to talk."

They did. It wasn't that Glo regretted what she said. She meant every word. She just hoped her actions hadn't made things harder on Asher. She slid a worried look to Elana, then Leland, who joined his wife and cupped her elbow in support.

Harder on everyone.

* * *

"Because I just don't want you to come in!" Gloria said after she stepped from her car and onto the sidewalk.

"Do you have eleven cats or something?" Asher asked.

"No. It's not that."

"Are you a hoarder?"

"Asher." Why did he insist on making everything light? She was traumatized, had possibly traumatized Hawk...

"Are you an undercover spy and your walls are covered in your latest top-secret case?"

"*No.*" She came to a stop outside her door and Ash stopped with her.

"I get it, okay? Things went south today. Jordan was in the center of that. I'm not surprised. But this is also the part where you let me in. You have to talk to me."

"I know." She fiddled with her key ring. She owed him

at least that. He would need to know what happened so he could react the right way.

"Sarge." He lifted her chin. Clearly, he wasn't leaving.

The idea of him in her house...She wanted to hide at the thought. *No one* came to her house. Sure, she'd hosted wine night when she had a rental here, but that was different. Rentals were like hotel rooms. Impersonal. Not her own. This rental, however, was full of her things. Her private things. Her private space.

She swallowed against the surge of anxiety and her keys shook in her hand.

Asher took them from her, palmed her back, and let them inside.

Fast was the only way to do this, so she pulled away from him and burst into her apartment. She dropped her purse on the kitchen table, flipped on the lights, then stood in the center of the living room and waited for Asher to follow.

He did, taking a leisurely look around. She saw what he saw. Standard brown carpet, khaki walls, basic light fixtures. A flat TV hanging on the wall and a bookshelf beneath it holding an array of movies and books. Kitchen table—small, oak with four chairs, not the most stylish but functional.

"Not alarmed, Sarge," he said, sliding her keys in his pocket. "Half expected a collection of weird dolls or a curio cabinet full of porcelain cats or—"

Then he saw it. He'd been turning as he'd been talking, and now that he'd turned around, his gaze landed on the biggest eyesore in the room. And stuck. Now she'd have some explaining to do. She didn't want to explain.

His eyebrows lifted and he shot her a look that said, *Oh, that.*

"Sarge."

"I know."

"That's...interesting." He frowned at the piece of furniture and she came to stand beside him and look at it with him. "Is that an authentic wine barrel couch from the seventies?"

"Whiskey barrels." Whiskey barrels. Deep brown Naugahyde. Rust, mustard, and red diamond design in the center of each of the three back cushions.

"It's—" he started.

"Hideous," she finished for him. She knew. The couch was hideous.

"Definitely a departure from your style."

It was. Anyone taking a look around at her black bookshelf, modern but comfortable gray-purple sofa with black and white floral print pillows, white chair with a purple chemise blanket thrown over the back would immediately balk at the extra couch in the room. It was one reason she didn't like to have company, but not the only reason.

"I don't even sit on it."

"Why? Is it worth a lot of money or something?" His brow scrunched. He was trying to understand.

"Not at all." In mint condition, and that one was not, the thing was worth about a hundred and fifty bucks. Maybe. Gloria sat on her much more stylish couch instead.

Ash took another possibly confused glance at the antique and crossed the room. "Let's hear it."

"The story behind the couch?" She balled her hands in her lap. It shouldn't be a big deal. She had just built it up to be a big deal, and because of that, it *felt* like a really big deal.

"Yes to that, but first, let's tackle what happened with Jordan." He sat on the lavender couch next to her and pushed her hair from her face. "And why you look green."

Gloria met his eyes. "She reminds me of my mother sometimes. In that she's not a very good one."

He nodded at the same time the corners of his mouth pulled into a frown. Glo didn't like that either. Hawk deserved the best.

"I overstepped my boundaries," she admitted, rubbing her knees with her hands. "I just want her to do better. I told her she needed to step it up or else her son would forever resent her."

"That's the truth," he murmured, putting his hands over both of hers to stop her incessant rubbing. "Not a bad thing, Sarge."

"I made a scene." She looked up at him to accept her punishment. Whatever it would be. Him getting angry with her. Him leaving. She'd deserve it. But it didn't happen.

"Honey, you *are* a scene," Asher said with a smile. "Jordan is so jealous of what we have, she can't see straight. I don't mean she wants what we have with me, but I do think she wants this with someone. She's all over the place. Can't focus that energy to a point. It's good you told her where her focus should be."

"Shouldn't it be obvious?" Gloria asked. He took one of her hands and she traced his skull ring with her fingertip.

"Yeah. It should be," he said, his voice low. "It was to you."

She lifted her head. Asher gave her a soft smile, then leaned back on the couch, wrapping his arm around her and pulling her back with him.

"Now let's hear the story of that beast." He nodded at the couch.

"It was my grandmother's. She died when I was twenty-four."

She saw the question on his face. If she had a grandmother who was alive when Gloria was young, then why had she lived with a pair of drug addicts?

"Her name was Rita. My mom's mom. She had a house full of things that were destined for the Dumpster, but she loved them and so she kept them. My grandfather, her husband, died when I was a baby. My mom and I lived with her on and off since my dad came into our lives as often as he went out. Rita always took us in, even though my mom was an addict. My mom stole from her a lot."

Asher ran his fingers along her arm and just listened.

"I was about four years old when she started forgetting things. The Alzheimer's was full-blown by the time I was ten. My mom moved back in with my father permanently, and he'd recently gone through rehab. Sobriety didn't last. He and Mom started shooting up a few months after we moved into our shitty apartment. Rita had to be put into an assisted-living home. I visited her when I was old enough to take the bus on my own, but she didn't remember me.

"Long story short, she died when I was living in Chicago. Word came to me late. The will left everything to my mom, who I had no contact with for obvious reasons. I drove to the facility in Indiana and arrived to find Rita's room completely empty, save for that." Gloria pointed at the Naugahyde sofa.

"The damn thing weighs a couple hundred pounds, which is the only reason it was left behind. Everything else of hers fit in boxes that they shipped to my mom."

She would never forget that day. Showing up to Grandma Rita's room, mourning and grieving her passing, along with regretting not having visited in months.

"I called local movers and paid them my next two months' rent if they'd load up the couch, drive it to Chicago, and put it in my twenty-eighth-floor apartment."

Her grandmother was the only bright spot of her childhood Glo could remember.

"That's it," she said.

"Eerily normal, Sarge." Ash threaded his fingers with hers. "I have an old guitar my dad gave me that he used to play when he was a kid. It's beat up, missing a few strings. I don't play it. I just want it. No shame in having that." He pointed to the couch with their linked hands.

It was a big deal to her. For the girl who had never kept a piece of anyone, who didn't give a piece of herself to anyone.

"I don't...talk about her." It hurt too much, to feel the weight of what she'd lost. Instead of admitting that truth, she shrugged and said, "I'm just not used to having people in my space, that's all."

"That's all," he repeated, but it wasn't in agreement—she could tell by his tone.

She was getting increasingly fidgety and feeling as if she was being challenged but not understanding why his knowing this about her made her so nervous.

"You don't let people in, Glo," he said.

She stayed silent.

"But you let me in."

She didn't like where this was going. She didn't like how exposed she felt. How bare.

"Like you said, no big deal. I have an embarrassing couch. Now you've seen it, and I'm tired, and you should go." She stood and pulled her hand from his, but Asher stood with her, wrapped a hand around her arm, and tugged her close.

"Stop," he commanded, and before she could point out that he wasn't the boss of her, he kissed her long and hard.

"Ash," she breathed when he tore his lips from hers. He tasted good, felt better, but she wasn't going to allow herself to be silenced by his kiss.

"Glo," he returned.

"This doesn't change anything," she snapped, trying to get a handle on the conversation. On her hectic feelings.

"This changes everything," he stated. "You let me in."

"So what?" She was getting angry now. Her posture grew rigid as she yanked her shoulders back. In her mind, she was busily piling bricks over the huge hole she'd just knocked in a wall, showing the ugliest parts of herself.

He knew too much about her. She thought it might help, but it only frightened her. She never should have let Asher follow her home. He was too close. This was too much.

"That"—he pointed to the couch—"makes this place a safe space to you. A space you don't let anyone into. But here I am."

"You didn't give me a choice," she said weakly. But that wasn't the issue. The issue was that after years and years of sealing herself up, of being alone, of longing to be a part of something, she finally felt like she was a part of something. Part of Asher's world.

Hawk. His parents. The I-love-you bomb. Even stupid Jordan and her irritating mother. Gloria was part of all of them.

"I have to get a shower and you're not invited." He didn't let her go and he needed to, before she lost her shit. She was okay when he was pushing her buttons to argue, or even spank her, but she needed him out of her space. This space that was hers and hers alone.

"You want me gone?" he asked, starting to sound angry.

"Yes," she answered, but her voice shook. She was used

to arguing with Asher, but this argument seemed worse—his anger more acute.

"Fine. Hide, Sarge. Weather it alone." He turned and stomped out her front door, slamming it behind him.

Gloria, justified, locked her dead bolt and the knob and watched out the window as Asher climbed into his car and sped down the street. Only then did she allow the tears balanced on her eyelashes to tumble down her cheeks.

CHAPTER 21

*S*he'd finally done it. She'd driven him off.

She climbed into the shower and took her time washing her hair, shaving and soaping up and down her body, and lying to herself about how she was glad to be doing this alone and without Asher's assistance. She didn't need him in here, plucking calloused fingers over her nipples. Working his hand between her legs while he kissed her mouth and she fought his tongue with hers...

She put her face in the spray in an attempt to power wash away those thoughts. She didn't need him for that. She could take care of herself. It wasn't like she'd never—

What was that?

She froze under the pounding water and listened to her front door open, then close. She'd locked it...hadn't she? The sound wasn't quite loud enough to make her think someone had broken in, but someone had just entered her apartment.

Quickly, she rinsed the soap away and turned off the shower. She'd just reached for a towel when she heard it. A guitar. And a familiar voice—a sexy one—began humming to a tune she couldn't quite make out.

How did he get in here?

Then she remembered. He'd slipped her keys into his pocket after letting them in.

Glo opened the bathroom door. She'd wrapped in her towel, but water dripped from her wet hair. She peeked down the hall to see the back of Asher's head, as he was sitting on her grandmother's couch. The one that Glo never sat on. She marched out with as much dignity as she could, considering she was dripping wet and naked beneath the terrycloth. But when she got there, Asher stopped humming and started singing.

"Blue eyes, blue skies…You, you, you. We're fated. Fated."

He kept singing, his eyes on hers. *"Long black hair and fire in her walk, beauty on the bend, wait'll you hear her talk."*

Glo sank onto her fancy, modern couch, Ash appearing oddly at home on the barrel couch in his all-black clothes, black guitar on his lap, silver rings on his fingers, a leather cuff on one wrist.

She soon determined that the words he'd started with were a chorus when he looped into it again after a few verses that smacked with an odd familiarity. Familiar, because he was singing about her.

"She's makin' me wait and want…and she can't see we're fated. Fated."

He ended with that part, fading off in a hum and meeting her eyes with his. One final strum of his guitar, and he smiled so tenderly, her chest constricted. She stared, her mind a tangle of emotion and confusion. Water dripped from her hair to her shoulders, giving her a chill.

"You're sitting on my grandma's couch."

"You need a better memory of it." He grinned. It was at once boyish and sexy and completely tantalizing. "Did you like your song?"

"Did I...like the song?" Her heart thudded hard against her breastbone.

"*Your* song, Sarge."

My song. He'd sang about her eyes, her hair, but he'd also sang that he was waiting. That they were fated.

"Like it?" he asked again.

"I..." And that's when her throat stopped working. Mouth open, she shook her head, not because she didn't like it. She did. She couldn't seem to unfreeze her vocal cords at the moment.

"The pieces connected tonight," he said, strumming idly while he spoke. "I had a few lyrics but couldn't nail down the chorus."

She can't see we're fated.

She forced her throat to swallow. She needed some water. Or a shot. Whiskey would go a long way to helping her cope with this moment.

Asher stopped strumming and rested his guitar on the barrel couch and Glo stared at it, trying to decide if she liked his guitar on her barrel couch. She did. She liked it so much, she could picture it there in the future. And Asher lounging on the couch in the future. Both of them, actually. Because wasn't that her sitting right next to him in her mind? Yes. Yes, it was.

Ash stood and took two steps to reach the sofa where she

sat. He knelt, grabbed the towel where she'd tucked it in at her breasts, and tugged her close.

His lips hovered over hers, but he didn't kiss her.

"Guy writes a song for you, you're supposed to swoon."

"I don't swoon." She shivered as the cool air puckered her nipples and brought goose bumps to her skin.

"You moan, though." He yanked the towel loose and dropped it to the floor. He palmed the back of her head at the same time he placed an openmouthed kiss to her throat. Then one on her collarbone. She tunneled her fingers into his hair, holding him to her as he kissed his way down her chest and took a nipple on his tongue.

"Oh, yes," she hissed.

Asher sucked her deeply, before sliding his mouth over to her other breast and giving it equal time and attention. As he tortured and pleased her, he laid her flat on her sofa. He slipped his fingers between her legs where she was wet and warm and ready for him.

"So hot. Let me taste." He backed away enough to give himself room and then dropped her legs over his shoulders, angling himself so he was in between. He went down on her, lapping and making her claw the couch and knock her decorative pillows to the floor.

"Oh God, oh God," she moaned, eyes closed, all of her in heaven as he laved her with determined licks. He added a finger, then two, and slid deep at the same time he sucked her clit. She nearly shot to the ceiling. "Ash!"

She bucked, her hand on his head, her eyes open to see what he was doing, the way he was turning her inside out. His deliciously muscled shoulders, visible even under his tight shirt, his stubble scraping her inner thighs, his tattoos on display. Her orgasm hit her with a ferocity, and she shouted, knowing it was too loud and her neighbors would probably hear, and not giving a damn.

Shattered, she lay writhing, only vaguely aware that Asher had pulled away and was doing…something. She forced her eyes open all the way and saw him fist the neck of his shirt and strip it over his head. He shed his pants and shoes next. With one hand, he stroked his length into even *more* length, watching her with hooded dark eyes as she lay, teeth stabbing her lip and anticipating more.

He rolled on a condom, put a knee on the sofa between her legs, and hoisted one of her legs over his hip. Then he drove into her in one long, smooth, mind-melting thrust. Her head tipped back and she held on to his shoulders as he stroked into her, moving to a rhythm that she matched. It felt like they moved to the beat of the song he'd written for her.

You let me in.

She did.

"Stay with me, Sarge." He drove deep, forcing her thoughts back to him. Asher was the only thought worth having and her body was attuned to his every micro-movement and each hard, smooth, and slick slide. "There she is."

His breathing was tight as he moved over her and she heard the sweet wave of release build to a deafening roar before she tumbled over again. It took her with it, her synapses exploding, lights flashing behind her eyelids, and her entire body clutching, pulsing, and drawing Asher's orgasm from him like they were connected—by more than their physical bodies.

He came with a long, low, sexy male groan, and she held him to her, not wanting to lose the feeling of his lips against her ear, or his hand wrapped sturdily around her hip, or the way his weight sank her deeper into the cushions.

Not wanting to lose any of it—any of him.

But he'd have to sit up eventually, and after they both caught their breath, his hold loosened slightly and he pulled his face away to look down at her. She let herself do what she wanted, refusing to temper her feelings for once, and put a hand to his face, appreciating his beauty and all that he was.

"Stay with me," he whispered, then that soft smile again. His lips brushed hers. He pulled out and made his way to the bathroom.

Stay with me.

Oh, how she wanted to . . .

On rubbery legs, she met him in the hallway. He kissed her, backing her to her bedroom as he did. They climbed beneath the blankets and shortly after, fell asleep.

And they did it wound around each other.

* * *

Asher wasn't asleep.

Gloria was, though, and snoring softly, which was so damn cute he wanted to wake her up and make love to her all over again. But he'd let her rest. She needed it after today, after tonight. He needed it, too, but there was no shutting his brain off.

He climbed from bed carefully, quietly, and padded to the kitchen on bare feet. One peek into her nearly empty fridge confirmed he'd be choosing something from the pantry for his snack.

Before he was finished rummaging, his cell phone rang from his jeans—jeans that were wadded on the floor of

Gloria's living room. He rushed to the discarded pants, recognized the number, and his heart promptly hit his feet.

"Emily."

"Asher! They're gone!"

"Say again?" His hold tightened on the phone.

"Jordan and Hawk. They're gone! I don't know what to do." Her voice was fraught with worry and fear.

His heart hammered, then almost stopped. Years ago, his buddy Evan had delivered a similar phone call about Rae. *She's gone.* When Ev had called Asher to break that news, he'd meant "gone" as in the permanent sense. That thought, combined with his lack of sleep, buckled his knees.

The barrel couch caught him.

"What's that mean?" he asked, each syllable shaking from fear.

"Jordan and I came home from the party and put Hawk to bed," Emily explained, sounding slightly less hysterical. "I woke at four this morning, feeling like something was off, and noticed Hawk wasn't in his room. And Jordan wasn't in hers. My car's gone, too. I called her cell phone. I texted her. Nothing."

"Okay." Asher held out a hand. It shook, too. "Okay, then she's just somewhere, and they're fine," he said as much for his own comfort as for Emily's.

"I don't know where they are!"

"Em. Calm down."

Gloria stepped into the living room, her eyes round with worry, her expression grave. She was wearing his T-shirt and panties and nothing else.

"I'll come over and we'll figure this out, okay?" He didn't know what the hell he'd do once he got there, but getting there was at least doing something.

"Thank you, Asher."

"Make coffee," he told her. "I'll see you soon."

He said good-bye and dropped the phone on the couch, then propped his elbows to his knees and put his face in his hands. He was aware of Gloria shuffling closer, then her hands wrapping around his wrists. When he pulled his hands away from his face, he found her on her knees in front of him.

"What's going on?" she asked, concern outlining each word.

"Jordan left with Hawk." He put his hands together and rested his chin on them. "Emily said she took the car, has no idea where they went."

Gloria's eyes slid to the side, her teeth clamped onto her lip.

"I'm heading over there to be with Em. She's going nuts."

"This is my fault." Gloria let go of his wrists, put her hands on his knees, and pushed herself to standing.

"No, Sarge." He stood and touched her arm. "It's not."

"I'm going with you," she said. He didn't know if it was out of a sense of ownership or obligation, but he didn't care.

"Good," he said. And he meant it.

Because he needed her.

* * *

During the drive to Emily Trudeau's house, one thought echoed through Gloria's skull.

Did I just cost Asher his son?

Gloria had always been ready, fire, aim, the method she tended to favor. To her credit, it was sloppy but effective. Being able to react in an instant and be brave enough to try new things was responsible for her career, her life. Her moving to Evergreen Cove.

But rolling the dice with her life was one thing. Taking chances on Asher's relationship with his son was another.

She glanced over at him from the passenger seat of his car. He looked downright grim with one hand at twelve o'clock on the steering wheel. Worry pulled his eyes tight and stubble surrounded his mouth, now pressed into a tight line.

"She'll come back," he said to the windshield.

Gloria wasn't sure how he knew, or if he knew, but thinking that way was the only way to get through any of this with a scrap of sanity. "Of course she will."

He flicked a look over at her and his mouth softened some. Then his hand landed on her thigh and squeezed.

"I shouldn't have said anything to her," Gloria said. And she shouldn't have. It wasn't her business or her place. Now Jordan had run off with Hawk to God only knew where. It didn't occur to her until just now that Emily might not be that happy to see her. "I probably should have stayed home."

"Sarge."

"If I'd had any idea Jordan would do something this stupid..." She watched the trees out the window.

"Sarge, come on." Another squeeze on her thigh had her turning her head. He spared her a glance, then refocused on the road.

"You should take her to court and sue her for kidnapping," Gloria said, suddenly angry. "If you ever had a shot at full custody, this is it."

His hand left her leg to steer into Emily's driveway. He turned off the car and unbuckled his seat belt, then faced her.

"Okay, Sarge. One thing at a time."

"Ready, fire, aim," she said.

His brow creased, but his lips curved into a tentative half-smile. "What?"

"I aim last. Problem-solve after I cause the problem."

He slipped a hand into her hair and curled it around her neck, gripping her gently but firmly. "You don't cause problems. You're helping me out of one now."

"Who do you need me to be in there?" she asked. "You need me to be bad cop? The heavy? Need me to threaten Emily and let her know her grandson will not be staying with his harebrained mother? Or would you like me to be gentle and say, 'Asher, calm down, we can work this out'? Or I could—"

His lips closed over hers for a brief but thorough kiss, trapping the rest of what she was going to say in her throat. When he pulled back, he kept his eyes on hers and his hand on her nape.

"I need you to stand next to me and keep me from freaking the fuck out," he said. "Jordan has my son and they're missing and I hope to God nothing bad has happened."

"Me too," Gloria whispered.

He kissed her again. "I know."

"I won't let Emily get to me. I promise."

"I'm not worried." He let her go, opened his car door, and got out. Gloria did the same and when she met him on the driveway, she slipped her hand into his.

CHAPTER 22

*E*mily Trudeau opened her front door, saw Asher, and her shoulders and face crumpled. She reached for him and he embraced her.

"It'll be okay, Em," he said.

Then her eyes opened and she caught sight of Gloria, and her face transformed. "What's she doing here?" she clipped.

"She wants to help."

"I think she's *helped* enough."

Gloria felt like shrinking, or maybe crawling into the azalea bush over there. Emily didn't like her, and that she could handle, but being partially responsible for Jordan's disappearance...well, Gloria couldn't blame the other woman. If she were Emily, she'd be pissed, too.

Gloria pulled in a breath but it was Asher who spoke.

"We're not doing this, Emily."

Her eyes rounded in surprise. "Doing what?"

"You know what."

The standoff was short. Emily looked from Asher to Gloria, then gave her a curt nod and stepped aside to let them both in.

Gloria entered a massive foyer, opening to a large, posh living room filled with expensive furniture and antiques. The exact opposite of how Gloria grew up. Hers had been a world of frayed, stained carpet and hand-me-down everything—usually from her grandmother. Her foster parents' homes were nice, middle-class, and stank of maxed out credit cards. Jordan's mother's home was the real deal. Wealth and country-club class.

"I'll get us some coffee," Emily said, taking a step toward the kitchen. She stopped, half turned. "Gloria? Coffee?"

"Make mine a double," she joked, but her smile felt brittle. At least Emily had called her Gloria instead of *Ms. Shields*.

"I'll bring the pot," Emily said, missing the joke entirely. For a second, Gloria felt sympathy for Jordan having to grow up in such an arid, humorless house.

Asher's hand slipped around her back and he put his lips to her ear. "Sarge, you okay?"

She should be asking him that. This was about Hawk and Asher being okay. Gloria straightened her shoulders, mentally digging out her big-girl panties yet again. There was no room to think of anything but the most important thing: finding Asher's son.

"I'm great. Don't worry about me."

"Lean, Sarge," he said simply, a smile playing on his tired face. Then he put his arm around her and pulled her close, and she did just that. Wrapped her arms around his waist and leaned. And Asher...he took her weight.

* * *

Em served coffee, and later lunch, and frankly, Asher was impressed she did it herself and didn't have her house staff do it for her. Then again, she probably called and told them not to come in because who would want the embarrassment of losing her daughter?

She was niceish to Glo, too, which he appreciated. He wasn't all that surprised. Once they'd formulated a plan, everyone got to work, and there wasn't a lot of room for petty arguments.

After last night, Asher understood more about Gloria than ever. Her world used to be a tiny sphere occupied by her and a few other people. When she was a kid, it was her parents and grandmother. Then just her mom, then just her. She'd opened a little to allow Kimber in, but then Kimber became Kimber *and* Landon *and* Caleb. Like Evan became Evan and Lyon and Charlie. And then Asher had come along, and Sofie and Faith crept in, and now? Hell, Gloria's world was packed like a too-tight elevator. Asher came with Hawk—who came with Jordan and Emily. Not even counting his band, his parents...

For a girl who flew solo, Gloria had taken on a lot of people. And her meltdown in her apartment was more about her not knowing what the fuck to do with it all.

But in the clutch and when it counted, Gloria was at her best. Asher may have had an air of calm and collected, but inside he was mess. All he could think about was Hawk and his safety. There was an incredibly creative part of his brain that made up scenario after scenario where Jordan harmed or abandoned their son, but he quickly suffocated each and every thought.

If he went down that road, there'd be no coming back from it. Besides, Jordan was a massive pain in the ass, but she wasn't insane. She just…did things without thinking. Like sneaking into his cabin barely clothed.

They spent a good chunk of the morning dividing and conquering Emily's address book. Gloria made more calls than anyone, her efficiency admirable. She was friendly, sympathetic, and yet able to get off the phone quickly. The bad news was that no one had heard from Jordan. Either that or someone was lying to cover for her.

After lunch and the final few phone calls, Ash and Glo left Emily's. One of her friends had come by to offer support, and once she was settled, Asher bolted. He had to do something, so he drove around the Cove and searched for Emily's Cadillac. It was a waste of time, and part of him knew that, and probably all of Gloria knew that, but she sat by his side in his convertible, holding her hair to the side as the wind whipped it, and helped him look around. She'd even suggested a few off-road places to check.

By the time Asher pulled up to Gloria's apartment and rested his head back to study the blue skies above, his body had started feeling signs of fatigue. Gloria's hand wrapped around his arm and he turned his head to find her looking as tired as he felt. Tired, but still beautiful.

"I should head back to the house in case Jordan comes to her senses and stops by. You probably need to grab a nap. It's been a tough morning."

"Okay." She watched out the windshield for a few moments. "Let me pack a change of clothes."

His eyebrows went up in surprise.

"Is that okay?" She gave him a tentative smile, then glanced at his lips like she wasn't sure if she should kiss him or not. One day, his girl would be comfortable enough to accept the fact that when they were near, they should just be near. No thought needed.

"Always okay, Sarge," he answered. He needed her there. Even if she was just snoozing in his bedroom while he paced the floors and played hide-and-seek with a pending breakdown. He sat up, put a palm on the back of her neck, and tugged her close for a kiss. She held her lips to his for a few moments, then drew back and climbed out.

"Always okay," he repeated to his empty car.

About then, his text pinged. He nearly fumbled the phone. He couldn't get to it fast enough.

Not Jordan. Instead it was Fonz. *Anything?*

Nothing, Ash typed.

I'm still coming over.

Ash smiled. He'd forgotten the band was due to come over that afternoon... He glanced at the clock. Shit. In a few hours. Tired as he was, he knew there was no way he could sleep. And he'd exhausted every contact searching, so now all that was left was waiting.

He hated waiting.

Practice is still on. Need the distraction, he pecked back in. Fonz responded with a *Yup* and Ash trusted him to take care of letting the band know the plan. He rested his head back and looked at the sky, waiting on Gloria to return so they could go home.

* * *

"Take five." Ash rose from the stool he'd been perched on for the last two hours. His ass was tired. His head was tired, but it was now a combination of creative and physical exhaustion. Still better than pacing the fucking floors by himself.

No, he couldn't stop thinking about Hawk. Or wondering where Jordan had taken his son. But he knew there wasn't much else he could do. It had been less than twenty-four hours, so he couldn't report them missing. Much as he wanted to bring in the police, and damn near every resource at his disposal, he couldn't negate the fact that Jordan had only been gone since this morning, and this whole situation might be nothing more than her forgetting to charge her phone.

Gloria hadn't napped right away, but after sitting at her laptop for an hour or so in the living room, she'd vanished in the direction of his bedroom, first giving him a tired wave that he returned through the soundproof studio glass.

"I feel like we got some good stuff out of that," Ricky said of the set they'd just played, going for encouraging.

Asher felt doubtful until Shiff agreed. "That last song jibed."

Well. Good. Because Ash couldn't tell if shit or sunshine was coming from his guitar. He pulled a hand down his face and set the instrument aside. "Whiskey?" he offered.

"I'm in," Ricky was the first to say. Shiff nodded and Fonz gave an indifferent shrug.

"I'll bring the bottle, but don't let me do more than one shot in case Jordan calls." He left the band in the studio and headed for the kitchen. Not halfway across the house, a knock came at the front door.

His heart hit his feet.

"Asher!"

Jordan.

"Asher!" Another knock, fast and constant. His blood ran cold, his heart thundering as Tank barked in alarm. He nearly tripped over the dog and the couch and almost bashed his head on the door when he pulled it open.

Hawk was in Jordan's arms, crying, but he wasn't bleeding and he didn't appear to be visibly harmed. Asher nearly collapsed with relief.

"Take him," she said, practically thrusting the boy into his arms.

But Asher was already poised to do just that. "It's okay, bud," he murmured into Hawk's ear. His face was warm. "Is he sick?" He pressed his cheek against his son's forehead.

"No," Jordan said, stepping into the house. "He's just… He won't stop crying."

Asher forced himself to calm down. Hawk's face was warm, but he didn't feel like he was burning up with a fever or anything. He tilted his head at Jordan. "Tell me what's going on. Right now."

"I just wanted to prove I could do it." She twisted her fingers, fresh tears streaming down her cheeks. Her brown hair was lank and she had black shit under her eyes from her makeup. Her clothes were stained, and a glance down showed her flip-flops were two different colors.

"Prove you could do what?" His hand went to his son's back; he was still whimpering but no longer at a full-blown wail.

"Be a mom." Her voice wobbled. Her eyes went to the band, who were filing out of the studio one by one. "Hey, guys," she said.

Hey, guys.

Asher closed his eyes and prayed for strength, then

opened them to find Shiff looking disgruntled, Fonz with his hands in his pockets, and Ricky lifting Tank to quiet him.

"How'd you do that?" Jordan asked, her sincerest expression on Asher.

"Do what?"

"Calm him down," she said, and Asher realized that Hawk was no longer crying. "I've been trying to get him to stop crying since we went to Grove Falls."

Asher felt his shoulders go stiff. Grove Falls was a theme park, like a mini Disney World, in Michigan. "You took him to Grove Falls?"

"Yeah. I wanted him to see he could have fun with me, too. Not just you."

Christ. This was about *him*?

Jordan grunted and folded her arms over her chest. "It totally backfired. He didn't appreciate it at all."

"He's three, Jordan," Asher said, hearing the edge in his voice. Hawk whined, uttered a string of incoherent words. "It's okay, kiddo," he told his son.

"Daddy," Hawk wrapped his little arms around Asher's neck.

Daddy. Asher nearly lost strength in his knees that his son was holding on to him. "Here for you, man."

"There a reason you didn't answer our calls and texts?" he asked, losing the calm he'd kept at hand throughout the day. Jordan had taken Hawk to a goddamn theme park a hundred miles away without telling anyone.

She shrugged.

Fucking typical. Hawk kicked his legs and murmured a few more random words, "doggie" and "down" among them. His boy. He loved this kid more than life.

"I'm done," Jordan said, her voice nearly a whisper.

"Done with what?" Fury ran through Asher's bloodstream like lava. He was pretty sure he knew what she was "done" with, and if he was right, he was about to go nuclear.

"Just...It's hard." She gestured at him, including Hawk in the sweep of her arm.

On the inside he was screaming, *Fuck yeah, it's hard! Kids are hard!* But with his son calm and warm in his arms, he said nothing and hoped Hawk couldn't feel his body literally vibrating from pent-up anger.

"He can't even stand me for one day by myself." Jordan wrinkled her nose. "He's been awful."

Asher closed a palm over Hawk's ear at the same time Fonz approached, arms outstretched. God bless him. His friend knew exactly what was needed here.

"Hey, Hawk, wanna play trains?" Fonz smiled and Hawk answered with a cautious smile of his own.

"That sounds fun," Asher said, pulling a hand over Hawk's hair. "Go with Fonz and see the trains, okay?"

Tank barked, and Ricky put him on the ground.

"Doggie!"

Tank. Also saving the day.

Asher nodded his thanks to Fonz, then set his son on his feet. Hawk tore off in the direction of the bedroom, giggling as Tank chased after him, barking at his heels. Fonz followed.

Once the three of them had disappeared down the hall, Asher faced Jordan again.

"Deck," he told her, pointing to the back door. Because he needed to say things to her away from everyone.

"Brother, maybe you ought to—" Ricky started.

"No, man," Shiff interrupted, placing a hand on Broderick's arm to stop him.

Asher and Ricky shared a long, hard glare. Ricky said no more.

Wise man.

Ash opened the back door and pointed out of it and Jordan stomped through it like a disgruntled teenager. She walked down to the dock before she stopped, facing the water.

Asher followed, slowing his roll on the way. When he reached her, she turned around and burst out with, "Mom is better with him. She's better at raising him than I am!"

Of course she was. Emily had been doing everything since Hawk was born. In Asher's absence, and Jordan's, apparently. She may have been around, but she hadn't participated as fully as she should have.

"Well, then get better, Jordan. Emily is his grandmother, but you're his mother. You will always be his mother." He bit off the sentence before he added, *So start acting like it.* Wasn't easy to do, but he was trying to be amicable. Screaming at her would feel good in the moment, but what he needed was a change from her that was more long-term. He needed her to step up.

"I want to have fun. You get to have fun! You have *all the fun.* You lead a life of fun and games and sleep around with everyone!" Her bottom lip jutted out in a feeling-sorry-for-herself pout. "I'm stuck with a toddler. I'm stuck with stretch marks! I'm just plain *stuck.*"

"*Stuck,*" he repeated. "Never say that shit in front of him, Jordan. Not ever. We are not 'stuck' with Hawk. He's our son and he's not going to grow up thinking he's a burden or feel as if he's kept you from doing whatever crap you need to do to have 'fun.'"

"He's not a burden for you!" She swiped her eyes but it only smudged her makeup more. She noticed the black on her fingers and lifted the edge of her oversize T-shirt and swiped her eyes. "You get him part-time. I have to be with him *all the time*."

"I want to be with him all the time!" He kept his voice just below a shout, barely. He'd leaned forward and gestured to himself when he'd said that, mostly to keep from grabbing her arms and rattling her until her teeth clacked together. "It's you and your mom who have been keeping me away from him *most* of the time. Christ, Jordan! I didn't even know he existed until last year!"

Guilt swam in her eyes and Asher felt a strange twinge of satisfaction at seeing it. She should feel like shit about it. She'd robbed him of so much. Hawk's heartbeat on a monitor. Cutting the cord. Holding him as a newborn. Watching his eyes change from blue to brown. It killed him to know he couldn't get a single second of that back.

"You don't want him?" he said, his tone calm but rigid. "Leave him with me. I'll send along custody papers as fast as my lawyer can draw them up."

He expected an argument, an indignant statement about how he could never keep her from her son. Instead, she said, "You'd do that?"

It sounded hopeful and she'd better not mean that—for her sake.

"No." A small frown pulled her mouth. "I don't want to give up custody of my son," she said as if she'd had a sudden realization. "Not completely."

"Good to hear," he said, meaning it. "I hoped I wouldn't have to pull your head out of your ass for you."

Her eyes narrowed.

"You need a break, take one. But you don't get to bail on him."

"And you do? You're the one going back to LA."

That had been the plan. Keep his apartment in LA. Visit here in the summer months and see Hawk as much as possible. But that'd been shortsighted, hadn't it? Next summer would be comprised of a countrywide tour for Knight Time's current album. He'd be away from both homes he had. Away from Hawk. *Away from Gloria.*

Well.

None of that would work. He'd have to make a call to Donny to get him to replace the fireplace sooner than later, because Asher would have to be here year-round. He'd missed enough of Hawk's life as it was. He didn't want to miss more.

"I'll be here," he said. "I don't want to take him from you any more than you want to keep him from me." He almost added *anymore* but figured they were on shaky ground as it was. Hawk had a trio of grandparents located at the Cove. He wouldn't deprive his son of his family no matter what Jordan was spouting right now.

"You're staying." Hope bloomed in her eyes.

"Yes." It was the right call, and every bone in his body reverberated with that knowledge.

Her face brightened. "So the band...they'll be here, too."

God. Groupie through and through.

"Sometimes." He could practice anywhere. He could tour from anywhere. He could fly the band in on his dime or fly to them as needed. Hawk was portable and Asher wanted him to come to a show. Hell, maybe even Glo would bring him out. Ash wouldn't deny Hawk the privilege to have her in his life, either.

"Can you keep him for a few days?" Jordan asked.

"Of course." He pulled in a deep breath of fresh air.

In the Cove permanently. He could dig this as his home base.

"I have his bag in the car with clothes and some toys..."

"I have shit for him, here, Jordan. He's got an entire wardrobe. All the toys he needs. You keep your stuff at your house for him. He'll be back to see you."

"Yeah, okay."

"Okay." Progress. He'd broken through.

"We can do better, right?" she asked.

Wow. Seriously broken through.

"We can," he said, a weight lifted from his shoulders. "Did you call your mom?"

"Yeah."

"Good. You should go home, help her call the people we called yesterday and put their minds at ease," he told her as they paced for the back door.

"Sounds like a blast," she said with a roll of her eyes. It was good-humored, though, and paired with a small smile.

The back door opened and Tank ran out. Ricky stood in the threshold, his eyes on Jordan, and the back of Asher's neck tingled.

"J, you okay?" Ricky called out.

"Yeah." She stepped into the circle of Ricky's arms.

Son of a bitch.

Ricky murmured something to her, then walked into the house, his arm around her shoulders.

Shiff appeared in the doorway next, shaking his head.

"What the fuck?" Asher asked. Because seriously. What was going on right now?

"Bitches, man."

"Shiff."

"Sorry."

Ash clapped him on the shoulder, watching Ricky and Jordan through the window as they chatted next to her car. "Know anyone who can play the keyboard?"

In a rare display of emotion, Shiff's shoulders shook with laughter.

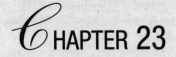

CHAPTER 23

$\mathcal{I}$ can't remember the last time I ate a fish stick," Asher commented.

"Really?" Gloria put the baking sheet in the sink and turned on the water, scrubbing the remnants of panko bread crumbs from it with a sponge. "I would think as a bachelor, you'd have a huge array of frozen foods at your disposal."

"Oh, I do," he said.

Glo peeked over her shoulder to see him cutting Hawk's fish sticks into manageable chunks and explaining calmly that he can't eat just yet because they were too hot. Hawk began wailing. Asher patiently picked up a piece, blew on it, and offered it to him. When Hawk cried again, Asher gave it to Tank, who ate it happily.

Hawk stopped crying and laughed.

Gloria and Asher exchanged a glance as Hawk accepted his next cooled bite from Asher without issue. Three-year-olds.

Gloria had woken from her nap disoriented and bleary-eyed. She'd listened at Asher's closed bedroom door to two things: Hawk crying and Jordan's muffled whining. She waited until they took to the deck and then ducked into Hawk's bedroom.

Seeing the kid sitting there, tears dry, playing trains with Fonz, was enough to make her lose the strength in her knees. By the time Asher came back in after the hullaballoo in the living room, he'd found Gloria snuggled next to Hawk, her lips pressed to his head.

She hadn't missed the heat and admiration that washed over Asher's face. And she hadn't hidden how happy she was that his little boy was home.

Home.

"I kept frozen food in my freezer in LA," Ash interrupted her thoughts to say. "Prepared by a local organic meal place that delivers, along with my sushi and nutritional shakes, on a daily basis. Then I'd go on the road, or come to the Cove, and I gotta remember how to cook things all over again."

"That's why you have so much cereal," she said, infusing her voice with wonder.

"Smart-ass."

She grinned.

"Smart-ass," Hawk parroted.

"No, bud," Asher began, ready to lay down the parental law.

Gloria turned her back to the kid before she laughed and encouraged more lewd language.

They ate, the scene homey and comfortable, and Hawk, with the exception of not liking her tartar sauce—which was epic if she said so herself—was a dream for the remainder of the meal. That was saying something considering how tired he must be. What a day he'd had. Being toted on a long car ride to a theme park. Jordan had set out on a quest to prove all of them wrong—Asher and Gloria and her mother. Or maybe she'd cooked up that quest as a way to prove to herself she was a good mom.

Who knows what went on in Jordan Trudeau's head?

What was most important was simple: Hawk was with Asher and he was safe. Nothing else mattered.

After dinner, Hawk proved more awake than he should be, watching the same cartoon three times before he gave up and closed his eyes. Then, he was out. Ash carried Hawk into his own bedroom, fully stocked with toys and everything a little boy needed, and laid him down to sleep.

Door shut behind him, Asher swaggered to her decked out in black jeans, a black tee, and black boots. He had a presence, a way of owning a room. Hell, he'd *owned* the entire conference center where Evan had first introduced Gloria to him. Only now, she knew Asher's layers intimately. He was older, he was a father, and the backdrop of blue water and green hills and deep forest pines lent a comfortable, homey vibe to his badass rock god demeanor. Possibly the most intriguing thing was that he was able to pull off both at the same time.

His lips twitched at the corner, a subtle smile, and then he sat on the couch—really close. "Gloria Shields."

"Asher Knight."

"Known you a long time."

Fact. She and Asher had known each other for a long time.

"Thing is, how can I know you for a long time and not get the least bit sick of you?" He reached over and twirled a lock of her hair around his finger. "How come you wear short skirts all the time, but I never get tired of seeing those legs? How come I've seen you naked over and over again and yet it's the only thing I can think about the second my son's head hits the pillow?"

She lifted and dropped one shoulder. She didn't have an answer to those questions either, but she felt the same around him. He was still as sexy as the first time she'd laid eyes on him. And when he was this close, his dark eyes on her, those long lashes casting shadows on his cheeks, she wanted to touch him and kiss him. And do a whole host of other fun and dirty things.

"You're gonna get sick of me long before I get sick of you, Sarge," Ash said this with a sad note to his voice. One that bent her eyebrows and made her smile fall.

"I'm not as sick of you as I should be," she said quietly.

"Excellent news." He put tension on the piece of hair he had wrapped around his fingers. Then he put his lips on hers so gently, she sort of melted into him, leaning closer and almost falling into his lap. He kept her in place by lifting his other hand to her jaw as he tasted her lips, tilting his head and raking her face with his stubble, erasing her worries when he pushed his tongue into her mouth.

A soft moan sounded between them, and Gloria was half alarmed to find out it was her making that sound.

Asher's lips left hers abruptly. "We were going to talk."

She shook her head. "No, no talking." She kissed him again, and he let her, but he tugged away first, still holding her face in his hands.

"There's more coming your way tonight, gorgeous. But since making dinner and eating dinner and watching *Mr. McGregor's Menagerie Emporium*"—his eyes went big and he gave her a look that pretty much summed up the way they both felt about the poorly drawn, poorly written children's show—"didn't allow us to catch up, I figure we should catch up. So we're talking. And when we're done talking, we're going to go to bed and fuck as quietly and as long as we possibly can before Hawk interrupts."

Her face went warm at that prospect. She liked the way that sounded. Every last bit of it.

"Okay," she breathed.

"I think you're right. You're not sick of me." He let her go, but his grin endured, and it was positively shit-eating.

She rolled her eyes.

He leaned back, arms splayed across the couch, eyes on her. "I don't think Jordan can handle things like an adult."

Gloria felt her head nod. "I would agree with that."

"She gets overwhelmed, and I think it's because Emily has coddled her to the point of uselessness." He shook his head, his eyes unfocused on the windows. "I didn't know her. I still don't."

"She brought Hawk to you."

Asher looked over, his brow creasing.

"Not Emily. You." That was the important part. "She needed help with him and brought Hawk to his father. That wouldn't have happened a year ago." Gloria smiled softly. "You're a great dad."

"That means a lot," he said, and she could tell by the quirk of his lips and the way his eyes briefly went to his lap that he was flattered. Humbled. Humility wasn't an emotion Asher Knight often showed.

"Hawk needs to know someone is going to be on his side no matter what. That's you. That's huge." *That's what I didn't have,* she thought, but didn't say. What she would have given to know her mother or her father would have turned their lives upside down to be there for her. Her grandmother was there for her as long as she could have been, but even that wasn't the same.

"Come here, Sarge." He flicked his fingers and when she moved to him, he closed an arm around her. His lips hit the top of her head. "Never could have done any of this without you."

"Sure you could've," she said, feeling slightly uncomfortable.

"You kept me even. I needed you."

Needed her. Her heart clutched.

"Hawk looked good nestled against you in his room earlier."

Clearly, he was trying to give her cardiac arrest. She stayed silent.

"You look good with a toddler, Sarge." Lips against her hair, he changed subjects yet again, giving her no time to catch up. "How do you feel about seeing more of me?"

She pulled back and trained her eyes on his dark, earnest ones. "I'm not sure how I could see any more of you than I have already," she joked. "I've seen every last inch."

"All nine," he joked back, but his smile wasn't as cocky as she would have liked. Then it clicked. He didn't mean that she would see more of his body. He meant she'd see more of *him*.

Him here.

"Oh," she said. Her hand curled into his T-shirt, beneath which she felt a strong and steady heartbeat.

"Yeah."

"What about...what about your place in California?"

He pulled in a deep breath. "I'll have my stuff shipped here and list the house under market so it sells fast."

"What about Knight Time?"

"Well, Ricky is going to find himself unemployed here, soon."

She frowned. "Why?"

"Him and Jordan."

She gasped. "No."

Asher shrugged. "I don't know. He hugged her and they talked for a few minutes and she left. Asshole had to slink back in here to get his guitar. Wouldn't look at me." He wound his hand in her hair. "Just want a little peace, you know?"

"Yeah. I know." She couldn't blame him. She wanted a little peace, too. She felt like she was close, but then the nervous part of her showed up and tore down that carefully structured peace wall brick by brick.

They watched each other, silence blanketing the house save for the crickets sawing away outside. Gloria tipped her chin and kissed him, and he kissed her back, allowing her to push him down on the couch. She lay over the top of him, kicking off her sandals as she settled, her hips over his hips, her breasts on his chest, her hands on his shoulders, her mouth sealed over his.

He shoved both hands into her hair and held her head, turning her face gently as he made out with her and then kissed a trail from her chin to her neck. She squirmed against him. The part of her and the part of him that fit best together did most of the moving, the rhythm and insistence conveying exactly what they'd rather be doing.

Rather than tear at each other's clothes, they continued to kiss and hold each other, rub and play and smile against each other's mouths. They did some heavy petting, Gloria rubbing a palm over the thick ridge of the erection pressing against his fly. She swallowed his groan to keep Hawk from overhearing. Asher thumbed her nipple over her bra and shirt and he returned the favor by keeping his lips to hers when she whimpered.

The last time she'd made out like a teenager, she *had been* a teenager. She'd since forgotten how exciting, how thrilling, how mind-blowing it was just to hang out around second base for a while. Asher kissed her until his stubble left a burn on her neck and along her lips. He held her hips tight in both palms and ground against her until she was panting.

"Please," she whispered.

"Please what?" he whispered back, raking his teeth along her neck and cupping her breast.

"Please let's get to the...other part."

"'Other part,'" he repeated, his voice lilting and clearly amused.

She didn't feel like being crass. She felt like being the girl she never got the chance to be—shy and curious about this new experience. She and Asher may have done lots of things together, but this was new.

"The doing it part," she whispered against his mouth.

His eyes glittered. "Slip outta those panties, Sarge."

"We can't do that here." But the thrill that had coursed through her veins intensified. Her voice rose a little higher than she anticipated. The baby monitor made a noise and Gloria pressed her lips together. Asher froze, hand on her breast, mouth on her neck as they listened in the quiet of the room for Hawk...and to find out if their plans had just been drastically derailed.

No noise came from the monitor...but neither of them moved.

"I'm suspicious," Gloria said, keeping her voice low.

"Me too. I'll look in on him." He gave her a peck. "Meanwhile, get naked from the waist down and start figuring out how you're going to keep quiet."

She eased off him, taking time to slide her body down the length of his, pausing with her mouth over his fly before sitting back on her knees.

Asher lay there an extra second, nostrils flared and eyes hooded. Then he adjusted his length and stood from the couch, shooting her a heated look that said she'd pay for that.

She could hardly wait.

* * *

Carefully, Asher poked his head into Hawk's room. His son's chest lifted and fell and his eyes were sealed shut. He couldn't have appeared more peaceful if there were a halo over his head.

Ash closed the door until it clicked and then made up his mind that while he could take Gloria to his bedroom, he wanted her on the couch. It would mean being more careful and more quiet, but he'd loved the passion in her eyes earlier when they made out. His entire body throbbed, ready for more.

With an anticipatory grin on his face, he came to the couch where she sat, legs folded under her. Her short skirt was in place, her eyes wide and innocent, but just beyond where she sat, oh yes...

Silky pink panties draped over the arm of the couch.

"Asleep?" she asked.

He nodded. "You ready?"

She smiled.

He sat.

The moment his ass was on the couch, he grabbed her up and kissed her and then said into her ear, "You're on lookout duty."

Not wasting time—because his son was part ninja and could wake at any moment—Asher assisted with the skirt lift. Palms on her thighs, he pushed his hands along her skin, sliding the material higher and higher. Glo threw one leg over his lap, settling over his fly, but not before her hands went to his pants. He watched her fingers work, slipping the thick leather from his belt buckle, popping the button-fly open.

"Oh," she said, her voice a sexy-as-hell breathy whisper.

No boxers, so he was free and so hard and absolutely ready to go. "We need to get you on the pill, Sarge."

Her hands flattened on his shirt.

He shoved his hands higher, cupping her bottom and moving her directly over him. "Imagine."

A short, tortured exhalation left her lips.

"Just imagine…" He tilted his hips and slipped his cock between her folds, finding her slick and wet and *mercy*, he was going to quite possibly die. This was a bad idea. All he wanted to do was plunge in there and pound them both into sweet, sweet bliss.

She leaned over him, her lips brushing his when she said, "I already am. But you…you're…"

"I'm what," he growled. His grip tightened on her ass.

"You," she finished.

He knew what she meant by that. That was fair.

"Sarge, I never would have done this"—he shifted her and slipped along her folds again—"if I didn't know I was squeaky clean." He moved along her again. "I think I could just do *this* if pressed." He put his mouth on hers, then pulled away to say, "You feel incredible."

"So do you," she panted, tossing her head back and closing her eyes.

Wet. She was wet and smooth, and so damn ready it
wasn't funny. He had no idea the last time he'd sat and
kissed a woman for as long as he and Glo had gone at it.
When he'd first talked her back to his place years ago, she'd
gone straight for his fly before he could get her undressed.
That hadn't bothered him in the past; he was all for getting
to the good stuff. But now since he'd had her on top of him,
fully clothed, kissing him for what was probably an hour,
he'd become a big, big fan of foreplay.

"Up to you. It's your body, gorgeous. I'm springing this
on you." His lips twitched. "Literally."

Gloria kissed him, letting out a muffled laugh. She rocked
against him and Asher's eyes slipped down to where they
were nearly connected, his fingers pressing into her hips, his
teeth stabbing his bottom lip. He watched their flesh slide,
and damn, there wasn't anything sexier than seeing that. Unless he had her shirt off, too, and her tits in his face. As it
was, he'd have to make do with the view. Not a bad one, admittedly, since her V-neck shirt gave him a tease of cleavage,
hinting at the fantastic rack she was hiding.

She kissed him gently, then paused, her mouth over his.
Her voice was husky when she said, "Yes."

Asher's spine snapped straight.

In answer, she rose to her knees and positioned herself
over the head of his cock. She brushed over him, and he
clasped on to her bare ass. She sucked in a breath through
her nose as he closed one hand around the back of her
neck.

Then he pushed her onto his length, impaling himself in
her smooth, silken heat.

He dropped his forehead to her chest and blew out a breath. Having sex with Gloria was awesome. Having sex with Gloria without a condom was...

He had nothing. No word in his vocabulary did her justice.

"Fuck," he growled.

Except for that one.

But this was deeper than that. This was her trusting him more than she ever had before. This was more than a quick lay, to get off, and had been for some time now.

She rode him bareback, thrusting her chest closer to his face with every stroke. She took turns watching him and watching Hawk's bedroom door. Ash grinned. Because, yeah, this was challenging in a way neither of them had been accustomed to pre-Hawk, but it was also just plain fun in a totally surprising way.

Watching Glo try to muzzle the very loud shouts she should be letting loose right about now was turning him on even more. His release built, putting pressure on his balls and vibrating down his spine like too much feedback from a hot mic. He was about to have a challenge of his own. Keeping himself from shouting his release or demanding Gloria to "come."

He kept himself in check, focused solely on her. She caught his eye there at the end and he fisted her hair in his fingers, pulled her lips to his, and spilled inside her, letting out a few sharp breaths as his orgasm slammed into him.

He was sure she went over at the same time, given the way he felt her clutching, pulsing around him as he continued pumping. He hoped so, because he was spent. If she needed to get off after this, he was going to have to go to the kitchen and make himself an espresso.

It'd been a long-ass day.

"Ash," she breathed into his ear as a shudder snaked down his spine. Lazily, he opened his eyes and found Glo over him, looking sated and relaxed. He released her hair, straightening her black locks as well as he could. Yeah, she came. He could see it in the highlighted pink of her cheeks and in the heat darkening her blue eyes.

"Yeah, Sarge," he croaked.

Her lips parted, then closed. Then her eyes flitted away from his, and her fingers played along the neck of his shirt. She let out a sigh. A frustrated one.

He lifted his hands to her jaw and turned her face gently toward his. Just a hint of shimmer swam in her eyes, and if he had a guess, there was something on her mind and it was something she hadn't quite worked up the courage to share.

She wanted to tell him. She just couldn't.

"Yeah, Sarge," he said, but this time his comment was a confirmation. "I see it."

"See what?" Her eyes widened the slightest bit.

"You, honey. I see you."

Her eyelashes fluttered and she leaned in and placed the softest, sweetest kiss on the center of his lips. "I like that you see me. And I...you know."

That shy look again. That was killing him.

"I...like you."

"Good to know." He smothered a laugh, but keeping the smile from his lips proved impossible.

"*Like* like." She was trying. God, he loved her for it.

"Also good to know," he told her.

"*A lot*," she said meaningfully.

"Get to bed, babe." With a gentle slap to her ass, he said, "You can work up to it."

He expected her to give him hell. She didn't. Instead, her eyes turned to his. "Thank you."

"You're welcome." He sat forward, still inside her, and kept his hands on her lower back to keep her from falling.

She pressed a finger to his lips, then replaced it with a kiss. It was the sweetest thing. Then she slid off him and tugged her skirt down. The moment the bathroom door closed, the monitor crackled and Hawk's voice cut in.

Ash didn't know what his son said or if he was sleep-walking or up and at 'em, but he was grateful he'd had these last few hours—and the next several—with Gloria. She was able to be her and he was him, and they were *them* even with Hawk down the hall.

This was fucking *working*.

Asher buttoned up his fly, buckled his belt, and shook off the post-sex buzz threatening to drop him into bed where he could easily sleep for twelve hours.

Instead, he popped open Hawk's bedroom door and dealt with his boy.

CHAPTER 24

*G*loria was beginning to wish she'd gone out with the bachelors instead. The bachelor party would probably consist of booze, bar-hopping, and pool or darts. Sofie's bachelorette party had morphed into a baby shower.

Sigh.

She needed a refill on her sangria by the time Sofie held up the eighteenth (*eightieth?*) onesie and everyone crowed, "Aww!"

With a polite smile, she slipped out of the chair in Sofie's mother's living room and went to the kitchen.

"I'm jealous."

Gloria turned, midsip, to find Faith in the kitchen with her.

"I want sangria."

Glo smiled.

"Wine is my other drug."

"And Connor is your first?"

Faith waggled her eyebrows and Gloria chuckled. She understood. Good sex could be like a drug. And there was no denying Faith thought her sexy ex-military landscaper hung the moon.

"Anyway," Faith continued. "I need to dish with you." She poked Gloria's arm. "We haven't had enough girl time. I'm not the only one who wants details on the aftermath of Jordan running off like a crazy person." She shot a thumb into the living room and mouthed *Sofie*. "That girl is gonna grill you. So after the baby shower hoopla is over, you're coming out with us."

An hour and a half later, Gloria, Sofie, Faith, and Charlie had escaped the family function and reconvened at Salty Dog. Salty had the best food in town when you wanted something fried and also wanted a good drink. And while Faith and Sofie weren't going to be drinking tonight, Charlie and Gloria, and Sofie's sisters, Kinsley (younger) and Lacey (older), were definitely going to be partaking in the spirits.

"Sofie," Gloria interjected, and Sofie turned toward her, her green eyes bright and smile broad. "We have given you baby presents, we have fed you dinner, and we have drank in your honor." Glo held up her martini and Charlie, Kinsley, and Lacey lifted their glasses and tapped them together in a silent cheers. "Now what would you like to do? The night is your oyster, sweetheart."

"Hmm…" Sofie rolled her eyes to the ceiling, then her mouth dropped open and her eyebrows rose. "Donny."

"Oh no, you get to *do* Donny every other night of the week," Glo argued. "Tonight is—"

"No," Sofie said with a giggle. "I mean Donny." She pointed. "He's here. They're all here."

Since Gloria sat with her back to the front door, she had to pivot in her chair to see a herd of men strolling in. Donny,

Connor, Asher, Evan, and two men she didn't know. One was average height, had close-cut hair, and was wearing khakis and a golf shirt—Lacey's husband, no doubt about it—and the other was tall, dark, slightly older, and incredibly attractive.

"Who's the new guy?" Gloria asked.

"Kenneth," Lacey said proudly, then wiggled her fingers at her new husband. Kenneth waved back, looking as out of place in the pack of bad boys as a taco at a sushi bar.

"I bet she means Alessandre," Faith guessed correctly. "Donny's friend and mentor lives in New York. Has a gazillion dollars."

"Approximately," Sofie said, and lifted her Perrier bottle to tap with Faith's.

The pack of bad boys didn't wave, but Glo could see in their eyes the very moment they found their women. Donny found Sofie, Connor found Faith, and Evan found Charlie. Gazes locked, then ignited. And quite possibly the coolest part was that Glo wasn't left out. Asher found her and winked.

God. They were *so* together. The realization that she was his made her tingle.

"Look at you," Kinsley murmured into Gloria's ear. "Think you can find me one of those rock stars?"

Gloria turned her head to take in Kins and automatically thought of Ricky. The long-haired, wily new guy to the band would be much better hooked up with Kinsley Martin than he would Jordan Trudeau.

"Trust me, sweetheart," she told Kins. "You don't want any part of Knight Time, but I'll keep my eyes peeled for you."

"My girl. At a bar." Donny crossed his arms over his chest

and looked down at his wife-to-be, his long black hair brushing his cheekbones and a smile twitching on his lips. "What are you doing here? You were doing baby shit or something."

Baby shit. Gloria laughed.

Donny peeled his eyes off Sofie to smile over at her. "How you doin', Glo?"

"Keeping her in line," she said with a lift of her glass.

"We're done doing baby stuff and decided we should come out and have a little party of our own," Sofie said to her fiancé. "You don't look like this is your first stop."

"Aless got us a limo. Surely the girls aren't making you drive them around on your bachelorette night."

"I'm doing it," Faith said, lifting her hand.

"That's why I love her." Connor crossed over to his wife and bent to kiss her on the lips. He lowered his voice and murmured and everyone close by looked away to give them privacy.

"Ace, you good?" Evan came to his wife next, standing behind her, his hands on her shoulders.

Charlie tipped her head, her honey-blond hair falling over the back of the chair, and pursed her lips. Evan rewarded her by bending and giving her a kiss.

Kenneth was next, smooching Lacey and squatting next to her chair.

"Why does everyone get kisses but me?" Sofie pressed her nails to her collarbone. "Am I not the bride?"

"I'm going to excuse myself to the ladies' room," Kinsley groaned. "I can't take it."

"I'll go with you." Gloria stood, too. She agreed that everything had suddenly become intimate. She didn't get far before Asher grasped her hip with one palm, pulled her to him, and took her other hand in his. He danced a few steps, leaning her back to dip her and she'd just figured out why. Over the din of diners and the blare of TVs, Knight Time's "Unchained" played over the speakers.

"How could I have possibly missed that?" she asked as Ash brought her to her feet again.

"I know my own song, Sarge." He stopped dancing but held her close. There was a twinkle in his eye and a curve to his lips that made her think he'd had a few brews before Salty Dog as well.

He kissed her, and Gloria melted into him. The kiss went on a little longer than socially acceptable. She knew, because a few whistles and howls came from her friends behind her.

"You guys have a limo? Why didn't we think of that?" Gloria shifted away from Asher and tried not to look like that full-body assault was the single best thing that had happened to her all day.

"I can get you a limo," came a smooth-as-silk voice. The man with the widow's peak and sharp, dark eyes offered a hand.

"Gloria Shields." My, but was he good-looking. He stood right around Donny's six-four, had the same black hair but with gray at the temples. He was dressed in designer faded jeans, his button-down shirt cuffed at the forearms, his hair falling rakishly over his forehead.

"Alessandre D'Paolo."

"Ohh, and an accent. Aren't you a catch?" she teased. Alessandre lifted her hand and placed a kiss there.

"Hey, hey, easy." Asher pulled Gloria flush to his side. "He has a ton of ex-wives. No idea what he's doing, so don't let that smooth accent fool you."

Alessandre let out a hearty laugh. *Of course.* Asher had already won over the newest in their boys club. The charmer.

"All right, us hens are going to get out of your cock house." Sofie frowned and looked to the side. "I'm pretty sure I said that backwards."

Everyone erupted in laughter, including Charlie, who was adorably drunk.

One by one, the girls stood from their chairs. Kinsley returned from the bathroom, and Gloria didn't miss Donny pulling Sofie over to the side, wrapping his palms around her ass, and pulling her up and into him for a deep kiss. Where her rear was concerned, the man was not shy. Glo had seen that ass-grab more times than she could count. Donovan set Sofie back on her heels; then his hand went to her tummy and paused there while he stared into her eyes.

Gloria put her hand on her chest, her breath catching. It may have been the first time she'd ever felt a real tug to have what those two had. The promise of family. A love so deep anyone looking on could see that they were going to make it.

"It's fantastic, isn't it?" Kinsley pulled her purse onto her shoulder.

"It is."

Then Kins echoed Gloria's thoughts by quietly adding, "*Want.*"

Exactly. Who wouldn't want that?

Kinsley sighed and then announced, "I'm good to drive, so don't worry about me, but I'm going to call it a night. Lacey? Time to go, hon."

"No! I don't want to go home!" Kenneth put an arm on her to keep her from stumbling as she stood. "Unless you come home with me." She pouted.

"Um, yeah, of course," he said, knowing his place. He waved at the guys. "See you guys. Good to meet you, Alessandre. Asher."

"Yay!" Lacey said.

"Yeah, yay," Kinsley repeated, a little less enthused. "Later, Gloria."

"Later, Kins."

They left and the remaining bachelor party guys straggled to the bar. Asher hung back and put his arm around Gloria again. Glo held up a finger to let Faith know she'd be a minute. Faith waved a hand, letting her know to take her time.

"What are you going to do tonight?" Asher asked her. "Where are you staying?"

"I'm staying in my own bed," Gloria stated, getting in his face on purpose. "Why do you ask?" She wasn't drunk but she was buzzed from the extra shot she had as a sidecar to her martini earlier. She hated to admit it, but faced with the option of hanging out with her girls for the rest of the evening and being this close to Asher when he smelled this good and looked even better, she'd choose the latter. Because with Asher, the evening would end with her and him and a lot of skin.

Yum.

"Just wanted to know in case I get frisky at four a.m.," Ash said. "Pull an all-nighter."

They grinned at each other.

"Hawk's at Mom's for the night. I am a free man."

"Not that free." Gloria narrowed her eyes. She felt bold, and brave, and as possessive over Asher as he'd been with her when Aless was faux flirting with her. "You're mine and no one else's," she added on a whisper. "Not anymore."

As long as she had a say, Asher wasn't going home with anybody but her.

His eyes warmed and the fingers resting on her back rubbed along the bare skin at the edge of her tank top. Then he broke the moment of seriousness, letting her go and bursting into a falsetto rendition of "I'm a Slave 4 U" by Britney Spears. Gloria gave him a shove toward the bar. He sent her a quick flash of a smile over his shoulder and shook his ass as he accepted the shot glass Connor was handing him.

Glo turned from the scene and put a hand to her very warm cheek. Her giant smile frozen on her face, she noticed Faith, Charlie, and Sofie giving her suspicious little smiles of their own.

Uh-oh.

"What?" Gloria asked, moving her hand away from her face.

"You said I could do whatever I wanted tonight." Sofie crossed her arms and looked ready for a fight.

"Uh…"

"I've decided, and these two agree"—she pointed to her left and right at Charlie and Faith—"that I want to finally see your apartment."

* * *

"That's it. That's everything," Gloria said.

Charlie, Sofie, and Faith had filed into her apartment and Glo had handed out a round of waters. Then she told them everything.

About her mom.

About her grandmother.

About her foster life.

Some details some of them knew, and some details none of them knew. But they were her friends, and Gloria was tired of hiding.

The monologue had drained her, had made her knees loose, and because Asher had already broken the rule of not sitting on Rita's couch by sitting on it, Gloria plopped onto the vinyl seat.

She was immediately surrounded by her friends.

Charlie on her right, Sofie on her left, and Faith on the end. Without prompting, Charlie took hold of Gloria's hand, Sofie wrapped an arm around Gloria's waist, and Faith leaned past Sofie's lap to rest her hand on Gloria's knee.

Her support system. These girls were here for her no matter what her story was. And knowing she had this kind of undying friendship was almost too much. They knew the dirty secret of who she used to be and knew it was something she'd purposefully kept from them.

Yet they accepted her. It needed to be acknowledged.

"Thank you," Glo said, eyes on her lap, smile and voice watery.

"You're welcome, hon," Sofie said. Then she pointed to the kitchen. "Charlie, pour her a shot. We're not done with her yet."

"Right." Charlie vanished to the kitchen and came back with two filled shot glasses. "You aren't drinking alone, sister," she said, handing one over.

Glo blinked back the few tears that dared pulse against the backs of her eyes and turned to Sofie.

"Now you're going to talk," Sofie said, green eyes bright and eyebrows high on her forehead.

"Is that so?" Glo challenged, feeling her smile crest her mouth.

"Oh, that's so, missy. You are going to tell me everything that is happening between you and our resident rock star. If I can't get drunk, I *will be* regaled with tales of debauchery."

"Told you." Faith grinned at Glo.

Glo grinned back. Charlie tapped their shot glasses together and they threw back the whiskey. "I'm ready. Hit me, Scampi," she teased, using Donny's nickname for her.

"Everything happening between you and Asher, and do not leave out the good parts." Sofie and Faith got comfy and Charlie cozied in, too. And there, the four of them smashed together on the ugliest couch ever to grace a living room, Gloria spilled.

She told her friends about Hawk. About Jordan. About Emily. About how Asher's mom, Elana, made Gloria feel like family. About how Asher was great in bed and great against the wall and great skinny-dipping in the lake. She told her friends everything...

Almost.

The spanking thing, that was hers and Asher's.

A girl couldn't divulge all of her secrets.

* * *

Oh, man. Donovan was plowed. But he could get plowed and handle it like a champ. And he'd better, because the man was getting married tomorrow and it was Connor and Asher and Evan's jobs to see that he sealed the deal come four o'clock. Which was...approximately fourteen hours from now.

Fourteen. That was a *lifetime*. Ash had gone on two hours of sleep more times than he could count. Coffee and cigarettes and whiskey were his *compadres*. So...maybe that wasn't the solution for Donny, but Asher had faith his buddy could rally.

Donny had asked Alessandre to go to the mansion to check on Gertie. His friend obliged, taking the limo back to check on the pooch that'd been home alone most of the evening and likely needed to go outside. Donny told Aless they'd be right where he left them, at Last Chance, a bar on Alps Way.

Only the second the limo pulled away from the bar, Donny had announced. "Let's go."

Ash and Evan were currently downing their shots and Connor was simultaneously downing his and throwing money on the bar. But Donny was already out the door, heading directly for Library Park.

A Penis Bandit Reunion was in full effect.

"You know you're an honorary member now," Asher commented to Connor once they were outside.

"I'm good, thanks," Connor said as he shoved his wallet in his pocket.

"Hey." Evan stopped Connor with a hand on his chest. "Not optional, soldier." Then that grouchy exterior faded into a smile and Evan clapped his friend hard on the back. "Don't worry, it's not like we're going to get arrested."

"Getting in the fountain nude is no longer frowned upon?" Asher asked. He enjoyed the brief look of horror that colored Connor's face before he figured out Asher was kidding.

"What do you think he's planning, anyway?" Evan asked, picking up the pace.

All three guys looked at Donovan, who, while he wasn't running, wasn't out for a leisurely stroll. At Library Park, he hung a hard right and walked directly to the fountain.

"Ah, shit. I was gonna keep my pants on tonight," Asher muttered.

But Donovan wasn't looking at the fountain; he was looking straight up at a wide tree with lots of low branches. His hands were on his hips and there was a gleam in his eye when he grinned over at Asher.

"No, man." Evan approached with one hand out. "There is a reason we decided you weren't going to the quarry. No climbing tonight. You fall and break your ass and then somebody else is gonna have to stand up front and marry Sofie. And only one of us standing here can do that legally." He slid a glance to Asher and raised one dark eyebrow. "And I'm pretty sure this one isn't single any longer."

Ash smothered a smile. Much to his surprise, he liked that he wasn't automatically assumed single. It'd been a while. No, correction—he had never been assumed to have a girl-friend. His mom knew—well, not *knew* but had a general idea—that he didn't spend a lot of time alone. When it came to past relationships, he favored slipknots in his attached strings.

All of which had changed. Hell, he didn't know if there were knots in the strings with Glo. They were more like one continuous loop he hadn't found the end of yet.

"I am climbing this tree. This is the last tree I will climb as a bachelor." Donny grinned, knowing how much shit he was full of and knowing his buddies knew it, too.

Asher stepped forward. "I'll spot you."

"Me too," Connor said.

"What the hell?" Evan asked, looking grumpier than usual.

"I may be a new member, but my vote counts." Connor shrugged. "You're outnumbered, Grandpa."

Evan muttered a creative expletive, and Asher laughed, throwing in, "Guess he told you." Yeah. Connor fit in just fine. Donovan started up the tree. The man could climb. Asher had witnessed him climb forty or fifty feet straight up a sheet of rock when they were younger. Without gear. Stupid. But then, they'd done all kinds of stupid shit back then. Hell, Asher just recently stopped doing stupid shit.

Donny could handle the quarry, so no doubt this squatty library tree was not a challenge. But he surprised them all by stopping when he'd barely climbed ten feet off the ground.

"Hey." He looked down, his black hair falling over his face, legs spread between two branches, arms holding on to the nearest limb. "Kids are trashin' the library."

"Oh, hell no." Evan's eyebrows slammed down.

"Yeah, time to interfere," Donny said, coming down as quickly as he went up.

"Penis Bandit Vigilantes," Asher said. Connor, next to him, chuckled.

Donovan hit the ground, landing on his feet and brushing the bark from his jeans. Then the four of them headed around the lawn to the front of the library. Asher had envisioned a group of kids spray-painting penises on the library's brick wall. Not so.

Three teenage boys—by the sounds of their punchy laughter, he assumed they'd been drinking or smoking something—stood in front of the library, but they weren't holding cans of spray paint. They had rolls of toilet paper.

White streamers dripped down the trees' branches, mummified the hedges, and wound around a line of new saplings like Maypoles.

"You have got to be shittin' me," Connor growled. "If they stomped my hostas, or bruised my lavender…"

"And you called me grandpa?" Evan joked. Then he shook his head as he looked around at the bits of tissue littering the normally impeccable manicured library lawn. "Mrs. Anderson is going to have a grand mal seizure when she looks out her front door and finds this."

In sync, they turned to Mrs. Anderson's house across the street. The porch light was on, but the windows were dark. Ash guessed she and Mr. Anderson had hit the sack after *Jeopardy!* was over.

For now at least, it appeared the kids hadn't been made.

"Wrap it up, guys," Donny announced, his baritone voice infused with authority. Like he *hadn't* just been trespassing and climbing a tree while three sheets to the wind.

Asher scrubbed his face to hide a smile.

The boys turned, startled at first but green enough that they didn't know who they were dealing with.

"Yeah?" the scrappier one called out. "What're you gonna do about it?"

"He isn't going to do anything about it," Connor said, balling his fists at his sides. "But I will. I dealt with rebels in Afghanistan, so believe me when I say I have ways of making you talk." His voice was steel and ice, and he wasn't lying about his experience.

Asher bit down on his lip to keep from losing it, but he had to commend Connor on his choice of threats. Asking them to stop trampling his tulips wouldn't have gone over nearly as well.

"I won't let him torture you," Evan said. "But I will supervise while you clean this up."

Two of the boys bent their heads close, whispering to each other. Then one of them grabbed a third boy, the scrappy ringleader, and pointed at Asher.

"Holy crap." The scrappy one stepped forward, reverence in his round eyes. He pointed at Asher with the toilet paper roll in his hand. "You're Asher Knight. You're the lead singer of Knight Time. Holy crap, I can't believe it." He turned to his buddies, a grin splitting his face. "Fucking Asher Knight, you guys!"

Evan, Donovan, and Connor wore matching expressions of burden.

Asher shrugged. Not his fault. It was gonna be harder to bust the kid's balls when he was this starstruck, though. And then the kid hit Asher's soft spot.

"I play guitar," the kid said. "I know the opening to 'Unchained' and I started writing a song. You can ask these guys. I play it all the time."

The kids behind him nodded in tandem, muttering, "Totally," and "All the time."

"Oh, man, I can't believe it's you!"

Way starstruck.

"Calm down, dude." Asher held out a palm and looked over his shoulder. "Listen. I get that you guys need to unwind and there isn't a heck of a lot to do in this boring, rich-folks town, but you can't be decorating the library or Mrs. Anderson is gonna have an aneurism. Know her?"

The boys shook their heads.

"She's the librarian and she lives there." He jerked his thumb over his shoulder, and the three boys followed his gesture. "She comes out here and busts you guys, you're going to wish you'd found something better to do with your night."

Hard telling if any of it was sinking in.

The scrappy ringleader smiled widely and took a step toward Asher. "Can I get your autograph?"

Yeah, so it probably hadn't sunk in.

"Sure. Pen?" Ash held out a hand. He didn't even want to know why the kid behind them had a Sharpie in his back pocket. One of those monster ones used to make the signs in the grocery store. He accepted the gargantuan marker and a roll of toilet paper to sign.

Yes, being a celebrity was truly glamorous.

Asher signed a roll for each of them. They took off, a spring in their steps and still talking about the autographed rolls in their hands.

"They were supposed to clean up this mess, genius," Evan said.

"They were drinking," Asher said, realizing he still had the Sharpie in his hand. He pointed at Evan with it. "Do you know what a vacation ruiner it is to be busted for underage drinking?"

"I do," Donny answered, his tone dry.

"I figured they needed a break," Ash continued, sliding the marker into his pocket. "You never know, those three might grow up to be like us." And before anyone could fill in the blank of what that meant, Asher said, "Though, a tattoo artist, mason, landscaper, and rock star are unlikely."

"Unlikely, but not impossible," Evan said, watching the boys retreat into the shadows. "Life takes weird turns sometimes. Turns you don't expect."

Too true. Evan's life had taken a turn when his wife died and left him in charge of their three-year-old son. And Donny's life had taken a turn when his grandmother passed and left him a mansion he swore he'd sell, but now lived in. Connor's life changed irrevocably last year after one of his best friends died. And Asher's life had been changing since he learned about Hawk's existence.

The turns his life had taken were intersected by more detours he hadn't seen coming. Asher couldn't have seen Gloria coming. And he never thought he would get a chance to win her back. Yet here she was, in his life, in his arms. Great with his son.

"Let's get to it." Donovan interrupted Asher's thoughts. He walked to the nearest tree and started tugging strips of toilet paper from the branches. "Least it's not raining."

"You've become more patient in your old age, Donny." Connor followed suit, carefully detangling the tissue from the library's decorative bushes and flowers.

"They didn't buy the cheap shit," Evan commented as he and Asher loaded their arms full of Charmin.

"Bored rich kids," Ash commented.

"We've come a long way, brother," Evan said, but he was smiling.

"Yeah," Asher said, and smiled back. "Guess we have." A long way since they'd come down here with spray cans drunk off their asses and looking to cause trouble. A way none of them had expected, but each of them had embraced. Asher included.

Evergreen Cove was beginning to feel like home.

Red and blue lights slashed across the library's brick wall and washed the lawn in color.

Asher and Evan took in the scene and exchanged glances. The officer, who'd parked his squad car on the edge of the lawn but hadn't stepped from it yet, was seeing four not-so-sober guys, armloads of toilet paper. And at least three of them had a rap sheet—the scene of the crime this very site.

Brady Hutchins climbed out of the car.

"You're kidding me," Connor muttered. He didn't have the best history with Brady after he and Legs had dealt with

the potential break-in at her apartment. Brady hadn't necessarily made a play for Faith, but he and Connor, from what
Asher had heard from the girls, had had some sort of pissing
match.

"Lock it up," Evan muttered to Connor.

"What's up, guys?" Brady called as he stepped onto the
lawn, a grin on his face. He was in his blues, thumbs hooked
on his belt, smug amusement coloring his tanned face. He
had shaggy blond hair and was tall enough to look Asher and
Evan in the eye. Which he did . . . right after scanning the TP-
covered grounds. "Feeling a little sentimental?"

"Our reputation precedes us," Ash mumbled to Evan.

"Don't be a dick, Hutchins." Connor dropped the wads of
toilet paper he'd just collected on the lawn.

"I wouldn't push me if I were you, McClain. I have
cuffs."

"Use those on your girl," Asher said, and because he was
supporting his friend, he added, "If you can find one."

"Pardon?" The cop's good humor erased as his jaw
ticked.

"Hutch," Evan said. "He's kidding. We're at the tail end
of Donny's bachelor party. We're not driving. We walked
down here to . . ." He paused, wisely, because the truth put
Donovan at the top of a very high tree. So he rerouted.
"Found some kids tearin' up the place. Thought it our civic
responsibility to run 'em off."

How Ev was able to say "civic responsibility" without
stumbling after the amount he'd had to drink was a remark-
able feat.

"I signed their toilet paper," Ash put in.

Brady blinked like he'd just noticed him.

Asher grinned. "I'm famous."

Hutchins did not look impressed.

"We're on cleanup duty, man," Evan explained, holding his arms out to reference the disaster on the library lawn.

"You guys are interested in cleaning up the city, I can arrange that for you," Brady said.

"Get that rod out of your ass, Brady. Lend a hand," Donny said, his speech slightly slurred.

"He's kidding, too," Evan said, but it was obvious to all of them that Donny was not kidding. Donny didn't "kid."

"Mrs. Anderson wakes up, she's gonna kick all of our asses," Asher pointed out, because he'd just seen an upstairs light come to life across the street.

"Yours included," Connor put in.

At the mention of Mrs. Anderson, Brady turned to look at the house behind him. Another light flicked on. This one downstairs.

"Ah, hell," the officer said in a tone that hinted he'd dealt with Mrs. Anderson a time or three.

A second later, the front door popped open and the elderly librarian came down her porch steps with the assist of a railing, wearing a fuzzy blue bathrobe and a scowl Asher could feel in his bones.

"Here we go," Ash muttered.

"Wait! You just wait one minute!" she shouted as she crossed the street without looking.

Not a surprise. Traffic stopped for Mrs. Anderson. It'd always been that way.

"Don't worry, ma'am, I'm taking care of this right now," Brady said in a calming, practiced tone, one hand making a "calm down" motion.

"Oh no, you don't, Brady Hutchins," she snapped. "I saw those hooligans out here toilet-papering my library, and these four boys ran them off. I suggest you don't give them any guff for trying to clean up what wasn't their mess."

Brady blinked at her.

"You could lend a hand, you know," she barked, fists on her hips.

Connor's face split into a grin.

Brady reached for his radio. "What did they look like? Any kids you recognized from the community? Maybe it's not too late to catch them."

"It's dark," Asher said, flicking a look to the librarian.

"Not talking to you, Knight," Brady growled, but he took his finger off his walkie. He turned back to Mrs. Anderson, but her eyes were on Asher.

Subtly, he shook his head. *Give 'em a break.*

"Mr. Knight is correct. It's very dark out here," she said.

Asher winked at her. He thought he saw the side of her normally flat mouth tip, but the shadow of a smile vanished a millisecond later.

"Doesn't matter anyway," she said, her tone hard. "What matters is getting my library cleaned up. You know this young man is getting married tomorrow to that lovely brunette event planner?" She pointed at Donny, whose chest puffed at the mention of Sofie. "We can't have the library looking a fright with out-of-towners filing in to the mansion for the big shebang, now, can we?"

Shebang, Evan mouthed, and Asher had to bite down on his lip to keep from laughing.

"This place covered in toilet tissue makes our town look like trash. I won't have it," she stated.

"I understand that, ma'am, but if we hope to *keep* the town clean—"

"Come on. Get to it." She looped an arm around Brady's

elbow and led him into the mess. They all may have been the town bad boys at one point, but they were grown men now. Grown men who respected their elders. Clearly, Mrs. Anderson respected them right back. Evan, for providing art for the library—though the content of his donated painting was questionable—and Ash for performing on her command at every festival he'd been in town for.

Mrs. Anderson and Sofie had been responsible for sending Connor business, what with him setting up for the annual Harvest Fest every fall and landscaping for them every spring. And evidently, Donny had accidentally wormed his way into the librarian's good graces thanks to Sofie.

"While you're here," Mrs. Anderson said to Donny, "I need that light replaced." She pointed to a lamp hanging over the front door that was dim.

"You got it." Donny nodded.

"I'll just get the bulb." She pulled the keys out of her robe's pocket and unlocked the front door.

"Bury that hatchet, boys," Evan said to Connor and Brady. "Just for an hour."

"I was at the end of my shift," Brady grumbled, looking around as if he couldn't figure out how he got into this mess.

"Next time, keep goin'." Connor slapped him on the back.

"Shee-it," Evan said through a laugh.

Brady only shook his head.

Asher and Ev bent and started cleaning again, and Donovan climbed a ladder and replaced the light.

CHAPTER 25

Always a bridesmaid, never a bride," Kinsley said with an exaggerated sigh.

Sofie's sister was beautifully dressed for duty in a strapless, knee-length baby pink chiffon gown with a sweetheart neckline. All the girls looked incredible in them—from gold bangles and earrings to tall, nude-colored shoes. Kins had paired hers with thick charcoal eyeliner, which was perfect for her rock 'n' roll style. Hmm. She really was well suited to a rock band guy.

"Have you been in as many weddings as me?" Kins asked, adjusting her simple bouquet of white roses.

"One," Glo answered. Kimber's wedding.

"Lucky," Kins said, but her grumble was good-humored. "Oh, I'm up!" She scuttled through the grass to Faith, Lacey, and Charlie. The other girls waved and Gloria waved back, that ping of loss radiating in her breastbone again.

"Sofie needs you."

Gloria turned toward Donovan's voice to respond but couldn't get her tongue untangled enough to do so. He wore a white dress shirt, open at the collar, beneath a bone-colored jacket he'd pushed over his tattooed forearms. A pale pink rose was pinned over the pocket, and his matching slacks were adorned with a thick, deep brown belt. Offset by his medium-length black hair and electrifying pale blue eyes, Donny was a sight.

"Wow," she muttered. "You look great."

"So do you." He glanced down, his lips curving like she'd amused him, then tipped his head. "In the library."

"Right." She blinked out of her stupor but slipped right back into it when Connor exited the house, Gertie at his side. The Saint Bernard mix was brushed and smooth, a grouping of white and pink roses attached to her collar with ribbon. Connor, dressed exactly like Donny, looked equally handsome. And so did Evan—turquoise eyes standing out like beacons. "Good Lord," she said, stepping through the grass as she passed him. "You guys do scrub up nice."

Lyon wandered out behind Evan, and Gloria nearly dropped.

"Wait," she said. "We have a winner." Evan's son, with his father's eyes and his mother's cocoa skin tone, wore a pale suit and was simply gorgeous.

"Hey, Aunt Glo," Lyon said with a shy smile. Shy? That was new. She figured he'd be going through a few varying levels of confidence but had no doubt he'd land somewhere around where Evan hovered: too confident to care what anyone thought.

"I'm off to see the bride," Glo announced.

She hesitated a few minutes to watch as the men ambled to the seating area where guests were sitting, then to an elaborately carved arch that Ant, a friend of Donny's and Connor's, had carved with a chainsaw. It was absolutely gorgeous. Ant wasn't bad either. He was hard to miss in a beat-up fedora in the third row, groom's side.

She pulled open the side door to let herself in and ran into Asher. He grasped her elbow to steady her when she wobbled. A smile surrounded by stubble tilted his mouth. Gorgeous men may be dotting the lawn behind her, but there was only one gorgeous man for her. Sexy, smoking-hot rock god, Asher Knight.

He wore an identical groomsmen suit, but somehow wore it better than the others. The tousled dark hair, eyes that sparkled with flecks of gold in the sunlight, bracelets on his wrist, rings on his fingers... and oh, yes. Boots.

Of course he'd worn his boots.

She opened her mouth to say excuse me, but he wrapped an arm around her waist and pulled her into the kitchen. Then he lowered his face to hers and growled, "Why are you wearing red lipstick?"

"Because it matches the dress?" she said innocently, her hands on his muscular shoulders.

"I want to kiss you so bad." His voice was low and gravelly and she realized that she'd made a terrible error with the lipstick. She wanted to kiss him, too.

"I can reapply," she said.

"No time," he growled some more. "After, Sarge. Take that off."

"Don't worry. Lipstick usually comes off on its own after cocktail hour."

"I wasn't talking about the lipstick." His lips curved into a feral smile and he ran a finger along the bodice of her dress. "Gotta walk," he called as he strode for the door.

She watched him do it, admiring the way his ass looked in those pants before smoothing a hand down her red dress. Low cut in the front, the V showed off her generous cleavage, and the waist nipped in, hugging her figure. Add to that an above-the-knee skirt and red strappy sandals, and she had just found the recipe for turning Asher Knight inside out.

And oh, she liked it.

On the walk through the mansion's dining room and foyer, Gloria pulled herself together, and put the sexy rock god on the back shelf of her mind. She tapped lightly and Sofie opened the door, looking fun and fresh and drop-dead gorgeous.

"Sofie, you're beautiful."

"Thanks!" She beamed. Her wedding dress was a frothy, airy confection, with layers draping to just above her knees thanks to a round baby bump pushing out the front of the dress.

"You are supposed to have a flock of bridesmaids at your beck and call," Gloria said. "Can I get you anything?"

She waved a hand. "No! I'm totally fine. I have something for you, and I didn't want an audience when I gave it to you."

"Something for me?"

"Yes," she said, walking to her desk and bending over a drawer. "I'm sorry I didn't give it to you sooner. It just sort of came to me last night."

Gloria knotted her fingers together, feeling nervous even though she wasn't sure why.

"I feel badly I didn't include you in the wedding." Her brows bent sincerely.

"It's okay." Because it was. Her feelings of being left out were just that, *feelings*.

"It's not. We've gotten closer this year and I feel like we weren't as close before. And I didn't want to burden you with the expense of a dress and I knew since Asher was a groomsman that could get hairy since the two of you weren't...you know."

"Honestly, Sofe. You shouldn't be thinking of this on your wedding day." She was so insanely sweet, Gloria wanted to hug her, but Sofie had already rounded her desk.

"I want to, Glo. Your friendship means a lot to me." Her pretty pink lips lifted.

Gloria couldn't speak around the lump forming in her throat. So she just nodded.

"There's a quirky tradition in my family where lighting the candles represents a fresh start." Sofie pulled open a drawer. "It's a symbol of illuminating the future while burning the past."

"Deep," Gloria said, more nervous than before.

"Yeah, well. My family has a flair for the dramatic." She pulled a stick lighter from the desk drawer. A white one, the handle decorated with roses and ribbon.

Gloria's face fell.

Oh no.

"Sofie..." She took a step back.

"Hear me out." Sofie came out from behind the desk, lighter in hand. "I feel like your fresh start is happening while we all watch. Who would have thought you and Asher after all these years..."

Gloria felt her shoulders tighten. This tradition bespoke of a lot of future and permanence.

"It's meant to be." Sofie grinned and held out the lighter. "Would you do Donovan and me the honor of lighting our wedding candles?"

Gloria's heart cracked. No way could she tell her friend no.

"Of course," she said, then caught Sofie in her arms. She hugged her carefully so as not to crumple her wedding dress.

"Thank you." Sofie's smile was positively radiant as she explained to Gloria that she would walk down the aisle ahead of the bridal party to do the honors.

Gloria nodded, her fingers tight around the lighter, and made it her job to calm down and keep her focus on her friends.

* * *

Gloria had no problem with crowds, or being watched. Walking up the aisle while music played softly in the background was no big *thang*. She pulled her shoulders back, put one foot in front of the other, and walked to the candles at one side of the arch.

You've got this.

The metal stand was painted gold and shaped like a tree, its branches surrounding several taper candles. The three top ones were out of Gloria's reach, but the stick lighter would make up for the lost inches.

The bottom tapers lit, she moved to the center, aware of her posture and the expression on her face since the photographer was snapping away at a distance. She reached the candles on the top row and fired the lighter. The spark flicked, but no flame came out.

Glo, unruffled, inspected the lighter, adjusted the little wheel setting for how high the flame should be, and tried again.

Spark, fizzle.

Hmm.

When she lowered the lighter this time, it was taken out of her hands and replaced with a silver Zippo. She locked eyes with Asher.

"Always be prepared, Sarge."

"Thanks."

But he didn't leave her side. He reached over her head and pulled one of the top tapers down. She opened the lid to the lighter, flicked the wheel, and watched Ash through the flame for a split second. The very man who had set her on fire on more than one occasion—both good and bad—looked back at her.

She'd been determined not to let the symbolism of this moment seep beneath her skin, but with him there, it was impossible. They'd been through too much together.

"Lotta ribbon around here," Ash commented as she lit the taper. He lifted it and carefully wedged the lit candle into the stand. "You want to be tied up with it, we could sneak out of the reception."

"Shh," she said, aware of keeping a smile on her face so the photographer didn't catch her frowning.

"Music's loud. Guys are lined up on the other side of you. Nobody can hear us, Sarge." Except for her, and his naughty suggestion was making her warm. He pulled down taper number two. "We could go back to *our* room in the mansion. The one from last year."

He offered the taper and she flicked the lighter, losing her grip on the wheel when he said, "Like to slip you out of those panties. Thong? Lace. Tell me."

"Asher." The photographer moved in her peripheral, clicking the shutter. She flicked the lighter smoothly this time. A feat considering how distracted she was.

"Don't tell me you're not wearing any or I'm going to

throw you over my shoulder and take you upstairs right now," Asher murmured, unfazed that they were in the middle of a ceremony. "Wedding be damned."

"You can't—" She cleared her very dry throat and kept her voice low. "You can't damn this wedding while we're lighting the fresh-start candles."

His brows pinched. "The what?"

"Tell you later."

He traded out the lit taper for a fresh one—the last one, thank goodness. "You're gonna do a lot of things later, gorgeous."

This time, the lighter's flame bounced off his whiskey-colored eyes. One of which he winked, and Gloria felt her smile go from posed to genuine. God. She loved him.

Loved him in a way she'd never loved anyone in her life. Loved him deep in her soul, in a way that scarred, leaving marks that would never fully disappear.

The thought wiped her smile away. She quickly pasted it back on, lit the taper, and returned Asher's lighter. She'd been trying so hard to keep her feelings to a minimum, to not make any major pronouncements. Not until she was sure she could handle what came with it. Which was what, she didn't even know.

She'd never been in love before. She'd never *allowed* herself to be in love before.

She didn't know what to do with the loving Asher thing. Especially now, in the midst of happily-ever-after dripping from every available chair, table, and person at the wedding.

Asher wasn't done with her. He offered an elbow. "Walk you to your seat."

She looped her arm in his and he sat her in the second row, then returned to his position. The music swelled and the women came to take their spots across from the men. Lacey stood at the matron of honor position across from Alessandre, who looked as dashingly handsome as the other men; Faith was at position two across from Connor; Kinsley had been paired with Asher; and Charlie and Evan stood in the final position.

And then the music shifted.

Gloria wasn't much of a weeper, but seeing Sofie glide down the aisle, the promise of her and Donovan's future rounding the front of her dress, almost did her in. She loved that Sofie didn't try to hide it but instead proudly displayed what was a son or daughter growing in her belly.

But it was Donny who caused Gloria to sniffle, and prompted the woman next to her to push a tissue into Gloria's palm. Donovan had had a hard life, and a harder adulthood. The man was as stoic as they came. But when Sofie came to him in white, her smile bright, it was the groom who looked like he needed a tissue. His eyes glazed with unshed tears; his jaw was clamped tight. And his eyes never once left his bride.

Gloria dabbed her eyes and managed to hold herself together for the remainder of the wedding. After they were introduced as husband and wife, Evan put his fingers to his lips and whistled. Shouts and claps infused the air. Then everyone got down to the business of partying.

The reception was informal—no required wedding party or parental dances. In place of a cake were cupcakes and Devil Dogs from Sugar Hi. A jazz band played from the huge brick patio running the length of the rear of the mansion, and dinner consisted of buffet-style small bites constantly replenished by bustling waitstaff dressed in black.

Gloria lifted a champagne flute off a passing tray and turned to see Charlie, her shoulder-length honey-blond hair done in waves, pink dress hugging all the right places, and shoes off. She was breathing heavy from dancing and smiling so big, Gloria couldn't help but return it.

"Smooth moves, Ace," Glo teased, using Evan's nickname for her.

"Thanks, *Sarge*." Charlie winked. "You were looking pretty cozy nestled against Asher Knight a few songs ago."

Glo sipped her champagne. Asher had asked her to dance to a fast song, kept her spinning until the music slowed, then refused to let her escape. He held her close, his hand in hers and her arm against his chest, his other arm low on her back while she held his neck. They talked, she laughed, and he muttered sexy, delicious things he wanted to do to her later into her ear.

There'd been zero opportunity to sneak into the house with the vigilant waitstaff swarming like an army of ants all over the mansion, so they'd settled for a lot of verbal foreplay and the promise of more later.

"It seems you two have worked things out," Charlie said, still smiling.

"We don't hate each other," Gloria quipped.

"Yeah, but did you ever?"

"No," Gloria admitted. Then mumbled, sort of to herself, "I never hated him." *I only ever loved him. Even before I knew I was avoiding admitting it.*

"Champagne! I'm so jealous!" Faith shook her fists in front of her.

Charlie pointed at Faith's stomach. "I'm jealous of you, mommy-to-be."

Faith pursed her lips. "No luck yet?"

"We're not trying again yet. Practicing"—Charlie waggled her eyebrows—"but not trying."

"You look like you're going to be getting some practice in tonight, too, Glo," Faith teased.

"Oh, well, you know." If Gloria's dress had a collar, she would have tugged it to allow room to swallow around her suddenly swollen throat. Her nerves were jittering and for some reason, her third (or fourth?) glass of champagne was not helping calm them. "I need whiskey," she said, abandoning the flute on a tray as it passed by.

"You'll be fine," Faith said, stepping closer.

"It's just like riding a bike." Charlie huddled in, too, unintentionally making Gloria feel caged in. "And in a few months, or maybe a year"—she tipped her chin at Sofie, who was holding on to Donovan while a guest admired her wedding ring—"that'll be you and Asher."

Time stopped.

Gloria's eyes went to Asher in his tux.

"Mmm-hmm," Faith agreed. "First comes love, then comes marriage, then . . . well, you know how it goes."

Love. Marriage.

Baby.

God.

A baby.

Gloria made a great lay, and as she was learning, a decent girlfriend, but a wife? Or a . . .

"Mom!" Lyon shouted, and Gloria nearly leapt out of her skin.

"Yes, my son," Charlie answered formally.

"Can I stay with Derek tonight?"

"That sounds like a question for your dad," she answered.

"He told me to ask you!" Lyon argued, mouth twisted into a frown of disgust.

"I'll be back," Gloria said to her friends. She made sure to slap a big smile on her face and pray they didn't see how she was really feeling. Half mortified, halfway to an anxiety attack.

Her fear of permanence and future and the idea of being a—*gulp*—mom all came to a head in an instant. Everyone around her had accepted this was a logical next step, but what if Gloria didn't know how to take that step? She had no idea what it was like to stick by someone. Everyone sticking by her made her realize how bad she was at returning the favor. She was better at walking away. Walking was easy. Walking was less painful.

Walking was what she was good at.

"Whiskey," she ordered from a bartender who looked to be about twelve years old.

"Shot or rocks?"

"Shot," she told him, biting her tongue so she didn't order a double. She needed to calm down, not start dancing on the tables. And she needed to think through the rather rash decision she'd made this morning.

This morning when Brice McGuire called her cell phone.

"Good morning, Heels," he'd said when she answered. She knew what he wanted. He wanted her answer about Chicago. And he didn't hesitate to let her know if she didn't accept, he would begin the hunt for her replacement.

Gloria, feeling smug, hadn't hesitated when she turned him down. The prospect of Chicago had dangled in front of her, tempting, for several weeks. In a way, Chicago had become her escape hatch. If she couldn't hack the Cove and Asher and life in general, she had options.

But then last night, Asher had kissed her in the bar in front of all their friends, and afterward, those same friends rallied around her on her grandmother's couch with hugs and laughter and for the first time in her life, she no longer felt like having a plan B.

The Cove had finally opened its arms, and her three girl-friends who lived here and had hunks of their own had opened theirs. And Asher not only loved her, but also needed her. And he was staying.

Gloria was home.

At least that's where her head was this morning. But she hadn't looked farther into the future than a few days...a few months. Now that she'd sealed her escape hatch, she felt...trapped.

The kid put the shot glass on the bar top. Gloria fished a dollar out of her clutch, plunked it in his tip jar, and threw the liquor back in one burning swallow.

"Hey, now it's a party," Asher approached, hands in his pants pockets. Then he caught her expression, which must have been dismayed because next, his smile fell. He pulled a hand from his pocket to touch her lower back. "Sarge, you okay?"

"Brice called," she blurted.

Asher's face scrunched.

"He offered me Chicago."

Asher's eyes went to the empty shot glass, then back to her.

"I told him no," she said, tucking her clutch under her arm.

"Good." He still looked confused and it was no wonder. She wasn't making much sense. "I want you here. With us."

Us.

God. She could puke. She blinked a few times, feeling

the burn of tears again—but this time not because she was emotional over the wedding. No, this time, it was because she was overwhelmed by how many things—how many *people*—she would need to make room for in her life. Gloria could barely handle herself. This was not good.

She sucked in a breath. "Can we leave?" They drove together. She knew that'd been a mistake. Now she was stranded.

Asher's eyebrows dropped so low, his eyes were barely visible through narrowed lashes. He girded his anger with a deep breath and tipped his head toward the side yard. "Over there."

"No," she said, then pointed to the valet waiting nearby. "Over *there*."

"Sarge."

"Asher."

He crowded her, putting his lips on her ear. "I will absolutely throw you over my shoulder in front of every one of these people."

"You would not," she breathed, angry and slightly exhilarated at the thought—a reaction that confused her as much as everything else about how she reacted to him.

His warm palm splayed over her hip. "Try me," he said into her ear, then drew away to peg her with a scarily serious glare.

She decided not to try him. Her dress was really short.

Turning, she made her way around the side of the mansion, through the yard, and across the cobblestone. On the other side of the garage, a huge oak tree offered privacy and shade.

"Let's hear it," Asher said, calmly advancing, hands in his pockets.

"Hear what? I'm just ready to go."

"That's one."

"One what?" She was fuming now.

"One slap on the ass for every lie you tell me."

Her mouth dropped open. "You can't threaten me, Asher Knight. I—"

"Now that I have you good and pissed off, care to tell me what you're running from?"

"I'm not running!"

"Two." The rage was gone...or maybe it'd transferred to her. He looked completely collected and in control of his faculties.

A low growl left her throat. Asher wasn't wavering, and he wasn't his happy, easy, jokey self. He was thoroughly serious.

"Our friends were married today, Glo."

"I know that," she mumbled, resisting the urge to grind the tip of her shoe into the grass. Was he trying to point out she was being selfish?

"Their reception is going on as we speak. I'm taking the mic in a few minutes to sing 'Unchained.'"

Of course he was. Asher would trot out any act his friends asked, because that's the kind of guy he was. Bad boy. Good man.

"I only have a few minutes, so you cooperating instead of being a pain in the ass would be helpful," he said.

"I'm not a pain in the ass!"

"Three." He let loose a weary smile. "Sarge. Out with it."

She swallowed, feeling overwhelmed and too warm, even standing in the shade of the tree, a breeze blowing. She adjusted the clutch under her arm, fiddled with the rings on her fingers, and decided how best to tell him how full her head was. How full her heart was. How everyone and everything lining up was beginning to feel like she was smothering beneath a ten-ton mattress.

Instead, she blurted, "I can't do this."

His head jerked like he'd been slapped. "What *this*?"

"*This* this." She lifted her arms and dropped them helplessly. "Us, Ash. My God! Sofie and her stupid fresh-start candles."

"What's wrong with that?" Now he looked angry. Earlier when they were dancing and Gloria explained what the symbolism was for, he looked happy. Which was the point. Asher needed to be happy. What if she couldn't make him happy?

"I don't know what I'm doing! I see everyone settling down, pairing up. Having"—she swallowed thickly and eked out the word—"families. I'm going to fail but this time it won't just be me in the wreckage. I can handle being in the wreckage. I've put myself together more times than I can count." She swallowed past another thick ball of emotion. "I won't take you down with me, Asher. I won't take Hawk down with me. Trust me, you don't want to risk—"

He cut her off with a kiss. His lips were so gentle, her eyes closed. He held his mouth over hers for a few lingering seconds and then pulled away. "Is there a time you're ever not in your head, Sarge?"

"Yes," she breathed.

"By my count"—he lifted his knuckles to her cheek—"You're up to eight."

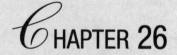HAPTER 26

*S*he was scared. He could see the fear on her face, broadcast from the worried sea of blue in her eyes. He could see it in her goddamn body language. Gloria stood, knees pressed together, shoulders under her ears. Like if she let go of the control strung through her body like cables, she'd collapse.

His girl.

She wasn't in full-on meltdown mode, but she was close. He wasn't going to let her get away with this, not any of it.

"I screwed up," he said.

Her eyebrows lifted into her black bangs.

"When I met you, I thought for sure you and I were gonna burn hot and heavy a few times and then fizzle out."

The first time he'd laid eyes on the curvy, modern-day pinup girl, his cock had stood on end. When she'd put that soft palm in his and introduced herself, he'd sent Evan a sideways glance that asked, *How have you not begged this one to go to bed with you yet?*

"I knew your type," he continued. "Businesswoman looking for a tumble with a guy she didn't have to commit to. I figured you were off a bad relationship or a marriage. Needed a rebound. I knew you didn't have kids, which also made you perfect for me."

He had her attention. Blue eyes held his and he just kept right on going.

"You liked me. Stroked my ego and stroked my cock and sucked it, too, and all of that worked for me." Once he'd dug beneath the outer layer of Gloria, he learned there was a whole lot more to her than he'd assumed. Smart. Sassy. Shrewd. And just a little broken. Then she'd shown her vulnerability dressed up like haughty anger, and he'd let her scare him off.

"I screwed up," he repeated, "when I let you go. You came at me with all this sass and the sharpest, barbed accusations I've ever heard, and I didn't fight for you. I thought to myself, 'Who needs the trouble?' Because I've long been a big proponent of easy."

Sadness crept in as the fear crept out. That was it. Her biggest fear. That she was too much trouble for anyone to love. He'd learned that about her and had baited her to this very point.

"Sarge, I love that you don't give me easy. I can be lazy. I can be careless. I can be self-focused. You force me to be other things. You force me to care too much about everything. About everyone. You challenge me and you don't even mean to. I didn't feel bad about taking a groupie backstage between sets until I met you. Then I only thought of you and what I was missing—what you gave me when we were together. What you gave me, baby...I can't get that anywhere else."

Her eyes were trained on his, and she was struck completely dumb by his speech. And he still had more to say. He stepped closer and brushed her smooth, porcelain cheek with his knuckles.

"No one makes me want like I want when I'm with you. You make me crazy in the best way possible. Never planned on getting married or settling down. When I was hit with the news about Hawk, the first thing I thought after the initial shock of having a kid wore off was that I'd lose you. I knew it'd hurt too much for you to have to see him knowing that Jordan and I made him. And I also knew I wouldn't walk out on my son. That I had to make up for lost time and that I had a long road ahead. That put me at your mercy. The big test of keeping you or not was outta my hands. You'd either stay with me in spite of how hurt you were, or you'd bail."

"A test I just failed," she said, her voice barely a whisper.

"Nine," he whispered back, then smiled. "I underestimated you yet again. Should've known you were tough enough to handle Hawk. To handle Jordan. Hell, you showed up and put a dent in her ass the second you thought she was doing us wrong."

A tiny smile tipped the corners of her lips. She was trying.

"You won't take me down, Sarge. You're too busy standing up for me." He moved his palm to the side of her neck, sliding his hand through her hair and pressing his fingertips into her nape. "You have changed my entire world, do you know that? And I get that you're scared. Hell, I'm scared. I've never done this before. I've never been a dad. I've never tried to have a relationship that was remotely normal. And you... Your mom bailed, your grandma died, and you're so terrified to trust anyone—to trust yourself, that you figure you should get out while the gettin's good. And the shit of it is, every foster family, every guy you've pulled this crap on in the past, has let you go." He nodded and added on another painful truth, "Me included."

Her delicate throat worked as she swallowed. He ran his fingers down to her necklace—a thin gold chain with a heart on the end. Then along the low-cut neck of her fire-engine-red dress. He loved her in red.

He just loved her, period.

"I'm not letting you go again," he said.

"You can't know I won't screw everything up."

He wedged two fingers into her cleavage, grabbed hold of the center of her bra, and dragged her close.

"I know," he said. His lips were almost touching hers and he smelled the slightest hint of whiskey on her breath.

"*I* can't know that," she whispered.

"You have to try." Before he could breach the minute distance between them and kiss her, Connor's voice came from behind him.

"Ash! You're on, man!"

He held a thumb overhead to let Connor know he heard him.

"Time to play famous, Sarge," he told her, leaving her tempting mouth in favor of stepping back. He extracted his fingers from her dress without sliding to the left or right to tweak a nipple, and for that show of self-control, he deserved a medal. "Do me a favor."

"What?" She adjusted her low neckline, then tucked her purse beneath her arm.

"Love me."

Her lips dropped open with a sharp intake of breath.

He took another step back. Toward the stage, toward their friends. Toward their future, if she chose to accept it.

"That's it," he said. "Everything will work out, but you have to commit to that one thing."

He turned and walked away when what he wanted to do was grab her hand and drag her with him. But Gloria didn't need to be dragged. He may be good at pushing her, but if they were going to make this work, the next step she took would have to be toward him.

* * *

Asher tuned his guitar, pausing to grin and say, "Dodgy F," into the microphone. The slightly boozed up crowd snickered.

Gloria stood among them, equally rapt with the man on-stage. The man who had made the simplest of requests. *Love me.* She watched him walk away from her, from the lawn to the cobblestone, until he vanished around the back of the house.

And then she followed.

Chairs were scattered on the patio and now people sat, cocktails in hand. The sun had just tucked behind the trees and bulbs on strings were laced overhead, giving the entire outside patio a relaxed feel. Almost everyone who attended the wedding had stayed to hear Asher, her included.

Asher Knight: resident rock god, children's book author, and man who had just committed to never leave her. She didn't know what to do with that. What to do with him. Yet here she was.

"Ah, there we go," he said when the chord struck true. A few soft chuckles sounded from the crowd. Asher, the entertainer.

He turned to the jazz band behind him and gave a few instructions and then started to play "Unchained."

A hush fell over the crowd as his voice cut in—perfect and soothing. Rasping and rough. He was a star, and he was meant to be one. Gloria had felt that same charge of charisma the first time she'd laid eyes on him.

I knew your type. Businesswoman looking for a tumble with a guy she didn't have to commit to.

He was half correct. She hadn't been looking for a tumble with a client, but when she'd laid eyes on Asher, her rules fell away. The rest of *the world* fell away.

He sang the line about being connected. Feeling rejected.

A lump formed in her throat.

I didn't fight for you.

She didn't fight for him either. He was right about everything he said about her. She'd accused him and made things hard.

I'm not letting you go again.

He was right about the fear that had carved a hole in her heart, too. The plain fact of the matter was that no one had fought for her. Until now. Asher had made one simple request.

Love me.

She'd never had anyone ask her to love them. She'd been told "I love you" before from guys wanting something or thinking that those three words would soften her. When Asher had admitted he loved her, he didn't ask her to say it back.

He didn't even say it today during his big speech.

He'd simply asked her to love him.

The thing about it was, she did love him. She'd loved him for a really long time and was only now just admitting it to herself. And she loved Hawk. She loved Asher's mother, too, and guessed after she got to know his dad better, she'd love him, as well. She'd caved the other night when her girl-friends from the Cove wrapped her in their arms. She loved every last one of them.

"You're still here."

Donovan, dressed in a black T-shirt and jeans, leaned a shoulder against the wall of his mansion. Yeah, that tux hadn't lasted long. His eyes were on Asher but sifted down to hers in a way that she felt dwarfed. Well, more dwarfed. The man was damn near six-and-a-half feet tall.

"Did you think I wouldn't be?" she quipped.

A small grunt that could have been a laugh followed the murmured, "You're braver than me. I'm a runner."

Gloria turned to face him, gesturing to the gold band on his ring finger. "You didn't get very far."

"She didn't let me."

"Smart girl."

They shared a smile. The thing about Donovan was, he and Glo had a lot in common. Raised by not-so-great parents—hers neglected her, and his father beat him—and facing their own demons about loving the people around them. Maybe that's why she confided in him just now.

"Does it get easier?" she asked.

"Yeah. It does. It's dropping the armor the first time that hurts like a bitch." He shrugged his mouth. "Then, after, it gets easier."

Her gaze tracked back to Asher.

"He's so gone for you, it's embarrassing," Donovan said, and when Gloria turned to him, he laughed. The smile lit his pale eyes and made him look approachable and warm. Beneath that concrete exterior he'd brought back to town, she guessed this side of him had always been there.

"He asked me to love him," she said, her cheeks going rosy with embarrassment.

"Do you?"

She sliced him a glare. "Of course."

"Yeah, thought so." He pushed away from the wall at the same time Sofie appeared on the porch, wearing a simple black dress. "Jeep's packed, Scampi."

"Thanks, baby." Sofie stretched up and kissed him, then gave Gloria a quick hug. "Thanks for lighting the candles."

"You bet." And now her eyes were burning.

Sofie hopped onto the porch and was promptly accosted by hugs.

"Whatever you do"—Donovan's gaze slid back to Gloria—"don't be so tough you miss out on the good, Sarge." He smiled at his bride, happiness saturating the air around him. "And trust me, you don't wanna miss it."

"Yeah, yeah. Go ride off in your coach, Prince Pate." She was playing off the tender moment, and he saw right through her. But he let her have it, leaning in to kiss her forehead in a rare display of physical affection before literally sweeping Sofie off her feet and into his arms.

"Gotta go," he announced to the crowd as his wife giggled and hugged his neck.

"Bye, everyone!" Sofie called.

"Where are you going?" Faith asked.

"Not telling," Donny said, halfway to the Jeep.

He was the perfect yin to Sofie's yang. Rough where she was sweet, forceful where she was careful. Their deep love for each other radiated in a wide arc around them. They'd been through hell together, and it had only made them stronger. Iron was forged in fire, after all.

"Grab those bags of rice, people," Asher ordered into the

microphone. "Mr. and Mrs. Pate aren't leaving here without getting pelted!"

The patio emptied, everyone going to one of two baskets filled with organza bags of rice. The white grains fell like confetti, sticking in Sofie's dark hair, dotting Donovan's black T-shirt, and pinging off the Jeep's shiny black hood as he reversed down the cobblestone drive.

And then they were off, leaving the mansion and friends behind.

Gloria's eyes brimmed with tears. It was beautiful. The entire journey. And she didn't miss the way her mind had strayed from Donny and Sofie's journey and focused on hers and Asher's.

Little by little, guests made their ways to their cars, waving good-bye and saying "nice to meet you" to new friends and acquaintances. The band packed up as well, chatting with Asher as they did.

Connor stepped out of the mansion as the caterer stepped in, Gertie at his side on a leash, a giant bag of dog food balanced in his arm.

"Guess I know where Gertie is staying during the honeymoon," Gloria said as Faith followed him out, a bag over her arm that Glo guessed was filled with treats and toys. Soon, Gertie wouldn't be an only child and she wondered how the pooch would feel about sharing her parents.

She bent to pet the dog and stood, her pulse kicking into high gear when she heard Asher right beside her.

"Key," he said.

"Oh, right." Connor dug into his front pocket and handed over a key. "Skeleton. Fits everywhere."

"Thanks." Asher tucked it into his pocket. "I'll check every room."

"'Preciate it," Connor said. "I have to get my wife home. And our new dog." He scrubbed Gertie's head and she smiled up at them all, tongue lolling.

Asher and Gloria said good night and watched as Connor and Faith loaded their temporary canine into the back of his Mustang, which would take them to the cottage on the back acreage of what used to be part of Donovan's estate but was now Connor's.

"You're checking every room?" Glo asked as she and Asher walked across the back patio.

"Can't have someone passed out in the library and wake to find themselves trapped in the mansion, now, can I?"

"No, I guess not. I'll help."

"Not yet." Asher clasped her hand and then grabbed his guitar. He led Gloria to one of the white plastic chairs on the patio, dipped his chin in an order for her to sit. She did. Then he took a chair across from her, played a few chords on his guitar, and said, "I'm calling your song 'Fated.'"

Then he launched into the song he wrote about her. The one he sang to her while he sat on her grandmother's couch, then stayed the night with her. Some of the lyrics had changed to include skinny-dipping in the moonlight, passing out on the beach, and breakfast in bed. The last line was *"We were always fated to be, you were meant for me,"* and Ash sang it looking right at her.

He strummed the guitar one final time, then peered up, chin down, eyebrows raised. He looked good in his tux. He looked clean and simple and like a man she could easily love for the rest of her life.

"Well?" He was asking for her opinion on the song, but what she gave was her answer to something else entirely.

Love me.

"I already do," she whispered.

In the light cast from the strings of bulbs overhead, she could see in his eyes he knew exactly what she meant. There was a fire burning in there, bright and hot. And solely focused on her.

Then, while she watched, that look of heat faded into pissed off.

"I'm adding one," he growled. "For saying something that fucking sweet when I have a thirty-five-room mansion to check before I can get you naked and under me."

She bit her lip.

"Adding one more for that cute look you're giving me." His eyebrow tilted.

Gloria grinned.

"One more for being cocky. And you're helping." He abandoned his guitar on a chair, took her hand, and walked inside. They checked the mansion, first floor and second, room by room. By the time they ended up in the last room down the hall, Asher smashed his mouth into hers, stripping her of her little red dress like he'd promised earlier.

He also delivered every slap to her ass as promised. She knew, because she counted each one.

Aloud.

$\mathcal{C}$HAPTER 27

$\mathcal{E}$ndless Avenue was quiet for a Tuesday afternoon. Gloria figured it was because most vacationers had gone home after the weekend. Hand in hand, she and Asher walked down the sidewalk, away from Torsett & Torsett—Scott Torsett's office. The lawyer had drawn up the paperwork for the custody agreement, and Jordan and Asher had just signed it.

"How do you feel?" Glo asked.

"Relieved. I get to have Hawk every other week." Until he started school, and then Jordan and Asher had agreed they'd reevaluate. Hawk needed as much permanence as possible and they were doing what was best for him. That suggestion had come from Emily, who'd also been present, no surprise there. What had surprised Gloria was when Emily approached her, thanked her for being so good with Hawk, and then apologized for the way she'd treated her in the past.

Gloria had accepted the apology, of course, saying she only wanted what was best for Hawk. Emily stated that she agreed, then went to the table and sat with Jordan, where she allowed the meeting to go forth without a single peep of interference. Gotta love the country club type. Emily did have a sense of decorum.

Asher's cell rang, bringing Glo back to the present.

"Yeah?" he answered, then smiled at Gloria. "Fantastic news. Send it my way. I'll look it over." He ended the call and pocketed the cell. Then he dragged Gloria by the hand to her office and instructed, "Open up."

"Okay, okay…" She pulled her keys from her purse and unlocked the door. The moment they stepped foot inside, Asher flipped that same lock and moved around the room, shutting the blinds.

"What's happening?" she asked with a laugh. Since the Pate wedding two months ago, she and Asher had been adhered to each other's sides. Glo had even flown to LA with him to help him decide which pieces of furniture to keep or sell. They'd gone round and round about a red couch in the shape of a giant pair of lips. Asher said he didn't need it; Glo insisted it reminded her of the Rolling Stones and that it would break every rule in the rock star handbook if he didn't feature the piece prominently in his cabin.

She won that argument.

Last week, she'd convinced him and Evan to write another series. *The Adventures of Mad Cow and Swine Flu* may have come to an end, but there was a definite fan favorite in Chicken Pox. Glo had plans for that hen. Old girl needed her own spin-off series where she could get into hijinks with some other animal…Cat Scratch Fever, maybe? Evan and Asher hadn't figured out the details yet, but they would. They were the dynamic duo when it came to this stuff.

Developing a routine with Asher and Hawk had been something of a revelation for her. She hadn't ever imagined herself playing with a three-year-old, and further, could never have imagined herself exclusively dating anyone—let alone Asher Knight.

He returned to her when the last of the blinds were closed. The entire room was muted gray, blocking out the late autumn sunlight. He kissed her, moving his hands to her back to hold her tight.

"Mmm," she hummed when he pulled away. "Are you intending to have sex with me on my desk?"

"Duh," he answered.

She laughed. It was fun to be in love. She'd decided not to miss the good stuff. Donovan was right.

"That must have been some good-news phone call," she said, raking her fingers through Asher's hair.

"That was my Realtor. She has an offer for my house in LA."

"Good one?"

He shrugged. "Don't care. I want it sold."

"You need to talk to your accountant, Ash." She arched a scolding eyebrow.

"I only need to talk to you."

She blinked. He looked so serious. Why wasn't he mauling her? Shouldn't they be having celebratory desk sex?

"Gloria Shields." His hands traveled down her back and he hugged her close.

Oh no. Her heart tripled in speed. This felt big...and scary. Asher grinned. A bad sign.

"Sarge." He lifted her and plopped her ass on her desk.

"You're going to get mushy, aren't you?" she asked as he cupped her face in his hands. "I can't handle it."

"Yeah, you can." He brushed his nose over hers.

"Let's just—"

"I wrote you a song. I moved to the Cove. I pushed my way into your apartment, your life, your heart." This was starting to sound like a speech. A confession. Goose bumps broke out on her skin.

"You did," she admitted. He was taking up so much residence in her life right now, she would feel lost without him.

"What do you want?" He moved his hands to her shoulders.

She felt her eyebrows close in. "What do you mean?"

"From me. What do you want?"

"I...Nothing."

"Not true. There's something you need. Something you want. You're gonna tell me what it is and I'm gonna stand here until you do."

She didn't doubt it. He looked comfortable standing there. Waiting. *Looming.*

"Aside from coffee in the morning and great sex at night, there's nothing else I need," she said, attempting to lighten the thick air between them.

He shook his head. "Try again."

"Okay." She let out an exasperated sigh. "I guess... staying with you is nice."

"You mean in the dream house you once fantasized of buying and growing old in?"

"I never said growing old!" she argued, her lips pulling into a pout.

He stayed silent, waiting for her to continue.

She fiddled with the cross around his neck. "I like having an automatic date for things like weddings and summer concerts..."

He nodded again.

"What about your office?" he asked of the very room they stood in.

"It's okay," she said. "Not ideal."

"What's ideal?"

She stopped playing with his necklace and rested a palm on his chest. His firm, delicious chest covered by a thin gray T-shirt. "A better view."

"Woods?" His hands slid from her arms to her hips.

She nodded, feeling suddenly shy. Exposed.

"Water?" He moved his hands to her thighs.

She nodded again.

"Beach?" he asked, his expression going serious, his voice low and intimate. "Dock?" With a smile added, "Giant lips-shaped couch in the living room?"

"Yes to all," she whispered.

"There's more."

How could there be more? The offer to share his home—on a more permanent than a here-and-there basis—was almost everything.

His hands moved to her ribs over her blouse and she squirmed under his warm palms. "You could take my name."

She quit breathing.

"Take my ring and a vow that lasts until our time on this planet stops." He pushed his hands under her shirt, his fingers tickling the bare skin of her back. His eyes burned into hers, filled to overflowing with love. And it was all for her.

She felt her lips curve into a shaky smile.

"There she is," he muttered, smiling back at her. "Love me?"

She nodded.

"Need to hear it," he said with a slight headshake.

"I do!" she barked. "I just…feel silly blurting it out."

"Sarge."

"Asher." She rolled her eyes. "Fine, I love you."

"Prove it. Marry me." He grinned.

A sharp gasp was the only thing between them. That was her. Trying to catch her breath. Trying to regulate her heart, which was galloping for the hills right about now.

"No one makes a better team than we do. You can be my wife, be Hawk's stepmom. Be the daughter my parents are thrilled they never had to rear through teenage years."

Oh, she wanted all of that. But wasn't it too much all at once? Moving in, marriage, being a stepparent…maybe being a real parent in the future. Yeah, she was going to hyperventilate.

"God, I'm scared," she admitted in a dry whisper.

"Don't be scared. You're marrying a Knight." His brow lifted and his lips formed a cocky smile.

"I didn't say yes yet," she said, eyes narrowing to block out his insanely attractive face.

"Yeah, you did."

"Well, then where's my ring?" She folded her arms, teasing him now, which she knew he expected

"There's a jeweler on Endless Avenue." Asher took both her hands in his and helped her off the desk.

"Do you ever plan ahead for anything?" Her knees shook as she followed him. He couldn't be serious.

He gestured her out the door and, still smiling, locked the office behind them. She hadn't even seen him swipe her keys. He threaded their fingers together and led her down the block. "It's across from Cup of Jo's, right? Want to get a coffee first?"

How could he be so casual? At her alarmed expression, he grinned. A few steps later, she froze on the sidewalk, mind whirring and blood rushing to her toes. Their arms stretched straight between them and her mind flashed back to one warm summer night on the beach, seconds before he led her inside and made love to her on the bathroom floor.

What are you doing?

Making you want it, honey.

He stopped walking and turned to face her.

"My God. You did it." She went to him, steps slow, her eyes on his and her heart in her throat.

"Did what?" A gusty breeze kicked the dark hair off his forehead. His brown eyes twinkled in the sunlight. Above his shadowed jaw, his lips flinched.

"You made me want it." Amazing. Years and years of practice at not allowing herself to want things, at denying herself connections and relationships... "You made me want you," she said. "A future. A son. A...husband. You made me want to love you. You made me want it all."

"Only fair, Sarge." Keeping hold of her hand, he towed her close and dropped a kiss onto her mouth. "You made me want it first."

She kissed him again and he returned it with enthusiasm—so much of it, she was vaguely aware of a passerby clearing his throat. Asher lifted his lips from hers and smiled.

Together they walked to the Cove's premiere jewelry store, Treasure Trove, and he picked out the biggest diamond ring they had in the place. Of course, Gloria argued and picked one with a few less carats. Asher argued back, and the clerk excused himself to give them a minute.

Gloria explained to him she didn't need a ring to knock against her desk or countertops, or one that would be in the way while she was chasing Hawk.

She didn't need a ring at all.

But she wanted it.

EPILOGUE

"I'm not sure I should go," Gloria mumbled around her toothbrush. She leaned forward, spit into one of the double sinks, then toweled off her mouth.

"Sarge, since when was you not going an option?" Asher hoisted an eyebrow, swiping the last of the shaving cream from his neck with a towel.

"I just want to be extra super double sure that it's okay." She dropped her toothbrush in a drawer and shut it, regarding his reflection dubiously.

A sexy smile tilted the side of his mouth before he turned toward her. The damn charmer.

He backed her across the bathroom to the open door; then his palm went to her belly, still blessedly flat thanks to her watching every single thing she put into her mouth. No coffee. No Brie. No fish. No food dyes. No preservatives of any kind...Mostly she ate organic fruits and veggies, while making sure she was taking her vitamins as the doctor ordered.

"Doc said a rock concert isn't going to be bad for the baby," Asher said, his warm palm moving from her stomach to her breast. "This is our kid we're talking about. He's going to attend a lot of rock concerts if I'm his old man."

"I know." She offered a pout.

"I wouldn't recommend you join the mosh pit in the front or anything…"

"A mosh pit," she said, her tone flat and disbelieving. "At Evergreen Cove's Starving Artist Festival."

"It could happen. I'm that good." Cocksure and sexy and yeah, he was that good.

"Billboard Top 100 good," she agreed.

Last summer, "Fated," the song he'd written for her, shot up the charts like a rocket set to Mars. Then there was the tour—which had included Broderick since he'd pulled his head out of his ass. Then a wedding—Gloria and Asher's—and then they had taken it easy over the winter and spent it lounging on their red sofa in front of the new fireplace Donny built for them as a wedding gift.

When she found out about the bun in the oven, Asher decided to focus on his children's book career because he didn't want to miss a single second of Gloria's pregnancy. He'd been especially excited about the ultrasound—they both had. Seeing that heartbeat…the baby they'd created. It was one of the most amazing moments of her life. Their lives.

"We have a few minutes before we have to pick up Hawk." Hands on his hips, his eyes went dark and molten the way they did before he stripped her bare and made her scream his name. Pregnancy hadn't changed that. If anything, it'd increased his chances. She had enough hormones to rival an entire bus full of teenagers.

He lowered her to the bed and she complied, but not before issuing the challenge of, "What if a few minutes isn't enough?"

"Then we'll be a few minutes late."

She wrapped her arms around her husband's neck and gave in to the happy. She'd been doing that a lot lately. After fighting it for so long, she figured she was due a little wallowing. He made it easy to wallow, to get wrapped up in what they were doing and completely lose track of everything but the two of them.

They were a few minutes late to pick up Hawk, but Asher hit the stage on time. He sang "Fated" directly to Gloria, while she and Hawk sang it back to him as loudly and badly as they possibly could. There was a moment Ash broke in the middle of the song and laughed through the verse, and that was a moment Gloria tucked into her heart to keep there for all eternity.

Because this? *This* was what mattered.

Not the past. Not old barrel couches. Not the hurt that people dealt out when they didn't mean to. Just Hawk's small hand warming hers and the promise of a new life and many sleepless nights in her belly. And Asher, of course. Without him, she'd have a radically different—and much emptier—life.

Asher Knight, who stood in front of a microphone on a plywood stage in the center of Evergreen Cove. Asher Knight, who strummed the last note of "Fated," grinned ear to ear, and sent Gloria Knight his patented rock-god wink.

A Recipe from
the Desk of Jessica Lemmon

Asher Knight's Green Rock God Smoothie

Because sexy rock gods can't survive on whiskey and gummy bears alone.

Ingredients:

- ½ green apple, cored and cubed
- 1 banana, peeled and cut into slices
- 1 rib of celery, cut into chunks
- 2 teaspoons of fresh lemon juice
- 2 handfuls fresh spinach
- water
- honey, to taste

Directions:

Blend apple, banana, celery, lemon juice, and enough water to make the shake smooth.

Add spinach to the blender a handful at a time, adding more water until you reach desired consistency.

Add honey to taste.

Enjoy.

Merina Van Heusen will do anything to keep her parents' boutique hotel in business— even marry cold-as-ice but hot-as-hell billionaire bachelor Reese Crane. It's a simple business deal: six months of marriage, absolute secrecy, and the Van Heusen is all hers again. But Merina never expected to fall in love with her husband...

Please see the next page
for an excerpt from

The Billionaire Bachelor

CHAPTER 1

The Van Heusen Hotel was the love of Merina Van Heusen's life. The historical building dominated the corner of Rush and East Chicago Avenue, regal and beautiful, a living work of art.

Her parents' hotel had once been the Bell Terrace, home away from home to celebrities such as Audrey Hepburn, Sammy Davis Jr., and, more recently, Lady Gaga and the late Robin Williams. The original structure perished in the Chicago fires, only to be resurrected bigger, better, and more beautiful.

There was a life lesson in there.

After the last heir from the Bell family died (roughly forty-some years ago), the hotel fell into disrepair. Enter a couple of dreamers a decade later: Merina's newly engaged parents and their fresh-eyed vision of restoring the Bell Terrace to its original glory. Jolie and Mark Van Heusen fell in love in this city and revived the hotel, their focus on preserving every meaningful nick and dent—right down to the table where James Dean scrawled his signature with a knife in the Bell Terrace Restaurant.

Latte in hand, Merina breathed in the air in the lobby, the scent a mix of vanilla and cinnamon. Faint, but reminiscent of the famed dessert invented right here back in the 1800s: the snickerdoodle. On her way past Arnold, who stood checking someone into the hotel, she snagged one of the fresh-baked cookies off a plate and winked at him.

The dark-skinned older man slid her a smile and winked an eye at her. Having practically grown up here, the VH was her second home. Arnold had started out as a bellman and worked here for as long she could remember. He was as good as family.

She dumped her purse in her office, finished her cookie, but held on to the latte while she meandered down the hallways, checking to make sure there were no trays outside the doors that needed collecting. At the end of the corridor on the first floor, she saw a man outside one of the rooms, drill whirring away.

"Excuse me," she called. Then had to call again to be heard over the sound. When she came into view, he paused the drilling and looked up at her.

He wore a tool belt and navy uniform, and the antique doorknob was sitting on the floor at his feet along with a small pile of sawdust.

"What are you doing?" she asked, bending to pick up the heavy brass. Her parents had done away with "real keys" the moment they took over, installing the popular keycard entry hotels now used. The uniformed man removed that next and dropped it at his feet. From his pocket, he pulled out a small silver pad with a black opening.

"Installing the fingerprint entry," he answered, then went back to drilling.

"No, no, no." She placed the doorknob back on the ground and dusted her hand on her skirt. "We're not doing any fingerprint entry." She offered a patient smile. "You need to double-check your work order."

He gave her a confused look.

"Ma'am?" He was looking at Merina, but his voice was raised.

Merina's mother, Jolie, appeared from behind the door, and her eyebrows rose into hair that used to be the same honey-eyed shade of blond as Merina's but now was more blond to hide the gray.

"Oh, Merina!" Her mother smiled, but it looked a little pained.

"Can you give me a minute with my daughter, Gary?" Like she was Gary's mother, Jolie fished a five-dollar bill from her pocket and pressed it into his palm. "Go to the restaurant and have Sharon make you a caramel macchiato. You won't be sorry."

Gary frowned but took the cash. Merina shook her head as he walked away.

What is going on?

"Sweetheart." Jolie offered another smile. A tight-lipped one meaning there was bad news. Like when Merina's cat Sherwood had been hit by a car and Jolie had to break it to her. "Come in. Sit." She popped open the door and Merina entered the guest room, another beloved part of this hotel.

White duvets and molded woodwork, modern flat-screen televisions and artwork. Red, gold, and deep orange accents added to the richness of the palette and were meant to show that a fire may have taken down the original building but couldn't keep it down.

Jolie gestured to the chair by the desk. Merina refused to sit.

"Mom. What's going on?"

On the end of a sigh that didn't make her feel any better, her mother spoke.

"Several changes have been ordered for the Van Heusen in order to modernize it. Fingerprint entry is one of them. Also, the elevators will be replaced."

"Why?" Merina pictured the gold decorative doors with a Phoenix emblazoned on them and her stomach turned.

Instead of answering, Jolie continued. "Then there's the carpeting. The tapestry design won't fit in with the new scheme. And probably the molding and ceiling medallions will all be replaced." She sighed. "It's a new era."

"When did you take to day-drinking?" Merina asked, only half kidding.

Her mother laughed, but it was brief and her smile faded almost instantly. She touched Merina's arm gently. "Sweetheart. We were going to tell you, but we wanted to make sure there really was no going back. I didn't expect the locksmith to arrive today." Her eyes strayed to the door.

Merina's patience fizzled. "Tell me."

"Your father and I sold the Van Heusen to Alexander Crane six months ago. At the time, he had no plans on making any changes at all, but now that he's retiring, the hotel has fallen to his oldest son. Evidently, Reese had a different idea."

At that pronouncement, Jolie's normally sunny attitude clouded over. Merina knew the Cranes. Crane Hotel was the biggest corporate hotel outfit in the city, the second biggest

AN EXCERPT FROM THE BILLIONAIRE BACHELOR   379

in the nation. Alexander (better known as "Big Crane") and his sons ran it, local celebrities of sorts. She'd also read about Big Crane's retirement and Reese's ascension.

But none of that mattered. There was only one newly learned fact bouncing around in her brain. "You sold the Van Heusen?"

She needed that chair after all. She sank into it, mind blanking of everything except for one name: Reese Crane.

"Why didn't you tell me?" Merina stood up again. She couldn't sit. She could not remain still while this was happening. Correction: this *had* happened. "Why didn't you talk to me first?"

"You know we'd never include you in our financial difficulties, Merina." Jolie clucked her tongue.

Financial difficulties?

"Bankruptcy was not an option," Jolie said. "Plus, selling gave us the best of both worlds. No financial responsibility and we get to keep our jobs."

"With Reese Crane as your boss!" Her mind spun after she said it aloud. My God. Would they all be answering to that arrogant, idiotic . . . "No." Merina strode past her mother. "This is a mistake."

And there had to be a way to undo it.

"Merina!" her mother called after her as Merina bent and collected the discarded doorknob. She strode through the lobby, dumping the remainder of her latte in the wastebasket by the front desk, and then stomped outside.

As luck would have it, the light drizzle picked up the second she marched through the crosswalk. Angry as she was, she'd bet that steam rose off her body where the raindrops pelted her.

"That stupid, smarmy jackass!" she said as she cut through

a small crowd of people hustling through the crosswalk. Because seriously, who in their right mind would reconstruct the Van Heusen? Fingerprint entry? This wasn't a James Bond movie! She caught a few sideways glances, but it was hard to tell if it was because she was muttering to herself like a loopy homeless person or carrying a disembodied doorknob around with her.

Could be both.

Merina's parents had sold their beloved hotel to the biggest, most ostentatious hotel chain in the world. And without telling their own daughter, who also happened to be the hotel's manager! How close to bankruptcy had they been? Couldn't Merina have helped? She'd never know now that they'd sneaked behind her back and unloaded the VH to Reese freaking Crane.

How could they do this to me?

Merina was as much a part of that hotel as they were. And her mother acted as if selling it was an inconvenience.

Focus. You're pissed at Crane.

Right. Big Crane had done her parents a favor buying it, but now that he was about to "peace out," sounded like Reese had decided to flex his corporate muscle.

"Shit!" She didn't just do that. She did *not* just drown her Louboutin pumps in a deep puddle by the curb. Except she had. She shook the rainwater from her shoe as best she could and sloshed up Rush Street to Superior, her sights set squarely on the Crane hotel.

Seventy floors of mirrored glass and as invasive as a visit to the ob-gyn. Given the choice between this monstrosity and the Van Heusen, with its warm cookies and cozy design, Merina couldn't believe anyone would set foot in the clinical, whitewashed Crane hotels let alone sleep there.

At the top of that ivory tower, Reese Crane perched like an evil overlord. The oldest Crane son wasn't royalty, but from the social media and newspaper attention, he sure as hell thought he was.

Halfway down Superior, she folded her arms over her shirt, shuddering against the intensifying wind. She really should have grabbed her coat, but there wasn't a lot of decision-making going into her process. She'd made it this far, fists balled and steam billowing out of her ears, her ire having kept her warm for the relatively short walk. She should have known better. In Chicago, spring didn't show up until summer.

Finally, she reached the Crane and stood face-to-face with the gargantuan, seventy-floor home base. The Crane was not only the premier hotel for the wealthy (and possibly uncultured, given that they stayed *here*) visiting the city, but it was also where Reese hung his proverbial hat. Rumor had it he slept here often, in his very own suite on the top floor, instead of in his sprawling Lake Shore Drive mansion. She wouldn't be surprised if he slept right at his desk, snuggling his cell phone in one hand and a wad of money in the other.

Stupid billionaires.

Inside the lobby, she sucked in a generous breath, her cheeks warming instantly. In here there was no wind, and despite the chilling whitewash of furniture, rugs, and modern lighting, the hotel was warm. But only in temperature. The Crane represented everything she hated about modern hotels. And she should know, because she'd fought alongside her parents to keep the integrity of the boutique hotel since she started running it. Her hotel was a place of rich history, beauty, and passion. This place was a tower of glass, made so that the lower echelon of the city could look but never touch.

Perfect for Reese Crane.

She bypassed the lobby, filled to overflowing with business people of every color, shape, and size. Flashes of suits—black, gray, white—passed in a monochrome blur, as if the Crane Hotel had a dress code and each and every guest here had received the memo. Merina, in her plum-gray silk shirt and dark gray pencil skirt and nude heels didn't stand out...except for the fact that she resembled a drowned rat.

A few surly glances and cocked brows were her reward for rushing in from the storm. Well. Whatever.

She spotted the elevator leading to Crane's office and caught it as an older woman was reaching for the button. The woman with coiffed gray hair widened her eyes in alarm, a tiny dog held snugly in her arms. Merina skated a hand down her skirt and over her hair, wiping the hollows of her eyes to ensure she didn't go to Reese's office with panda eyes.

"Good morning," she greeted.

The older woman frowned. Here was the other problem with the Crane. Its guests were as snooty as the building.

Attitude reflects leadership.

The doors opened only once, to deliver the woman and her dog to the forty-second floor, and then Merina rode the car to the top floor without interruption. She used the time to straighten herself in the blurry, reflective gold doors. No keys or security measures were needed to reach the top of the building. Reese Crane was probably far too smug to believe anyone would dare come up here without an appointment. And she'd heard his secretary was more like a bulldog that guarded his office.

And there she was. The elevator doors slid aside to reveal

an angry woman wearing all black, better suited for a funeral home than a hotel.

"May I help you?" the woman asked, her words measured, curt, and not the least bit friendly.

"You can't," Merina said, pleased the rain hadn't completely drowned out her rage. "I need to speak with Mr. Crane."

"Do you have an appoin—"

"No." Merina stood firm.

The phone rang and the woman slid her acerbic glare away from Merina to the phone. She waited as the other woman answered a call, spoke as slowly as humanly possible, and then returned it to the cradle. The woman folded her hands and tilted her chin. "You were saying?"

Even with her nostrils flared, Merina forced a smile. There was only one way past this gatekeeper. She called up an ounce of poise—an ounce being the most she could access at the moment. "I'm here to see Reese Crane."

"Without an appointment, I can't help you."

"My last name is Van Heusen." She supposed she could make an appointment, could have called ahead, but no sense in robbing him of the full effect of her face-to-face fury.

"Ms. Van Heusen," the woman said, her tone flat. "You're here regarding the changes to the hotel, I presume."

"You got it," Merina said, barely harnessing her anger. How come everyone was so damn calm about dismantling a town landmark?

"Have a seat." Crane's bulldog gestured one manicured hand at a group of cushy white chairs, her mouth frowning in disgust as she took in Merina's dishevelment. "Perhaps I could get you a towel first."

"I'm not sitting." Merina wasn't about to be put in her

place by Reese's underling. A set of gleaming double doors behind the secretary's desk parted like the Red Sea. *Jackpot.* She barreled forward as the woman at the desk barked, "Excuse me! Ms. Van Heusen!"

Merina ignored her. She wouldn't be delayed another second...or so she thought. She stopped short when a woman in a very tight red dress—the neckline plunging into plentiful cleavage, her heels even higher and potentially more expensive than Merina's Louboutins—swept out the doors and gave her a slow, mascaraed blink. Then she sashayed around Merina, past the bulldog, and left behind a plume of perfume.

Well. That was interesting.

Reese's latest date? An escort? If Merina believed the local tabloids, one and the same. He wasn't known for his personable side, and paying for dates certainly wasn't above his pay grade.

Before the doors closed, Merina slipped into Reese's office.

"Ms. Van Heusen!" came a bark behind her, but Reese, who stood facing the windows and looking out upon downtown, said three words that shut up his secretary instantly.

"She's fine, Bobbie."

Merina smirked back at the sour-faced, coal-eyed secretary as Reese's office doors whooshed shut.

"Merina, I presume." Reese still hadn't turned. His posture was straight, jacket and slacks impeccably tailored to his muscular, perfectly proportioned body. Shark or not, the man could wear a suit. She'd seen the photos of him in the *Trib* as well as *Luxury Stays*, the hotel industry's leading trade magazine, and like every other woman in Chicago, she hadn't missed the gossip about him online. Like his more professional photos, his hands were sunk into his pants pockets, and his wavy dark hair was styled and perfect.

Clearly the woman who had just left was here on other business...or past business. If something more clandestine was going on, Reese would appear more mussed. Then again, he probably didn't muss his hair during sex. From what she gleaned about him via the media, Reese probably didn't *allow* his hair to muss.

But the snarky thought paired with a vision of him out of that suit, stalking naked and primed, golden muscles shifting with each long-legged step. Sharp, navy eyes focused only on her...

He turned toward her and she snapped out of her imaginings and blinked at the stubble covering a perfectly angled jaw. What was it about that hint of dishevelment on his otherwise perfect visage that made her breath catch?

Thick dark brows jumped slightly as his eyes zoomed in on her chest.

She sneered before venturing a glance down at her sodden silk shirt. Where she saw the perfect outline of both of her nipples. A tinge of heat lit her cheeks, and she crossed her arms haughtily, glaring at him as best she could while battling embarrassment.

"Seems this April morning is colder than you anticipated," he drawled.

And that was when any wayward attraction she might have felt toward him died a quick death. The moment he opened his mouth, her hormones pulled the emergency brake.

"Cut the horseshit, Crane," she snapped.

The edge of Reese's mouth pulled sideways, sliding the stubble into an even more appealing pattern. But she wasn't here to be insulted or patronized.

"I heard some news," she said. "Your father purchased the Van Heusen."

"He added it to the Crane Holdings portfolio, yes," he responded coolly.

Portfolio. She felt her lip curl. To him, her beloved home away from home was a number on a spreadsheet. Nothing more. Which also could mean he didn't care enough about it to continue with the ridiculous changes.

"There's been an error. My mother is under the impression that many of the nostalgic and antique fixtures in the building will be replaced." She plunked down the heavy doorknob on his desk and watched, smiling as a pool of rainwater gathered on a leather blotter.

Reese sucked in a breath through his nose, wrenched his eyes from the puddle, and pulled his hands from his pockets. He moved to his desk—a heavy block of black wood—and rested one hand on the back of a shiny leather chair. Black. Of course.

He gestured with his other hand—manly hands for a guy who spent his days in an office and spare time eating souls, and about as disturbingly masculine as the scruff lining his jaw—for her to sit in one of the two matching guest chairs parked in front of his desk.

But she didn't want to sit. What she wanted was to march over there and slap the pompous smirk off his face. Then she remembered her compromised top and decided to keep her arms over her breasts.

She sat.

You win this round, Crane.

Reese lowered himself into his chair and pressed a button on his phone. "Bobbie, Ms. Van Heusen will need a car in fifteen minutes."

"Yes, sir."

So he'd deigned to carve out fifteen minutes for Merina. Lucky her.

"I don't want a car."

"No? You're planning on walking back?" Even sitting, he exuded power. Broad, strong shoulders filled out his dark jacket, and a gray tie with a silver sheen arrowed down a crisp white shirt.

"Yes." She wondered what time of day he finally gave up and yanked the perfect knot out of that tie. When he surrendered the top button. A flare of heat shot through her. She hated the way he affected her even though she hated him. She was just so damn aware of him.

It was unfair. She frowned.

"You were saying something about horseshit," he said smoothly, and she realized she had been sitting there glaring at him in silence for a long while.

She cleared her throat and plowed through what she needed to tell him.

"You can't redesign the Van Heusen Hotel. It's an historical site. A landmark. Did you know the hotel was the first to install elevators? The hotel's chef created the snickerdoodle. That building is an integral thread woven into the fabric of this city."

She pressed her lips together. Perhaps she was being a tad theatrical, but the Van Heusen did have historical importance to the city, and beyond that, a personal history to her. She'd grown up half at home, half in the hotel. She'd gone to college straight from high school and graduated with her business degree, her dream to run the Van Heusen and continue the rich, rewarding work of maintaining a building with such a meaningful history.

"Born and raised in Chicago, Ms. Van Heusen. You're not telling me anything I don't know," Reese said, sounding bored.

"Then you know remodeling the Van Heusen makes no sense," she continued, using her best ally: reason. "Our hotel is known for its style. Guests come there to experience a living, breathing piece of Chicago." She stopped short of going into a monologue about how even the fires couldn't destroy the dream.

"My hotel, Ms. Van Heusen," he corrected.

His. A fact she'd only gleaned a few minutes ago. A dart of pain shot through the center of her chest. She should have demanded to see the contract her parents signed before sloshing over here in a downpour and parading her nipples for Mr. Suit & Beard. She was almost as pissed at them for keeping this from her as she was at Crane for thinking he could strut in and take over.

"No matter who owns the building, you have to know that robbing the Van Heusen of its style will make it just another whitewashed, dull hotel," she said.

Her stomach churned. If she had to bear witness to them ripping up the carpeting and replacing it with white shining tile, or see a Dumpster filled with antique doorknobs, she might just lose her mind. The hand-carved molding, the ceiling medallions...Each piece of the VH had been preserved to keep the integrity of the past. And now Reese was erasing it.

She heard the sadness creep into her voice when she ventured, "Surely there's another way."

He didn't respond to this; instead he pointed out, "Your parents have been in the red for nearly two years."

She felt her eyes go wide. Two *years*?

"I gather this is new news to you," he added, then continued. "Your father's hospital bills put them further in debt."

Her dad's heart attack was last year, but Merina had no idea the bills had buried them. She lived in the same house. How had they hidden this from her?

"They came to us to buy the building and we did," Reese said. "I could have fired them, but I didn't. I offered a generous pension plan if they stayed on through the remodel."

A shake worked down her arms and over her shoulders. Pension?

He sighed. "I take it you didn't know that either."

"They didn't want to worry me," she said flatly, but it didn't take the sting from the truth. They'd kept everything from her.

Her pie-in-the-sky parents who loved that building arguably as much as they loved each other had gone to Big Crane as a last resort. They'd overlooked he had Satan for a son.

"They trusted your father to take care of them," she said, her anger blooming anew. "Then you waltz in and wipe them out."

"My father likes your parents, but this isn't about what nice people they are," Satan continued. "He mentioned how well they'd maintained the local landmark with what funds they had available."

Merina's nostrils flared as she inhaled some much-needed oxygen. Her parents had cared for and upgraded the Van Heusen as best they could, but face it, her family didn't have the billion-dollar bankroll Crane's had.

"Your father is a wise man," she said, pitting the two men against each other. Sure enough, a flicker of challenge shone in Reese's navy eyes. "I doubt his intention when he purchased the Van Heusen was to turn it into a mini-me of the Crane."

"My father is retiring in a few months. He's made it clear the future of the Van Heusen is in my hands." Reese shrugged, which made Merina's pulse skyrocket at the same time it made him look relaxed. "I fail to see the charm in a funky, run-down boutique hotel, and I gather most visitors do as well."

Funky? Just who did this jerk-off think he was?

"Do you know how many Hollywood actors have dined in our restaurant?" she blurted. "Hemingway wrote part of his memoir sitting on the velvet chair in the lobby!"

"I thought he mostly wrote in Key West."

"Rumors," she hissed.

A smirk slid over his lips in a look that melted his fan club's collective underpants, but it had no effect on her. Not now that she knew how far he was taking this.

"You have outdated heating and air," he said, "elevators that are so close to violating safety codes, you may as well install ladders for the guests on the upper floors, and the wood putty isn't fooling anyone, Merina."

At the cool pronouncement of her name, she sat straighter. She'd been told last month the building inspector had come by for a reassessment for property value, having no idea he'd be feeding information to the vulture sitting across from her now.

Then again, she was learning she'd been left out of a lot of discussions.

"The elevators are original to the building."

"It shows." He offered a slow blink. "The Van Heusen is stodgy and outdated, and revenue is falling more each quarter. I'm doing your parents a favor by offering them a way out of what will be nothing but a future of headaches." Reese folded his hands on the desk blotter, expertly avoiding the water gathered there. A large-faced watch peeked out from the edge of his shirt, the sleeves adorned with a pair of onyx and platinum cuff links. "The Crane branding is strong, our business plan seamless. If you love the building as much as you claim to, you'd support the efforts to increase the traffic. We'll see profits double with an upgrade." He shook his head. "But not with your parents there. And not with you there."

A shiver climbed her spine, the rain and Reese's words having sunk right into her bone marrow. Was he suggesting... "You're...firing...me?"

He remained stoically silent.

"My family's goddamn name is on the marquee, Crane!" She shot out of her seat and pressed her fingertips onto the surface of the desk. Shining, perfect, unscarred. No character. No soul. No history.

Like Reese Crane himself.

"Your family's name will remain on the building," he stated calmly. And while those words tumbled around her brain and set fire to the fury that he'd put on to sear, he added, "Your parents are getting close to retirement age. Are you sure you swam over here on their behalf? Or is this about you?"

"Of course I'm sure," she said too quickly. She wasn't sure at all. Her world had been upended. It was like when she'd found out there was no Santa Claus. She thought back to her mom telling her about the sale of the Van Heusen and recalled a dash of hope in Jolie's expression.

Did they want out?

"Think about it, Merina. What I'm offering is more than

retirement, and at their age I'm sure they don't want to find work," Reese stated. "Running the Van Heusen is all they've known."

If she had said that, the sentence would have been infused with passion hinting at the fairy tale by which they came to own the Van Heusen. When Reese said it, he made the hotel sound like it was a lame, deaf, blind dog needing to be put down.

No. She would not accept this. Not from Reese. Not from her parents. It was possible they'd forgotten how much the hotel meant to them. Not having money created desperate feelings. Her father wasn't as spry as he once was given his heart condition. Maybe all they needed was her intrusion.

Reese's phone buzzed and Bobbie stated, "Ms. Van Heusen's town car is here, sir."

"I don't want it," Merina, still leaning over his desk, bit out.

He angled his eyes up to her and they stayed locked in a heated staring contest until "Very well" came from the phone's speaker, then clicked off.

Merina straightened. Outside the rain started coming down in sheets. Didn't it figure? An involuntary shiver racked her spine, and possibly her lips were turning blue from her wet hair, but she kept her back straight, her knees locked, and her arms folded securely over her peekaboo breasts.

"I have an appointment I can't miss, but I won't leave you in suspense." Reese stood, deftly unbuttoned his jacket, and shrugged out of it. Those shoulders. My God. He was a mountain of a man. Tall and broad and the absolute opposite of what anyone might expect a hotel owner-slash-billionaire to look like.

"Suspense?" she repeated, her voice dipping low when he came out from behind the desk. "Do you have more to tell me?" Her eyes screwed up to meet his as he draped his suit jacket over her shoulders.

"I'm not going to put you out on your fantastic ass, Merina." His lips tipped—lush lips. His was a mouth made for sin. But then, Satan. So it made sense.

She gripped the jacket when he let go. She should be throwing it at him, but it was warm and she was freezing. And it smelled of leather and money and power. Three things she wished didn't make her feel safe. What was it about this man? She'd seen pictures of him before, and yes, she'd recognized he was attractive, but in the flesh...he made her feel utterly feminine. Even at the worst possible times. Like him dangling her job over a lava-filled pit and daring her to grab for it.

"I appreciate you reconsidering. I belong at the Van Heusen." Until she figured out a way to get the hotel back, at least she could be there. She could come up with a way to delay the remodel.

"No, you misunderstand me. I can't keep you there," he said, a frown marring his otherwise perfect brow. "But I can offer you almost any position you'd like at Crane Hotels. We have openings in Wisconsin, Virginia, and Ohio. I know it's not Chicago, but chances are you can stay in the Midwest."

He slid past her while she stared at the sheeting rain, her fingers going numb around the lapels of his jacket. Not only was he firing her, but he expected her to work for him? Expected her to leave Chicago? This was her city, dammit! He didn't reserve the right to boot her out.

When she turned, Reese was pressing a button on the wall. His office doors whispered open.

A balding, smiling man appeared in the doorway and gave Reese a wave of greeting. He noticed her next and offered a nod.

Merina didn't care who he was; he was about to get an earful. She wouldn't allow Reese Crane to dismiss her after dropping that bomb on her feet.

She stomped to the doorway between him and his guest.

"You listen to me, you suited sewer rat." Disregarding their current third party, she seethed up at Reese. "I'm going to find a way around your machinations and when I do, I'm going to march back in here with the contract my parents signed and shove it straight up your ass."

Reese's eyebrows rose, his lips with them. Instead of apologizing to his guest, Reese grinned over at the balding man, who to his testament was appropriately shocked, and said, "You'll have to forgive Ms. Van Heusen. She doesn't like when she doesn't get her way." The balding man laughed, though it sounded a tad uneasy. Reese tilted his head at Merina. "Will there be anything else?"

"Your head on a pike." With that parting blow, she left, holding fast to the suit jacket. She wore it on the way down the elevator, through the bland lobby, and out onto Superior Street, where she wadded it up and threw it into a mud puddle gathering near the curb.

Then she walked back to the Van Heusen in the rain, telling herself she'd won this round. But Merina didn't feel victorious.

She felt lost.

Fall in Love with Forever Romance

RETURN OF THE BAD BOY
By Jessica Lemmon

Fans of Gena Showalter, Olivia Miles, and Jaci Burton will love Jessica Lemmon's hot alpha heroes with dark pasts and hearts of gold. Rock god Asher Knight is forced to put down roots when he finds out he has a three-year-old son. But is his newfound stability enough to convince Gloria Shields to finally surrender her heart to this bad boy?

THE WAGER
By Rachel Van Dyken

Seattle millionaire Jake Titus has always made Char Lynn crazy. He's too rich, too handsome, and too arrogant. But now Jake's stopped acting like a jerk and turned on the charm, and Char knows she's in trouble. The *New York Times* bestseller from Rachel Van Dyken is now in mass market.

Fall in Love with Forever Romance

THE WEDDING PACT
By Katee Robert

New York Times and *USA Today* bestselling author Katee Robert continues her smoking-hot series about the O'Malleys—wealthy, powerful, and full of scandalous family secrets. In THE WEDDING PACT, Carrigan O'Malley has a parade of potential suitors, but the only man she wants is the head of a rival ruling family. To be with Carrigan, James Halloran will have to fight not only his enemies—but his own blood.

HER KIND OF MAN
By Elle Wright

I'll never let you go… Allina always dreamed of hearing those words. But when her fiancé utters them—it's a threat. Forget walking down the aisle; it's time to run. Back to Michigan. Back to Kent. Kent will do whatever it takes to make Allina feel safe, beautiful, and desirable. But as the two grow closer, and their passion pushes deeper, it's clear that something bigger than a botched wedding still lingers between them…

Fall in Love with Forever Romance

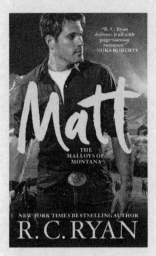

MATT
By R. C. Ryan

In the *New York Times* bestselling tradition of Linda Lael Miller and Diana Palmer comes the first in a beautiful new series by R. C. Ryan. When lawyer Vanessa Kettering and rancher Matt Malloy are forced to weather a terrible storm together, they're drawn to each other despite their differences. Can they survive the storm without losing their hearts?

HOW I MARRIED A MARQUESS
By Anna Harrington

When an old family friend comes to retired spy Thomas Matteson about a rash of mysterious robberies near Blackwood Hall, he jumps at the chance to be back in the field. What will he do when the suspect turns out to be the most beautiful—and beguiling—woman he's ever seen? Fans of Elizabeth Hoyt will love this sexy historical romance.

READ MORE FROM
JESSICA LEMMON

THE LOST BOYS SERIES
BOOK 1

MEET THE ULTIMATE BAD BOY...
AND A LOVE THAT CROSSES
ALL BOUNDARIES